THE STOLEN

THE STOLEN

An American Faerie Tale

BISHOP O'CONNELL

HARPER
VOYAGER
IMPULSE

An Imprint of HarperCollins Publishers

THE STOLEN. Copyright © 2014 by Bishop O'Connell. All rights reserved under International and Pan-American Copyright Conventions. By payment of the required fees, you have been granted the nonexclusive, nontransferable right to access and read the text of this e-book on screen. No part of this text may be reproduced, transmitted, decompiled, reverse-engineered, or stored in or introduced into any information storage and retrieval system, in any form or by any means, whether electronic or mechanical, now known or hereinafter invented, without the express written permission of HarperCollins e-books.

EPub Edition JULY 2014 ISBN: 9780062358776

Print Edition ISBN: 9780062358790

10 9 8 7 6 5 4 3

For "The Boot" and to Dennis Morgan,
who believed in me before I believed in myself.

Faeries, come take me out of this dull world,
For I would ride with you upon the wind,
Run on the top of the disheveled tide,
And dance upon the mountains like a flame.

—WILLIAM BUTLER YEATS,
"THE LAND OF HEART'S DESIRE"

THE STOLEN

THE STOLEN

CHAPTER ONE

Brendan Kavanaugh smiled and examined the wrought silver claddagh ring, admiring its fine details. The small hands holding the crowned heart were gleaming perfection, a stark contrast to his thick fingers and scarred knuckles. The small emerald in the center of the heart sparkled in the flickering light of the jewelry store's single kerosene lamp.

"A finer piece of work I've never seen," Brendan said to the jeweler, leaning on the counter. "Nicely done, sir."

"Glad you approve of it, lad," Patrick said. "I'm sure Áine will as well."

"Not a gleaming diamond though," Brendan said, his smile fading.

Patrick smacked the back of Brendan's head. "Oh, for Finn's sake! Any good and proper Irish lass would prefer an emerald."

Brendan stood to his full height. He towered over

Patrick, as he did everyone. He gave the old man a sharp glance and rubbed the back of his head, but he couldn't keep from smiling. "Aye, and that she is, to be sure."

"You're a lucky man, Brendan Kavanaugh," Patrick said, pulling a small leather box from behind the counter. "And with God's mercy, your children will take after their mother."

Brendan laughed. "Oh aye, that's God's truth there, to be sure." Brendan handed the ring back and fished the cash out of the pouch on his hip as Patrick boxed the ring. "Thanks again, Paddy. For staying late and all, I mean."

"Just doing me part for young love."

Brendan put the money on the counter, took the box, and closed the now empty pouch.

Patrick frowned. "Oh, and now we've got a problem."

Brendan knitted his brow. "Aye? What's that, then?"

"You've gone and paid me too much."

"But your man said—"

"He didn't know about our special Fian wedding discount."

Brendan's face fell.

"Now don't give me that bleeding look. Firstly, it's ridiculous on a fella your size. Secondly, I don't give a rusted shilling what happened in Ireland, and neither do any of us what know you. We know it was you pulled them dark *bastúin* off of old Joseph. Besides, this is my bloody shop. For discounts, I'm the one what decides who's a Fian and who ain't." Patrick handed a few bills back. "You can't give a girl a ring and not take her for a meal, wouldn't be right."

Reluctantly, Brendan took the offered money with a nod and a faint smile.

After a moment, Patrick let out a sigh. "Oh, bloody hell, man. Off with you now. Wouldn't be right to keep her waiting, neither!"

Brendan's smile widened. "You're a wise man. *Mile buiochas.*"

Outside, the night bore the chill of early autumn, but Brendan didn't feel a bit of it. The sky was clear, the stars shone their blessings from the heavens, and he didn't care that he was smiling like a fool.

The Boston streets were quiet, the streetcars having finished their runs. Brendan caught the scent of cooking food drifting from the tenements, mingling with the smell of burning coal, wood, and leaves. In the distance, a lone gasman lit the last of the streetlamps. Brendan knew the old fella. They'd arrived in Boston on different ships, but in the same year and, by all outward appearances, at the same age. But, unlike Brendan's, the old man's face now bore the lines of the decades that had passed since that day.

The old man looked over from his work as Brendan drew near. He saw the kilt, then he looked to the pin worn on it like a badge, a claddagh encircling a wolf's head. He met Brendan's eyes, smiled faintly, and gave a firm nod of approval. The dark green kilt and gleaming pin clearly identified Brendan, to the older generations at least, as a Fian, a protector of mortals from things that go bump in the night. The older immigrants were the only ones who remembered Ireland. To their children, the first generation born in America, Brendan was just a strange, albeit large, redheaded fella in a skirt.

Brendan returned the smile and nod. As he did, he saw a glint from the man's ring finger. He squeezed the box in his sweaty hand tighter and felt his stomach churn. He increased his pace, focusing instead on Áine's smile, the way her eyes shone, and the surety that they would sparkle just the same when she was old and gray.

In minutes, he was just around the corner from where they were to meet at O'Connell's Athenry Inn. He stopped, swallowed, and looked down at the modest leather box.

"*Dar fia*, it's really going to happen, ain't it?"

After letting out a long breath, he continued on to the inn. He didn't see Áine waiting for him, so he stuck his head inside.

She wasn't waiting inside the door, or sitting at a table either.

His stomach twisted. He wasn't early. He was actually a little late. She never was.

He closed his eyes and focused on the scents and sounds around him. He could hear the people inside the inn and the houses around him. He could smell the food, the smoke spewing from the chimneys, and the garbage in the alleyways, but not Áine.

After a moment of consideration, he tucked the box in his pouch and began walking the path he knew she'd take. He ignored the stab of regret that he didn't have his knives.

The minutes dragged like slices of eternity with no sign of her.

Brendan rounded another corner and came to a street lined with mills and factories; the farthest brick building was the textile mill where Áine worked a row of looms. The gas lamps were out, and the street was draped in darkness.

The hair on the back of his neck stood on end as he scanned up the street. He thought he could smell her scent, just a whisper on the air. It made him think of the green fields of home right after a heavy rain, but he couldn't be sure he wasn't imagining it. The odors of burned coal and textile dyes were strong, ugly, and overwhelming. He sniffed the air again and there was something else. Something wound through the industrial stench. It was the smell of flowers, but fetid, tired, and wrong. As if someone had forced the perfume from them long after they should've been dead—

A scream split the air and turned his blood to ice water.

Long-forgotten whispered threats from the dark faeries whose mischief he'd stopped now shouted in his ears. He could no longer ignore their threats of exacting revenge.

Brendan sprinted toward the sounds of a struggle down an alleyway. When he reached it, he slid to a stop on the slick cobblestones and stared in horror.

Three oíche, small and childlike, with hair of deepest black and clothes of poorest street urchins, had Áine pinned against the wall with their inhuman strength. One made to lift her long dress, while the other two held out her arms. She twisted and pulled, trying to wrench out of their grasp. One small, calloused hand came free, and she drove it into the face of an attacker, but the faerie shook off the blow.

The two grinned, bearing pointed teeth, and yanked her back against the bricks. As they did, she brought a leg up and kicked. The heel of her black, laced boot caught the oíche in front of her on the bridge of his nose and sent him stumbling back. Before her leg came back down, the oíche had wiped the black blood away, seized her leg, backhanded her, and then lifted her skirt once more.

Time stopped and Brendan stood frozen, unable to believe what he was seeing.

Áine turned her lovely green eyes to him, eyes that should've been filled with light and joy but were instead filled with pain and terror.

Hell churned inside him, crying out to be released.

Brendan obliged.

Fury overtook him as he surged forward, steps pounding the cobblestones like the thunder of a deadly storm. He howled, and it was a sound not of this world.

All three oíche turned their solid black eyes to him, their alabaster skin almost luminescent in the moonlight.

He struck the dark faerie violating Áine first, seizing him by the shoulder. The oíche still had a grip on Áine's skirt when Brendan twisted and hurled the faerie into the wall fifteen feet away. The sound of ripping fabric filled the alley.

Before that one had fallen to the ground, Brendan seized another by the wrist and spun, driving the oíche face-first toward the opposite wall. He hit a wide iron drainpipe instead of brick.

The oíche shrieked in pain as the flesh of his face burned away amid a cloud of darkness swirling with motes of white light.

Hearing the scream only fed Brendan's rage, and he turned to face the last attacker.

The oíche's hand blurred as he raked his claw-like nails down Brendan's face.

Brendan moved aside, but one claw dragged down his left cheek, missing his eye by a hairbreadth. He swung his fist and felt it connect with flesh and bone. He heard the smack of the faerie hitting the wall.

Brendan wiped the blood from his eye just in time to see the oíche coming at him again, his snarl revealing rows of sharp teeth.

Again, Brendan made to dodge, and again a single claw made contact. This one caught the left edge of Brendan's mouth and tore a gash across his cheek.

The taste of blood filled his mouth, stoking the fiery rage in his heart.

The oíche slashed out again, but this time Brendan was faster. He caught the tiny wrist and twisted, spinning the fae around him. There was a pop as the faerie's shoulder dislocated, followed by the snap of his wrist breaking.

The oíche who'd hit the drainpipe had recovered enough to come at Brendan again, the darkling's face half-skeletal as he shrieked in rage.

With all his strength, Brendan hurled the broken faerie at his companion. Both hit the ground and slid a dozen feet away.

Brendan heard footsteps behind him. He turned as the first oíche he'd tossed ran along the wall and leapt at him.

The rage boiling in Brendan now sang in delight. The pain in his cheek faded, and fresh strength filled his arms and legs.

He caught the flying oíche and drove his face into the drain. Both bone and iron shattered amid a howl of pain, and it was like an angel's chorus to Brendan.

Brendan snatched a length of broken pipe and drove into the chest of the oíche writhing on the ground. The faerie vanished in a cloud of darkness and twinkling white lights.

Cold iron in hand, Brendan turned to the remaining two oíche.

Both stared at him with wide black eyes, frozen in place.

Brendan pounced, slashing the end of the pipe across the throat of one. He then drove the pipe into the chest of the other so deep his fist broke rib bones. The second oíche exploded into nothing but a wafting darkness and tiny lights.

Brendan's hands shook as the battle rage continued to grow, unsated.

Something moved in the mouth of the alley, and half a dozen oíche approached.

"What's going on here?" one asked.

Brendan attacked. Each blow felled another, and still the rage inside him grew like wildfire. With each he killed, he moved faster. Now it wasn't even a fight, it was a slaughter. In moments nearly a dozen oíche lay dead around him without having scored more than a blow or two of their own.

Brendan roared in the delight of battle and the hunt.

"Brendan! No—"

He spun, saw a final oíche, and was on her before she could finish her spell. He drove the pipe, now saturated with blood and gore, into her belly, and twisted.

There was no scream, no darkness, and no lights.

He looked into the oíche's tear-filled green eyes and knew something was wrong.

Cold washed over him and the rage vanished. As it did, he saw Áine underneath him, impaled on the pipe in his hands.

"Oh God, no!" He let go of the pipe, not daring to pull it out. He tore his shirt off and used it as a makeshift bandage. "Stay still, Áine. I'll get you a doctor, you'll be fine, love." His tears and shaking hands betrayed the lie, but he made to stand.

Áine caught his wrist. "No, stay with me."

Brendan took her face in his hands. Even now, there was no malice in her eyes. Her curly, fiery red hair was soaked in blood. He brushed it away from her face, leaving streaks of blood across her smooth, and freckled, pale skin. His vision blurred with tears. "*A ghrá mo chroí*, I'm so sorry."

Áine lifted her left hand and put her fingers over his lips. "Shh."

The tears broke free. "No! Don't you leave me! You hear me?"

"I love you so much, remember that," she said, her voice weak.

He took her hand and kissed it, shaking his head. "No, don't you give up on me."

Áine smiled. "I never have, love. I never will."

"You can't go. We've a long life to live together."

"You live it for us both." She blinked, and tears rolled down her face. "Tell me you love me—"

"*Tá grá agam duit, m'aingeal.*"

Áine smiled, then Brendan watched as the light in her eyes vanished and her small body went limp in his arms.

"*Dia ár gcumhdach!*" he screamed and pulled her close. She felt so small against him. Barely five feet tall, she'd always felt small in his arms despite her womanly curves, but now it was like holding a whisper. Even through the coppery scent of blood, her sweet smell of Irish summer rain was there. It only made him weep harder. It had become the smell of home to him.

In time, he looked up and saw the bodies of what he'd thought had been *oíche* at the alley entrance. They were mortals. *Ceapa* and passersby who'd come to see what had happened. He'd killed them too, all of them.

In that moment, it was decided. He'd wait to be arrested and hanged. He might even see a trial. The rest was between him and the devil. Running footsteps, quick and light, came down the street. He lowered his head and waited for the constable to drag him away.

"Shadowed dawn!" a familiar voice said between heavy breaths. "Brendan, is that you?"

Dante. Worse than the bleeding *ceapa*. Brendan couldn't bear to face him. "Aye."

"What happened?"

"It was me. I murdered them."

"What?"

The footsteps drew closer, and Brendan clenched his jaw tight when he sensed, rather than saw, Dante notice Áine.

"No—" Dante stepped around Brendan and knelt on Áine's other side. His black frock coat skimmed the ground as he leaned forward and touched her neck with two fingers, looking for a pulse that Brendan knew wasn't there. Light blond hair that was normally oiled and slicked back on his head fell across his temple, revealing the tips of his pointed ears. After a moment his shoulders slumped, his head bowed, and the solid green glow of his eyes dimmed.

Brendan pulled Áine closer and kissed her brow. "Kill me."

Dante's head snapped up. "What? No."

"If you call yourself me friend," Brendan said, "don't let me live with this." His voice broke, and it took a moment before he could speak again. "I let it get control. It's just like they said would happen."

"What happened? I mean, what would cause you to—" Dante's head turned, and Brendan saw him look at Áine's torn dress, then at the bodies. "Who . . . ?"

Brendan didn't say anything.

"Oíche." Under the surface of Dante's voice simmered a long-held anger.

There was silence for several minutes. Brendan just held Áine closer to him.

"You can't stay here," Dante said. "Let me get you out of here."

"No."

"Brendan—"

"It was me what done it, and I have to account for it," Brendan said. "I'll stay here and get what's bloody well coming to me."

"They'll kill you."

"Aye, but not if you do it first."

"Don't ask me to do that."

Brendan let his head fall forward, and he buried his face in Áine's neck. He knew Dante was right. This was Brendan's to carry, but he had to make sure this could never happen again.

"Can you get it out of me?"

"Get it out—?"

"Can you get the bleeding *deamhan buile* out of me?"

"I don't even know what your parents did to put it there."

"So, no, then."

"I'm sorry."

Brendan inhaled Áine's scent and gritted his teeth.

"Can you bind it, then? Chain the bloody thing down at least?"

Dante sighed. "I don't know, maybe, depending on how strong it is. Even if I could, there's no telling what effects it could have on you. It might kill you."

Brendan forced a chuckle. He wouldn't be so lucky. "You do what you have to, then I'm leaving Boston."

"You're not in any shape to make a decision like that!"

"*Dar fia,* man," Brendan said. "Word will spread fast, people will know. I have to leave, don't I? Maybe if I can find some way to make this right—"

"And where will you go?"

"Away." Brendan took a breath. "I'll be needing me a horse."

"I—"

"What else can I do, then?"

"I don't know, maybe . . ."

Brendan felt Dante's eyes on him. He tried to resist meeting the bright green gaze of his friend. He failed, lifted his face, and they stared at each other in silence for several long minutes.

Dante closed his eyes and bowed his head. "All right, I'll do it."

CHAPTER TWO

Brendan took a final drag from his cigarette and flicked the ash out of his old truck's open window. Traffic was light on I-93 as he crossed into New Hampshire.

Sure, he'd taken the long route, but it kept him far enough away that he didn't even have to see Boston's skyline. He'd have gone back more, but the first time he'd risked a visit to Áine's grave, when he'd heard her friends speaking about the child, their child . . . Well, he still wasn't ready to face Dante again, not yet.

He turned his attention away from his current line of thinking, but it was too late. Somewhere inside, something stirred, restless and hungry.

You can't keep me locked away forever.

"We'll see about that, then," Brendan said to the empty truck.

Distantly, he could almost hear laughter.

Absently, he scratched at the sigils tattooed on his

sternum. When he noticed what he was doing, he lit another cigarette and ignored the twisting feeling in the pit of his stomach. He didn't have the luxury of doubts. There were things to be done.

A car with Massachusetts plates cut him off, but he didn't flinch. He just slowed down, and as he did, he noticed the car's bumper sticker.

Time heals all wounds.

(And so does revenge)

Brendan half smiled. "Aye, we might just be finding the truth of that, then."

Caitlin Brady walked out of the Manchester, New Hampshire hospital, her nurse's scrubs in the bag slung over her shoulder and her daughter Fiona's small hand in hers. The four-year-old girl was skipping and humming a happy tune. She was always like this after a visit with Eddy. Caitlin completely understood. He'd always made her feel better, too. In fact, without him, she wasn't sure how she would've made it these last few years.

Kris's car pulled up in front of them, and the willowy young woman got out with a smile.

Fiona struggled with the back door for a moment before Caitlin opened it for her and the little girl climbed up on the seat.

"Thanks again," Caitlin said to Kris. "I know it's short notice."

"No problem," Kris said, smiling. "You go out and

have a good time. You could use it. We're going to have a night with everyone's favorite pixie."

Fiona cheered as she settled into the child seat.

Caitlin leaned in and buckled up Fiona. As she did, it struck her again just how much her daughter took after her. They both had the same curly, fiery red hair, unmanageable, to be honest. The same green eyes, though Fiona didn't have the matching set of luggage under hers. They were both light skinned and liberally dosed with freckles, though Fiona, like all children, pulled off the look better. Caitlin silently hoped that Fiona wouldn't also inherent the extra twenty pounds Caitlin carried around, or that she'd at least be tall enough for it not to be as obvious; Caitlin was several inches shorter than every other woman she knew. If she just worked less and slept more, she knew it would make a world of difference, but she had more important things in her life than sleep.

Caitlin ran her hand down Fiona's cheek and let out a breath. "You behave for Kris, okay, peanut?"

"I will, Mommy." Fiona's green eyes lit up. "I love you."

Caitlin felt a twinge at the words and smiled; even that matched her daughter's. "I love you, too. Now give me a kiss." She leaned down, got her kiss, and gave one back before closing the car door with a sigh.

She waved and tried to ignore the pang of guilt as the car pulled away. Eddy was probably right. No, he was always right, and it was annoying as hell.

After a minute or two, she convinced herself it was okay to go to the art show. She closed her eyes and took a deep breath of the crisp autumn air. When she exhaled, she found the guilt assuaged enough that she could probably do an hour or two with the girls. Baby steps, right?

Emerging from the parking garage stairwell, she pulled her keys from her purse and pointed the fob at her car. A sudden, overwhelming chill of dread and hopelessness washed over her. It stopped her so abruptly that she nearly fell on her face.

Caitlin could sense someone behind her, watching her. She could almost feel cold breath on her neck.

She stood there, frozen in place. The only sound was her shallow breathing. She struggled to move her legs, but fear had them cemented in place.

"Come on, Caitlin," she whispered. "Just remember the self-defense class." For the first time she could remember, she was glad Fiona wasn't with her.

Hands still shaking, she gripped her keys so that they protruded from between her knuckles. Then she sucked in a breath and turned to confront whoever it was, spiked fist at the ready.

An empty lot stared back at her.

She blinked and looked around, knowing that she should be relieved, or at least feeling silly, but she wasn't. Her heart still pounded, and a cold fist still held her stomach in a death grip.

The garage looked empty, but she knew it wasn't. More disconcertingly, she couldn't explain how she knew. When she saw the shadows at the far wall, her stomach lurched and her breath came up short.

She inhaled, then exhaled. It was a patch of darkness, that was all. She could see the wall through it. Nothing was hiding in the shadows. Nevertheless, she knew with absolute certainty that something, or someone, was staring back at her. A primal and desperate need to flee seized her and returned life to her legs. She bolted for her car, fell into the driver's seat, then slammed and locked the door.

Fumbling with the keys, she stabbed at the ignition. "Come on, damn it!"

Finally, the key went in. She turned it, and thank God, the motor came to life. The sound of the engine evaporated the terror and dread. She let out a breath and leaned her head against the steering wheel as her body slowly stopped shaking. When it had, she started laughing.

She lifted her head and looked at her reflection in the rearview mirror. "You're losing it, girl."

In the mirror, she saw the shadows again. The cold and empty feelings returned.

She backed the car out, shifted into drive, and sped out of the garage, almost certain that she heard laughter buried under the squealing of her tires.

There's comfort in lit spaces filled with other people, even if they're strangers, which is why Caitlin still went to the art show that evening. That, and going home would be admitting her brief lapse of sanity in the garage hadn't been a delusion.

Also, a beer sounded absolutely divine just then.

The shaking in her hands was fading as she walked into the warehouse turned art gallery. The space retained much of its industrial history; the walls were exposed brick and the ceiling was all ventilation ducts. Scattered about the space were several temporary walls, on which hung various paintings and photographs. Caitlin's friends stood around a small, high table, waving her over.

As Caitlin approached, Casey motioned to a pint glass of brown ale. "I ordered you a—"

Caitlin lifted the glass and downed half of it in a series of large gulps. The cold beer poured down her throat and smoothed over the last of her frayed nerves. She set the glass down, sucked in a lungful of air, and closed her eyes. When she opened them, her friends were staring at her.

"Uh, rough day?" Janet asked.

"Just some neuroses and hallucinations."

"What?" Casey asked.

"You sound like Eddy," Janet said with a smile.

Caitlin waved her hand. "I'm fine."

The friends left the table and wandered around, examining the various pieces of art on display and making small talk. Caitlin was only half listening to them. The show was Celtic themed, so every piece stirred memories of Ireland and James.

As she forced her eyes away from a black-and-white photo of the Dingle coastline at sunset, she noticed something out of the corner of her eye. A tall, slender couple in their early twenties stood several feet away, examining a painting. They were both blond, tan, and so put together it looked as if they had a staff that did nothing else. Aside from that, they looked normal, but just moments before, she could've sworn they'd been looking at her and that their eyes had been, well, glowing.

She took another drink of her beer and brushed the incident off. Until it happened again, this time with a teenage girl, who was clearly the creator of a large painting, and then a third time with a large and ugly man who looked as though he might live under a bridge and harass young goats as they tried to cross. An old saying came to mind; if one person calls you a duck, you ignore it; if two people call you a duck, you begin to wonder; if three people call you a duck, you're quacking.

The door to the gallery opened. Caitlin glanced over as a man who had to be at least six foot four stood in the doorway, guitar case in hand. Powerful, working-man muscles strained his black shirt. His long, copper red hair was pulled into a ponytail. He wore old work boots and a hand-folded olive green kilt, held in place with only a belt. Instead of a sporran, an old leather pouch sat on his hip. At the bottom front of the kilt was a pin so battered Caitlin couldn't make out the design.

Caitlin started to look away, but her gaze locked on his face. Not because he was handsome, though he was in a classic sort of way. No, it was the two wicked scars that crossed his face. One ran from just above his left eyebrow, over his eye, and down to his chin.

The second went from his mouth, across his face, and bisected the first, leaving lines of bare skin in what seemed to be several days of scruffy growth. She knew scars like that came from either serious injuries, poor treatment, or both. In his case, she leaned toward option C.

Before she could look away, he met her gaze. His face drained of color, and she thought his electric blue eyes went wide for an instant before he took half a step backwards. Caitlin looked away but could feel him still staring at her.

She looked back and opened her mouth—

"Brendan!" someone shouted.

He and Caitlin both saw one of the musicians on the makeshift stage waving at him. Brendan shook his head as though trying to clear it, nodded, and started to look back at Caitlin, but he stopped short instead and walked over to the stage.

Caitlin watched him for a moment before lifting her glass and taking a couple large gulps.

Quack, quack.

"Testing. One, two, three," Brendan said with a heavy brogue into the microphone. No sound came from the speakers. "Riley, is it any use back there?"

"You going to be okay?" Sharon asked from behind Caitlin's shoulder.

It wasn't just the accent. Even the timbre of his voice was like James's. Caitlin nodded to answer Sharon's question and closed her eyes as unwanted memories broke through.

James had been charming, romantic, and handsome: not the kind of man who usually went for her. His attentions had made her trip to Ireland seem like a dream. In retrospect, she knew that she'd been naïve, but she'd been fresh out of college then. It had taken four days for him to wear her down and get her into his bed. It'd been sweet and tender, everything she'd hoped and more. The next morning, he was gone. Only his backpack and guitar had been left behind, and no one in town had seemed to know anything about him. Eddy said she'd never found closure, and now, five years later, she only really thought about him on Fiona's birthday. But then, he was Fiona's father.

"The microphone isn't on, Brendan," Riley shouted from behind the bar, and when he turned his head just right, the tips of his ears looked pointed. Caitlin blinked as Riley looked away and the illusion was gone. Must've just been the lighting.

Caitlin shifted her attention back to the stage as one of the other musicians switched on the microphone and said something to Brendan while pointing to the amp.

Brendan looked at it as if it were some sort of alien technology.

A guitar strum sounded through the speakers. "Aye, this better, then?" Brendan asked.

The bartender gave a thumbs-up.

"Right, then. How about a pint of plain, if you please?" Brendan cleared his throat.

Caitlin drank the last of her beer as Brendan leaned forward again and spoke into the mic.

"Well, as you might've guessed, we'll be playing for you tonight. If there's something you'd like to hear, just let us know."

He turned to the others on stage, and they started a nice pub song. The band was good, but Brendan was exceptional. Caitlin just watched and listened, until he started to sing "The Fields of Athenry." She found herself being drawn in by the emotion and power of his voice.

Caitlin could picture the scene. Ireland, 1847, and a young woman, ravaged to nothing but skin and bones by the famine. Leaning against a stone wall, she spoke to her love, imprisoned on the other side for stealing food to keep their children alive. Every word Brendan sang was a brush painting emotions in Caitlin's heart. She could feel the lamenting sadness and pain as the man was led to the ship bound for Australia. The young woman's heart broke, and Caitlin's broke for her.

Caitlin opened her eyes, unaware of when she'd closed them, and shook herself from the daze. She looked up at Brendan; his eyes were wet, and he stared off into space as his fingers made the guitar sing. He looked almost, well, wistful was the only word for it. If she hadn't known it impossible, she'd swear he was singing his own story.

As she glanced around the room, her mouth went slack. The entire place was watching him. Every single person, including the staff, was staring in rapt silence. No one was moving. No one was talking. As the last note faded, her hands began to shake again.

There was a long and heavy moment of silence before abruptly, as if someone pressed the play button, life returned to the room. People applauded, or returned to their earlier conversations, and no one seemed the wiser.

"Thanks." Brendan looked around the room. His eyes found Caitlin's and held them for a split second. He looked like he wanted to say something, but instead he turned away. "Bit of an emotional one, I know. I think for the next, maybe something a wee bit easier on the heart."

The band began an instrumental, Brendan staring intently at his guitar strings.

"Caitlin? Are you okay?" Casey asked.

Caitlin struggled to find words as her friends shared a concerned look.

"Why don't we sit down?" Janet said.

They led Caitlin back to the small table and resumed their idle chatter while keeping a watchful eye on her. She struggled to put the weird happenings aside or explain them away, but soon it all combined with the beer, the music, and exhaustion from too many sleepless nights. She reached her limit.

"I need to go."

Her friends looked at her, then over her shoulder at Brendan.

Casey put her hand over Caitlin's. "Go home, kiss Fiona goodnight, and get some sleep."

"Thanks, I'll make it up to you, I promise." Caitlin hugged each of her friends and made for the door.

Outside the air was brisk and, after the events of the night, she could describe it only as delightfully real. She breathed it in and leaned against the wall. Once calm, she headed to her car. As she rounded the corner, she fished out her keys and was about to unlock her car with the fob when fear hit her like a sledgehammer and it felt like her heart went into ventricular fibrillation.

This was the same feeling she'd had in the parking garage, only now it was amplified. This wasn't a normal, everyday fear that she could push aside. This was a soul-freezing, primordial dread that spoke to an ancient part of her psyche, a part born from staring into the darkness and knowing that in its depths there are creatures born of nightmares.

"It's not safe for a pretty girl to be out this late all by herself," a soft, melodic voice said from behind her.

The voice was beautiful, almost hypnotic, but very, very cold. Gooseflesh erupted over Caitlin's entire body, and every instinct told her to run. Instead, she closed her eyes and let her logical, rational mind wrestle the panicked, screaming part into submission. Her heartbeat slowed to something slightly less than a scared hummingbird's and her muscles eased their tension, reluctantly giving control back to her.

She shifted her keys into the spiked fist configuration again. "Well, I'm just about to my car, so . . ." She let the sentence trail off as she started walking away.

Laughter erupted from behind her, and it hit like a physical blow. It wasn't jovial or even a forced chuckle. It was a derisive, mocking laugh. It made her think of kids at recess encircling some poor outcast, everyone pointing and jeering.

Then the laughter wasn't just behind her. It came from the shadows ahead of her, too.

Her heart dropped and her body tensed.

"You're not going anywhere," the voice behind her said.

The knot in her stomach began to tighten, but she thought of Fiona and her resolve hardened. She clenched her jaw and turned, ready to fight.

"Leav—" Caitlin stopped when she saw who'd been speaking to her.

An eerily beautiful boy, perhaps thirteen, looked at her with more confidence than anyone that young should have. His skin was white—not just pale, but unreal, alabaster white. His hair was sheer black, as were his clothes and fingernails, and he must've been wearing some kind of special contact lenses, because his eyes were all black, no whites at all. He was thin and not much over five feet tall, just about her height.

He smiled, showing his teeth. Every single one, upper and lower, came to a sharp point.

Caitlin felt the blood drain from her face and her heart skipped a beat.

The boy's eyes narrowed and he looked at her for a moment before he smiled wider. "Boo!"

Caitlin flinched and he laughed again. She could feel his black eyes bore through her. This child exuded evil. She tried to slow her breathing or bring her heart rate back down, but nothing worked. She couldn't even cry out for help.

"Listen to her heart pound," purred a voice from behind Caitlin, this one more feminine. "Oh, I think you scared her, dear brother."

Light footsteps sounded on the concrete as whoever it was drew closer and the screaming part of Caitlin's brain kicked the rational side to the ground and locked it in a closet.

"Now," the voice said, this time in her ear. It was soft, almost seductive. "While we'll enjoy you trying to fight, in the end it will only be worse for you."

The breath was as icy as the voice it carried was alluring. Soft fingers ran along her neck, sending waves of pleasure through her, and she found herself enthralled by the cold touch and voice.

"But if you just go along with us . . . ," the voice cooed, "oh, it will be so much better."

Caitlin had a flash of all the horrible things that were going to befall her. As desperation set in like a raging river, she found a handhold in steely resolve. She wouldn't go without a fight, if not for herself, then for her daughter. Her parents had left her at an early age. She wasn't going to leave Fiona. She gripped the keys in her sweaty fist and spun to see the female counterpart to the Goth boy, clad in Doc Martens, fishnet stockings, and a black dress.

The girl gave her a pouty look. "Uh-oh. She's mad now."

Caitlin set her jaw.

"I don't think she likes us." The boy laughed and stood next to his sister.

"Get out of my way, right now." Caitlin began to plan where and how she would strike if it came to that. Part of her hoped it would.

"Tisk, tisk," the girl said, then gave a disapproving look, a shake of her head, and even a wag of her finger. Black eyes, like her brother's and just as empty, locked on Caitlin's, and the girl bared her sharp teeth in something closer to a snarl than a smile. "I tried being nice."

Caitlin had to swallow before she could find any words. "Don't, don't make me repeat myself." Her muscles went tight, ready to strike.

Both sets of black eyes blinked at her, turned to each other, and looked back to Caitlin.

The girl's look went back to the haughty sneer. "Well then, if that's how you'll have it. Brother, would you like the pleasure?"

The boy moved much quicker than Caitlin expected, but she'd been waiting for something to happen. She punched with all the strength she could muster, and her fist connected hard with the boy's neck, the metal keys sinking into his white flesh.

His eyes went wide as he staggered back a step.

When she pulled her hand back, it was coated with a cold, black sludge.

"That hurt, you bitch," the boy said through gritted teeth. He licked the pad of his thumb and dragged it over the wound. When he was done, the punctures were gone.

Caitlin's brain locked up trying to process what she'd just seen.

The boy rotated his neck as if stretching it, causing it to crack a few times before he leveled his gaze at Caitlin. "Just for that, I'm going to take you slow." He bared his teeth and drew back.

"That's a *skawly* idea there, Tinker Bell," said a familiar voice at the corner.

Caitlin turned. James? No, it couldn't be.

Brendan stepped out of the shadows and folded his arms over his broad chest. "Best you and that oíche-bitch let the *cailin* go on her way."

"Mind your own—" The girl stopped midsentence when she saw Brendan. Her eyes moved from his scarred face to his kilt pin. "The Fian!"

The boy's mouth turned up into a wicked grin. "Oh, I could go for a piece of that as well." He held his arms out, extended his fingers, and his nails grew to sharp claws.

"I'm about to lose me head here, bucko." Brendan smiled. "And if I do, then you'll be losing yours. Let her go. Mind, if I have to be asking again, I won't be nearly so polite about it."

"He's mine!" the girl said, then leapt at Brendan.

Brendan drew a large, curved knife out from behind his back. It glittered in the streetlight as he stepped to one side and slashed.

If Caitlin had blinked, she would've missed it. The blade cut across the girl as she flew past, and when she fell to the ground, shrieking in pain, Caitlin could see what looked like thick black smoke filled with tiny motes of light wafting away from the wound.

Caitlin's mouth opened, but the boy went for her again. She punched with the keys, this time hitting his face and one eye.

He grunted in what sounded more like annoyance than pain.

She kicked his groin, but he didn't crumple. He just grunted and sucked in a breath.

She swallowed hard and stumbled as she tried to back away.

"You're starting to piss me off, *a bhitseach dhaonna!*" The boy glared at her with one good eye as black fluid poured down his cheek. He rubbed his injured eye, and when his hand came away, his eye was whole once more. A streak of black across his face was the only evidence of her punch.

Reason stopped banging on the door and decided it was nicer in the closet. "What are you?" Caitlin asked.

The boy lunged again.

Caitlin punched, but he caught her fist in one hand and took her by the throat with the other, lifting her off the ground as if she weighed nothing at all.

Caitlin clawed with her free hand at the vise of flesh and bone squeezing the life out of her. Her back slammed into a wall, hard, her head bouncing off brick. Her vision began to spin and fade to blackness as she tried to draw in a breath that wouldn't come.

No, please, God.

"Mind yourself!" Brendan shouted, but it sounded far away, or like it was underwater.

The hand came loose and Caitlin fell to the ground. Cool air rushed into her lungs as her vision, though still blurred, opened back up. Sharp pain lanced through her head as she gulped air and struggled for any kind of coherent thought, but each just slipped away.

Brendan crouched down and lifted Caitlin's face by her chin so he could look her in the eyes. "You all right there, love?"

He glanced over, and Caitlin followed his eyes. The girl was gripping her side and grunting as she struggled to her feet, the black smoke still seeping from between her fingers. Behind Brendan, Caitlin could see the boy clear on the other side of the street, also getting to his feet.

"Are you all right?" Brendan asked again.

"I, I think so." She put a hand to her head and kept blinking, waiting for this all to make some kind of sense. "What's going—" She stopped.

"What?" Brendan asked.

"My purse!"

"Go, Brother!" the girl shouted through clenched teeth.

"No, you don't!" Brendan spun in his crouch and threw his knife at the boy. It turned end over end as it sped to its target, the blade flashing in the streetlight.

The boy jumped several feet up to grab an overhang, swung himself up into the air, and landed on the roof of a ten-story building.

The knife passed where the boy had just been and stuck in the bricks.

Caitlin stared, openmouthed, hoping that any moment she'd wake up.

The boy turned and ran, vanishing into the darkness, his laughter fading behind him.

"You fecking coward!" Brendan screamed.

Caitlin's heart was trying to escape her chest, then her vision snapped into clarity as she saw the girl charging Brendan. The warning moved up her throat, but she knew she couldn't say it in time.

With one hand, Brendan snatched the girl out of the air like a lobbed softball and, with a grunt of effort, drove her into the wall. The girl's skull made a cracking sound as it hit the bricks.

Caitlin gasped and reflexively turned away, eyes closed tight. She covered her ears with shaking hands, desperate to deflect the sounds of the girl's struggle. A nightmare, this had to be a nightmare. Nothing this bad could be real. It had to be bits from a horror movie she'd seen as a kid that her subconscious had dredged up and formed into this.

The girl screamed in pain. Caitlin pressed her hands harder against her ears, but the shriek pierced into her brain. She wanted to scream, or vomit, but instead she chanced a glance and saw the girl pinned to the wall by a knife in her shoulder. Darkness, not smoke, Caitlin realized, poured from the wound, and again tiny white lights danced in it. She jerked back around, closing her eyes and bending near double to shield herself from this horrific scene. Why was no one coming? Someone had to have heard all this. Where the hell were the cops?

Brendan said something, but Caitlin couldn't hear it over the wailing. The girl screamed back in that glass-shattering shriek, and while Caitlin couldn't understand the language, there was something familiar about it.

There was the sound of metal against stone, followed by another scream. Caitlin heard the unmistakable sound of splintering bone, and the girl's voice became a pathetic gurgling sound.

Caitlin pressed her head against the brick wall beside her and drew in deep breaths to try and keep the sudden dizziness at bay. This wasn't like the things she'd seen at the hospital. That was always after the fact, always insulated from the actual violence. She'd never been in the midst of it. Now she was drowning in it.

The gurgling finally stopped, and the sudden silence was overwhelming. Caitlin turned and opened her eyes in time to see the girl disappear into a cloud of darkness sprinkled with lights. In moments, the cloud had dissipated, leaving only a knife handle sticking out of the wall.

Brendan knelt down beside Caitlin. "You still with me, Áin—" His breath caught in his throat. "Uh, love? Did they hurt you?" He looked at her arms and face, his gentle hands moving over her neck and shoulders.

Caitlin's mind was grasping for anything that even

resembled normal, but she couldn't find it. She still felt dizzy, and nothing seemed to hold in her mind, until finally, a single thought rose to the surface of the maelstrom when she looked at the knife still in the wall. She kicked at Brendan. "Get away from me!"

He stumbled back and stared at her.

"I don't know what, who you are, but just stay back." She began inching away from him.

He raised his hands and his eyes looked sad. "I'm not going to hurt you, love. If I wanted that, I wouldn't have stepped in, now, would I?"

He kept talking but Caitlin didn't hear it. She tried to speak, but nothing would come out. Tightness in her chest made it hard to breathe, and things started to go black again.

"Don't lock up on me," Brendan said. "Come on back, love. It's over. You're safe now. They're gone."

"You—" She stopped, and looked from Brendan to the knife buried in the wall. With a great deal of effort, she pointed a shaking hand at the blade. "You killed—"

Brendan made a pained expression, but it was gone in an instant. "Breathe. You've got to breathe." His eyes seemed to radiate something that was oddly comforting, but the streetlights cast shadows over his face that made his scars more prominent, almost feral.

"I, what just happened?" The logical voice in her head was now out of the closet and ranting.

"Oíche-sidhe."

"I'm sorry? What?"

"Dark fae."

Caitlin blinked.

"Faeries? The sidhe, fair folk?" He glanced over his shoulder. "Though the oíche aren't what I'd call fair."

"No, that's not possible." She shook her head and started laughing. "No, there's no such thing as faeries."

"I think they'd beg to differ with you on that, love." He stood and offered her his hand. "Come on now, up with you."

She stared into his eyes and somehow knew he was telling the truth. Her floundering mind seized on this ridiculous explanation as a refuge from the unexplainable events.

"Faeries?" She thought of all the stories her grandmother had told her, but the faeries in those stories were nothing like these. No. Faeries don't dress like Hot Topic refugees. They dance in mushroom circles or drink the bowl of cream left out for them.

This was all too much. Caitlin had to get home, back to the sanity of her life. She looked around. "Damn it, where are they?"

"Where are what?"

Her eyes darted to a glint in the streetlight. She grabbed the keys and got to her feet.

"Would you wait a bleeding minute?"

Caitlin got to her feet and shoved Brendan aside. "Just stay away from me." She moved on shaky legs to her car. "I have to get home."

Brendan followed her. "I can help."

Caitlin unlocked her car, opened the door, and got in. She paused when she saw Brendan, then forgot to shut the door. She tried to put her key in the ignition, but her hands were shaking so badly she dropped them. Brendan bent to pick them up for her, but she got to them first.

"I—thank you, but—" She closed the door as she jammed the key into the ignition and turned the engine over.

"Wait, you should ride with me. You're in no shape to drive, and me truck is just—"

Caitlin put the car in gear, stepped on the gas, and sped away from the curb, leaving Brendan with nothing but the smell of burned rubber.

CHAPTER THREE

Caitlin gripped the wheel so hard that her hands ached as she tore down the street. She reached for her cell phone, only to remember it was in her absconded purse. She cursed under her breath and pressed the accelerator. She had to distance herself from all this; if she could just see Fiona, everything would be okay. The high speed almost caused her to lose control of the small car, but she somehow managed to keep it on the road. She tapped the brakes and slowed down, but no matter how many miles passed, the feeling of dread wouldn't abate.

After what seemed like a century, she skidded to a stop in her driveway and leapt out almost before the car had stopped. She started to push her key in the house's lock, but the front door was open.

Caitlin fought to ignore the knot in her stomach as she stepped into the living room.

The place was quiet and still. She looked around. "Fiona? Kris?"

No answer.

She spotted Kris lying on the floor behind the coffee table. Caitlin ran to her friend and knelt down beside her. She found no obvious injuries, but Kris was unconscious.

"Fiona?" Caitlin called as loud as she could manage.

"Mommy!" Fiona yelled from upstairs, and the tone of her voice froze Caitlin's blood.

Before the sound faded, Caitlin was on her feet and running up the stairs. As she reached the second floor, Fiona's door flew open and the little girl ran out. Before she could reach Caitlin, white hands and arms sheathed in black fabric grabbed her.

"Mommy!"

"No!" Caitlin roared and charged into the room.

Amid the bright colors and stuffed animals, the boy who had attacked Caitlin was placing a stump of wood in Fiona's bed and muttering over it. It shimmered and almost looked like Fiona, but the body was pale and lifeless.

Caitlin tore her eyes away from the simulacrum and saw a second boy, almost a twin of the first but without the black streak on his cheek, struggling to keep hold of Fiona, who was kicking and punching him.

Caitlin lunged for her child's outstretched hand.

The boy trying to restrain Fiona muttered something and a cold shiver passed over Caitlin.

Fiona's tear-streaked face went quiet and her body went limp.

"No! My baby!" Caitlin screamed.

The boy on the bed, who'd just turned around, said something Caitlin couldn't hear. She felt another wave of cold, but it vanished in an instant, and she drove her fist into the faerie's face.

"Son of a bitch, I'll kill you!" she said. Bone cracked under her knuckles and the oíche released Fiona as he spun and fell to the floor.

Caitlin grabbed Fiona and turned to run from the room.

"*Codail!*" a soft voice said into her ear as the voice's owner threw dust into her eyes.

Caitlin shook away a wave of dizziness and drove an elbow into the ribs of whoever was behind her. She heard the person grunt, stumble back, and hit the wall outside the room.

"Sleep!" the one on the bed shouted, and threw more dust at her.

As Caitlin took a step forward, her leg went out from under her. She drew Fiona close and turned so the child fell on her rather than the other way around.

Sprawled on the hardwood floor, her body wasn't responding to her commands, and her eyes grew heavy as she watched the boy casually climb off the bed. He smirked as he pulled Fiona from her arms.

Inside her mind, Caitlin screamed that he was supposed to be taking her, not Fiona. She willed her body to grip her child and pull her back, to stand and fight. No sound came from her and her body didn't answer.

The boy snickered as he lifted one of Fiona's arms

and waved it at Caitlin. "Bye-bye, Mommy," he said, his words soaked with derision.

"No," Caitlin managed to say. In a final push of will, she reached with one arm for her child.

The oíche slapped her hand away and it fell to the ground.

Tears poured from her eyes.

The oíche she'd punched gave her one last look before picking up a pink blanket from the bed and stepping over her. The one holding Fiona kicked Caitlin in the stomach before following his compatriot out of the room.

Her eyes closed and darkness overtook her.

CHAPTER FOUR

Brendan sprinted down the street to his truck. As he opened the door, Riley came running around a different corner. The elf stopped when he saw Brendan.

"What the hell's going on?" Riley asked. "I thought—"

"Plan's changed, boss," Brendan said as he climbed in and started the engine. "The fecking oíche made a move we weren't expecting."

"Brendan, wait, what are you—?"

The old truck bounced over the curb and sped off. Thankfully, the streets were nearly empty. It was late enough to avoid people heading out for the evening and early enough to avoid them going home, and thanks to Riley, there wouldn't be a copper for miles. Brendan rolled down the window where he'd seen Caitlin last. He focused for a moment, then his senses came to life and he sniffed the air.

Nothing.

"Dar fia!"

He began to fear he'd truly lost her trail, when, beneath a mix of exhaust, damp asphalt, and cooking food, he found her scent. It was faint, but it was there, and it was Áine's.

The truck came to a stop in the middle of the road as his breath caught in his throat. He inhaled again, desperate for more, but the scent was gone.

Then he realized what he was doing. Cursing his stupidity and the delay it was causing, he leapt out and redoubled his focus as he turned in all directions. After a few seconds, he found Caitlin's scent again, and while it was so very close to Áine's, it had more powder and flowers to it. It was not Áine's. He reminded himself of that repeatedly as he got back in the truck and sped off.

He tore around corners and through the vacant streets. Soon the city shifted from businesses to houses, and Caitlin's scent was diluted amid the smells of a thousand homes. He stopped the truck, clenched his shaking hands into fists, and closed his eyes. The garbage left out for pickup in the morning wasn't helping.

A breeze blew in the open window from the south, bearing the faintest hint of her. His eyes opened, and he turned his truck in that direction. The streets all began to look the same, and her scent again became more sporadic.

"Go hifreann leat. You won't win this time." He spotted her car in his peripheral vision and sped down the street.

The car was parked in the driveway of a modest home, driver's side door still open, as was the front door to the house.

He parked behind the car, shut off his truck's motor, and opened the door with one hand as he grabbed a knife with his other. As he passed her car, he closed the open door and looked around.

Nothing was moving; no birds, no insects, nothing. He hated the suburbs.

He crept to the open front door. Caitlin's scent poured through it and into the night air. He took a deep breath and moved closer. As he did, he smelled it. Just beneath Caitlin's was the scent of the fae. It was strong, which meant they'd just left or were still here. The combination of familiar smells stirred the sleeping monster inside him, but he pushed the beast back down.

He stepped to one side of the doorway and turned his head so one ear was angled in. He heard a slow, steady heartbeat just inside. At the sound of the soft, even breathing, his heart sank.

Knife at the ready, he scanned the room. Several crayon drawings hung on the fridge door in the kitchen to his right. A living room with children's toys scattered about was to the left. The couch, chair, tables, and large wooden television stand showed no signs of struggle.

On the far side of the room lay a woman with brown hair, facedown. She was the source of the breathing and heartbeat, but she wasn't who he was looking for. He rolled her over. She was a young girl, and pretty.

"Fecking slumber," he muttered. He saw the stairs and could hear another heartbeat and slow breathing. He took them two at time without making a sound.

Upon reaching the second floor, he found to his right an open door leading to the bathroom. To the left, the hallway vanished around a corner. Halfway down was a second open door.

You're too late. The oíche are long gone, else they'd have been on you before this.

"Shut it, you." He tucked the knife behind his back.

It was a child's room with soft pink walls and white furniture. Stuffed animals were everywhere. When he saw the stump of wood tucked under a blanket on the bed, he gritted his teeth and forced himself to stay calm. At his feet lay Caitlin, one arm outstretched.

He sighed and put the events together as he rolled Caitlin onto her back. "I tried to warn you, didn't I?"

Well, doesn't this all seem familiar—?

"Come on, then." He carried her down the stairs to the living room. There, he laid her on the couch and put a pillow under her head, then set the other girl in the chair.

Running a hand through his hair, he paced and considered his options. There weren't many, and those weren't appealing. He was too far outside Boston to know anyone he could ask for help, and that meant—

His head jerked around as he heard a car racing down the road. He peeked out the door. The car was heading this way, fast. The headlights prevented him from seeing the driver.

"*Damnú air!*" He went into the kitchen, found a shadow, and ducked out of sight.

Tires screeched as the car came to a stop. A door opened and slammed closed, then someone ran up to the house.

Brendan drew the knife out, slowed his breathing, and readied himself.

A tall, thin man, who couldn't be much into his thirties, stepped inside. He was well dressed, with tousled brown hair, an immaculately trimmed goatee, and wire frame glasses.

"Oh my—Caitlin?" He knelt beside the couch, shook her, and touched her face. "Wake up. It's Edward." He slapped her face gently, then shook her again.

Brendan studied Edward, then glanced around the room at the pictures. They were all of a little girl, or Caitlin and the child together. Ignoring the stabbing pain in his heart, he turned his focus back to Edward. Whoever he was, he wasn't important enough to be in any of the photos.

Edward passed a hand over Caitlin's face and muttered something.

Brendan's eyes went wide as he smelled magic. While Edward focused, Brendan moved silently.

"Who did this to you?" Edward wondered aloud, and ended the spell.

"Faeries," Brendan answered from right behind him. "*Oíche-sidhe*, if you're wanting to be exact about it."

Edward jumped and spun around at the same time, or he tried to. His knee caught the couch, and he fell backwards. His shoulder slammed against the coffee table and his head hit the couch, bouncing him back. He settled on the floor, looking up at Brendan with huge eyes, glasses askew.

"Graceful that was," Brendan said. "But there's something I don't understand here, boss."

Edward began inching away on his backside. "Who, who are you?"

Brendan ignored the ammonia-like smell of fear that was filling the room. "How is it you didn't sense the fae slumber right away?"

"What did you do to them?" Edward's face hardened. He moved to his knees and drew a hand back.

"It weren't me, you *gobdaw*. Now, answer the bleeding question. What kind of fecking wizard doesn't recognize a fae sleep?"

"What?" Edward blinked at him. "How did you—"

"I'm not asking again, who the bloody hell are you?"

Edward gnashed his teeth. "*Tân!*" A small ball of flame appeared in his shaking palm. "No," he said. "Who are you?"

Brendan couldn't help but chuckle. "You'd best be putting that out, boyo, unless of course you mean to be burning the place down." He stared hard into Edward's eyes.

Edward flinched and the flame snuffed out. "Crud."

Brendan sheathed his knife, grabbed Edward by his shirt, and lifted him clear off the ground. "I didn't do this. Would I just be sitting here having me a cup of tea if I had?" He pulled Edward close. "Now, answer me question. Who are you?"

"I, I'm a friend of Caitlin's." Edward nodded to the couch. "I'm a doctor. I work at the hospital with her."

"And what are you doing here?"

"She'd told me she was having night terrors. I placed a protection spell on her earlier tonight, just to be safe. I came over when it was triggered."

Brendan studied Edward for a moment, then set him down.

Edward straightened his glasses and looked down at Caitlin. "So, who did this?"

Brendan rolled his eyes. "I told you already, didn't I? It were oíche-sidhe."

Edward's eyes went wide, and for a moment he stopped breathing. "They took Fiona, didn't they?"

Brendan muttered something under his breath. "Aye, they got Caitlin's purse—"

"Her purse?"

"She likely had something of herself in it."

Edward just stared.

"To get past the hearth protections?" Brendan said.

Another blank stare.

"Bloody hell, what kind of wizard are you?" Brendan asked. "You don't know a fae slumber, you don't know the oíche, and you don't know the hearth protections. What is it you do know, then?"

"Is, is that really relevant right now?" Edward stammered as he looked away.

"Aye, a bit, don't you think?" Brendan took a step forward, forcing Edward to take one back. "Where'd you learn your craft, then? A fecking mail-in course? Or did an uncle leave you his magic books?"

Edward blanched and looked away.

"Ah, bloody hell. That's it, isn't it?" Brendan laughed. "Jesus, man. What're you thinking, getting into this business?"

"It was my Taid, I mean, grandfather," Edward said. "Besides, I wasn't even sure there were other—" He waved his hand. "Others like me."

Brendan nodded. "Oh, well, that makes all the difference, then."

"Is the sarcasm really necessary?"

"You needn't worry, amateur night is over." Brendan moved toward Caitlin. "Stand aside, bucko."

Edward put his hand out to push Brendan away, but Brendan caught his hand and twisted it around. Edward fell to his knees with a cry, and Brendan held him there, on the edge of breaking his arm.

"I'm getting these two out of this house before the dark faeries what made off with the child decide to come back and collect them as well." He pushed Edward face-first onto the floor. "I suggest you get your arse out of here as well." He picked up Caitlin. "Or don't. It don't bother me a whit, either way."

"Wait," Edward said from the floor. "Please, I can help!"

Brendan closed his eyes and sighed. "I've got no time for someone stumbling about. This is a dangerous business, and if I'm to get the *girseach* back from those dark bastards, I can't be spending time hand-holding the likes of you."

"But—"

"Look, I can see she's a friend, and I respect your wanting to help—"

"We can take them to my place, they'll be safe there."

Brendan looked away and drew in a long breath.

"I have wards around my house." Edward waited for Brendan to look back at him. "Those I can do very well."

Brendan sighed. What else was he going to do? Leaving them in a dell somewhere wouldn't work. The oíche weren't the most nature-bound fae, but plenty of the Rogue Court fae were, and some of them were friendly to the oíche.

"Please, I really can help."

Brendan looked him in the eye again.

Edward gritted his teeth, but he didn't flinch.

"How far is it, then?"

"Not far." Edward got to his feet. "It's just outside of town. We can be there in twenty minutes."

"All right, then."

"I'm Edward, Edward Huntington," he said, offering his hand.

Brendan looked down at Caitlin's limp form in his arms and raised an eyebrow. "You think maybe we should hold off on all the pleasantries till we get them out of here?"

Edward lowered his hand.

Brendan nodded at the dark-haired girl. "Get that one and put her in your car. I'll follow you with this one."

Edward nodded and went over to Kris, who was still sleeping.

Brendan looked outside. No neighbors were nosing about, so he carried Caitlin to his truck and secured her in the passenger seat. When he finished, he saw Edward carrying the other girl. His face was red and he was sucking in sharp, short breaths.

"What've I gotten meself into?" Brendan watched Edward struggle. "A wizard what's useless as a chocolate teapot and as strong as a nine-year-old girl." He opened the passenger door of the black luxury sedan parked in the street, then took Kris from Edward's arms and buckled her in the front seat.

"All right, then," Brendan said. "You're leading the way. If you get stopped, just tell the coppers you're taking her home after a few too many down at the pub."

"I'm sorry, did you say 'coppers'?"

"Aye, the fecking constables, man."

Edward opened his mouth.

"The police?"

"No, I got that, I just—"

Brendan swore under his breath and started walking back to his truck.

"Wait. Can I at least know your name?"

Brendan eyed him.

After a moment, Edward winced. "Right. Wizards, names, all that. Sorry."

As Edward walked around the car, Brendan let out a deep sigh. "So, not completely clueless, then?" Edward stopped, and Brendan held out his hand. "Brendan Kavanaugh."

"Thank you, Brendan." Edward smiled as he shook Brendan's hand.

After a few seconds, Brendan looked down. "Are we done holding hands?"

Edward winced again and let go. He muttered something as he got into his car.

Brendan shook his head as he walked to his truck. "Let's just hope Merlin doesn't get lost on his way home."

CHAPTER FIVE

Memories threatened to consume Brendan, but he pushed them aside again as he followed Edward. He instead tried to convince himself that the mounting similarities in this mess were just coincidences and didn't mean anything.

It is uncanny, isn't it?

Brendan focused on the road, and soon the streets of identical homes turned into a wooded country back road. He kept an ear on Caitlin's breathing and heartbeat. He even glanced over a few times, but he never allowed his gaze to linger.

Edward's car pulled into a driveway, and Brendan parked behind him. The neighborhood was the old New England style, big colonial homes, large lots, and plenty of trees.

Keeping a watchful eye on the trees and shadows, Brendan got out and opened the passenger door. Another quick glance, this time at the neighbors, told him that even if someone was watching, they wouldn't be able to see anything. He sniffed the air, but the only faeries he smelled were on Caitlin.

As he lifted her, her head fell against his chest and unruly red hair brushed his chin. His knees threatened to buckle. Instead, he closed his eyes and sucked in a breath.

"Leave her for now, boss," Brendan said as he walked past Edward, who was retrieving the other girl. "Just get the door. I'll come back for her once we get this one safe inside."

Symbols of warding were carved into the wood frame of the house, and a hint of magic was in the air. They were good wards. Brendan hadn't sensed them until he was almost on top of them. Odds were, most people would never see them at all, even if they looked for them.

Edward reached the front door, but instead of putting his key in it, he passed his hand over the knob and spoke something. The door opened and the symbols vanished from sight.

Brendan nodded as he walked past. "Not bad there."

"Thanks." Edward flipped a switch on the wall and the room lit to show an entryway and living room decorated in dark brown leathers and rich hardwoods. It could've been something out of an Old English gentleman's club. "You can set her on the couch." He pointed to the large overstuffed sofa.

Brendan placed a pillow behind Caitlin's head and gingerly brushed hair from her face.

Edward cleared his throat. "Kris is, uh, still in my car."

Brendan winced and stood quickly.

Edward eyed him as he walked by. Brendan could feel it. He returned with the other girl, and Edward motioned to a love seat as he laid a blanket over Caitlin. "Over here."

Although the girl wasn't tall, her legs still reached past the armrest. Taking a cue from Edward, Brendan found another blanket and draped it over her.

"So, what do we do now?" Edward sat on the arm of the sofa, putting himself between Brendan and Caitlin.

Brendan looked Edward up and down, then in the eye.

"What?" Edward leaned back as his eyes twitched.

"You're staying here and watching over them," Brendan said. "Keep your wards up and going till I come back. The oíche might've tracked us here."

"What are you going to do?"

Brendan let out a long sigh. He'd been trying to put off the inevitable, but it wouldn't be ignored any longer. He wasn't going to find any useful information without an older friend's help. "Well, I'm off to have a bit of a chat with someone who might know about where the oíche took the girl." He turned and made for the door. Maybe there was another option though.

"Wait a second." Edward stepped in Brendan's path. "We going to do this dance again, then, are we?"

"Would you please tell me what's going on here?"

"You're dense as a block of Connemara marble. I told you already, didn't I? Faer—"

"Yes, I heard you the other eight times. Faeries accosted Caitlin, then used her purse or something in it to get past some kind of protection and kidnap Fiona. But why would faeries take her?"

"It don't matter."

"What? Of course it matters! Does this kind of thing happen all the time?"

Brendan swallowed. "Not like it used to, but—"

"Look, I'm the closest thing she has to family." He pointed at Caitlin. "I don't know anything about you, though."

"Easy there, buc—"

"No!" Edward took a step closer. "Maybe you don't care why they took her daughter, but I've known that little girl since she was born. She's like my own daughter."

"Will it help get her back?"

"What?"

"Will knowing why they did it help get her back?"

"It might, actually. I'll be the first to admit I don't know much about all this, but I can help."

Brendan laughed.

"You dismiss me out of hand and I'm just supposed to trust you with getting my friend's daughter back?"

After watching Edward for a moment, Brendan half smiled and nodded. "Aye, you're right."

"I, what?" Edward furrowed his brow. "I am?"

"Time is an issue here, boss. There are all kinds of things they could want the *girseach* for, but figuring out that kind of thing isn't what I do."

Edward waited.

"I don't have time to go into it all, either way," Brendan said. "You're right, you've got no reason to trust me, but we need to get past that now, don't we?"

"I suppose you're right." Edward narrowed his eyes. "Do you swear?"

"What?"

"You seem the sort who values honor and your word. Do you swear that you're only in this to help Caitlin get her daughter back?"

"No."

Edward's face dropped.

Brendan smiled and stepped close. "I'm also interested in giving the oíche a dose they won't soon forget. And that's the truth of it, lad. You've my word."

Edward looked at Brendan for a long moment before he nodded. "All right." He stepped to one side. "What do I do if they wake up while you're gone?"

"They won't stir till dawn at the earliest." Brendan put a hand on Edward's shoulder. "Just watch over them and keep them safe. I'll be back when I find something or, God willing, the *girseach* herself."

"Why'd you help her?" Edward asked as Brendan started to leave. "You don't know Caitlin or Kris. So . . ."

Brendan shrugged. "Well, it's the right thing to do, isn't it? You can't just leave someone to the mercy of this like. They've got none, you see." He let out a breath. "I told you figuring things out wasn't what I do."

Edward nodded.

"Well, this is what I do." Brendan didn't look away from Caitlin. "I don't just walk away."

Not anymore.

"A lot of people can and do. It's human nature to look out for ourselves above anyone else," Edward said.

"Well, it's not my nature, then." Brendan stepped outside. "Raise the wards as soon as the door is shut, and don't lower them for nothing. I'll be back, I swear it."

Brendan closed the door behind him and glanced over his shoulder when he felt the thrum of the wards. He got into his truck, turned the engine over, and headed back to the highway.

CHAPTER SIX

Edward passed his hand over the knob and focused his intent. The familiar tension of the wards coming to life put his heart a little more at ease, but apprehension ate at his insides as the headlights of Brendan's old truck flashed through the window. The vehicle vanished down the street, and Edward was alone in the overwhelming silence.

He let out a deep sigh and ran his hands through his hair.

"All right, genius, what now?" he asked, but the darkness didn't answer. "Sure, now you've got nothing to add."

He retrieved a stethoscope and a sphygmomanometer from his black doctor's bag. There were upsides to being a psychiatrist besides being able to prescribe meds. While he didn't often use his medical training, he remembered it in pristine detail. Actually, he remembered everything in pristine detail. He'd always had an eidetic memory, or as close to one as he'd ever heard of, but it had proven to be both a boon and a hindrance for him. He'd always done well in school, never having to study something more than once, which had earned him a full scholarship. Unfortunately, as a general rule people didn't like spending time with a walking, talking encyclopedia.

He checked the girls. Their blood pressure was good, their breathing and heart rates were slow but not dangerously so. This fae slumber was fascinating. The effect was more powerful than the strongest anesthesia. It made him wonder if Rip Van Winkle was more than just a story.

As he put his equipment away, he found himself staring at Caitlin, and he thought back to their first meeting, when she was just a nursing intern. She'd been so lovely that he'd actually walked into a wall when he'd seen her. He'd been mortified, but she'd just smiled and helped him up. He smiled now as well, remembering so many shared lunch hours at work after that, and those wonderful Saturdays he'd spent with Caitlin and Fiona at the park. He couldn't help but smile as he thought of Fiona's laughter and Caitlin's radiant smile as she'd pushed the giggling little girl on the swing. She was his best friend. Hell, she was his only friend, and he'd contented himself with that eventually.

He let out a sigh, turned the large leather chair to face the couch, and collapsed into it. His head fell back, and, as he stared up at the ceiling, he slammed his hand on the arm of the chair. That was another problem with having an eidetic memory. He was so used to knowing things that when he didn't, it really, really, REALLY bothered him, especially when it was something he should know, like, say, a wizard knowing about faeries.

He rolled his head to one side until he was staring at the open door to his study.

So do something. You're a wizard, do some wizarding.

Nghalon, as he'd named the voice, just to have something to call it, was one of the less comforting aspects of the house. Edward wasn't even sure it was the house, because sometimes he heard Nghalon in his office as well. No one else could hear it, and as a result, he frequently wondered if practicing magic was causing him to lose his mind. Of course, he'd never heard of an auditory hallucination being quite so sarcastic. It was like being haunted by the ghosts of Waldorf and Statler from *The Muppet Show*.

"Sure, now you have some advice," Edward said. He extricated himself from the chair. The study was large, and like all the rooms in the house, it didn't fit the layout. The house was larger on the inside than on the outside, literally. He'd taken measurements once to be sure.

The blaze in the fireplace, which took up nearly a third of the wall, was crackling as always. Someday he'd have to figure out how to extinguish it. It was like a giant version of a trick birthday candle. Shelves covered the walls, and they were filled with books ranging from recent medical references to ancient tomes in languages he couldn't even identify. An old wooden desk and chair near the center of the room, a small wet bar, and a love seat not far from the desk finished the décor.

He poured himself some whiskey, took a sip, then set the glass on the desk and walked to a bookcase. He went along the shelves, reading the titles. Of course, in any other setting, he'd be able to remember every title and its location, but another treat of this house was the library's tendency to rearrange the books on its own. Oftentimes he'd find entirely new books. They usually had to do with whatever he was considering at the time, so that rather made up for the rearranging thing, which really annoyed him.

A familiar title jumped out at him. He removed the book and sat down at his desk. He turned on some music to settle his nerves, and Tom Waits's gravelly voice filled the silence as Edward took another drink. He flipped through the book's pages.

Hadn't he seen some kind of tracking spell before? Maybe he could use it to find Fiona. Alternatively, maybe he could find a way to wake Caitlin.

"No, let's solve problems, not create new ones," he told himself.

After several minutes, he hadn't found anything. He rubbed the bridge of his nose and sighed. When he opened his eyes, he flipped more pages, his patience faltering.

Then he stopped.

He adjusted his glasses and turned back a couple

pages. The symbols were familiar. He read the description and noted the symbols were related to connections and scrying. Scrying! If he could see Fiona, then he could not only find out where she was but also make sure she was okay. He examined the page; it looked simple enough.

Famous last words.

"Not now," he said to Nghalon. "Besides, you were wrong about the protection spell, weren't you? I told you I knew what I was doing then, and I still do."

He pulled a sheet of paper and a pen from the desk drawer. Thankfully, this spell didn't require blood over ink. He copied the circle from the book on a little bigger scale. He slowed his breathing and focused on the intent behind the symbols, filling them with power. When he finished, he looked the drawing over and compared it to the original. It was a perfect match. Now he just needed to collect the ingredients.

He opened a large steamer trunk behind the love seat and looked over the labeled boxes, collecting what he needed. A crystal, a small silver bowl, and—

"Angel's tears?"

He looked closer at the book to make sure he'd translated it right. When he knew he had, he looked in the trunk and, sure enough, found a small glass bottle labeled such. When he saw the last item on the list, his heart sank.

"A piece of the one you seek."

"You stupid . . ." He should've known he'd need something of Fiona's, blood, hair, something. But where would he get anything like that? Caitlin didn't have her purse, and he couldn't leave to go to her house.

He carried the items he'd collected to the desk and considered the problem. A sip into his second whiskey, the answer came to him, and he wanted to kick himself. Of course, it was going to be a bit awkward, but he resigned himself to the task, rose, and walked to the living room.

Caitlin was still sleeping, her chest rising and falling in a most appealing—

He clenched his jaw. It was the only way. He just had to treat it like an examination. He took a deep breath, pulled the blanket away, and knelt down.

Slowly and deliberately, he began looking over her blouse for stray hairs. He reminded himself of the reason he was doing this, and that it didn't make him a pervert.

He didn't find anything.

When another thought came to him, he closed his eyes and rubbed his temples.

"You're not just dreaming these things up to satiate some perverse fantasy," he whispered. "There's no other option." It was a sound argument and he intended to cling to it, desperately.

He opened his eyes, reached down, and slipped a hand into the front pocket of Caitlin's slacks. They were tight, which made it hard for him to keep his hand away from her leg. The shaking of his hand didn't help either.

Again, nothing.

He looked at the other pocket, sighed, and cast a beseeching look skyward. After a moment, he shoved the voice that was calling him a sad little deviant down, next to the one telling him to enjoy it. They could keep each other company and let him focus on the task at hand.

He slid his hand into Caitlin's other pocket, and his fingertips brushed something. He gripped it between two fingers and pulled it out. When he saw the spots of discoloration on the handkerchief, he couldn't help but smile.

"Oh, thank God for kids and snot."

He covered Caitlin with the blanket and went back into the study. He placed the bowl inside the inner circle on the paper. Next, he poured in the angel's tears until the bottom of the bowl was just covered. He wrapped the crystal in the handkerchief, took a deep breath to focus, then slowly lowered the wrapped crystal into the bowl.

"*Yn dangos i mi beth sy'n cuddio. Dangos i mi Fiona,*" he said slowly.

There was sudden pressure in the room. It kept building with the magic, and soon he was having trouble keeping hold of it all. He gritted his teeth and redoubled his efforts, but it was like trying to hold a fire hose at full blast. At the edges of his senses, he could feel sweat beading on his forehead.

He had to focus. He could do this.

Inch by inch, the power started slipping away from him, but at the same time, his senses began to expand out of the room and he almost thought he could smell Fiona, maybe even hear her voice. Exhilaration flooded him, then he was falling, and he fought to keep his focus.

There was a flash, and he saw Fiona!

She was lying on a concrete floor holding a pink blanket, apparently sleeping. He reached out for her, but the world around him vanished and he found himself in complete and utter darkness. He took a cautious step forward, but there was no sense of movement, or even of distance. A cold and pervasive fear crawled up his spine.

He sensed something else in the darkness. He wasn't alone.

He fought to break the connection, to end the spell, but panic had shattered his concentration and now the magic had a life of its own. He felt like a little kid again, only this time he was trapped under the bed and the monsters were real.

The presence drew nearer. Glowing red eyes emerged from the darkness. He could feel it reach out for him.

"NO!"

His mind raced. In a flash of desperation, he reached out to his body and slammed his hands down onto his desk. When the presence seemed mere inches away, he felt a flood of pain as the whiskey glass shattered and the shards bit into his hand.

His eyes snapped open. The bowl was shaking inside the circle.

"Oh fu—"

The crystal exploded and threw him backwards. His legs struck the bottom of the desk, the chair tipped over backwards, he smacked into the chair, and his head bounced on the hardwood floor.

He lay there in a cold sweat, bleeding and trying to get his emotions under control. The music continued to play. He closed his eyes tight and felt tears roll down his cheeks.

When he got to his feet, he bandaged his hand and started pacing. Fiona's image came to him again, clear and just out of reach.

"Damn it all!" He shoved the items off his desk and they crashed to the floor. He righted the chair, sat down, and put his face in his hands.

"Nicely done." How many times did he need to learn the same lesson? Knowledge and practical application were two different things. He was just glad Nghalon wasn't saying "I told you so," even if he was the only one who ever heard it. Glass shards and powdered crystal were everywhere, and the handkerchief was scorched. Somehow, the bowl had survived.

All he could think of was those two glowing red eyes and the presence reaching for him. His heart stuttered and his hands started to shake as if it were in the room with him even now.

When the image passed, his face was wet from tears and his body was shaking. Once he calmed down, he cleaned up the debris of his failure and ensuing tantrum. He found comfort in both the familiar task and restoring order to his home. Once the wreckage was disposed of, he got a fresh glass, poured two fingers of whiskey, and downed it in a single gulp. He leaned back in the chair. The wiser course would be to listen to music and drink until Brendan came back. Leave it to someone who knew what he was doing.

He glanced at the living room. "I don't know if I can—"

Something shifted on a bookcase.

He ground his teeth and scanned the titles. They'd moved again. On the third row, he saw the newest addition to his library. He pulled the book out and looked at the cover. In gold embossed Welsh, he saw the words *Llyfr y tylwyth teg.* The Book of Faeries.

He looked around the empty room. "Perhaps you could do this a little sooner next time?"

As he opened the book, the shaking in his hands stopped. Maybe he could do something after all.

CHAPTER SEVEN

After a long, quiet time on I-93, Brendan saw the Boston skyline rise on the horizon. It hardly looked like the same city. The towers of glass and steel, and the haze of light that hung over them, seemed to swallow the city he'd once called home. As expected, Brendan's memories threatened to get the better of him, but he dragged them away, tossed his cigarette butt out the window, and accelerated across the Bunker Hill bridge.

The city seemed to now grow and change faster than ever. Hopefully, he'd still be able to find his way around.

As he emerged from the tunnel, it struck him how attempts to preserve the city's history had only served to change it. The pungent smell of glass, steel, concrete, and car exhaust poured through the open window. True, coal, wood smoke, and rotting garbage hadn't been pleasurable, but it all felt so artificial now.

He parked his truck and pulled a black sweater over his head. He grabbed one of his sheathed knives, tucked it behind his back, and pulled the sweater down to conceal it. Before shutting the truck door, he grabbed a small wooden box from under the seat. Most of the night's stars were obscured by the glare of the city or blocked by the tall buildings, but near as he could tell, it was about one in the morning. He headed to a nearby alleyway, hoping the old tunnels and haunts were still there.

Cars rolled by as he walked. They added to the constant noise that seemed to permeate the city. He'd never really adjusted to the noise. Ireland had been so quiet. He missed that quiet, even more so as the years went by. He found hints of it in the more secluded reaches of New England, but it wasn't the same.

When he turned down the alley, the large ogre standing guard outside the door told him the tunnels were still in use. Of course, mortals would just see some big guy with no neck in front of a nondescript door.

Perhaps you'll be remembered.

The ogre was typical for his kind; pushing seven feet tall, muddy green skin, and bald. He had two enormous canine teeth that jutted up from his lower jaw and extended over his upper lip. The jeans, motorcycle boots, and long-sleeved black shirt stretching over his muscled form were apparently new fashion, as were the piercings in his lip, nose, and eyebrow.

"This here is a private club, sir," the ogre said in a

muddled cockney accent. He looked closer at Brendan and furrowed his brow. "Fian?"

Brendan clenched his jaw and nodded once. "Aye."

The ogre sniffed the air. His lip pulled back into a sneer, exposing yellow teeth, and he glared with his beady eyes. "I smell iron."

"I'm looking for information, not a ruckus." Brendan opened the box.

The ogre's eyes went wide and his mouth opened. "Is that—?"

"It is." Brendan closed the box. "Now, I'll not be leaving me blade with you."

The ogre glared.

"But I swear if no one gives me cause, it'll stay where it is."

The ogre laughed. "Someone breaking wind could be cause to a Fian."

Brendan stared at the ogre and took a long, slow, deep breath, then let it out even slower. "I'll ignore that insult this once, but don't be doing it again. Let me pass, mate. If no one means me harm, I'll do none."

The ogre considered for a long moment.

"I haven't got all bloody night here, tiny."

The ogre chuckled and opened the door. "All right, you're bound by your word. Any violation will be reported to the magister."

"Wouldn't want that," Brendan said under his breath as he walked through the door.

The tunnels were lined with old bricks and industrial lights set at ten-foot intervals, the kind with brass cages around the glass. No cords ran to the lights, and glowing crystals replaced bulbs.

Soon the tunnel split into three directions. It'd been a long time, but Brendan still remembered the way. He turned right and took some stairs down to another hallway. It ended at a plain wall. He reached down and pressed a brick. There was a clicking sound and a section of the wall swung inward. As he walked into Have-Nots Hall, the familiar smell of fae, sweat, blood, and beer hit him.

The entryway led to a catwalk around a massive stone chamber, dimly lit by no apparent source of illumination. Below was a patchwork bar fashioned of mix-match planks, and a line of rickety stools stood in front of it. Tables and chairs collected over the years filled the remaining space. The centerpiece of the room was the large copper cage, the makeshift ring it housed, and the fighters inside it. The place hadn't changed much, just more dust and dirt. The smell hadn't improved much, either.

As the bar's name suggested, the have-nots of the Rogue Court filled the place. The ogres appeared much like their counterpart at the front door. The trolls were as tall as ogres, but leaner, with skin more yellow in color. Dwarves, gnomes, and various other fae also packed the chamber and looked down at the fight from the catwalk.

In the ring was a troll, large even amongst trolls. His opponent was a pixie. From where Brendan watched, it appeared as little more than a ball of light.

"Poor bastard," he said and made for the stairs to the main floor.

He got several dark looks as he walked by, and everyone gave him a wide berth. He ignored them and their mutterings.

When he reached the ground level, he scanned the room, looking for a familiar, and hopefully friendly, face. In the cage, the troll swung a fist down. The pixie, hovering in the air, caught the fist and didn't move an inch. There was a high-pitched grunt as the tiny fae spun and hurled the troll across the ring and into the cage.

Cheers erupted from the patrons.

Brendan laughed.

"By summer's blooming flowers! Brendan? Is that really you?" a small, childlike voice asked.

A boy of about ten stepped out of the crowd, large mug in hand. His long ears were pointed and extended past the back of his head. He was dressed in brown corduroy pants and a black shirt with white lettering that read, "I'm huge in Japan." A mess of unkempt brown hair and a giant toothy grin finished the look.

Brendan smiled at the brownie. "Abán?"

Abán offered his hand. "It's good to see you again, old friend. It's been a long time." There was a crash from the cage behind them, but Abán didn't flinch. He glanced at the fight, then back to Brendan. "If you're looking to make some coin, I've got just the—"

"Sorry, mate. I told you before I was done with that, and I still am."

Abán nodded. "Well then, come have a drink with me and we'll catch up."

As Abán led Brendan away from the cage, a cracking sound was followed by a bellow of pain from the troll and the noise of a fist pounding the mat. A chime announced the fight was over, and the crowd headed off to drink and make wagers before the next bout.

Abán climbed into a seat at an empty table.

"What'll you have?" Abán asked. "On me."

"I've got no time, I'm afraid."

"Oh?" Abán's face sagged in disappointment, which made him appear even more childlike.

"I need me some information."

Abán sighed. "As ever."

"Haven't I always made it worth your while?" Brendan looked at the cage and back to Abán.

"You have." Abán nodded. "What do you need to know?"

"You hear anything about a stolen child?"

Abán looked around in quick, jerky motions. "Not so loud! You know that's against the Oaths. Why don't you see the magister?"

Brendan cleared his throat. "I thought I'd see if I could resolve this meself first. It were the oíche—"

Abán made a choking sound, then leaned in close and lowered his voice. "No one here will tell you anything about them, stolen child or no. They've been getting real nasty of late."

"Oh, aye, they're normally all sunshine and light, they are."

Abán rolled his eyes. "They've gotten nasty, even for them. They're collecting on all kinds of debts. Everyone is too afraid to talk about it. You never know when they might be watching in the shadows." He looked around again. "I know a pixie who said they broke her wings when she wouldn't do what they wanted."

Brendan looked at the now-empty ring, then back at Abán.

"A young pixie." Abán took a drink. "Dusk Court." He turned and spat.

Brendan leaned back in his chair and pursed his lips. The oíche were schemers; thuggery wasn't their style. "Any idea what's got them in a twist?"

"I can venture a guess, but you're going to need to talk to the magister if you want to know anything for sure. If the oíche did break the Oaths, he'll want to know anyway."

"Aye, I know." Brendan let out a breath. "So, where's Dante keeping himself these days?"

"He's got a club where he and the other court nobles hang out. Probably find some oíche there as well." Abán turned and spat again.

He gave Brendan the address. "Sure you can't stay for just one drink?"

"Sorry, mate. Wish I could." Brendan got to his feet and looked at the box in his hand. He set it on the table and smiled. "Thanks for the information. If you hear anything else, let me know?"

Abán nodded. "I'll send a messenger, as usual. It was good to see you, Brendan."

"And you."

Abán opened the box. His eyes went wide and his mouth went slack. "Is that one of Nuada's tears? How?—"

"Take care of yourself." Brendan turned and walked out.

CHAPTER EIGHT

The man working the door stared at Brendan through eyes caked in black liner. His dark blue painted lips twisted into a smirk.

"You're kidding, right?"

Brendan didn't say anything, though he was thinking the same thing about the doorman. He just crossed his arms.

The cocky smile vanished and the doorman cleared his throat. "I just, you know, meant that I, I don't think this is your kind of club." He laughed. "That's all. No offense or nothing, man."

"Oh, I see why they got you working the door." Brendan leaned in close. "That finely tuned sense of reading a man's character, yeah?" He stepped around the man. "At least the ogre had a set of bollocks on him," he muttered.

"Um, cover charge is—" The doorman stopped when Brendan grabbed the door handle.

"Why don't you go after him and get it?" a man in line said with a laugh.

"Why don't you—" The door closing behind Brendan muffled the rest of the doorman's words.

As soon as Brendan passed through the second set of doors, his senses were assaulted by pounding techno music and flashing lights. The smells of sweat, perfume, and fae were overpowering. He had to look away and get a grip on his overloaded senses.

Once he acclimatized, he saw that everyone was staring at him with expressions ranging from concern and confusion to outright disdain. The crowd was a mix of mortals and some of the lesser Rogue Court nobles. A few mortals had telltale signs that made him wonder if they were changelings.

Ignoring the glares, he scanned the room and wondered if Dante had lost his mind. How could he have gone from frequenting vaulted concert halls and theaters to building this disgraceful pit of empty noise? Above the pipes, cable trays, and other industrial hardware covering the walls grew large vines and tangles of ivy. There were even trees, the smallest of which was an oak well over twenty feet tall. Brendan could smell that it was real.

He didn't see Dante, which drew both relief and anxiety in equal parts. He headed to the bar, pushing past sweaty, writhing bodies, and earning more than a few dirty looks. The bartender wore a black button-down shirt, black trousers, and no makeup at all. Apparently Dante and the other sidhe hadn't completely lost their minds. The barman handed a glass of red wine to a young girl, who was, against all odds, dressed totally in black, then leaned toward Brendan.

"You've got to be lost," the bartender said with a smile.

"I'm afraid not, I'm looking for Dante. Know where could I find him?" A few people around him laughed with their best snotty, indifferent chuckle.

"VIP room." The bartender pointed across the crowd of dancers to a second level that overlooked the dance floor.

"Don't suppose you have any decent beer back there, do you, boss?"

The bartender reached down into a cooler, brought out a bottle of Sam Adams, and popped the cap off. "Some of us aren't big on wine."

"How much, then?" Brendan pulled a mess of wadded bills out of his pouch.

"On the house."

"*Sláinte.*" Brendan lifted the bottle to his lips and dropped a bill on the bar anyway. After swallowing a mouthful of beer, he looked at the dance floor. He had to fight back the sick feeling in his stomach and remind himself the room wasn't actually closing in on him.

"So," a feminine voice said. "What's under that kilt?"

A girl, barely old enough to order the drink in her

hand, gave him a wry smile. She was a pretty enough thing, but she wore too much makeup and a black dress made of some shiny material.

"Boots and socks," Brendan said. "Excuse me, love." He took another drink and waded into the sweaty throng on the dance floor, heading for a pair of double doors on the far side.

Bodies rubbed against him. He got several glares and even a few winks and smiles. He clenched his jaw and cleared the writhing horde. A man in a black suit and a deep red tie stood off to one side of the wooden doors. His bald head and large build probably did more to turn people away than any actual threat he posed. Brendan had another drink of his beer and took measure of the man. A big fella, all muscle, no finesse, and he wasn't any good at hiding it. Hell, he probably relied on it.

Brendan opened his mouth to speak, but the man cut him off.

"Members only," the man said with a scowl and a heavy Boston accent. He looked at Brendan's kilt. "And I know you're not on the list."

Brendan drew in a breath through his nose and let it out. "Listen, mate, Dante knows me. If you just tell him—"

"Mr. Dante knows lots of people." The man puffed out his chest. "If they're not on the list, they don't get by either. You're not on the list. Get it? Or do I need to draw it in crayon?"

Brendan counted to ten. "Just step aside there,

bucko. I'll be up and back before you know it. There's no need—"

"Not going to happen," the man said. "Now, why don't you go back to your renaissance faire before something bad happens to you?"

"Sorry?" Brendan leaned in close. "I don't think I heard you right. Did you just ask how far I could put me boot up your arse?"

The man cracked his knuckles. "Oh, you don't want none of this, skirt boy."

Brendan laughed. "That must get the kids wetting themselves, aye? Sure, I don't want any." He finished his beer and looked at the bottle, but he knew bashing the fella over the head with it would likely put him in the hospital and piss off Dante, when this was going to be bad enough.

"Well, princess? You're mo—"

Brendan hit the man's forehead with an open palm and knocked him into the wall. Brendan's other hand brought the bottle up, and he pressed the bottom of it against the man's neck, pinning him in place. Brendan leaned in with an outstretched arm. The man swatted at him, but he couldn't reach.

"I tried to be civil about this, but that's done now. I'm going through that door there." He nodded to it. "You can either step aside, or I can step over you. Which is it you'd prefer, then?"

The suited goon gurgled something, then stopped trying to pull the bottle off his neck and gestured to the door for Brendan to enter.

"Smartest one in your class, you must've been." Brendan let go and the big man fell to his knees, hands going to his throat as he gasped. Brendan dropped the bottle. It bounced on the man's head and hit the ground. "Be a dear and toss that in the bin for me, would you, love?" He opened the door.

The second floor was a large, open space with a view of the bar and dance floor. Like the rest of the club, it was a mix of industrial and natural, the same ivy-and-vine-covered walls. In the middle of a large V-shaped sofa sat Dante. He was a beautiful man—beautiful, not handsome—whose appearance was locked in his midtwenties. His skin was a deep tan, his hair was a light blond tousle reaching just above his shoulders, and his eyes were a vivid green. Like the other high sidhe, his eyes had no pupil or whites, just solid color that bore a faint glow.

He'd traded in his stiff collar and frock coat for jeans and a fitted pale gray blazer over a light blue striped button-down shirt. Aside from his fashion, he hadn't changed a bit. Like everything else in the last few hours, this was both comforting and disconcerting.

Clustered about Dante—or, rather, hanging on him—was a collection of attractive women. Other Rogue Court nobles—sylphs with hair and eyes a matching blue or green and large, translucent wings; a nymph with dark brown skin and hair the color of leaves; a nixie with a bluish tint to her white skin; and several tall elves, all of whom could make supermodels feel inferior—sat in the chairs and love seats scattered about. Brendan saw a half dozen oíche in a far corner, and he noticed them noticing him.

Of course, the glamour kept the mortal women hanging on Dante from seeing the radiant eyes, pointed ears, and wings around them, or, in the case of the oíche, black eyes, pointy ears, and sharp teeth.

After a deep breath, Brendan started to walk toward Dante. One of the oíche boys gave him a dirty look, then got to his feet and blocked his path.

"What the hell do you want, Fian?" the boy asked with a sneer.

Brendan was almost two feet taller than the oíche, so he stared at Dante over the faerie's head, hoping Dante would look up. The women around him seemed to have his undivided consideration.

"Hey, I'm talking to you!"

"Step aside, Justin," Brendan said. "I've something to discuss with your man over there, and it's no concern of yours." He looked down. "Not yet anyway."

"Well, I'm making it my concern right now. You're not welcome here, *díbeartach*." Justin spat the last word out.

Brendan clenched his fists and drew in a long, slow breath through his nose. Then he closed his eyes and exhaled. He wouldn't let them manipulate him, not again. The time for reckoning would come. He'd waited this long for his revenge, he could wait a little longer, especially with a mortal child at risk. Of course, in the meantime, he could play this game as well.

He opened his eyes and smiled down at Justin. "I ran into some friends of yours tonight. Afraid the girl won't be home for tea."

Justin's lips twitched. "You dare to strike down nobles of the Rogue Court?"

"Only those what accost an innocent mortal—"

"And you know for certain we didn't have an agreement with her?"

"Never said she was a *cailín*, did I?"

Justin's eyes widened for just a moment.

"Now, I got legitimate business with the magister. Are you going to let me by, or would you rather raise a bit of hell?"

"Make your move." Justin leaned in and whispered, "*Díbeartach*."

Brendan ground his teeth.

Do it, rip him apart. Let me loose here and now. We can get the lot of them. You know you want to.

Brendan focused and pushed the rage back down.

"Step aside." Brendan paused for a moment, then added, "Justarisheeth."

Justin flinched as if he'd been slapped, then froze in place. The soulless black eyes glazed over and his mouth twitched. The muscles in his arms and neck flexed and shook. Then, slowly, fighting it the whole time, Justin stepped to one side.

"That's a good little fella." Brendan patted him on the head.

"We're . . . . not . . . . finished," Justin said through gritted teeth.

"Oh, now you're making me sweet promises." Brendan shouldered past Justin so hard it knocked him to the ground. "Careful there. And here I thought your kind was supposed to be graceful like."

Brendan stood in front of Dante, waiting for him to acknowledge his presence, and kept one eye on the other oíche. They were helping Justin to his feet and watching Brendan as closely as he watched them.

"So then he ordered a virgin martini," Dante said, finishing his joke.

The girls around him giggled.

Brendan rolled his eyes and cleared his throat.

As the laughter faded, the girls looked at Brendan, then away. They seemed convinced that if they ignored him, he'd disappear.

"The prodigal Fian returns," Dante said without taking his eyes from the buxom brunette to his right. "Do tell, what brings our wayward *Seanchaí* back to Boston?"

"I need a word with you, Dante." Brendan looked at the collection of women. "Alone, if you don't mind. It's important."

The women gave Brendan looks that were equal parts derision and dismissal, then leaned back against the couch.

"Well, I'd imagine it must be." Dante flashed a bright white smile at Brendan. "I don't imagine you'd reappear, completely out of the blue, after"—he looked away, then back—"my, how many years has it been?"

"Dante—"

"Then you crash my club," Dante continued, unfazed, "and no doubt knock out my security man. It can't be all for something minor."

"I didn't knock him out. He's fully conscious, though he might be having a bit of trouble breathing."

Dante stroked the brunette girl's cheek. "You left, after I did everything you asked. You left without even saying good-bye, and never felt the need to drop in during any of your 'clandestine' visits."

Brendan looked away. "Look, I'm sorry about that—"

"As you can see, I'm very busy just now. What makes you think I'll find it as important—"

"Stolen child." Brendan punctuated each word.

For a heartbeat, Dante didn't blink, move, or even breathe. When the moment passed, he closed his mouth and drew a sharp breath in through his nose.

"Ladies," he said, smile returning. "Would you be so kind as to give my old friend and me a moment? Why not head downstairs and have another drink. On the house, of course."

The women pouted, flashed Brendan suspicious and scathing looks, then got up.

Brendan stepped aside so they could pass. "Mind the big fella what's a shade of blue on the other side of the door."

Dante watched with a pained look as the girls vanished down the stairs.

"You know the one in the red dress is a fella, right?" Dante arched an eyebrow and took a sip of his drink.

"Bleeding faerie," Brendan muttered under his breath.

"You still have all the charm and subtlety of a hydrogen bomb." Dante turned to Brendan and smiled. "Oh, and it's nice to see you again. How have you been?"

"Aye, I was a right and proper ass, but bloody hell, man, could we do this later?"

Dante motioned for Brendan to sit as he took another drink. "All right then. Tell me what happened."

"A couple of your lot attacked a mortal girl in Manchester. They broke the hearth protections, and they took her daughter."

Dante rubbed his forehead with his free hand. "And this week was going so well. Every time my stocks go up, something happens." He looked at Brendan. "I know you don't think I personally had anything to do with it, so that means someone else in the court." Dante's voice became monotone. "Gee, I can't imagine who would do such a thing."

"Aye, two guesses."

"Give me a second to get over the shock." Dante's words dripped sarcasm. He took another drink. "There. Now, how do you want to handle this?"

"I need to know where they took the girl." Brendan glanced at Justin and the other oíche, who were whispering in a tight group.

"You think he had something to do with it?"

"Maybe not directly. He's not the kind to get his hands dirty, but sure he knows something. He's still the top oíche around here, yeah?"

"He is," Dante said. "Though I'm not entirely sure how that happened. I don't like delving into their side of things."

"It was oíche I pulled off the girl and what got away with her purse."

"Got away? How very uncharacteristic of you."

Brendan glared.

Dante shook his head. "That was uncalled for. I'm sorry."

"Well, I suppose I had it coming."

Dante sighed. "No, you didn't, but as you said, there are bigger issues to address. Please, present your case."

Brendan took a moment to choose his words. "Now, I'm not saying every oíche are vile things that need to be wiped from the face of—"

Dante laughed. "Well presented. Of course you're certainly not saying they aren't."

"Aye, fair play that." Brendan shook his head. "I'm no use at this business. You and I both know they don't like playing by the rules. They were never happy about the hearth protections to begin with, and it was them what figured out the loophole."

"Well, as magister, I find the evidence sufficient. So it falls on me to resolve this."

Brendan laughed. "I'm sure they just love answering to a former high sidhe of the Dawn Court."

Dante smiled, with teeth. "I don't really bother myself with trivial matters like that."

Brendan laughed again.

"Well then, let's see what he knows, shall we?" Dante beckoned Justin over.

Justin whispered something to the other oíche before answering the summons. He flashed a murderous glare at Brendan, then bowed to Dante. "Yes, Magister?"

"Where's the *girseach*, you *cac ar oineach*?" Brendan said.

"Wow. You know, I do so love how you can just dance around a subject for hours on end," Dante said to Brendan. "It's like a verbal ballet, really quite remarkable. Now, if it's quite all right with you, may I handle this?"

"Fine, handle it, then." Brendan sat back and crossed his arms.

Dante looked at Justin and lifted his hands. "The stolen child?"

"I don't know what this *díbear*—" Justin stopped when Dante's eyes narrowed. "I don't know what this Fian is talking about. What child?"

Dante rolled his eyes and let out a breath. "I know you think you're renowned liars, but that's really only with mortals. There were two—not one but two—violations of the Oaths." Dante held up two fingers.

Brendan opened his mouth, but Dante glanced over, so he stayed silent.

"If you know something," Dante said, "now is the time to tell me."

Justin looked at Brendan and scowled. "So, now we answer to this—"

"YOU ANSWER TO ME!" Dante stood and spun, kicking Justin's legs out from under him. He grabbed Justin's neck and stopped his fall just before his face hit the couch. "I've had just about enough of your snide comments." Dante lifted Justin to his feet by his neck. "I don't care where you came from, you're a subject of the Rogue Court now, and you'll damn well respect its nobles!"

The whole room froze.

Brendan watched in silence. He'd forgotten how tall Dante was. He had several inches on Brendan, so he towered over Justin. This was, of course, in addition to the imposing presence that all high sidhe carried, slight of build or not.

"I." Justin cleared his throat. "I don't know anything about it, Magister." He spoke quietly, eyes locked on the floor.

"That's bollocks," Brendan said. "He's shoveling more shite than a potato farmer. It was an oíche kidnapping, and we all know you lot are thick as thieves."

"He makes a compelling point," Dante said.

A long moment passed in utter silence as Dante stared Justin down.

Justin cursed under his breath. "They weren't my people."

"So, you've got rogue, rogue fae?" Brendan shook his head. "Isn't that lovely?"

Dante closed his eyes. "Brendan—"

Brendan lifted his hands and sat back.

"Where did they take her?" Dante asked Justin with a calm and even voice. "There can't be many places they could keep a mortal child and not raise flags."

"I didn't approve of it!" Justin said. "I'm just as upset about the breaking of the Oaths as you."

"Then answer me."

"You can't ask me—"

Brendan's jaw started to ache.

"Well then, it's fortunate for you that I'm not asking, isn't it?" Dante said.

"I don't know where they took her."

"But . . . ?"

"But I'll find out." Justin looked at Brendan and then Dante. "I'll let you know as soon I find out anything, Magister."

"Dante," Brendan said. "Time is an issue here."

"You'll know before dawn," Dante said. "Yes?"

Justin nodded once.

"Get to it."

Justin went back to the other oíche and whispered. Brendan thought he saw a fleeting smile on Justin's face, but he couldn't be sure. Then the whole group of them went to the stairs and left the club.

Dante sat down, took a drink, and looked at Brendan. "Are you going to wait?"

"Aye," Brendan said. "I don't like it, but if they brought her to Boston, I don't want to have to come all the way back." He ran a hand through his hair and scratched his head. "I just need to get to the mother before the slumber wears off."

"They used a slumber on her?"

"Aye, and the babysitter as well, not much older than twenty, I'd say. They even tried to leave a glamour child."

"Oíche . . ." Dante rubbed the bridge of his nose. "The whole lot is still Dusk Court through and through if you ask me." He leaned back into the sofa and looked at the ceiling. "You know, there was a time when the Rogue Court had honor. Back when it was about the freedom to rule ourselves and live amongst the mortals."

"We both know the only reason you and your lot broke from the Dawn Court was because Teagan ordered you to."

"That doesn't mean we don't enjoy being on our own, or that she didn't have good reason. The noon fae don't have any nobles. That's also not to say some of us haven't been expecting the oíche to cross the line and planned accordingly." Dante winked and went to take another drink. Then he paused.

"What is it?"

"I'm just wondering, why take the child? This isn't just crossing the line. This is leaping miles past it. Why violate the Oaths like this when they've worked inside them, bargaining for children without any issue before now? Plenty of mortals are willing to bargain, so why take this one? And the glamour child, that's seriously old school." He shook his head. "It doesn't make any sense. There hasn't been a stolen child in over a century."

"I don't understand them any better than you."

Brendan leaned back and let out a breath. "It don't matter to me why they took her, just that they did. I don't get why you care so much about motives. It don't change a thing, does it?"

"Because it could be part of something bigger," Dante said. "Maybe they're setting someone up to take the fall for it. Get Teagan and Fergus involved."

"The oíche are schemers, and I wouldn't trust one to come in out of the rain. They know there'll be hell to pay. I just don't think they care."

"I don't think they're that stupid."

"I could argue that one there with you, boss. I'm sure they have some bigger plot at work, but I leave that to you and others like you to figure out."

"Thanks, I appreciate that," Dante said with a smile. It faded a moment later. "You've got your own motives, though, don't you?"

Brendan didn't answer.

"Don't pretend this is charity. It's beneath you."

"It's about doing the right thing," Brendan said.

Dante leaned his head back and let out a deep sigh. "Of course it is. I didn't mean to imply it wasn't." He watched Brendan fidget for several moments. "While I appreciate this attempt at small talk, we both know you don't want to wait here."

Brendan looked around the club. "I just don't know how you manage, or what got you to this bleeding state at all."

"It's the burden of good taste."

"Aye? That what you call it, then? I can remember when good taste was concert halls and art galleries."

There was a long silence between them.

Brendan looked at Dante, who gave him a warm smile.

"I never thanked you for all you did," Brendan said. "I'm sorry for that."

Dante's smile widened. "It's just good to see you. Now go on. I'll call you when I hear something." He pulled a cell phone out of his pocket and opened it. "What's your mobile number?"

Brendan's mouth twisted. "Oh, aye, I've loads of use for one of them, don't I?"

Dante let out a breath. "Of course, why would you have a mobile phone? That would put you well into the current century. Can't have that, now, can we?" He gave Brendan a sidelong glance. "You do know what year it is, right?"

"I do just fine, thanks."

Dante called one of the elves over. "I know it's not easy keeping up with trends, but I'm a great deal older than you, and I manage."

"And you wonder why I don't visit," Brendan said. "I just love the *craic* around here."

"Kevan, give him your phone, please," Dante said through a laugh without looking at the elf.

"What?" Kevan's head snapped from Dante to Brendan and then back again. "You can't be serious, Magister. Give my phone to him?" He motioned up and down at Brendan. "To him?"

Dante arched an eyebrow.

"But I just got it."

"You'll get it back." Dante glanced sideways at Brendan. "He will, right? Intact, I mean."

"Oh, sure," Brendan said. "I'll put it at the top of me to-do list. Right before retrieving the little girl and—"

"I'll get you another if he doesn't," Dante said.

Kevan handed the phone to Brendan like a child told to give up his favorite toy.

Brendan looked at it as if it was going to explode. "How do you work the bloody thing?"

"For Finn's sake, Brendan, how do you manage?" Dante took the phone. "Thank you, Kevan."

Kevan bowed to Dante and walked away, muttering.

"I'm surprised you drive that truck instead of a horse-drawn cart. You know they have plumbing indoors now, right?"

"Just explain the fecking thing and be done with it, if you please."

Dante laughed and held the phone up. "Don't worry about calling anyone. I'll call you. When I do, just press this." He pointed to the Send button. "Before you ask, it'll say it's me when I call."

"Deadly." Brendan took the phone and got to his feet. "I'm off, then. I need to get me some air."

Dante stood as well. "Where are you going to go? You're not likely to find a bar—I mean a 'pub'—that isn't packed at this hour."

"I'll just wander about for a bit. Reminisce with

some ghosts and all that." Brendan held out his hand. "Thanks, Dante. I appreciate the help."

Dante shook Brendan's hand, then pulled him into a hug. "What are brothers for?"

"I've told you before. You're not me bleeding brother."

"I know that." Dante laughed. "I'm much too good looking to be related to you. But I'm the closest thing you've got."

"Aye, don't be reminding me," Brendan said through a smile.

Dante chuckled and motioned to the stairs. "I'll call you when I hear anything. Try not to cause any trouble out there. We can use this to our advantage, but only if—"

"No promises." Brendan waved to Kevan. "Thanks for the phone, lad!"

Kevan gave a wistful look, then went back to his conversation with a nymph.

"Brendan," Dante said. "In all seriousness, I hope it doesn't take something like this for you to stop in next time. It's been too long, and Boston isn't the same without you."

"Thanks again," Brendan said as he made his way down the stairs. He waved at the bald man, who was checking the bruise on his neck in an ornate pocket mirror, moved quickly through the crowd, and made straight for the doors. As soon as his senses were no longer being assailed and he breathed the relatively fresh air, he felt more at ease.

He went over things in his head as he walked back to his truck and wondered about Dante's comment: "using the situation." Maybe they could both find the *girseach* and settle scores with the *oíche* as well.

He grabbed his other knife from the truck and tucked it behind his back. Word would be out shortly that he was back in town. He locked the truck, tucked the keys away, and looked around at the skyline.

"Like it'll be as easy as all that. Just wait, the other shoe will drop anytime now," he said to no one. "I just hope it drops instead of coming up and kicking me in the bollocks."

CHAPTER NINE

Brendan walked the streets, passing people who were headed home from a night out or just wandering like himself. He was lost in his own thoughts and memories. Changed as the city was, it was still familiar enough that each step only served to stir all the sleeping ghosts of his past.

As Brendan walked past one of the many pubs in Boston that played on the Irish theme, he heard a familiar song: "Thousands Are Sailing." He smiled bitterly at the irony. If he didn't know better, he'd say God had finally taken notice and was trying to offer comfort. Of course, he did know better. Besides, God's attention was better spent on lost little girls right now.

Brendan was still singing along in his head when he reached the waterfront. Past the New England Aquarium, he stopped to look out over the harbor. Logan Airport was a mass of lights across the water, but he didn't see it. He just saw the bay and the years that had gone by. Even now, he could still smell the coffin ship. Starved bodies, packed like cattle into the hold, praying to every saint they knew that they'd survive the voyage. Even after all this time, he could see the gaunt faces staring up at him and lifeless eyes that somehow managed to still have some hope.

Then another pair of eyes came to his memory.

"I know I can't make it right, but I'll get them for what they did, love." He rested his head on his hands clutching the railing and took long, deep breaths, trying to keep the tears from breaking through. Years had passed, the city had grown and changed, but her dead face still haunted him like a banshee.

Of course, it was no less than he deserved.

It was there, with the chill wind blowing off the harbor and specters of his past surrounding him, that the other shoe finally dropped.

Brendan nearly jumped out of his socks when the vibration and techno beat erupted in his hand. He almost dropped the bloody thing in the water twice. Dante's face appeared on the screen above his name.

Brendan pressed the Send button and lifted the phone to his ear. "Aye, Dante?"

"Yeah," Dante's tone was uncharacteristically somber and flat.

"I take it Justin found something out, then?" Brendan glanced up at the stars. About an hour had passed.

"He did." Dante took a breath. "They have her in an abandoned building in South Bos—"

"What's the address?"

There was silence on the phone.

"Bloody piece of . . ." Brendan looked at the phone, then put it back to his ear. "Are you there?"

"I'm here."

"Then what's the bleeding address, already?"

Dante relented and gave him the location of the building. "Look, Brendan, something about this feels wrong. You should wait. I can meet you there with some marshals—"

"You can if you like," Brendan said as he began jogging back to his truck. "But I'm not waiting for your bloody committee to decide what needs doing. And I'm not going to promise I'll be leaving anything for you."

"Shadowed dawn, Brendan, don't be stup—"

Brendan hit the End button. He couldn't wait for the politics of court to be resolved, and neither could the *girseach.*

His heart began to pound.

This is your chance. You'll be able to tear them apart, to hear their screams and taste their blood. Vengeance, at last.

He pushed the voice down and ran faster.

When he got to the truck, Brendan was breathing heavily, but he wasn't winded. He climbed in, started the engine, and sped off.

The roads were unusually quiet, and he didn't pass a single copper. Nearly a mile from his destination, he turned off the lights and crept into the industrial area. He parked well away from the building, climbed out of the truck, and pulled his sweater off. There was no point in concealing the knives now. There was no telling how many oíche he'd find, but they wouldn't hand the girl over without a fight. He needed to be able to move, and the sweater hindered that.

As he walked down the street, he took in all the scents and sounds. The air was heavy with the smell of fae from every direction, but South Boston was full of them. He didn't hear or see anything as he approached the warehouse, but oíche were especially stealthy buggers. Silently, he moved around the building. They had to know he was coming, but no need to make it easy for them.

He decided to start with the closest steel door. Standing against the wall, Brendan reached over and tried the handle. It was locked. Drawing his knives, he took a breath, said a silent prayer, then turned and kicked the door much harder than he'd intended.

It came off its hinges and flew several feet into the building.

"*Damnú air,*" he whispered, then stepped inside.

It was silent and black as pitch. He was cautious of every step and made as little sound as possible. His stealth wasn't out of fear of being detected. Even if they hadn't heard the door smashing in, which was unlikely, they'd hear his heartbeat. He just didn't want to miss any sound they might make.

Moving through what looked to be old offices, Brendan came to a closed door. There was something on the other side; the smell of fae and magic was heavy. Again standing to one side, he tried the handle. This one was unlocked, so he pushed the door open a little. Looking through the narrow slit revealed a large, empty warehouse. Everything was quiet, so he pushed the door open all the way, his back still to the wall.

Nothing happened.

He swallowed, almost wishing there'd been a bomb, or gunfire, or a flock of oíche pouncing on him. He chanced a quick look and saw a single light across the large expanse of darkness. Nestled in the ring of illumination was a form wrapped in a pink blanket. Curly red hair poked out of one end.

Through gritted teeth, he let out a breath.

Closing his eyes, he focused on the sounds and smells. There was the faintest hint of something he couldn't place. Shampoo, maybe? He also thought he could hear breathing and a heartbeat, too fast to be an adult.

Let me loose on them. You know that isn't the girl. Take your vengeance. You want the blood and you know it.

"No chance in hell!" Brendan said silently. "I'm not going to risk the *girseach*. And even if it isn't her, there are plenty of innocents outside."

So what? It would serve them right to die if they didn't escape. Hunter and prey, you know that. No one is truly innocent.

Brendan closed his eyes and fought the monster back down. It wasn't going to happen, not again, not here.

It took a lot of concentration to get his hands to stop shaking and his heartbeat back to normal. When he was sure he had the beast under control, he looked at the bundle. If it was Fiona, he couldn't just leave her there. He sheathed the knife in his left hand and took a deep breath.

"Nothing for it, then," he whispered.

He sprinted through the doorway and across the dark open space. As he passed the blanket-wrapped form, he snatched it up with his free hand and kept running. When he reached the far wall, he turned and put his back to it.

The door he'd entered through slammed shut.

No surprise there. The surprise would've been if the doll in his left hand had actually been Fiona. They must've wrapped it in her blanket to get her scent. He dropped the lure and drew his second knife.

This part had been inevitable, and in fact, Brendan had been looking forward to it. The only thing that pissed him off was that odds were Fiona wouldn't be here at all. Justin had set him up and he'd walked right into it.

The single light went out and darkness swallowed the room.

While Brendan had keen eyesight, he did need some light. The oíche, however, didn't. The walls had no cracks, and the windows had been painted over to block any light.

Laughter filled the room, bouncing off the brick walls and making it difficult to find the source.

"You killed my sister, Fian!" said a voice from the darkness. "I'm going to enjoy hearing you scream as I rip you apart."

Brendan closed his eyes to combat the instinct to try to see. He focused on using his nose and ears. "Don't you worry none, Tink," he said. "You'll be seeing her soon enough."

More laughter.

Brendan couldn't be sure, but he thought he counted twelve of them. At least they couldn't sneak up behind him. They'd have to face him head-on, and that was something, anyway.

A flurry of sound came at him.

Brendan ducked and rolled.

Claws raked across his shoulder. He shoved the pain aside and spun, cutting through empty air.

"Missed me!" mocked a new voice. "Here we thought you were supposed to be this big, scary warrior."

More laughter came from all directions.

"Let's get on with it, then," Brendan said from a crouch. "You lot are boring the hell out of me."

Another rush of air and he thrust his knife into the darkness where he'd just been. A scream of pain pierced the black, followed by a wafting trail of white lights that escaped the wound as he drew his knife back.

Brendan pounced on the wounded oíche, catching him from behind, and dragged his knives across the dark faerie's neck.

The shrieks stopped as the head came off and a shower of white sparks erupted like a volcano, momentarily casting away the darkness.

That's when Brendan saw his mistake.

He'd miscounted. There were easily two dozen oíche staring at him from around the huge room. Some sat on the rafters. Others clung to the walls, and still more crouched on the ground in front of him. All of them stared at him with murderous black eyes.

Now, driven by rage they attacked en masse just as the darkness returned.

Brendan spun, twisted, rolled, and slashed, but it wasn't enough. There were just too many of them. Claws raked over his body, shredding his shirt. Warm blood ran over his skin and soaked the tattered fabric. Small trails of lights were visible here and there as he landed the occasional hit with his knives but it wasn't enough to help.

A hard blow across Brendan's face sent him spinning and he landed hard, the fall knocking the wind out of him. His knives slipped from his hands and skittered across the floor.

The oíche were on him before he could get his breath back, or even blink. They pummeled him with fists, kicked him with heavy boots, and tore into him with claws. He could hear maniacal laughter, but it seemed far away. He wasn't going to stay conscious much longer.

Let me loose!

No, never again!

Someone rolled him onto his back.

"Oh, look at you," the oíche said. "The big—

scary—Fian," it said, punctuating its words with blows to Brendan's face.

Brendan's mouth filled with blood. The taste brought his senses back, and the monster inside him fought against the chains of his will and the magic of the tattoos with renewed vigor.

Let go! You want it! Let them reap the whirlwind! You know it's the only way!

"Where's the girl?" Brendan asked, and he spat blood in the face of the oíche kneeling over him.

Raucous laughter came from all around. "Shut up!" the oíche shouted at his companions. Leaning down close to Brendan's face, he said, "I guess you'll die never knowing. Don't worry, though. We have special plans for her. Mmm mm."

If you don't let me loose, the girl dies!

Brendan clenched his jaw and closed his eyes tight.

There has to be another way, he thought. If I can hold on, Dante will show—

There's no time! You're dying! Stop fighting it! They've brought this on themselves. If you don't and the girl dies, it'll be on your soul, again.

Brendan set his jaw and whispered, "*Tar amach, a Bháis.*" The tattoo in the center of his chest started to burn.

Rage, pure, unbridled fury, burning with the heat of hell's furnace, made its way through him, and Brendan smiled up at the oíche as his blue eyes smoldered.

Though the change happened in an instant, Brendan felt time slow to a crawl. Strength surged from the tattoo, renewing and boosting his own. The injuries were buried beneath the wrath and thirst for death and blood. The pain didn't go away, it just didn't matter anymore, and neither did the darkness.

"*Díoltas!*" Brendan shouted. His knives slid across the floor and leapt into his hands.

The oíche's eyes went wide as Brendan loosed a roar that would've given the devil himself pause, then he drove the blades into the sides of his prey, using the knives and his knees to toss the faerie over his head like a rag doll. It flew through the air and smacked into a pillar headfirst, its skull cracking, and was consumed in a roiling cloud of swirling lights.

Brendan was on his feet in an instant. He bellowed as he cleared the dozen paces between him and another oíche in a single leap, slamming into the wretched little thing. Landing on top of it, Brendan drove his knives into its shoulders. The blades went through the bone and into the concrete, pinning the creature down.

The oíche screamed, high, shrill, and laced with pain and fear.

Brendan felt his blood sing in response.

Your claws! Use your claws! Letting the darkness take them is too good for them, too fast. Bathe in their blood!

Brendan clenched and unclenched his fists, then extended his fingers. Sharp claws emerged from the tips, and he tore into the screaming prey. Thick black blood poured out. Now, there was only the fire burning in Brendan's heart, the enthralling feeling of their gore on his hands, the panicked shrieks, and smell of death that soaked the air.

Brendan looked around the room, absently drawing one of his knives from the pinned oíche's shoulder. Seeing the mayhem and pain he'd caused sent another wave of exhilaration through him. Without looking down, he drove the knife into the oíche's heart. There was a sudden eruption of darkness and lights beneath him.

"What is that thing?" one screamed.

"How the hell did he do that?" another asked.

Brendan listened and noted the locations of the remaining oíche around him. While his senses were exceptional before, now they were unparalleled. Even over the noise that echoed in the warehouse, he could hear the hum of the streetlights outside. Beneath the overwhelming blood and fear, he could smell the perfume of a woman who'd walked by hours ago.

A female oíche sprang at him. Brendan grabbed her from the air by the throat. He'd heard her muscles and tendons stretch when she'd leapt.

She kicked and raked her claws over his extended arm. With all his considerable strength, Brendan drove her down to the floor. Concrete and bone broke as he lifted, then slammed, her repeatedly. When she stopped moving, he tore her throat out.

"Shoot him, damn it!" someone screamed. "SHOOT HIM!"

Automatic gunfire and muzzle flashes exploded from several places in the room. Brendan leapt to evade the fire. While the shots were poorly aimed, several shattered the painted-over windows and let in dim street light, the oíche were dumping enough bullets to make up for it. A couple of shots ripped through Brendan's shoulder, causing him to lose his balance and fall to the ground. However, this pain, like the other, was of no consequence. It was just a nuisance.

Let them fight, but tonight, death has come for the immortal fae!

When the guns clicked empty, Brendan lifted himself from the ground and smiled. He watched the herd fumbling to reload. In a series of long strides, he crossed the room and tore into the stomach of one, then another, and they fell to the ground in lifeless heaps before a cry of pain could escape their lips.

Brendan roared, and it was a dirge on their behalf, undeserving though they were.

"Everyone out, now!" someone shouted.

Brendan recognized the voice as belonging to the one who'd gotten away earlier, the one whose sister he'd killed. He focused on that one.

The oíche saw Brendan charging at him. His black eyes widened, then he leapt into a dark corner and vanished, leaving only the tingling scent of magic behind.

With nothing there to slow him, Brendan slammed into the wall. He screamed in frustration and turned to see the remaining oíche leap into other dark corners and disappear.

Brendan fell to his knees and screamed his rage into the night. Blood and vengeance had been denied him!

Now, with no one left, his conscious mind began the fight for control. His body shook as the rage called for more blood.

Outside, there's more blood outside! Go out and take it! There is so much more! Can't you smell it?

He could, sweet and alluring. It was a balm to his fury and frustration. Others, so many others could fall in the place of those who'd escaped—

"No!"

Digging for every drop of willpower he could find, Brendan struggled to push the raging beast aside.

A door creaked, faint footsteps approached, and Brendan looked up as a familiar smell hit him, ancient oaks and meadow grass grown wild.

No, not now!

"Brendan?" Dante's voice called from across the shadow-laden room. "Are you in here?"

"Get out of here!" Brendan struggled to say, but it came out as a guttural scream.

Dante froze, eyes wide, when he saw Brendan. The three elves behind Dante, likewise dressed in black and holding some kind of small machine gun, took aim at Brendan.

"Lower your weapons," Dante said.

"But Magister, look at him," one of the elves said.

"Do it now!"

Take them. They're just like the others. You know they can't be trusted! Take them all, right now. Purge this world of their kind—

"No!" Brendan said.

"It's me," Dante said. His tone was calm and even, his hands up.

Brendan drove his claws into the cement floor.

"Magister, we need—"

"Shut up," Dante said in a harsh whisper to the elves. "You can fight it back," he said to Brendan. "You're the stronger one. We made sure of that."

Brendan screamed, struggling against the monster and wanting nothing more than to tear the flesh from Dante's bones. To feel his hot blood—

"Brendan, she wouldn't want this. She would want you to save the child."

Brendan saw Áine standing before him, as real as Dante. She smiled, and he felt the warmth of her love like a noonday sun.

"I love you," she said. "And this isn't who you are, my love."

Cold washed over him, quelling the inferno, and he felt a rush of strength as his will hardened to steel. He pushed and fought the beast back, one inch at time, until, at last, it faltered and Brendan got the upper hand.

Relief flooded through him as the heat extinguished and the beast retreated.

You'll not keep me locked away forever!

The pain and injuries that were of no consequence before leveled Brendan now, and he collapsed, gasping for air. When he managed to open his eyes, Áine was gone and his heart broke all over again. In the distance, he could see the handles of his knives glinting in a small pool of light leaking from a broken window. His eyes drifted over to Dante and the elves. They were watching him, warily.

Brendan lay there for several minutes, struggling to draw in a breath and get the better of the pain, physical and emotional. His muscles burned as he rolled himself onto his side.

"Is it you?" Dante asked.

Brendan couldn't speak, but he did manage to nod.

Dante started to move forward, but one of the elves grabbed his shoulder. "Are you sure it's safe, Magister?"

The hesitation in Dante's eyes was like a knife in Brendan's heart.

"On your feet, Fian! There's still work to be done!" Brendan told himself. With effort and pain, he got to his knees. He gritted his teeth and groaned as he lifted himself to his feet. His legs threatened to give out, but he managed to make it to the wall. He leaned against it and turned to look at Dante.

Dante pulled free of the elf and ran over to Brendan. He tore the remnants of Brendan's shirt off and used it to clean away some of the blood, but there was so much that his efforts did little more than spread it around and mix it with the evaporating oíche gore.

Brendan sucked in a breath and tried to take stock of just how bad off he was.

"Well, you've looked better," Dante said. "Sorry about that, but—"

"Nothing to be sorry for." Brendan didn't look up. "Just being smart about it."

Brendan's left shoulder had at least three bullet wounds. His ribs felt cracked or broken, which explained why he was having trouble breathing. His face had taken a beating that left his skull throbbing with a dull pain, but somehow they hadn't broken his jaw. There were cuts all over his chest, and he was sure under all that blood would be plenty of bruises. His legs had escaped with only a couple of grazes from stray bullets and shrapnel from ones that had broken apart when they'd hit the floor.

"You look pale," Dante said.

"I'll live," Brendan said. "We need to get out of here before the coppers show."

"Don't worry about them." Dante motioned for one of the elves to help him. "We've taken care of that." When the elves faltered, Dante glared at them. One came to stand beside Dante while the other two watched the room.

Brendan's eyes were wet. "I didn't have no choice. I wouldn't have let it loose, but—"

"You don't have to explain to me. I know how bad it had to be for you to go there."

Brendan knew Dante couldn't really understand, but he smiled anyway.

"So, ambush, huh?" Dante asked as he looked Brendan over.

"Aye." Brendan nodded. "They set me up, and did a fine job of it, too."

"Looks like." Dante squinted at Brendan's wounds. "I won't say I told you so."

"Appreciate that, boss."

Dante turned to the elf at his side. "I can't see anything. I need some light."

The elf removed a small sphere from inside his coat and held it in his open palm. The sphere lifted and glowed brighter and brighter until the area was filled with soft white light.

"Ouch," Dante said. "Something tells me you look even worse under this blood. Hand me the kit, Liam."

The elf to his right pulled a black case from his jacket pocket, opened it, and held it out.

Dante removed a long, thin crystal rod with a black tip. "We need to get the bullets out, Brendan. This is going to hurt like hell."

"Well, that'll be a nice break, then," Brendan said between labored breaths.

"I just—"

"*Dar fia!* Just do what you have to."

Dante gripped Brendan's shoulder and pushed the rod into one of the bullet holes.

Brendan closed his eyes as all of his muscles tried to flex at once.

"Got it." Dante withdrew the rod; encased inside the crystal, just below the black, was a single bullet. "That's one. Are you sure—"

"*Mo mhallacht ort,* just do it already!" Brendan said without opening his eyes.

Dante retrieved the second and third bullets. As he pulled the rod out for the last time, the bullets were lined up in a row inside the crystal. "You okay?" he asked.

Brendan nodded, and his breathing began to return to something approaching normal.

Dante put the rod back in the case and brought out a small jar. He dipped a finger in and removed a generous amount of greenish ointment. "This'll help with the pain."

"You're talking like we've never done this before."

"It's been some time, and some could say you still haven't learned not to bring a knife to a gunfight." Dante applied liberal amounts of the ointment to the bullet wounds.

"Well, I brought two knives, didn't I?"

Dante chuckled and shook his head.

"Trust those bloody things if you want," Brendan said. "Like as not, they'd explode in me hands."

"Sure, cause that happens all the time." Dante smiled. "You know, it's so cute that you don't let things like progress affect you." He returned the jar to the case. "Let's get a bandage on that."

Dante rolled a small, flesh-colored ball between his palms. After a moment, he pulled and stretched it into a flat disk. When he was happy with the size, he placed it on Brendan's shoulder.

The bandage stuck, then drew itself tight. The ointment was working, and the pain in Brendan's shoulder was almost gone. He looked away as Dante tended to his ribs and face.

Dante closed the case. "That should do it for now. How do you feel?"

"Better, thanks." Brendan found that his legs were

steady once more. One of the elves handed him his knives. He sheathed them behind his back. "We've a problem."

"A new problem, I assume?" Dante asked. "Not one of the myriad of other problems we already know about?"

"Aye."

"Just like old times. What is it?" Dante saw the look on Brendan's face and turned a little pale. "What's wrong?"

Brendan drew a breath. "They crossed."

"What? No, that can't be. That's impossible."

The elves gave each other quick glances.

"I know that, don't I?" Brendan said. "But they did. I saw them with me own eyes. They leapt into some shadows and was gone."

"I don't need to remind you the Rogue Court can't cross without a gateway," Dante said. "Even if they had one, it isn't an instantaneous trip. Only the trouping fae can do that, and I know the oíche didn't join their ranks."

"I saw what I saw," Brendan said. "I didn't say I could explain it. Is there no way they could do it?"

Dante shrugged. "I suppose they might have prepped it, but they'd still need a gateway."

"What if they had help?"

Dante considered for a moment. "A mortal wizard might be able to do it. If he were good enough, he could make a talisman that would work as a gateway."

"Maybe that's who they stole the *girseach* for?"

Dante ran a hand through his shoulder-length hair. "That's possible, I suppose. Where'd they find a wizard, though? It's not like they're listed in the yellow pages under *W*."

"We could ask Justin when we're asking about the girl."

"We could," Dante said. "But, shocking as it may be, he and his entourage disappeared shortly after I talked to you."

"Aye, monster surprise there," Brendan said. "But it don't matter none. We don't need to search him out." He smiled. "I've got his name."

"You've got Justin's true name?" Dante asked. "Do I want to know how you got it?"

"Not likely," Brendan said. "I got it the same place I got yours."

"I'm going to pretend I didn't hear that," Dante said. "Now all we need is a wizard of our own to compel Justin to appear and answer our questions."

Brendan's smile widened.

Dante's eyes went wide. "Do not tell me you found a wizard," he said, then gave Brendan a hard look. "Is there something I should be worried about?"

"Relax, mate," Brendan said. "It were just by chance. He's a friend of the wee one's mother. I don't know if he has the skill to pull it off, but if it'll help, he'll likely try."

"Try? That doesn't sound promising."

"Oh, you got a better plan in mind, then, aye?"

Dante sighed. "Let's go. We've got a car parked outside." He took a few steps, with the elves close on his heels.

"No, I'll be taking me truck, thanks," Brendan said.

"You think you're good to drive?" Dante asked. "Just because you don't feel the pain doesn't mean the injuries are healed."

Brendan opened his mouth to comment, but Dante cut him off.

"I'll ride with you."

"Magister," Liam said, "I don't think it's a good idea for you to be without protection. This mess could be the start of a war with the oíche, and you'd make a great target."

"Follow me then if you like," Brendan said as he limped toward the door. "But I'm not leaving me bleeding truck here. Besides, I need a clean shirt, and that's where I keep me wardrobe."

"You follow," Dante said to Liam. "I'll ride with Brendan." He watched Brendan limp by. "But stay close."

CHAPTER TEN

Edward closed the book slowly, as if doing so quickly would cause it to explode, and slid it away. He'd expected to find at least some similarities between cultural faerie stories and fact, but there didn't seem to be any. Shakespeare didn't even get the names right.

He pulled off his glasses, put his head down on the desk, and tried to get a handle on the situation. The twinge of curiosity—and, he had to confess, excitement—at the thought of all this happening was gone now. In fact, it was taking a determined effort to keep from curling into a fetal ball and wetting himself.

A sound from the living room brought his head up with a snap. He got to his feet and stopped in the study doorway.

Caitlin was stirring on the couch.

He looked at his watch, then out the large window

in the living room. It was still dark and at least a few hours until sunrise. Kris was still sleeping soundly.

"No, no, no. You're not supposed to wake up yet," he whispered.

Caitlin grunted as she opened her eyes and looked around. She blinked repeatedly and looked around again. Confusion settled on her face as she drew her knees up to her chest.

"What's going on? Where am I?"

Edward knelt next to the couch, taking her hand in his. "Easy. It's okay. I'm here."

"Eddy?" She shook her head and wiped her eyes. "What? What are you doing here? Where am I?"

"You're at, uh, my house."

"What happened to your hand?"

Edward moved his bandaged hand away. "It's nothing, I just cut myself. Listen, you've had a, well, a bad night. What's the last thing you remember?"

"Bad night? What are you talking about?" She tried to stand up, but her eyes closed and she started to wobble.

"Don't push yourself." He helped her sit back down and propped a pillow up behind her.

She looked around again. "Wait, your house? What am I doing at your house? How'd I get here?"

Edward scratched his head. "Well, it's kind of a long story. I think it'd be best, right now anyway, for you to concentrate on what you recall." He leaned in closer, squeezing her hand. "What can you remember?"

Caitlin put her free hand to her head and closed her

eyes. "I, um." She swallowed. "God, I have a splitting headache. I didn't think I drank that much."

"Here." Edward handed her a bottle of water and a couple of Tylenol he'd gotten out earlier.

She took the pills and emptied the bottle in a series of deep gulps. She set it down, then held her head. "I feel like I got hit by a—" She winced. "By a . . ."

"A what?"

She looked at Edward, as if by trying hard enough she'd find the answer in his eyes. "Last thing I remember, I was out with the girls. I don't think I got drunk, but . . ." She ran her hand through her hair. "Weird things had been happening all night. I remember leaving and then, I, uh, I got stopped by a couple of kids."

"Good, go on."

"They tried to mug me, or something. No, I think they were going to take me—" Her eyes went wide. "Oh God, Eddy! Fiona!" She gripped Edward's shoulders. "I have—"

"Breathe," Edward said, knowing he had to act fast to stop her from hyperventilating and passing out. "You have to slow down your breathing." He ran to the kitchen and retrieved a fresh bottle of water. "Here, drink this, slowly."

The bottle shook as she lifted it. After a couple of swallows, her breathing began to return to normal. Her eyes were still wide, but her face had turned to stone.

"It's a blur. Eddy, where's Fiona?"

Edward opened his mouth to speak.

"Where's my baby? Something's happened to her. I can't remember what, but I know."

"Well." He hesitated. "She's—"

Caitlin's face went pale. "She's dead. I saw her body—"

"You what?"

"No." Caitlin shook her head. "No, that's not right. I mean, I did, but it was wrong. I remember seeing her, but I know . . ."

"She's not dead. They took her."

"They took her?" She paused, and then her mind engaged. "They took her! We have to call the police. Where's your phone? Wait, you already called them, right?"

"Well, no—"

"What? Why not? We need to call them, right now. Your phone?" She made to stand again, but her legs gave out and she fell back down.

"Easy. Normally, I'd agree with you." He was struggling to find the right words. He'd told people their worldviews and concepts of reality were wrong before, but Caitlin wasn't one of his schizophrenic patients. "Under typical circumstances, I would've been the first to call, you know that, but this isn't typical. Caitlin, they can't help us."

At the sound of her name, she seemed to snap out of it a little more.

"The things I need to tell you, well, they relate to that. I promise you, we're going to get her back. In fact, Brendan is already out there, trying to find her."

"Who?"

"Brendan, do you remember him?"

"No—" She furrowed her brow. "Wait, I know that name. I, I can't place it though." She put her hand to her head. "Jesus, did they drug me?"

"Sort of." Edward gently touched her cheek and turned her face to look at him. "Brendan? Do you remember him? He helped you when you got attacked?" he said.

"Big Irish guy with scars?" She started to laugh. "No, he can't be helping. Eddy, he said they were—" She shook her head and laughed again. "He said they were faeries."

Edward cleared his throat. "It turns out he was telling the truth."

"What? No." Her smile faded. "No! This is a joke, right? Where's Fiona?"

Edward looked down.

She scowled. "No! There's no such thing as faeries!" Shaking hands went to her face and through her hair. "That's insane, faeries aren't real! Eddy, this isn't funny. Where's Fiona? Where is she?" Tears began to run down her cheeks.

"Brendan's out looking for her—"

"Some stranger is looking for my little girl and you're okay with that? Are you insane? What is going on?" She pushed him away. "Tell me, damn it!"

"I would've gone, but I had to stay here and look after you and Kris." He looked at his watch, then back up at Caitlin. "And, well, he knows more about all this than I do."

"He knows more about this? What's that mean? He knows more about what? Kidnapping little girls?"

"No! Faeries, he knows more about faeries." Edward lifted his hands. "Caitlin, please, focus on what I'm saying, this is important, okay? I know it's hard to believe, but tonight you were attacked by faeries. Oíche-sidhe."

"What the hell is that?" She covered her ears. "No! Stop it! Just stop, we don't have time for this! We have to—"

"Caitlin," he said with more force in his voice. He pulled her hands from her ears, then held them tight. "This is me, okay? Are you listening?"

She swallowed and looked at him. Anger still burned in her eyes, but she squeezed his hands, and not in an attempt to break them.

"Everything that can be done is being done," he said, never breaking eye contact. "I swear to you, if I thought we could do anything more, we'd be doing it. I'd be doing it. Now, please, this might really help. I need you to think back, concentrate. The kids, was there anything strange about them?"

"Why?"

"Just humor me."

Caitlin sighed. After a brief pause, her mouth closed and she blinked.

"What is it?"

"Their eyes."

"What about them?"

"They were all black." She gestured around her face. "No whites, no iris, nothing, just all black."

"Good, anything else?"

The color started to drain from her face. "Their teeth."

"All of them were pointed?"

She nodded.

"Pale skin? Angular features? Very pretty? Too pretty, in fact?"

"How did you—"

"Oíche-sidhe." He swallowed. "Dark faeries."

"They were after me." She put her hands to her mouth. "No, they weren't. Dear God in heaven, faeries took my little girl." Tears streamed down her cheeks. "I remember. I fought them, but I couldn't stop them. They took her." She hugged herself and looked at him with pleading eyes. "Eddy, they took her from my arms."

"I know this is hard—"

"You know?" Her eyes turned to steel and bored into him. "Really? How's that? Has your daughter been taken? Was it by faeries?"

Edward winced. "No, but—"

"No!" she shouted. "She's my daughter, not yours! I'm all she has and I need to find her."

"You're not all she has," Edward said in a whisper, but Caitlin didn't hear him and stood up. "Wait! Where are you going?" Edward grabbed her shoulder.

"Don't touch me!" She turned on him, pointing a finger. "Stay here if you want. Trust Brendan if you want. I'm going to find my daughter!"

"No! You can't leave."

"Oh, really? Watch me." She started walking to the door.

Desperation ran through Edward. When her hand was less than an inch away from the doorknob, he felt a flood of power rush through him.

"*Peidio!*"

Magic enveloped Caitlin and she stopped, frozen in place, hand hovering above the knob.

Heart-stopping dread clawed at his stomach. "Caitlin?"

It was as if someone had pressed the pause button. There weren't even the telltale signs she was breathing. Not even her eyes moved.

He started pacing. "What have I done? I'm so sorry, Caitlin. I, I didn't mean to, I just—" He pointed to the door. "You can't—"

A glance at her eyes told him that although they didn't move, emotion and consciousness were behind them.

He put his hands behind his head, trying to figure out how to undo what he'd done. Of course, he'd first have to figure out what it was he'd done. Dedicated focus, and he'd botched a scrying spell. Panic, and he'd hexed Caitlin into a statue.

Well done, Nghalon said.

"Shut up! That's not helping."

There is a practical side to consider. You kept her from going outside. The minor consequence of her entire sense of reality collapsing, then being frozen by her friend the wizard . . . well . . . that doesn't even merit considering.

"Knock it off," he said and looked at Caitlin.

She couldn't move, but the look in her eyes made his heart twinge and he felt his resolve harden. "I'll figure out what I did and undo it. But first, you need to listen."

With Caitlin like a statue, and a literal captive audience, he recounted the events of the evening; meeting Brendan, bringing her and Kris to his house for protection. He told her everything.

"I'm sorry," he said. "I'll fix this. The paralyzing thing, I mean. Wait here." He winced. "I mean, I'll be right back." He went into his study.

It took the better part of half an hour, but he found what he needed. A section of an old book, in Latin no less, explained the deconstruction of magical effects. He returned to the living room and lifted his hand. Reaching out with his magical senses, he felt the spell surrounding her. Slowly and carefully, he began to pull it apart. After several tense moments, he heard a faint popping sound.

Caitlin jerked her hand back from the handle.

"I'm sorry, I didn't mean to. It was an accident," he said as he stepped close, reaching out a hand to touch her shoulder. "You see, there's wards, and if you—"

She punched him in the face, really, really hard.

Edward fell back and landed on the floor, glasses askew. Caitlin's fists were clenched, and her eyes burned with anger.

"You son of a bitch." She took a step forward.

Edward backed away as he straightened his glasses.

"Listen very carefully. You're going to answer some questions," she said. "If I find out that you or that Brendan guy had anything to do with this, I swear to God, I will kill you both."

Edward wiped blood from his nose, then looked up at her. "I'd help you do it."

CHAPTER ELEVEN

Edward felt the heat of Caitlin's stare as she sat in a chair and held a mug of tea, still full.

At the far end of the couch, Edward held an ice pack to his face and avoided looking at her. "I'm sorry I didn't tell you before. It's not something that comes up in casual conversation."

"Wizard? Like robes, towers, all that?"

Edward shrugged. "The only robe I have is a bath-robe and I don't have a tower, but otherwise, yes. I don't have much practice, which should be abundantly clear. You told me you were having nightmares and strange things were happening. I just wanted to help, so I, uh, used a protection spell." He didn't mention the debates he'd had about whether or not he could pull it off. "Anyway, when the spell tripped, I didn't know what it was. As soon as I figured it out, I went to your house as fast as I could—"

"I suppose that explains how you always manage to show up or call just when I need you."

Edward looked down. "Actually, that was the first time I ever did that, or anything like it."

She looked at him. "How long?"

"I don't know. I guess it took me about twenty minutes to—"

"No. How long have you been a . . ." She swallowed. "A wizard?"

"Oh, right." He chuckled a little. "You wouldn't care about—"

"You're not exactly what I would've imagined a wizard to be, if I ever imagined them being real."

He smiled, but there was no joy in it. "Join the club. Brendan wasn't impressed either. I'm not very good. Turns out, learning magic isn't something that you can do without—" He let out a breath and his voice became shaky. "If I'd just known it was the protection spell, maybe I could've gotten there sooner and done something."

There was a long silence.

Caitlin shook her head. "It's not your fault, it's mine."

"What?"

"I used to see them when I was little." She took a drink from her mug. "Faeries, I mean."

"Caitlin." He reached and she didn't pull away; she just shook her head. "Lots of kids believe in faeries and monsters under the bed, but—"

"No. I saw them. I used to play with them. Mom

always told me I was just imagining it, but not Nana. She always smiled and made sure I put a bowl of cream for them on the doorstep." Caitlin snorted. "I grew up and just convinced myself that my mom was right. That Nana was just humoring me."

"You're still not being fair to yourself."

"Nana used to tell me the stories she learned in Ireland. They even have stories about children being taken, like that poem by Yeats."

"'The Stolen Child.'"

Caitlin stared out the window and let out a long sigh. "The poem makes it sound so magical. I guess it's not like that." She scrunched her face. "I should've known." She looked up at him. "And you should've told me."

There was no anger in her eyes, just sadness. Edward wasn't sure which was worse. "You're right, I should have, and I'm sorry, but would you listen to yourself? Because your grandmother told you stories about faeries, you should've seen that they'd take Fiona? That's absurd."

Their conversation continued, and Edward just let her talk. He did his best to reassure her and get her thinking clearly, making sure to give her plenty of space and time. He took every shot from her, too. He deserved each one.

Eventually, the turn in topic told him she was as coherent and in control as anyone could expect under the circumstances.

"Why did they take her?" she asked.

Edward felt a twinge in his chest.

"Why'd they take my baby?"

"I don't know." Edward tapped his knee. "I did do some research though. Apparently faeries enchant a stone or stump of wood to look like the child—"

Caitlin looked like she might throw up.

"What?"

"It was that piece of wood in the bed; it looked like Fiona, but like she was . . ." The heat in her eyes vanished. "If I'd been just a few minutes later, I would've thought that changeling was her. I'd have buried it and never known . . ."

"Don't go down that path. You did get there in time, that's what matters." Edward's mouth continued without consulting his brain. "And not that it's important, but a changeling is a half human, half faerie."

"What?"

"Nothing, it's just that what you saw is called a glamour child. Sometimes they'd leave a changeling, though. I guess the term got applied to both."

"Oh. Well, did you learn anything useful? Say, like how we could get her back? Or maybe how we could find where she is?"

He swallowed. "It was really just an explanation of types of faeries, their courts, things like that."

"Oh, well, that's great. At least you can write a dissertation about them."

He looked away and muttered a curse to himself.

She began pacing. "When's Brendan supposed to get back?"

"I don't know. Soon, I think."

"You think?" Caitlin sighed. "And we can't leave?"

"Not a good idea." Edward folded her blanket and draped it over the back of the sofa.

"Well, I'm not going to just sit idly by. You're a wizard, isn't there something you can do? Call her back, or find her, or something?"

Edward covered his bandaged hand with his good one.

"What is it?"

He explained his botched attempt earlier, omitting the glowing eyes from his story.

"So, why didn't it work?"

"I must have screwed it up somehow." He ran his good hand through his hair. "It might have been what I used, but I don't—"

"What are you talking about?"

"I needed something of Fiona to track her down; hair, fingernail clippings, blood, whatever. I didn't have any, so—"

"Can you use mine?" Caitlin asked. "Genetically, half of her blood is mine. Wouldn't that work?"

"I don't know." Edward thought about it for a moment. "It might. I mean, there's a bond between you—"

"So, we'll try?"

His stomach twisted and his hand started to throb.

Caitlin stepped toward him.

He flinched and took a step back.

She closed her eyes and took a breath. When she

opened them, the remaining traces of anger were gone, and all Edward could see was fear and desperate hope.

"I'm sorry, Eddy. I shouldn't have snapped like I did," she said.

"Well, if ever there was an excuse to lose your temper—"

"But if you think that means I'm taking no for an answer," she said, her voice soft, "or that I'm just going to sit here till Brendan gets back, you're wrong."

He wanted to tell her that he couldn't, that he'd tried and failed, and that he'd seen something that terrified him to his core, but a tear fell from Caitlin's eye and he tried to look away.

She put a hand on his face and looked him in the eye. "I'm truly sorry about before. But Eddy, she's my baby, and I need your help."

He swallowed.

"Please."

Caitlin watched Edward draw the circle while she chewed on her nails. She could see the fear in his eyes, and it worried her. She'd never seen him scared before. He'd always been her rock, there for her when she'd needed him most. She stopped pacing as she realized just how many times that had been. She thought of when she was pregnant, her ankles swollen to the point of excruciating, and she'd panicked about being a single mother; he'd rubbed her feet and assured her that everything would be okay. And all the times she'd gone by his office after work to find him still there, staring out his window, not a scrap of work to be seen. He'd been waiting for her just in case she'd needed him. He was always there waiting, and she knew he would be, though neither of them ever said it. Neither of them ever had to. She closed her eyes as her heart twisted. So many times and he never once seemed hurried or tired. He always greeted Fiona with a huge smile and a giant hug. Never once did he ask anything of Caitlin.

She opened her eyes and watched him. He was perhaps a hundred and sixty pounds soaking wet, a definite bookworm, and deathly afraid of spiders. He was terrified, but it wasn't stopping him, because she'd asked. She let out a sigh. He was still waiting for her, and she knew he would for as long as she needed him to.

When the circle was finished, Edward went to an old trunk and began gathering items.

"How long—"

"I know this isn't easy, but you have to be a little patient, okay?"

She shook her head and closed her mouth.

Edward walked to the desk, arms full of various items. "What about Kris?"

Caitlin glanced out the study door. "She's still sleeping."

"No, I mean, what about when she wakes up?"

Caitlin looked out again at her friend, then at Eddy. "I have no idea. It's not like we just explain it to her."

Edward stopped, arms still full, and nodded, a smile edging across his face. "I don't think I can take another punch."

Caitlin put her face in her hands. "God, I can't believe I punched you. I'm so sorry about that."

Edward set the items on the desk and wrapped his arms around her. "I deserved that—"

"No, you really didn't," she said. She pressed her cheek against his chest and realized it felt different than the other times he'd held her; it wasn't just comforting, it felt right, as if she was meant to be there. She felt some of her fear melt away, not much, but some. She pulled back just enough to look up at him.

He swallowed.

Had his eyes always been that pretty shade of green? Almost like summer moss. She shook her head, then hugged him tight. "Thank you, Eddy."

"For what?" he asked.

"For this, and for everything else," she said.

He stroked her hair and hugged her back. "We'll get her back, I swear to you."

She nodded and just hugged tighter.

"We'll figure out what to do about Kris when the time comes. Right now, maybe we focus on one problem at a time."

She stepped out of the hug and turned away to wipe her eyes. "Can I help with anything?"

"Not really."

Arms wrapped around herself, Caitlin watched him work as the seconds ticked by and she tried not to think about Fiona surrounded by prepubescent Goth monsters. Edward's voice snapped her out of her daze.

"It's ready."

"What do I need to do?" she asked, stepping forward.

"I need blood or hair." Edward pulled a slender knife from a drawer.

Caitlin took the blade from him. "Which, and how much?"

"Not much. I think blood would work best, but—"

Caitlin dragged the blade across the palm of her left hand, leaving a short and shallow cut. "Where do you want it?"

"Um, okay then." He handed her the crystal. "On this, please."

She flexed her hand a few times until a reasonable amount of blood collected, then she wiped it over the outside of the crystal and handed it back. "Is that enough?"

Edward nodded, passing her a monogrammed handkerchief for her hand, then took the crystal at the ends with his fingertips. With his free hand, he poured a clear liquid from a delicate bottle into a small silver bowl and set the bowl inside the circle.

"I'm going to need to concentrate, okay?"

Caitlin nodded and took a couple steps back.

After taking a slow, deep breath, he placed the crystal into the bowl and whispered something in a language she didn't know. Welsh, maybe? She flinched when his body jerked and straightened. She took a step forward but drew up short when his eyes opened, then rolled back into his head. Then his lips began to move as if he were speaking.

Seconds passed, then minutes. Caitlin watched in silence and focused on keeping her fear at bay.

After several torturous minutes, the crystal began to spin inside the bowl and stopped, pointing at her. Edward sucked in a breath and the crystal spun again. His hands pressed onto the desk harder. Color drained from his face, his jaw clenched, and sweat started to bead on his forehead.

She didn't know what to do. Would it be dangerous to interfere? Would it be worse not to?

Edward's eyes went wide, his body stiffened, and then he went limp.

"Eddy?" she whispered, rushing forward and catching him by his shoulders.

He lifted his head and took several shuddering breaths as his body shook.

"Did it work?" she asked, still in a whisper.

Edward ran his hands through his hair. He didn't look at her.

"Eddy?"

He licked his lips and shook his head. "No."

His voice was hoarse, and his words came so slow it made Caitlin nervous.

He swallowed. "I didn't find her. I'm sorry."

Caitlin stared at him. His eyes didn't have their

usual brightness and warmth. It was the spell, right? It had just taken a toll on him. They hadn't actually changed color . . . .

No, it had to be her imagination.

Or was there really someone else looking at her from behind his eyes?

CHAPTER TWELVE

Edward sat with Caitlin on the couch, but didn't look at her. He took another swallow of water, and the color began to return to his face. He shook his head. "I don't know if your blood won't work, or I couldn't do it."

She watched him, anxiety eating at the edges of her brain.

"I'm sorry, if I were just better, stronger—" Tears brimmed in his eyes, and he wiped at them.

Caitlin inched closer and reached out for his hand.

Edward took it.

His eyes were sad, but they were his. She sighed as relief flooded her. All she saw was the same strength, kindness, and compassion she'd come to rely on over the last five years.

"It's okay," she said softly, squeezing his hand. "I know you tried."

"I'll, um, I'll try again," he said with a shaky voice. "We'll keep trying until—"

The sound of an engine just became audible outside.

They looked at each other, holding their breath.

When the sound grew closer, Edward stood and walked to the door.

Caitlin followed, hope welling up inside her.

"It's him," Edward said with obvious relief as he looked through the peephole.

Caitlin wiped sweaty palms on the legs of her pants. The knock on the door made her jump.

"Open the door, lad. It's me," Brendan said.

Edward passed his hand over the knob and said something under his breath.

Caitlin's heart climbed into her throat, and it seemed to take months for the door to open.

Edward stepped back. "Jesus! What happened to you?"

"Had a bit of a run-in with the oíche—" Brendan's eyes went wide when he saw Caitlin.

"Oh, merciful God!" She gasped at the sight of him covered in dried blood, his shirt soaked through.

"They're going to keep watch outside—" a tall, blond man with pointed ears said as he walked up behind Brendan, but he froze when he saw Caitlin.

Through the open door, Caitlin saw three tall, slender forms in long black coats taking up positions around the outside of the house. She looked around, hope fading. "What's going on? Where's Fiona?"

The blond man seemed to blanch, and he stared at

Caitlin for a long moment before turning to Brendan. "She's the child's mother? The one who was put under a slumber?"

Brendan looked away.

Caitlin grabbed the doorframe, a sob overtaking her. "Fiona?"

Edward's arms went around her, helping her stand.

"Please," Edward said. "Tell me that's not—"

The blond man blinked, regaining his composure.

"No, the blood's not hers," Brendan said. "She wasn't there. It was a trap. They used this."

Caitlin took the pink blanket from Brendan's hand. It was Fiona's, her favorite.

"I do hate to be a bother," the blond man said to Edward, "but would you be so kind as to invite us in?"

Edward pointed outside. "Who are they? And who are you?"

"Dante," Brendan said through gritted teeth. "He's the Rogue Court Magister—"

"Rogue Court?" Edward asked.

"Jesus, man," Brendan said. "We can have class once we're through the bloody door. Just invite the nice elf inside, would you?"

Edward stepped back. "Elf?" He looked at Dante's ears, then back to his face. "But you don't look—I mean, sorry. Please, come in."

Caitlin watched Dante put Brendan's arm over his shoulder and help him inside. She gripped the blanket and brought it up to her face. It still smelled like Fiona's baby shampoo.

Edward closed the door and raised the wards. "She woke an hour or so ago. I don't know why or how."

Caitlin took a long breath, then eased her grip on the blanket.

"Doesn't matter right now," Dante said. "Brendan took quite a beating. Do you have some place I can get him cleaned up? I treated his wounds, but I still want a closer look at him."

"You're not me mother," Brendan said. "I just need me a stiff drink and a place to have a sit down, is all."

"What now?" Caitlin asked, just above a whisper.

Brendan looked at her and his countenance softened. "Don't you worry none, love, I'm not done looking. Not by a da—" Brendan's breath caught when he turned, as if he was having trouble breathing, then he tried again. "Not nearly done."

"We have an idea on how to find her," Dante said. "Assuming the wizard can manage it."

"Eddy?" Thoughts of the recent failure raced through Caitlin's mind, and she felt terribly ashamed.

"Me?" Edward asked.

"Eddy?" Dante stifled a laugh.

"Aye," Brendan said. "All fear Eddy, the great and powerful."

Edward stiffened. "I prefer Edward, actually."

Brendan and Dante both chuckled but stopped when they saw Caitlin's scowl.

"I really need to look Brendan over and make sure I didn't miss any injuries," Dante said.

"I told you," Brendan said. "I'll be fine—"

"No, he's right," Caitlin said. Brendan needed medical attention, even if he was a condescending ass. "I'm a nurse, and I've worked in the ER. I'll look him over." She turned to Eddy. "Where's the bathroom?"

"Listen, love, I appreciate it. But you're not me moth—"

"Shut up," Caitlin said, glaring at him.

Dante smirked. "Well, that clears up some questions. I'd listen to her."

Brendan shot Dante a glare before nodding to Edward, who led them all to the bathroom.

It was immaculate, which wasn't surprising, considering Edward's personality. A large clawfoot bathtub was against one wall, sink against another, and countertops of what looked like marble were reflected in a large mirror hanging behind them. Caitlin flinched when she saw her reflection.

"I'll get the first-aid kit and my bag," Edward said.

Caitlin turned Brendan so he could lean on the counter. "Take off your shirt." She began to lift it for him. "Let me have a look."

Brendan pulled his shirt off, grunting in pain.

Caitlin gasped when she saw his upper body. There were cuts, scratches, and bruises, and that was just what she could see through the blood. Nothing had been spared.

"What's this?" she asked, examining the bandage on his shoulder.

"*Dóu craiceann*," Dante said. "A bandage we grow. It works like artificial skin."

Caitlin blinked when she saw his almost luminescent, solid green eyes in the bright light of the bathroom. A shiver ran through her. Memories of the art opening and glowing eyes flashed in her head, but she swallowed and pushed them aside.

"Could you hand me that washcloth?" she asked Dante. "Where's Eddy with that first-aid kit?"

Dante handed her a collection of cloths. "I have my healing kit." He pulled the black case from inside his jacket. "Nothing against your skills, but I doubt a mortal kit will be as effective."

Caitlin almost stepped aside, a habit from working at a hospital. Like all nurses, she'd learned to defer to doctors, but she reminded herself that Dante wasn't a doctor, or at least she didn't think so. "Just set it there."

She cleaned the blood off while Brendan filled her in on what happened in the warehouse. She tried to listen, but she'd slipped into a numb sort of daze, her mind focused on Fiona.

When Dante took one of the soiled cloths, she watched him twist it under the running water as the blood ran down the drain.

"Who are you, anyway?" she asked.

"I told you," Brendan said.

"But what's a Rogue Court Magister?" Caitlin asked. "You have a healing kit; are you a doctor?"

"Not in the technical sense, no," Dante said. "Magister is a sort of local government official, but not."

"Can we chat later?" Brendan asked. "It's a bit cold in here, and I am half naked."

"He's shy around women," Dante said.

Caitlin cleaned the last of the blood away and saw the scars that ran over Brendan's body and the intricate Celtic knot tattoos that went from both elbows, up over his shoulders and onto his back and chest, as well as a small line of symbols tattooed up his sternum. She glanced into his eyes for just a moment, and she could see that the search for Fiona was personal for him too, though she couldn't say how she knew. She might not know his reasons, but he obviously wasn't someone who gave up. That, at least, gave her some reassurance.

While cleaning the blood from Brendan's back, she found more gunshot wounds and a few cracked ribs. Reluctantly, Caitlin moved away and let Dante step in. She tried to push aside her growing sense of being useless and focus instead on piecing her sense of reality back together. Feeling like the damsel in distress was leaving a rancid taste in her mouth.

"What's that?" Edward asked as Dante applied the last bandage. He held a black doctor's bag in one hand and a large red bag with a white circle and red cross in the other.

"Later," Dante said.

"I have some painkillers in my bag and a suture kit," Edward said.

"Thanks," Dante said. "But not necessary." He finished setting the bandage and patted Brendan's shoulder. "You're all set."

Caitlin noticed Edward glance at Brendan, then avoid her gaze.

"Me bag is by the door," Brendan said. "I need to get me a fresh shirt."

"And we need to ready the wizard," Dante said.

"For what?" Edward's face was pale again.

Caitlin bit her lower lip. She knew he wasn't fine, but he was putting on a brave face. Her heart filled with warmth at the gesture. She couldn't help but wonder what he was so afraid of, and what, if anything, it had to do with the spell.

Unbidden, another thought came to her: what had taken him so long to get his black bag? He always kept it close by.

CHAPTER THIRTEEN

Caitlin's eyes moved in time with her pounding heart, darting from Edward, to Dante, to Brendan. After a few rounds, her eyes settled on Kris, who looked even younger than usual. She'd been pulled into this for no other reason than being Caitlin's friend. How many more people would be dragged into this before it was done?

"What about her?" Dante asked, looking at Kris.

"I have no idea what I'm going to tell her," Caitlin said. "I still don't believe any of this myself." She let out a long breath and bit down on the foul taste of the words she was about to say. "But she's safe here, for now. At the moment, Fiona is the most important thing."

Edward stood close to her. "That's true, but won't it be dawn soon?"

"Let me." Dante sprinkled something in Kris's eyes as he whispered to her.

Caitlin felt a familiar shiver pass over her.

"That will keep her from waking," Dante said.

Brendan gave him a questioning look, but neither of them said anything.

Dante turned to Edward. "Now, to the business at hand?"

"What exactly is it I need to do?" Edward asked, standing a little straighter.

"We're going to be summoning an oíche what's probably hiding in Tír na nÓg, by using his true name," Brendan said.

"Okay . . ." Edward said.

"We think one of the higher-ranking oíche knows where your daughter is," Dante said to Caitlin. "Brendan has his true name. True names can be used to summon and compel fae and other beings of magic."

"But not," Caitlin said, then tried to think of the right word, "mortals?"

Dante shook his head. "No, I'm afraid not. Mortals aren't bound to magic that way."

"I've only read about summoning," Edward said. "I've never actually tried it. It seemed a little dangerous." He looked terrified, and somehow that fear was comforting to Caitlin.

"I just . . ." Edward looked at Dante. "I'm not saying no, but wouldn't you have better odds of success than me?"

Caitlin ignored the stab of guilt she felt for agreeing with him.

"No, I can't do it," Dante said. "I'm a fae and so is Justin, however much I dislike the notion. King Fergus and Queen Teagan can summon fae against their will and compel them to give information or perform a task. A human wizard can too—"

"If you use their true name," Edward said.

Dante nodded. "Just so. You're not bound by the same laws."

"So he won't be happy with me yanking him from wherever he is and depositing him here to answer to me. Something only the king or queen should be able to do," Edward said.

Dante nodded again. "That's pretty much it."

"Well, put like that, this should be a piece of cake," Edward said, forcing a smile.

Caitlin took Edward's hand in hers and squeezed it. "You can do it, Eddy." She tried to pack the words with confidence she wasn't feeling.

Edward turned beseeching eyes to her. "But if I screw up—"

"Oh, for feck's sake," Brendan said. "Man up and grow a set of—"

"What my tactless oaf of a friend means to say," Dante said, "is that I'll be helping you."

Edward looked at Caitlin for a long while . . . at least it felt like a long while. Then his lips turned up in that crooked smile that always made her feel better. "I'll do whatever it takes."

Caitlin leaned her head against his shoulder so he wouldn't see the tears. "Thank you," she whispered.

Dante stood up. "All right. We're going to need a circle."

"There's one in the basement," Edward said.

Caitlin, Brendan, and Dante all looked at him.

"What?" he said, shrugging. "This was my grandfather's house. This was all here when I got the place."

Dante chuckled under his breath. "Okay, lead the way."

Edward opened a door in the hallway to reveal stairs that ended in an empty room fifty feet across and forty wide. The whole room was made of cut stone, and in the middle, carved into the bare floor, was a large circle. It was much like the one Edward had drawn in his study, except this one was nearly five feet across.

Dante came to an abrupt stop and gaped. "I wasn't expecting this." He knelt down and examined the circle. "This is really, really well made. I can't see any flaws in it."

"So it'll work?" Edward asked, relief in his tone.

"It will at that," Dante said. "Let's go over what you'll need to do."

"Love, you probably ought to wait outside," Brendan said to Caitlin. "This is like to get ugly, and it won't be easy."

"No, I'm not going anywhere," Caitlin said. "Not like it could be worse than what I've gone through so far."

"Aye, fair play that." Brendan turned to Dante. "You tell our man the bad news?"

"Bad news?" Edward said. "What bad news?"

Caitlin glared at Brendan.

Dante sighed. "I was getting to it. We think they might be getting help from a wizard."

Edward licked his lips and swallowed. "What does that mean? You don't think it's me, do you?"

"No," Dante said. "It's just he might try to protect them. Summoning Justin could be dangerous if that's the case. More dangerous."

"Isn't the circle supposed to protect me?"

"It will, but only from what you're summoning." Dante put his hand on Edward's shoulder. "This is a good circle, best I've seen in a long time. It should protect you from mortal magic as well. You just need to be ready."

"Ready for what?" Edward asked. "I still don't understand what I'm supposed to do."

"Ready to fight back," Brendan said. "I take it the fire I saw in your hand earlier wasn't just for show?"

Caitlin stared at Edward, mouthing "fire?"

Edward shrugged "No. I know some offensive magic. I haven't really had any need to use it though."

"Well, you still may not," Dante said. "We just want to make sure you understand the risk of what you're about to do."

Edward smiled at Caitlin, and though it was faltering, it was that crooked, dimpled smile she knew so well. "I'm not backing out," he said to her. "I know she's not my daughter, but she means a lot to me, too."

Caitlin winced, but she knew she deserved that.

"No, I didn't mean—" Edward said. "I'll do whatever it takes." He turned to Dante. "Just tell me what to do."

"I'll be right back, lads," Brendan said.

"Where're you going?" Caitlin asked, but he was already up the stairs, so she looked back to Edward. "You can do this," she whispered to herself.

"First, you'll need to close the circle," Dante said. "Once that's done, you need to open the conduit and hold it open. Be careful not to cross over the circle's edge. The circle holds magic and magical beings, which means I can't break it, but you can. If you do, the protections will shatter."

Edward nodded.

"Brendan will give you Justin's name and you'll compel him three times to appear. The third time, he should manifest in the center of the circle, which will also serve to hold him."

"What then?"

"You'll compel him to answer our questions. When you ask, use his name. I'll tell you what to ask so he can't give us misleading answers. When he's first summoned and with each question, there'll be a battle of wills. That's where the compulsion comes in."

"Battle of wills?" Caitlin asked. "What happens if Eddy loses?"

"Thanks for the vote of confidence. I can be stubborn when I want to be."

Caitlin looked apologetically at Edward.

"Justin would escape," Dante said. "He could also get a shot off on his way out."

"So, don't lose," Edward said.

Dante smiled. "You'll have the advantage. You've

got his true name, you'll have the circle protecting you, and this is your demesne."

"You'll be fine, boss," Brendan said as he came back down the stairs. "Just be sure of yourself."

"He's right," Dante said. "That's the most important part of this, or any other kind of magic. You have to believe you can do it. If you don't, there's no point in trying."

"I can do it." Edward laughed a little. "No pressure, right?"

Caitlin gave him a hug and kissed his cheek, her lips lingering a bit longer than ever before. "I believe in you."

Edward hugged her back. "We'll find out where she is and we'll get her back."

"I know." Caitlin broke the embrace and stepped back.

"Back here, love." Brendan pulled Caitlin several paces away. "If you're going to stay, you need to keep out of harm's way and let the man work."

All her concerns and questions about Edward's ability and behavior threatened to bubble up, but she pushed them back down.

"Tell him Justin's name." Dante put his fingers in his ears.

Brendan stepped up to Edward. "Justarisheeth. Just-are-ee-sheeth." He said each syllable slowly, pronouncing each part. "Repeat it back to me."

"Just-arr-ee-sh-ee-th," Edward said. "Justarisheeth. Is that right?"

"Aye, that's it." Brendan patted his shoulder. "Make sure you pronounce it just like that."

"I'll get it right. Don't worry, I got it." He repeated it a couple more times under his breath.

"Okay then." Brendan nodded at Dante, who took his fingers from his ears. "Don't worry, you'll do fine. Just keep focused."

"Why'd Dante cover his ears?" Caitlin asked Brendan.

"He's forbidden from getting another fae's true name from anyone but the owner."

"Take a minute and clear your mind," Dante said. His voice was calm and even. "Let your worries and doubts drift aside."

Edward closed his eyes and took in long, slow breaths.

"Let the magic flow through you and over you," Dante said. "Don't push it, don't force it. Instead, guide it, direct it."

Caitlin watched as the seconds ticked by. After what felt like a week, Edward opened his eyes and whispered as he touched the circle. Tension filled the room, as if it had become pressurized. Instinctively, she found herself yawning to try to pop her ears.

"Won't do no good," Brendan said. "You'll get used to the feeling soon enough."

The circle began to fill with a soft blue radiance, as if someone poured the fluid from a glow stick into the etching. The intensity increased, and the lighting of the room seemed to diminish.

For a brief instant, Caitlin wondered what they'd do if this didn't work. No, it would work. It had to work. Eddy wouldn't let himself fail.

Dante spoke into Edward's ear. The air in the room grew heavier, and Caitlin felt like she was trying to breathe through a wet wool blanket.

Edward spoke softly and his fingers moved in the air.

The minutes dragged.

There was a cold stab of panic in Caitlin's heart when she saw Edward wobble. She took a step forward to help him, but Brendan caught her arm.

"Stay back. Dante will take care of him. It'll be all right. He's just not used to exerting himself. It can take a toll on you if you're not used to it."

"Are you sure?"

Brendan nodded and didn't let go of her arm. "He'll be fine. I wouldn't have suggested this if I didn't think he could pull it off."

The room lurched. Caitlin's stomach knotted and her knees went weak. Brendan's arm wrapped around her and pulled her close, holding her up.

"I got you, love."

A whirling mass of white clouds emerged in the center of the circle and electricity arced off them. It was like watching a miniature lightning storm.

Dante covered his ears. "Now."

"Justarisheeth! I summon you!" Edward shouted, his voice reverberating oddly, as if echoing from several directions at once.

An explosion of white light erupted in the center of the clouds and drew them in. It was like a star in the center of a nebula.

"Justarisheeth! I summon you!" he shouted again. He wavered as the clouds began to turn gray, growing darker as they churned.

The room began to shake.

Edward opened his mouth to speak the third time, and red lightning shot out from the center of the clouds. It hit the air at the circle's edge and lashed out at different points.

Caitlin looked from Edward to Dante and then to Brendan. The latter was staring with hard eyes at the circle, his jaw muscles flexed.

She gasped as Edward stumbled forward, but he caught himself inches from the edge of the circle. Her body tensed and her hands started to shake. "Please . . ."

Edward closed his eyes and lifted his right hand, palm facing the circle. "Justarisheeth! Oíche-sidhe! I summon you, now!"

Caitlin could hear the strain in the command, even though it was shouted. Her stomach did an intricate gymnastics routine and she held her breath.

The red lightning stopped, the clouds were pulled into a violent implosion, and the room shook again. Bright light drew itself in, then exploded against the unseen wall. When the light faded, a beautiful young man stood where the swirling clouds had been.

Familiar fear poured over Caitlin. The terror

fought against the relief of knowing that the spell had worked and her desire to make him pay for kidnapping Fiona.

Black eyes burned as they scanned the room. His pointed teeth flashed as his mouth twisted into a snarl and his gaze settled first on Edward, now on his knees and breathing hard. Contempt poured from the faerie's eyes, and they moved from Edward to Dante. The pure and raw hatred in them made Caitlin look away. She'd never seen anyone look at someone like that, and she hoped she never would again.

"Magister," Justin spat, more than said. "You'll pay for this." Sharp claws grew from his fingertips and he dragged them down the invisible barrier created by the circle. Long, bright blue scratches hung in his wake before fading.

"Get on with it, already," Brendan said, then whispered to Caitlin. "It'll be fine, love. It's nearly done. Be strong."

Strength, warmth, and confidence radiated from Brendan. She looked into his face and saw resolve. Something burned under the surface though, and it melted the cold fear, filling and feeding a slow burning anger in her. She'd scarcely had a violent thought in her adult life, but right now, she wanted nothing more than to beat the information out of Justin with her bare hands, to feel the satisfaction of his flesh and bone breaking under her fists.

Justin laughed at Caitlin. She flinched, and as images of her first encounter with the oíche returned, fear ate at the edges of her anger and she found herself drawing closer to Brendan.

"Fian, *díbeartach*," Justin said, each word soaked in venom. "I'll have repayment from you for giving my name to another." He glanced at Edward and a smile emerged on his face—the kind that's usually accompanied with an axe. "Do you think this sad little mageling can hold me? He's growing weak already."

Brendan unfolded Caitlin from his arms, and she felt vulnerable as he moved to stand inches away from the edge of the circle.

"Oh, he's a fine wizard," Brendan said. "Strength to spare. Don't you worry, cuddles, when we're done here, you're all mi—"

"Justin, you and your kin are in violation of the Oaths," Dante said, putting a hand on Edward's shoulder.

Edward took several short gasps and nodded.

"You've no jurisdiction on me now, Magister." Justin smiled at Caitlin.

She wavered a little but didn't look away; she wouldn't give him the satisfaction. Even so, he was clearly enjoying this, and it was getting to her.

"You're not in the Tír anymore, now are you, you *mac mallachta*?" Brendan asked. "That puts you back into his care." He smiled and crossed his arms. "Ask your questions, then," he said to Dante. "The sooner we get what we need, the sooner we get the girl back, and then Justin and I have a dance waiting."

Caitlin could see Edward struggling as Dante helped him to his feet. Edward glanced at her, and something changed in him. A look of focused determination solidified in his face. The self-doubt, fear, and worry that had plagued him before were gone.

Dante said something in Edward's ear, but Caitlin couldn't hear it. Edward's jaw clenched and he stared unblinking at Justin, who returned his stare. The room filled with a new tension as Edward and Justin began their battle of wills.

Caitlin's heart began to pound.

Edward's bandaged hand started to shake, but he tightened it into a fist until it stopped.

Hope welled up inside Caitlin. Edward was standing taller and straighter than she'd ever seen, and Justin was faltering. It was as if she was seeing Edward for the first time. Now the word *wizard* seemed fitting.

Justin's body began to shake with effort. Then he groaned and took a step back.

Edward gritted his teeth and smiled. "Take that, jerk."

"Good," Dante said. "First question: where is the stolen child, known as Fiona, who was taken from her mother's home this night?" Dante covered his ears. "Use his name."

"Justarisheeth," Edward said, and Justin winced. "Where is the stolen child, known as Fiona, who was taken from her mother's home this night?"

Justin gnashed his teeth. "No . . . I'll . . . not . . . say," he said between labored breaths.

"Again!" Brendan said. "Use his name at the start and compel him at the end. Don't ask, force him, the bastard!"

"Justarisheeth, where is the stolen child, known as Fiona, who was taken from her mother's home this night? *Trwy dy enw, yr wyf yn eich gorfodi*, Justarisheeth!"

This time, Justin staggered as if he'd been punched, dropped to his knees, banged his fists on the invisible wall, and screamed. "She's—no!" Again, his claws dug into the barrier, dragged down, and once more blue scratches hung in the air before fading.

"Again!" Brendan shouted.

"Justarisheeth," Edward repeated. "Where's Fiona? *Trwy dy enw, yr wyf yn eich gorfodi! Yr wyf yn eich gorfodi*, Justarisheeth!"

Justin's body shook as his muscles tensed, and he screamed, longer than any mortal would ever have been able to. Caitlin covered her ears.

"No!" Justin collapsed and writhed on the floor. "She's—" He convulsed and dug his claws into the stone. "She's between shadow and light." He screamed again and left deep gouges in the floor as his claws dragged across it.

"What?" Brendan clenched his fists. "No. You're lying. You wouldn't."

Justin's laugh was maniacal. He looked up at Brendan, still cackling. Small lines of black ooze ran out of his left ear and down his neck.

Caitlin saw what looked like fear in Brendan's eyes, and her heart turned to ice.

"I'm compelled, *díbeartach*!" Justin said with the same madness that tinged his laughter. "She's out of your reach!" He looked right at Caitlin and grinned. "And yours as well."

Caitlin took several steps back until she felt the wall behind her. She leaned against it as tears began to run down her face. "No, no, no."

Brendan grabbed Dante and turned him so they were face-to-face. "Your plan didn't work," he said once Dante had uncovered his ears.

"What? What did he say?"

"She's in the Tír!" Brendan shouted.

Dante's eyes went wide. "What?"

There was only a moment of confusion before Caitlin's mind went back to the stories from her childhood. "Tír na nÓg? No!" she screamed, or thought she did. However, no sound came from her open mouth.

Brendan bellowed and turned, arms reaching out for Justin.

"Brendan, no!" Dante grabbed the big man, pulling him back. "Not yet!"

"Get off me!" Brendan roared.

Meanwhile, Edward was perfectly still. He appeared unmoved by what was unfolding around him, except for the slightest tremor and small trickle of blood that ran from his nose.

Cold fear and hollow doubt were consuming Caitlin. It's all gone wrong, so terribly wrong.

Dante managed to pull Brendan back a few feet, then he stepped between him and the circle. "The wizard, don't forget about the wizard!"

Brendan seethed as he and Dante began shouting at each other in what Caitlin presumed was Irish.

Justin's black eyes locked onto Caitlin. She could feel his gaze burning through her and piercing her heart. It felt like he was violating her, delving into her very being.

He smiled knowingly, and his lips moved as he spoke silently.

Her heart stopped as she realized the truth. She'd lost Fiona.

A strange sigil, drawn of green fire, appeared high above Justin's head. As it did, the symbols of the circle shifted from blue to green.

Edward's eyes opened wide and he gasped as his body tensed, his hands began to shake, and sweat poured down his face.

Caitlin tried to scream, move, or do anything, but her body wasn't responding. Hopelessness weighed her down.

The sigil flared and there was a pop in the air. A bolt of green fire leapt from the burning symbol and struck Edward in the chest. He cried out and fell backwards, hitting the floor.

Caitlin's heart stopped. "Eddy, no!"

Dante and Brendan turned just in time to see Justin lunge at Brendan, claws first and mouth wide in a roar.

Brendan shoved Dante to the ground and, as Justin collided with him, twisted and used the momentum to hurl Justin across the room. The oíche hit the wall and fell to the floor with a thump, but he rolled and was on his feet in less than a second.

A second, apparently, was too slow.

Before Caitlin could even gasp, Brendan, a large knife appearing in his hand from nowhere, was on Justin.

"I'm going to make this hurt!" Brendan drove the knife into Justin's midsection.

Justin shrieked as lights and tendrils of darkness welled up from the wound and drifted away.

Justin swiped at Brendan, but Brendan caught his small hand and twisted his wrist until a snapping sound echoed through the chamber and was drowned under Justin's cries.

"You've had this coming," Brendan said as he slashed Justin's face with the knife. Justin's skin turned black and cracked at the edge of the cuts. Nearly invisible darkness wafted from the torn flesh. "And this is just the start!"

"Brendan!" Dante shouted from Edward's side. "Stop it, Brendan! Not yet!"

"I've waited long enough," Brendan said. There were flashes of silver as he cut Justin over and over.

Caitlin could see Justin slipping away. Part of her screamed for Justin's blood, to hear him shriek in pain. However, the larger part wanted her daughter back and knew her best chance was fading away right before her eyes.

She looked from Brendan back to Edward, who still wasn't moving. It was like standing on a hill and watching the whole world end. Then something broke inside her and she couldn't just watch anymore.

"No!" she screamed, and her muscles sprang to life. She grabbed onto Brendan and tried to pull him off Justin, but she might as well have been trying to move a tank.

Justin's howls of pain diminished and turned to choking laughter. His once beautiful face was now a black, dried mask. He looked every bit the monster. Unfortunately, he was a monster Caitlin needed.

"She's gone, *dibeartach!*" Justin laughed. "And you'll never get her back!"

Caitlin felt shaky, and her grip on Brendan grew weak as tears began to flow.

But it wasn't true. Justin was lying. He had to be. She'd know.

"You've lost another one, *dibeartach*," Justin said, between a mix of laughs and hacking coughs. He smiled at Caitlin, sharp teeth covered in black gore. "I hope you said good-bye, Mommy. No one comes back." He laughed and coughed again as his head rolled back.

Caitlin let go of Brendan as Justin, and her last hope, vanished in a cloud of black and tiny white lights. The weight of everything, the enormity of it all and the stark reality of what was happening, chose that moment to crash into her like a tsunami. Tír na nÓg? Fiona might as well be on the moon.

No, as long as Fiona was alive, there was hope. As long as Caitlin could still draw breath, there was hope. Wasn't there?

The possibilities ran through her head. She considered all the horrors her baby must be seeing, what these monsters might be doing to her. Caitlin gasped for air and leaned back until she felt the cold stone of the wall.

Her baby had been taken by faeries. Now Caitlin found herself in a world of darkness she'd never imagined could exist. A world she was unprepared to face.

"Find the courage! Find the strength! This is your child!" she told herself silently.

Disgust welled in her. Not at Justin, or the creatures who'd taken Fiona. Her revulsion was reserved for herself and her utter failure as a mother. Her heart began to beat more erratically. She reached out for strength, for hope, for courage, for any kind of comforting thought. Her baby needed her now, more so than ever before. But she couldn't get to her.

The room appeared frozen in time, and she was outside herself. Brendan was against the wall, his hand and knife buried in the cloud of darkness that had been Justin. Dante knelt over Edward. She sat against the wall in a fetal position as tears poured down her face.

A warrior, a wizard, and an elf had all failed. What could she possibly do? She tried desperately to cling to hope, even to the hope there was hope, but it was empty and hollow. She looked down at her small, pathetic form. Never before had she felt so minuscule, so insignificant, and so useless.

Everyone, everything in her life, even before this moment, had turned to ash. Her grandparents had cared for her when her parents had died, but she'd still taken the weight of that pain all on herself. She'd loved her grandparents, but she hadn't trusted them to stay. How could she? Her parents had died and left her. If they could be taken away, anyone could.

James had seduced her and then disappeared. Cold washed over her as she remembered waking up in that small bed and breakfast, seeing his bag in the corner but his clothes and shoes gone.

He'd left, just like Mom and Dad.

Again her grandparents had tried to help when she'd found herself pregnant, but they'd died and left her too, never even having had the chance to see their great-grandchild. And now Kris, caught in a dangerous situation, might end up being the latest casualty of Caitlin's cursed life. All of them suffering tragedy for nothing more than trying to help her.

She looked at Edward, limp in Dante's arms. Her heart began to crack. She knew the childhood he'd had. A skinny, awkward, and bookish child, for most of his life he'd been an easy and constant target for bullies. And yet after each blow that knocked him down, he got back up again. She thought of the failed spell. He'd seen, or maybe even been touched by, something terrible. And still, he'd put aside his doubts, his fears, and faced it all, for her and for Fiona. He'd always been there for her, perhaps even when he shouldn't have been, when she hadn't really deserved it.

Something flashed in the corner of her eye, and

when she turned to look, a tiny light, no larger than a spark, hung unmoving in the air. It was hope, but it was so small.

Caitlin closed her hand around it. Heat radiated from it, and she wondered if this was all real or just a hallucination.

There was no way she could do this, not by herself. She held the hope and looked from one face to another. When she looked at Edward, she saw his chest slowly rise and fall. He was still here. He was still alive.

She wasn't alone.

The hope in her hand grew warmer, and light leaked from between her fingers. That thought should've been obvious, but she only really understood it now. She needed others, to trust in them. She looked at Dante, then at Brendan. Strangers to her, but both putting their lives on the line, Brendan quite literally. They were all still fighting, all of them.

The light in her hand was blazing, casting streaks of white across the floor and walls. The consequences of their failure raced through her mind, and she gripped the hope as the weight of it all tried to pull her down.

That was it then; there really was no choice to make. She knew how this could end, but it didn't matter. Whatever the cost to herself, or even those around her, she'd find a way to live with it. Nothing else mattered, and everyone in this room knew that. They were willing to fight, and so was she. She could live with anything but losing Fiona. But there was always hope, however small.

She blinked and was back in her body, viewing the chaos around her. The light was gone, but the hope it represented remained.

Then her vision went black.

CHAPTER FOURTEEN

Caitlin had the vague sensation of being lifted from the ground and carried up the stairs. She felt hardly any sense of motion, and even her mind was quiet. Her body, however, continued to gasp between sobs so hard her stomach convulsed.

"Easy there, love," Brendan said. "Breathe. It's going to be all right, I promise."

"Please, help me," she whispered.

She felt soft cushions around her and tried to open her eyes but couldn't. Everything was dark and still.

"You all right, lad?" Brendan's voice asked.

"I'm sorry," Edward's voice said. It was shaking. "I couldn't hold him. It's my fault, I wasn't good enough."

"Your skill had nothing to do with it," Dante said.

There was the sound of pacing footsteps.

"Aye," Brendan said. "He's right. Don't blame yourself, mate. We told you the risk and you rose to meet it. You did fine, it was nicely done. We've both had our challenges tonight."

"How's—"

"Stay where you are," Dante said. "Caitlin's fine, she just fainted. All things considered, I'm surprised she held out this long." The sound of footsteps moved away, the fridge door opened then closed, and the footsteps returned. "Here, drink this."

"Thanks, I'll be okay," Edward said. "I just need a moment to get my head back on straight."

There was a sigh and weight on the couch near her.

"At least we know where the *girseach* is," Brendan said.

"Yes, but we still don't know what part the other wizard is playing in all this," Dante said. "Aside from breaking through one extraordinary protective circle and freeing Justin, I mean."

"Why'd the other wizard just release him?" Edward asked. "I mean, why didn't he return Justin to wherever I'd summoned him from? Why leave Justin here? The wizard had to know Brendan would kill him, right?"

The voices were silent.

"That's a very good question," Dante said.

"We should get this one clear," Brendan said. "Have one of your boys take her home. Use some hair to get her inside—"

"Are you mad?" Dante said.

"Well, it's not like she can invite them in," Brendan said. "*Dar fia*, you're only setting right an earlier violation."

"Can't you use her hair without cutting it off?" Edward asked.

"Oh aye," Brendan said. "But like as not she'd be a bit upset waking up bald."

"The hair is consumed in the charm," Dante said. "So you cut some off to separate it—"

"Water," Caitlin managed to say. "Please." Her voice was dry and her mouth felt like it was full of cotton. With some effort, her eyes opened. Blurry shapes of various colors moved like ghosts in front of her.

"Here you go, love," Brendan said.

A cold bottle was pressed into her hand and a strong arm against her back helped her sit up. She put the bottle to her mouth and drank the icy water, relishing the sensation of it pouring down her throat.

"Take your time. Get your breath back," Brendan said as he eased her back against the cushions.

"You had a panic attack," Edward said.

Caitlin's vision came into focus and the images became clear. She was lying down, and Brendan was sitting over her. She lifted her head and felt a flood of relief when she saw Edward collapsed in the chair. He looked pale and exhausted, but he was alive and unhurt. Dante was pacing. Caitlin's head pounded, but each gasp of air seemed to ease it a little.

"It was a bad one." Edward forced a smile. "But you just hyperventilated and passed out. That's all."

No, that wasn't all, she thought.

Caitlin's head fell back to the cushion. She was exhausted, but there was more to do. "Please, you have to get Kris out of this," she said.

Dante let out a breath and nodded. "I'll take care of it."

"Promise me she'll come to no harm," Caitlin said.

"I swear to you," Dante said. "She'll arrive home safe. My marshals will protect her."

Caitlin nodded. "Now, twice more please."

Dante, Brendan, and Edward looked at each other.

"Thrice promised, right?" she asked.

"And bound," Dante said with a nod and approving smile.

"I figured everything happening in sets of three meant it was true."

"It is," Dante said. "And you have my promise she'll arrive home safe. On my honor, no harm will come to her while in my charge."

Caitlin told Dante Kris's address as Edward removed the wards. Dante summoned a marshal inside, and the two whispered before the marshal relented, picked up Kris, and headed for the door.

"Wait a minute." Brendan went into his bag and came out with a cell phone. "Here you go." He tucked it into the elf's pocket.

"Don't waste time, Kevan," Dante said.

When the door shut and Edward raised the wards, Caitlin felt a slight sense of relief knowing Kris was out of this at least.

No one said anything for a long moment. Caitlin noticed her hand was still clenched into a tight fist.

She was still holding on to that small hope that Kris wouldn't be the only one to walk away from this. She looked at Edward and couldn't help but smile. His color was returning, slowly. He still had hope too, and that made hers a little brighter and warmer.

"I'm sorry if this is a stupid question," Edward said. "But I keep coming back to something that doesn't make sense."

Everyone looked at him.

"What did Justin mean?" Edward asked. "I thought he had to answer the question."

"He did," Dante said. "Unfortunately."

"Fiona is in Tír na nÓg," Caitlin said, then sucked in a breath and tried to sit up.

"Aye." Brendan helped her.

The room started to spin, but slower this time. Caitlin put a hand to her head, closed her eyes, and struggled to keep her breathing even.

"So, what do we do now?" Edward asked.

Caitlin had to push the taunting sound of Justin's last words from her head.

"And what do you think we do, then?" Brendan let out a breath. "Only one thing to be done, isn't there? I'm going to go and get her back."

Caitlin looked at Brendan and could see the steely resolve in his eyes. She drew on the strength and surety he was radiating. But there was something more beneath that. Emotions roiled inside her, but she said nothing. She just swallowed.

"Don't you worry, love." Brendan smiled. Caitlin

noticed for the first time that his scars caused it to fall a little unevenly. "I'll get her back to you. I promise you that, and I keep me promises."

Dante cleared his throat. "Brendan? A word, if you please," Dante said, then turned and walked out of view.

"Aye, keep your knickers on." Brendan stood. "I can guess what that word is." He nodded at Edward. "Keep an eye on her, lad. I'll be back as soon as Dante is done with me bollocking."

Brendan walked away and a door closed.

Edward sat down next to Caitlin, put his arm around her shoulder, and took her hand in his. She felt weak in every sense of the word, but she squeezed his hand. The faint sound of voices came through the door.

"Do you hear that?" she asked.

"No, I can't hear anything," Edward said. "You can hear them?"

"I think so."

The voices were muffled, and she strained to make sense of them.

"I know that, don't I?" Brendan asked. "But maybe by doing the right thing I can tip the scales—"

Dante cut him off, but she couldn't make out his words.

"What are they saying?" Edward asked.

Caitlin struggled, but she couldn't decipher anything else. "I don't know." Her head felt like it weighed a ton. She looked at Edward and squeezed his hand again. "Thanks, for everything."

"You don't have to thank me."

"Yes, I do." She drew in a breath. "It seems apropos I'm saying this to a psychiatrist."

Edward looked at her the way he always did, without judgment. "What?"

"I've got trust issues, especially where Fiona is involved."

"Well, gee, I wonder—"

"Please, let me finish," she said. "I know I can't do this alone."

Edward turned to face her fully. "You never need to ask for help from me."

She swallowed and looked at the closed door of the study. "I know, but I need their help, too."

Edward's smile faltered a little for just a fraction of a second, but then recovered. "I told you, I'll do whatever it takes." He looked over his shoulder at the closed door. "I'll make sure they do, too."

She closed her eyes and her head fell back against the couch. The sound of Justin's screams and the image of him disintegrating into darkness filled her head.

"What is it?" Edward asked.

"I think I enjoyed watching him die," she said. "In fact, I wanted to do it myself."

"He wasn't human," Edward said. "He was a faerie, and part of the group that took your daughter. Caitlin, he taunted you." He put her hand between both of his. "Things like that can cause people to . . . well . . . break. To grossly oversimplify a complicated psychological condition, feeling and acting screwed up during a screwed-up situation does not make you screwed up. Even if he didn't have it coming, which he did, no one can blame you for feeling the way you do. She's your daughter."

In Edward's eyes, Caitlin saw just how much he loved both her and Fiona.

"Don't you dare lose a moment of sleep over it," he said. "You understand—"

"Damn it, Dante!" Brendan's voice came through the door, causing both Edward and Caitlin to look up.

"I did hear that," Edward said.

The door opened and Brendan stormed out.

"Stop your talking. It's settled. I'm not going to just leave that girl at their mercy." He rounded on Dante and pointed a finger at himself. "I know what kind of mercy they got, don't I? This time, I'm finishing it. I'll do it meself. No one else need be involved."

Dante followed, but he didn't speak until Brendan sat in the chair. "You're not in any shape to go. You may not feel it, but you got your—"

"I'll be fine," Brendan said, not looking at Dante. "I just need me a few hours sleep is all." He turned to Edward. "You got a spare bed in this place I can use, then?"

"I do," Edward said. "Of course you're all welcome to stay, if you'd like."

"*Míle buíochas.*" Brendan looked at Dante. "I appreciate your concern, but what else can we do? You can't tell me you're fine with the notion of just leaving her there."

Dante sat on the arm of the couch that Edward and Caitlin were sharing and shook his head. "You know I can't go with you."

"I know," Brendan said. "I know you want to, but this one I need to do on me own." He took a deep breath and let it out slowly. "I can't cross till after nightfall. That'll give me a chance to rest and your handiwork time to heal me a bit. There's a gateway not far from here, in Vermont, that I can use. It's no more than a handful of hours away."

"I know it." Dante bowed his head. "Okay. I've said my piece."

When she lifted her head, Caitlin saw something in Brendan's eyes. She looked from Brendan to Dante then back again. In that glimpse, she understood what Brendan was saying. Moreover, she didn't have a choice but to let him.

Edward cleared his throat. "I'll go with you," he said, eyes focused on his shoes.

Caitlin's head snapped to Edward. "I—".

"Not bloody likely," Brendan said with a chuckle. "I appreciate the sentiment, lad, I do. But this is well beyond what you can manage."

"I know," Edward said, "but you can't go alone. You'll need someone to watch your back, as it were." He glanced first at Caitlin, then at Brendan. "I know I'm not the ideal choice. My skill may be lacking, but if Dante can't go, I should. I'll be able to help, even if it's just—" He swallowed. "Just to give you a chance to get out with Fiona."

Caitlin's heart caught in her throat. She knew this was what asking for help meant, but it didn't make it any easier.

"It's not like that," Dante said. "That's not what Brendan meant."

"I have to give you credit." Brendan smiled with genuine pride. "You've got a warrior's heart in you, mate. But you'd do me no good."

"He means your magic won't work there," Dante said. "You'd just be a normal mortal. That has all kinds of consequences in Tír na nÓg. It pains me to say it, but Brendan would move faster and have a better chance on his own."

"It's nothing against you," Brendan said. "But I can't be looking after you and trying to get the wee one back at the same time."

Relief poured through Caitlin, followed by an absolute certainty. "I'm going."

Six wide eyes below lifted brows stared at her.

"Don't take this wrong, love," Brendan said. "Not just no, but hell no. No bloody way, no. Did you not hear what I just said?"

"I heard you." Caitlin didn't look up. "I'm not going to sit here while others go after my daughter. I'm her mother, and she needs me."

Brendan opened his mouth.

"I'm not stupid. I know I can't do it alone, but neither can you." She looked Brendan hard in the eyes. "Besides, what if she needs medical attention? Or what if you do?"

"Look here, love," Brendan said. "I understand what it is you're saying, but—"

"I know what the risks are," Caitlin said. "I'm willing to take them. She's my daughter, and losing her—" Caitlin closed her eyes and shook as the thought of it passed through her. After a moment, she opened her eyes. "Well, that would kill me anyway."

"Is that so?" Brendan asked. "And who'll take care of her if you get yourself killed, then? I can't watch out for you the whole time, and it might take a while to find her. The Tír is a mighty big place."

"Eddy would." Caitlin squeezed his hand then looked at him, knowing there was desperation in her eyes. "Wouldn't you?"

"Yes, of course." Edward blinked. "But I'd prefer not to have to. Caitlin, this is way, way past what either one of us is prepared to deal with. It's one thing for me to go, but you're her mother. She needs you."

"I understand, love," Brendan said. "More than you can know, but you're not going. It's going to be hard enough on me own."

Caitlin felt her tenuous hold on her anger slip, and her face flushed. Her hands shook, but her voice was calm and flat. "You are not going without me."

"Well, I'm not going with you," Brendan said. "That's it, nothing more to say, then. You can't cross without me, and I'm not taking you. So it's done." He stood up.

"No." Caitlin said through gritted teeth.

"What?" Brendan asked.

"I said, no. You're not leaving me here to go insane, waiting to find out if she's okay."

"I told you—"

"No!" Caitlin stood up and glared at him.

Brendan took a step back.

"I'll fight. If I have to tear the whole damn place down to get to her, I will. She needs me. She must be scared. She's been with strangers for so long already." Tears rolled down her cheeks. "She doesn't even have her teddy bear with her. I didn't get to kiss her goodnight, or tuck her in." She took a step closer to Brendan and pointed a finger at him. "No one, not God in heaven, not all the demons in hell, and certainly not you, will keep me from her. That's not your decision to make. You understand that?"

Brendan lowered his head and let out a breath.

Edward stood between Caitlin and Brendan and put his hands on her shoulders. "I think we all could use some sleep."

She shrugged him off, stepped around Edward, and glared up at Brendan again. He wouldn't meet her gaze. "I asked you a question."

"Caitlin," Edward said. "What if Brendan agreed to not say no and to hear you out after some rest?"

"Aye," Brendan said. "I can do that."

Caitlin nodded once. "Fine."

"Good," Edward said. "Now let's all get some sleep. We'll go over this again when we have clearer heads. It's obvious I'm not the only one who's tapped out."

"Good idea." Dante's pocket started ringing. He

reached in and pulled out a phone. "Yes?" He listened and nodded. "Well done. Come back here and take up positions around the house. We're going to get some rest. If you need to call in others to relieve you, do it." He listened again. "That's right. And tell the Cruinnigh what's happened." He ended the call and turned to Caitlin. "Your friend is home, safe and sound."

"Thank you."

Dante looked out the window. "Sun's coming up. Edward, could you wake everyone by noon? That should give us time to rest, prepare, and then make the drive."

"Us?" Brendan asked.

"I can't cross," Dante said, "but we don't have to wait here."

"No, we don't," Edward said. He squeezed Caitlin's hand and gave her a small smile. "And we won't."

CHAPTER FIFTEEN

Caitlin felt numb; if asked, she wouldn't be able to swear she was even awake anymore.

Brendan and Dante vanished into their respective rooms, leaving Edward and Caitlin alone in the hallway. When Caitlin started for her room, Edward touched her shoulder. She turned and looked at him.

"I know it won't be easy," Edward said, "but you really need to try and get some sleep." He held out his hand. "I want you to take this." A small pill was in his palm.

"Eddy, I appreciate it, but I don't need—"

"Yes, you do." He put the pill in her hand. "You have trouble sleeping when your world isn't upside down. Just take it, please."

Caitlin looked at the pill, back to Edward, and let out a breath. "Okay."

He smiled. "Look, don't worry about Brendan, okay?"

"I'm not. He's not leaving me behind."

Edward opened his mouth to speak, but apparently thought better of it. "If you need anything," he said, pointing to a door at the end of the hall, "that's my room."

She hugged him, tight. "Thank you." She held up the pill. "For this, too."

"Just get some rest."

Caitlin stepped into her room and closed the door. Light was beginning to fill the sky and pour in through the window. She thought back to her college years. She'd never been a big party girl, but she'd still been up for her share of sunrises. Like now, it had never really hit her until she'd seen the morning sun. Then it was as if her body realized how long it had been moving.

She saw a bottle of water on the nightstand and laughed. That was Eddy, seeing to every detail, even as the world burned around him. When she picked it up, she thought of her lost little girl and sighed. Where was Fiona sleeping? Who, or what, was watching over her?

Caitlin looked at the pill in her hand. She needed rest, but it just didn't seem right. Of course, she wouldn't be any good dead on her feet either. She swallowed the pill with a mouthful of water. When she pulled the curtains closed, darkness swallowed the room, and for a moment, she felt like a little kid herself. She opened the curtains a little to allow some light in before collapsing on the bed.

Tears began to fall as she lay there waiting for the

pill to knock her out. Her mind drifted back to the night Fiona was born, and she smiled despite herself. Edward had paced in the waiting room, and anyone observing would've thought he was the father, the way he'd smiled when he'd finally seen Fiona. In fact, hadn't he been a father to her all these years? The only thing missing was the word, the title. In a slow progression of memories, Caitlin saw all he'd done for Fiona. She remembered Fiona's first time trick-or-treating, when the little girl had tripped, skinning her knee and tearing her princess dress. Edward had reached Fiona first, wiping away her tears. Caitlin could still hear his words, telling Fiona that it would take more than a little dirt or a torn dress to keep her from being the most beautiful princess ever. Caitlin's heart swelled, and she remembered when Edward gave Fiona Paddy Bear, her beloved stuffed animal. He was a good man, and if anything happened to her, he'd take good care of Fiona. She imagined Fiona safe in his arms and found it brought a mix of emotions, both comforting and heart wrenching.

She held a pillow tight in her arms and tried not to think about how unnatural it felt to be in bed without having hugged or kissed Fiona goodnight, or read her "just one more" story. A shuddering sob gripped her as she imagined Fiona, scared, hungry, and surrounded by monsters, crying for her mommy.

Burying her face in the pillow, Caitlin screamed and started punching the bed. It wasn't right! It wasn't supposed to be like this!

At a faint knocking on her door, she looked up. As

she stood, twinges of drowsiness began to settle in, but she walked across the room and opened the door.

"Sorry, I didn't—" She stopped when she saw who it was.

"I." Brendan cleared his throat. "I'm sorry about earlier. I behaved— Well, I was an arse, wasn't I? But there's things here you don't know, about me, I mean."

Caitlin thought he seemed smaller somehow. "It's okay. We found out where she is. That's what matters, right?"

"All the same, I can be a bit of a hothead. I just want you to know, I'm not going to let any of that get in the way. I meant what I said. I'll get her back."

Caitlin fought the growing heaviness in her eyes. "Thank you." She realized this was the first time she'd actually said that to him. "I don't know why you're helping me, I'm just glad you are."

His blue eyes seemed much softer than they had before, almost as if they'd changed color, shifting from bright blue to a duller gray. Again there was something behind them, and it made her feel a sudden rush of warmth.

"No need for all that, love." He looked at his hand. "Oh, right. I also thought you might want this." He lifted the blanket he'd brought back from Boston. "I thought you might sleep easier having it nearby. Not as good as the real thing, I know, but, well, in the madness, you left it downstairs."

Caitlin felt a lump in her throat as she took the blanket. How could she have forgotten it?

"Thank you," she said, and it came out much quieter than she'd intended. She lifted the blanket to her face, and Fiona's smell filled her nose. A couple of tears broke loose, and she wiped them away. When she looked back up, Brendan was staring at her in a way that made her heart pound a little harder. Her thoughts returned to his arm around her down in the basement.

After a long moment of silence, Brendan cleared his throat yet again and looked away. "All right, then." He turned, looked over his shoulder, then shook his head. "Just get some rest, aye?" He took a step back and made for his room.

"Brendan."

He stopped and turned around.

"Thank you." She kissed his cheek and felt rough stubble on her lips, then she hugged him, and his muscles tensed under her touch. Pulling back, she was unable to look him in the eyes and stared instead at his scars.

"You're welcome, love," he said, his voice shaky. "Goodnight." He returned to his room.

Caitlin shut the door and collapsed on the bed. She rolled onto her side, drew her legs up, and buried her face in the blanket. Thankfully, in just a few minutes, sleep rose up and took her into darkness.

Edward ground his teeth and balled his hands into fists as he stood behind his slightly open door and watched the scene unfolding in the hallway. When Caitlin closed her door, he shut his and began pacing.

"Who the hell does he think he is?" He ground his teeth and kicked at the air.

"He's no one," something inside him answered.

"That's right, no one!"

"What does he really have anyway? Knives? Muscles? Scars?"

"Exactly!"

"He doesn't have your power. He couldn't even conceive of the power you wield."

"Tân," Edward whispered. Fire answered his call and filled his hand.

"You can control the elements, the very power of life! What are blades when you can bend the very forces of the universe to your will?"

"Yes," Edward whispered as exhilaration surged through him.

"And you've barely touched your true power. Soon they will cower, and you can take her for yourself!"

"Yes! That's—" Edward blinked, and the fire snuffed out. "What? No." The room spun, and he stumbled toward his bed. He put his hands to his head and tried to get his suddenly racing heartbeat under control.

What was that?

He thought back over the night, to the scrying attempts, particularly the second one, and then the summoning. He thought of the way it felt to best Justin. A rush of adrenaline was still pumping through him. He'd felt connected to his magic tonight, more so than ever before. It was invigorating. True, Justin had escaped the circle, but in one night, he'd made more progress than he had in months. But that wasn't all, was it? He'd touched something tonight, something dark.

And it had touched him back.

He saw in his mind burning red eyes and felt the cold touch of it reaching into him again.

There'd been power in that darkness, huge power. It had made itself available to him. He'd felt it course through him, and he had to admit, it was amazing.

"No." He stood and paced. "What if it—"

He stopped and focused, desperate to get his jumbled thoughts in order. Could he control it? What if, just what if, he could? He could use that power against those who were working against them; he could turn it back onto itself. Was there even such a thing as dark power? A gun isn't intrinsically evil. It's how something is used that defines whether it's good or not. It all made sense. He could do it. After all, he made his living helping others use for good the darkness that had come into their lives.

He smiled as he lay down and closed his eyes.

CHAPTER SIXTEEN

Brendan woke and sat up with a yawn. He climbed out of bed and stretched, wincing when he went too far. He straightened and felt around his side. The ointment and bandages seemed to have done their job, or started to. In the mirror above the dresser, he saw that the bruises, scratches, and swelling in his face were all gone.

He poked at the bandage on his shoulder, which was still a little tender. He rotated it and found he could move it with only a slight stiffness and pain. No doubt the elfin bandages had closed the bullet holes, but it would be more than a week before they fully healed the internal damage.

"These ribs are going to be a problem," he said to his reflection.

He began to work out the stiffness in his muscles by gently stretching. He needed to find the limit to his range of motion. When he finished, he nodded. He wasn't in too bad shape after all. He just had to be careful. The pain wasn't the issue; he could push that aside. What he had to be mindful of was making the injuries worse. He couldn't let that, or anything else, cause him to fail.

He'd given his word to Caitlin, and in the end, that was all he had. He pushed the thought of her aside and gave his reflection a dirty look. As he pulled a clean shirt from his bag, a leather box fell to the floor. He picked it up, and slowly he opened it to stare at the shining claddagh ring. It didn't take him long to make the decision.

He closed the box and put it away, then looked out the window. The sunlight nearly blinded him, but he studied the trees, the clouds, and the sky. When the tears were about to break through, he chided himself, sucked in a breath, and turned to the nightstand.

The clock said 10:53. He knew the others would be up soon. It was time to get moving. He pulled clean clothes out of his bag, opened the door, and stepped into the hallway.

Caitlin woke with a start and sat up to find her head filled with lead. She hated sleeping pills, but at least she'd gotten some rest. Well, sleep anyway. As she rubbed her eyes, she heard something from the room next to hers—Brendan's room.

Panic rose and her breathing became shallow. He'd promised not to go, right? Thinking back, she realized he'd never actually agreed to that, only not to say "no" about taking her. She pushed back the swelling fear, rolled out of bed, and stepped into the hallway.

The door to his room opened, and Brendan stepped out, wearing only his kilt. He saw her and flinched, nearly dropping the bundle of clothes he clutched in his hand.

"M'anam, cailín!" He said. "You scared the life out of me."

"Sorry." She saw his bloodshot eyes and knew he probably hadn't gotten much sleep.

"I told you last night that I wasn't going to leave without talking to you, didn't I?"

"You did, that's right. I just heard you moving around and, I don't know."

He pointed to the bathroom. "I understand, love, but the only place I'm going is to get me a shower."

"I'm going with you."

"What?"

Caitlin's eyes went wide, and she felt herself turn bright red. "To get Fiona back, I mean."

Brendan laughed, then sighed. "It's going to be a violent and bloody event to get her. I can get her out. It isn't going to be easy, even if I were on me own. With you there?" He shook his head.

"I know, but I just can't sit and wait anymore. I can't let everyone else do it for me. I have to do more than just wonder what's happening," she said. "They took her from me. They literally pulled her from my arms. I don't even know why."

"I know—"

"No," she said. "I want my daughter back, that's all. She's everything to me."

Brendan opened his mouth.

"Let me finish."

Brendan nodded.

"I'm not ignorant." She shook her head. "Well, okay, I am. All I have to go on are the stories Nana used to tell me, and they seem to have gotten at least as much wrong as they did right, but I understand the risk. I'm sorry it'll make it harder for you." She swallowed. "Do you have kids?"

He stiffened and looked away. "No."

"I can't explain it to you then, but I can help. Like I said, I'm a nurse—"

"Stop." Brendan raised his free hand. "Just stop."

"But—"

"Bloody hell, woman. You can come, all right." He looked at the ground and shook his head. "I told you what lies ahead. If you want to go, I'm not going to stop you."

"Thank you." She felt, at long last, that she was taking an active role in this mess.

"Show's over," Brendan said over his shoulder. "Come on out. You might as well go and knock up Edward."

Caitlin blinked and was about to ask what he meant, then she remembered the phrase from her visit to Ireland.

"Like sands in the hourglass," Dante said as he stepped into the hallway.

"You won't regret this," Caitlin said to Brendan. When she looked at Dante, her mouth fell open. "You wake up looking like that?"

His eyes were bright and clear, his hair was perfect. She half expected to see a glint off his teeth and smell mint when he smiled.

Dante shrugged. "It's a curse."

"Can I take me fecking shower now?" Brendan asked. "It's been weeks since I've had a proper one."

"I could've done without hearing that," Dante said. "Although, it does explain—"

Brendan smacked the back of Dante's head, then disappeared into the bathroom, shutting the door behind him.

"I'll wake Eddy," Caitlin said.

"I'll see about some food," Dante said as he headed down the stairs. "I'm starving."

Caitlin knocked. "Eddy, are you up?" When she heard no answer, she turned the knob and opened the door. She peeked around it and saw that his curtains were open and his form was lying buried beneath a heap of blankets. It felt strange seeing him like that, as if she was invading his privacy.

Well, she supposed, in point of fact, she was.

There wasn't any way around it, so she reached out to wake him but stopped short. Guilt at drawing him into this caused her stomach to churn. But then he'd never willingly just stand by, not for anyone, much less someone he . . . Her eyes moved over his face, following the line of his jaw. Always right in front of her, and she'd never seen it. How much else had she missed, and missed out on?

Edward grunted and opened his eyes. He blinked a few times before his eyes focused on her. She felt her face flush, but when she saw the creases in his obviously ironed flannel pajamas, she just smiled.

"What time is it?" he asked.

"Almost eleven."

He sat up and ran a hand through his mess of hair. "Did you get any sleep?"

She nodded and tried to figure out how to tell him that Brendan had agreed to take her with him.

"Good." He yawned and looked at her. "What is it?"

She could feel his critical eyes on her, dissecting facial expressions and body language. "You know, sometimes it's so aggravating, having a friend who can read people." She let out a breath and sat on the edge of the bed. "I convinced Brendan to take me with him."

"You did?" His expression flashed fear, but it melted away and he nodded. "Okay."

"Okay?"

"I still don't think it's a good idea. Apart from the danger, you've got no idea what you're getting into. I think you should let Brendan go alone. He knows what he's doing, and he's the expert in these things."

"Wait, what?"

"Having said that . . ." He sighed. "I understand you wanting to go. I don't like it, but I get it, and I'll respect your choice."

Caitlin was speechless.

"But I'm going, too."

"What? No! I know you'd do it, and I love you to death for that, but you can't."

"Cait—"

She held up her hand and he stopped. "Eddy, I need you to stay here. In case—" She drew a breath. "In case something happens to me, I need you to take care of Fiona."

"Nothing's going to happen to you." He leaned toward her. "If Brendan agreed to let you go, it's because he believes he can protect you."

"Just promise me."

He looked at her for a long moment, then drew in a breath. "I can't do that."

She felt her stomach drop. "You have to, she doesn't have—"

"No. I'm not giving you an out." He smiled. "You'll just have to make sure nothing happens so you can raise her yourself."

It all made sense. His promise hadn't come in the words she'd expected, but he'd agreed to take care of Fiona all the same and now he needed her to make a promise in return.

"Okay," she said. "I will. And thank you."

"I told you—"

"Not just for that, or for last night, or this morning, or whenever it was. Thank you for everything. I feel like you've been a much better friend to me than I've been to you."

"Well, you're wrong."

Caitlin saw him looking at her lips. Her heart beat a little faster, and she knew her cheeks were turning pink. He started to lean toward her, but she turned her head at the last moment. Guilt tore at her heart when she realized what she'd done. When she looked back, Edward's faltering smile made her heart crack.

She reached out a hand to take his. "Eddy, I'm sorry, I just—"

"No, I'm sorry." He stood and stepped away.

She opened her mouth, desperate to explain it wasn't him but the timing.

"I, uh, I just—" He turned away. "Look, I just." He turned one way, then back before stopping and pointing to a door. "You go ahead and use my bathroom." He started pulling clothes from his drawers. "It'll give you more privacy. I'll just use the spare one."

"Eddy—"

"No, it's—" He turned as if to say something, but he just shook his head and closed the door behind him.

Caitlin stood there in stunned silence with nothing but her own stupidity to keep her company. She put her face in her hands and sighed. "I don't need this right now."

She ran a hand through her tangle of hair. At this point, there was nothing to be done. This wasn't the time to get into it. Right now, the only thing that mattered was Fiona and getting her back. This would just have to be added to the pile of crap she'd deal with later. So she did all she could do. She went into Edward's bathroom to shower and, hopefully, wash away more than dirt, sweat, and dried tears.

CHAPTER SEVENTEEN

Caitlin showered quickly. As she put on her dirty clothes, she pushed every thought and emotion down deep, until the only thing left was numbness and a focus on the task before her. This was how it had to be. She wondered if this was how soldiers felt before a battle. A "violent and bloody event" is what Brendan had said. She worried that Fiona might get hurt, or see some terrible things. But Caitlin also felt a twinge of excitement at visiting some of the pain back on those who'd taken her little girl. Violence and blood sounded about right.

All the doors in the hallway were open, and she heard faint voices from downstairs. She descended to the large eat-in kitchen, where the three men were sitting at a table, picking at food.

"You should eat." Dante offered her a plate.

She hesitated.

"You can eat quickly, but you need to eat," he said.

She accepted the plate of red grapes, neatly cut chunks of cantaloupe, slices of apple, and perfect squares of cheese, even though she wasn't sure she'd be able to keep anything down.

"Hope you like fruit and the like." Brendan drank from a mug. "Damn fae are all vegetarians."

"There's the stove." Dante popped a grape into his mouth. "There's nothing stopping you from cooking up some kind of dead animal."

"I'm enjoying my tea, thank you very much." Brendan glowered and sipped from his mug.

After a few bites, Caitlin realized how hungry she'd been. Like sleep though, eating didn't seem right under the circumstances. The sense of dread hung so thick in the air she could almost taste it; it was a bitterness that spoiled the taste of the food, but she ate anyway.

Brendan and Edward were as dour as she was, and it seemed that they somehow comforted each other in that silence.

Dante, on the other hand, acted as if it was just another day. He always seemed to be smiling when Caitlin looked at him. She did a double take when she saw him pop a handful of small, colorful candies into his mouth and chew with an almost euphoric smile.

"Are you eating M&M'S?"

Dante's smile vanished as he stopped chewing. "Maybe," he said with his mouth full.

"For some reason, he and his fellows got a weak-

ness for the damn things," Brendan said without looking up.

"It's not a weakness," Dante said.

"Aye, whatever you say, then," Brendan said.

"Well, maybe, but just the peanut butter ones."
Dante held a handful out to Caitlin. "Would you like
some?"

"No, thanks." She turned to Brendan. "So what's
the plan? What do we do first?"

"First, you get some food in you," Brendan said.
"Then we get you some fresh clothes and proper
shoes."

"Okay." Caitlin quickly ate the last of her food, then
stood. She reached for her plate, but Dante grabbed it
from her.

"I'll get this."

"All right, then." Brendan slid his mug away and
stood as well. "Let's get moving, then."

Caitlin glanced at Eddy, who was staring at Brendan with a hard, almost resentful look she'd never
seen before. After a moment, Eddy turned to her and
smiled, but she could tell it was forced. She fought back
the sense of doom that hung over her like the sword of
Damocles, dismissing the feeling as nerves.

Brendan picked up his bag and the four of them
walked together towards the door. When they reached
it, Edward muttered and began to pass his hand over
the knob. Everything slowed down as Edward's hand
finished its pass.

Brendan and Dante traded a glance before Brendan leapt at Caitlin and pinned her to the wall.

The door exploded inward.

The concussive force of the blast shook her entire body, all the way to her insides, even through Brendan's body.

A wave of intense heat rolled over her face as everything went white. For what felt like an eternity, the only sound Caitlin could hear was her own pounding heart and a faint ringing in her ears. As the droning faded, another sound took its place. Growing in volume, she could hear splinters raining to the floor.

"Bloody hell." Brendan winced. "Dante, you and Edward still whole?"

"Look to be," Dante said from the floor, where he'd tackled Edward. "You know what this means, right?"

"Aye," Brendan said. "Not much room for misunderstanding in that message, is there?"

"What's it mean?" Caitlin asked.

"It's a bleeding civil war." Brendan lowered his voice. "You're all right, love? Everything still attached as it should be?"

Caitlin nodded and swallowed. "If it's okay, I'm just going to start banking my thank-yous. I get the feeling it could delay things if I stop to keep saying them."

"Sense of humor intact as well, aye?" Brendan said. "Don't move. I'm going to check it out and make sure there's no one waiting to take another shot." He angled his head to look out the open space previously occupied by the door.

"No! Brendan, wait!" Edward shouted from the floor.

"Wha—"

A boom shook the room and knocked Brendan to the floor, even sliding him back a dozen feet. A bolt of red lightning jumped from a small ball of crimson light floating just outside the doorway. It struck the floor between Brendan's legs and left a black mark in the wood.

Brendan lifted his head. He looked at the scorch mark, and his eyes went wide. "*Dar fia*, that was a bit close." He scooted back some more and took a moment before getting to his feet. "Right, never mind, then."

Dante helped Edward to his feet. "It's the wizard," Edward said.

"How do you know?" Dante asked.

"I've read about those, but I've never actually seen one before now. I think it was a thread bomb. They're traps tied to wards and set to go off when the wards drop." He looked at Brendan, then Caitlin. "You two okay?"

"Aye," Brendan said. "Knocked me arse over tea-kettle and nearly changed me religion, but I'm none the worse for it."

Caitlin saw the subtle wince of pain as Brendan moved.

"Caitlin?" Edward asked.

"I'm okay," she said. "Brendan got me out of the way for the first hit, and I think he blocked the second one with his body."

"No offense, but it weren't intentional," Brendan said. "Dante, you still with us?"

"I am." Dante rubbed his head. "All fingers and toes accounted for."

"So," Brendan said, turning to Edward, "any more surprises I should know about before I go looking about outside?"

"Maybe," Edward said and shrugged. "But I'm pretty sure that last shot was the spell exhausting itself."

"You two wait here, then," Brendan said to Caitlin and Edward. "Dante, keep an eye on them."

"No," Edward said. "I'll go with you. I can watch your back. If someone's out there and takes a shot at you, I might be able to get them first."

Brendan looked at Dante, who shrugged. "All right," Brendan said, "but keep your wits about you."

After they disappeared through the doorway, Caitlin looked at Dante. He leaned against the wall. His smile was gone now.

Once again, an oppressive silence fell on the room.

After a long while, Caitlin felt a surge of relief as Brendan and Edward came back inside. Their faces were grim.

"Well?" Dante asked.

"Got good news and bad news," Brendan said. "Good news is, whoever set the trap is long gone. Bad news is, so are the marshals."

"Is the car still here?" Dante asked. The look on his

face said he knew the answer, so he didn't react much when Brendan nodded.

Edward winced and shook his head. "This is my fault."

"What?" Caitlin asked.

"The wizard must've tracked me down when I summoned Justin."

"It ain't your fault," Brendan said. "The oíche are making a play for the leadership of the Rogue Court."

"And they're using a wizard to help them do it," Dante said, then cursed under his breath.

"Wait, what are you talking about?" Caitlin asked.

"You might as well tell her," Brendan said.

"Tell me what?" Caitlin's hands tightened into fists.

"We don't know anything for sure," Dante said.

"Really?" Brendan pointed to the gaping hole. "You see some ambiguity in this, then, do you?"

"Tell me what?" Caitlin repeated, but her voice had gone flat and even.

"We think the oíche might have taken Fiona," Dante said, "as payment to a wizard for his help in their attempt to grab control of the Rogue Court."

Caitlin swallowed a mouthful of fire and rage. After a moment she asked the most obvious question. "Why would a wizard want Fiona?"

"That's not something to be thinking about just now," Brendan said. "Thoughts like that won't do no good. We're still going after her, and we're still bringing her home."

"Why would they bring her to Tír na nÓg then?" Edward asked.

"They probably figured it was a way to keep her out of reach until they made the exchange," Dante said.

Caitlin shook with the anger that roiled inside her as she fought the nightmarish images of what the wizard might have in mind for a little girl.

"Caitlin?" Brendan took her by the shoulder. "I'm sorry we didn't tell you, but nothing's changed. You can't let yourself be getting carried away with thoughts like you're thinking. If you're still coming with me, then you need to keep focused on that. If your mind is wandering, you'll be no use to me."

"But—"

"But nothing. We're going to get her back before anything happens, yeah?"

Caitlin nodded and fought hard to push the images from her mind.

"What's to keep them from crossing back here with her once they find out you've gone after them?" Edward asked.

"He's got a point," Dante said. "I should see if I can find the wizard. Block the back door, so to speak."

"Whoever this wizard is," Edward said, swallowing, "he's tracking me. I might be able to lure him away. Maybe even help Dante find him and take him out."

"That's a good plan." Dante nodded. "If we can remove him from the equation, the oíche will lose their advantage. Moreover, if they do cross back, they'll be headed to the wizard's location themselves. Not only will this make sure they don't slip away, it might even help by distracting them."

"It's settled then, yeah?" Brendan turned to Caitlin. "We'll get to her. Nothing is going to happen to her, all right?"

Caitlin stared hard at Brendan. After a brief moment, she managed a single nod.

"I mean it. I need you here and now. I know what I'm asking of you, but you have to put all that aside. She needs you to." He leaned in close and looked into her eyes. "You understand?"

Caitlin sucked in a breath. "You should've told me sooner."

"Aye, we should've at that."

"That was my fault," Dante said. "I'm sorry. We had only suspicions, and I didn't want to scare you unnecessarily. We'll get her back before anything happens. I'll bring in every resource at my disposal."

"Are you with me, then?" Brendan asked her. "Are you here?"

She steeled her resolve. "I'm here. Nothing's going to happen to her."

Brendan turned to Dante, and they spoke to each other in what sounded like Irish.

Caitlin threw her arms around Edward, hugging him tight. The earlier drama was shattered with the door and lay lost in the debris.

"I'm sorry," he said into her ear. "I know the last thing you need—"

"Shut up," she said and squeezed him tighter. "You

better be careful. If you get yourself killed, I'll never forgive you."

"What could go wrong?" he asked. "You're going into the faerie world to get your daughter back. I'm going to take on a wizard and prevent the overthrowing of a fae court. It's just another Saturday."

Caitlin's laugh was mixed with a sob. "Did you just make a joke? A good one?"

"Don't tell anyone. It'll ruin my image." Edward kissed her forehead, softly, then pulled back and looked at her. "Listen, you be careful, too. I look forward to seeing you come walking through the front hole of my house with Fiona in your arms."

She chuckled, then squeezed him again. He returned the embrace.

"Take this," Brendan whispered in Irish and held the leather box out to Dante.

Dante's eyes went wide. "Is that—?"

"Aye, it is." Brendan looked at Edward and Caitlin as they hugged, then back to Dante. "When the time is right, offer it to them. If they want it, it's theirs. If not, it's yours."

Dante didn't speak; he just took the box.

"You've done right by me over the years," Brendan said. "More than I for you, that's for sure. I'm sorry for that, but I need this one last thing."

Dante nodded and slid the box into his pocket.

After too short a time, Caitlin stepped back from Eddy, took a breath, and wiped some tears away. As she turned to the doorway, Brendan and Dante traded smiles, though they weren't joyful ones. Brendan took Dante's hand and drew him into a hug. Then he picked up his bag and turned to Caitlin and Edward.

"Godspeed," Edward said and held out his hand to Brendan.

"Aye, and to you as well." Brendan shook the offered hand and motioned to Dante with a nod. "Listen to him, he knows his business." He let go of Edward's hand, then turned to Dante and said, "*Ádh mór, mo dheartháir.*"

Dante drew in a sharp breath.

"*Slán agat,*" Brendan said.

"*Slán go fóill,*" Dante said.

Brendan smiled, then walked out of the house.

Caitlin looked at Dante, but he motioned with his head for her to follow Brendan. She gave a last look to Edward. Fear was eating at her insides, but she just kept pushing it back as she turned away.

Brendan was putting his bag behind the driver's seat of his old truck.

"What did you say to Dante?" Caitlin asked as she opened the passenger side door.

Brendan climbed behind the wheel and started the engine. "I said good luck and good-bye." He smiled. "He said good-bye for now."

Caitlin fastened her seat belt. She knew that wasn't all they'd said, but she let it go. After a few deep breaths, the knot came undone in her stomach. This wasn't any different from the hospital. Put it all aside, do what had to be done.

CHAPTER EIGHTEEN

Brendan put on a pair of battered sunglasses and drove, staring straight ahead, not saying a word.

Caitlin watched the neighborhood roll by. It was a lovely and mild autumn day. The sky was a brilliant blue, lightly spattered with clouds, and the trees were awash in colors. Closing her eyes, she savored the warm sun on her face and the gentle, cool breeze coming in the open window. It was sad to think such a beautiful day could hold something so ugly. Normally on a day like this, she and Fiona would've gone to the park. She allowed herself a moment to picture the familiar scene in her head, but only a moment.

"Why Fiona?" she asked Brendan.

"What's that, love?"

"Why would a wizard want Fiona?" Caitlin looked out the window. "I mean, why her instead of any other kid out there?" The fact that she'd actually said that aloud made her wince.

"I honestly couldn't say." Brendan didn't look from the road as he spoke. "There are a million different things that could make her stand out. Her name, the day or hour she was born, anything really." He gave her a quick glance. "It don't matter none, though. We'll get her back, and Dante and Edward will take care of the *drochairteagal* what wants her."

That answer didn't help, but Caitlin wasn't sure he could say anything that would. She looked at Brendan and considered him. Who was he? Where'd he come from? She didn't want the simple answers; she wanted to really know him. Didn't she owe him at least that much?

"I'm Caitlin Brady," she said, offering her hand.

Brendan glanced at her, confusion breaking through his stone mask.

"We never were actually introduced," she explained.

"Oh, right then. Brendan Kavanaugh. Pleasure to meet you Miss Caitlin Brady, wish it were in better times though."

"Me, too." She sighed and decided not to let the silence swallow them. "Do you know where you're going?"

"Aye, I think so. I'm nearly sure I remember the way, but feel free to let me know if I'm about to miss a turn somewhere."

"How did they get into my house? And what happened to the marshals' bodies?"

"Smart girl, you are."

"Am I?"

"Aye, it's never a bad thing to want to know more about who you're up against."

"Oh, well, thanks. Turn left here, it's quicker."

Brendan turned onto a side street. "The fae are bound by a set of rules called the Oaths. Part of that is the hearth protections."

"That's why Dante and the others needed Eddy's permission to come inside."

"Aye, but the oíche found the loophole. With a piece of someone what lives there, you can sidestep those protections."

Caitlin closed her eyes and thought of the lock of Fiona's hair she always kept in her purse. "So it really was my fault."

"What?"

"Nothing. What about the marshals?"

Brendan made another turn. "When fae die, they never leave bodies behind. If they're killed with iron, they burn away in either darkness or light, depending on their nature."

"I remember that." Caitlin shivered as she thought back to the darkness and small, swirling motes of light.

"I'm not entirely sure why their bodies vanish," Brendan said. "The best explanation I've heard that makes any bleeding sense at all is that since the fae aren't of this world, when they die they return to their home. They might've called this place home a long time ago, but not anymore."

"Oh, well, I guess that does sort of make sense."

Brendan laughed. "Usually, if you hear something about the fae and it makes sense, you'd best ignore it."

"What's that word? The one you keep using to refer to Fiona."

"*Girseach?*" Brendan asked.

"That's it. I like that. It means 'young girl,' right?"

"Aye."

Caitlin was about to ask how long Brendan had been in this country when he stopped the truck across the street from her house.

"That was quick."

"Aye, and we need to be. There's another stop to be made later on, and it's best not to linger." He opened the door and got out. "Let's be done with this, love."

Caitlin walked around the truck, and Brendan took up step beside her as they walked to her house.

"Is it safe inside?" she asked.

"I'm betting it is, but I'll go in first to be sure."

Caitlin fought her unease as flashes of the previous night came back to her.

Brendan must have sensed it, because he put his hand on her shoulder. "You're not alone this time."

She smiled at his choice of words as she knelt to get the spare key hidden under a rock.

Brendan took it, but he found the door unlocked. He handed the key back and stepped inside. After a moment, he opened the door wide. "Nobody's home."

The inside felt more alien to Caitlin than the outside

had. Without wanting to, she looked around the room and finally understood what *violated* really meant.

"Don't think on it." Brendan closed the door. "You can't be letting your mind wander. Focus on the business to be done."

"Right."

When Caitlin reached the top of the stairs, she saw Brendan still standing in the living room. "Would you mind coming with me?"

"Flattering as that offer is—"

"No, you oaf," she said through a smile. "I mean come upstairs and wait outside my room while I change. I just don't like being alone in here right now."

"Oh, right, then. Sorry." He bounded up the stairs and followed her down the hallway.

She went into her bedroom but didn't close the door all the way. "You have any suggestions on attire?" she asked.

"Something loose and comfortable is your best bet. Think of going on a hike, and dress for that. Bring a jacket with you as well."

She tossed clothes on the bed as she came across what she wanted. A pair of jeans, a long-sleeved shirt, fresh socks, sports bra, clean underwear, and a pair of hiking boots.

She stripped off her dirty clothes and slipped into the clean ones. It felt nice to change, but she wished she could've done it after the shower. After she tied her boots, she grabbed a light jacket from the closet and opened the door.

Brendan was looking at the wall opposite her room. He turned to her as she stepped out. "All done, then?"

"Will these work?" She held out the coat and showed him the boots.

"They'll do fine, yeah. If you're ready, I think it's past time we were getting out of here."

"Almost. I need to get something else before we go. It's important." She paused at the door to Fiona's room long enough to take a deep breath, then pushed the door open with shaking hands. The first thing she noticed was the stump of wood still in the bed. The sight of it made her knees a little weak, and she had to look away to swallow back the rising emotions.

"Now's not the time to face this," Brendan said from behind her. "You're best saving this for when the business is done."

"No." Caitlin scanned the room. "That's not why . . ." She started to worry that it wasn't here. Finally, she saw what she was looking for.

She picked up the small brown bear. It had a green shamrock on its left foot and a green bow around its neck. She squeezed it tight when the tears started up again.

"Paddy Bear." She held the bear up to Brendan. "It's Fiona's favorite."

Brendan smiled. "I'm sure she'll be happy to be seeing him again."

Caitlin played with the bear's ears and straightened its bow.

"Love, we need to be going," Brendan said. "What say we get the little fella to her, aye?"

Caitlin tucked it into one of her jacket pockets. "All right, could you—"

Brendan grabbed the stump before she could ask and they headed for the stairs.

He glanced out the sidelight before resting his hand on the front doorknob.

"What is it?" she asked. There were no wards here, so she knew it couldn't be one of those thread bomb things. She wondered, with some concern, if faeries or wizards ever used real bombs.

Brendan didn't speak. He just waited. Then he threw open the door. It bounced against the doorstop and went to close again. Several small knives streaked in and stuck in the wood. A large sword blade cleaved the air a moment later, but Brendan stepped to one side and avoided it. As the sword struck the ground, he reached out the door with one hand, then twisted and heaved a form, still holding the giant blade, screaming through the air.

"Get to the truck!" Brendan shouted as he tossed Caitlin the keys. "Get the hell out of here!"

"But—"

"I'll find you, love. Just go!" Brendan grabbed one of the slender knives from the door, hurled it at the form getting to its feet, and followed it up with the stump.

Caitlin watched, frozen in place, as the knife sank into the creature and the stump slammed into its chest, knocking it back down.

"*Damnú air*, I said go!" Brendan charged the creature. Its skin was dark green; its huge eyes were red and far too big for its head. It had no nose to speak of, but it did have pointed, bat-like ears. It snarled at Brendan and showed its long, pointed canine teeth. They wouldn't have been out of place on a wolf, or maybe a tyrannosaur.

Brendan leapt at the creature and tackled it to the ground.

Caitlin ran through the door, grabbing a knife for herself on the way. Halfway down the walkway there was a blur of darkness in the corner of her eye. She turned and saw nothing, but when she looked back, an oíche was standing in her path.

In an instant, she made her choice. She didn't stop or even slow down. Instead, she increased her speed. This tactic seemed to catch the oíche off guard. He didn't move, and she slammed into him, hard. She used the momentum to drive the knife deep into his chest, then shouldered him out of the way.

The oíche fell to the ground and Caitlin didn't look back. She just focused on the truck and kept running.

The driver's side door seemed miles away, and she could feel someone on her heels. Reaching her hand out in desperation, she grabbed the handle and pushed the door out, slamming it hard into the pursuing faerie. Though he'd seemingly recovered from the knife wound, the steel in the old truck's door wasn't so forgiving.

A cloud of darkness and twinkling lights burst from the other side of the door, and the creature fell to the ground, writhing and screaming.

Caitlin jumped in the truck, shut the door, started

the motor, and, after putting the truck in gear, stomped on the gas.

Creatures of every size and shape began leaping at her.

She didn't bother trying to dodge them—quite the opposite. She plowed right over them, using the steel bumper of the truck as a battering ram. Puffs of darkness exploded in her peripheral vision, and satisfaction rose in her.

"Take that, you bastards!"

Throwing the steering wheel hard to the right, she took a corner much faster than she'd normally be comfortable with, but with the rush of adrenaline, it didn't seem to matter.

After several blocks, she slammed on the brakes and came to a screeching stop. Her heart was pounding and her breathing was shallow.

None of these attacks made sense. They weren't subtle, but nothing and no one around her seemed to stir. There'd even been an explosion at Eddy's house. Eddy might live in a secluded area, but this neighborhood was in the middle of suburbia. Where were the sirens? Where were the police cars? Someone had to have seen that attack, or at least heard the noise. She knew most of her neighbors, and many of them were well armed. It didn't make any sense.

Her hands began to shake, and she realized that she had no idea where to go. Brendan had just told her to leave, that he'd find her, but how would he? Come to think of it, how had he found her last night?

Movement drew her attention to the right.

With her foot ready on the accelerator, she turned to see Brendan vault over a fence that was easily six feet high and run to the truck.

"Oh, thank God."

He ran around the truck to the driver's side as she put it in park and slid over to the passenger's side.

"I'd intended you to get a bit farther away than this," he said as he climbed in.

"I didn't know where to go. You didn't say—"

"It's okay, love," he said and put the truck in gear. "You were brilliant."

Caitlin returned his smile as the truck sped off down the street.

"What happened?" Caitlin asked. "What was that thing in the house? It didn't look like an oíche."

"It weren't," Brendan said.

Caitlin could hear something in his voice.

"It was a goblin."

"A goblin?" Caitlin looked over her shoulder as if it were right behind them. "I don't get it, what's a goblin doing coming after us? Are there goblins in the Rogue Court?"

"I don't know every faction of the Rogue." He turned down another street. "I do know the alternative isn't promising." He slowed to a more reasonable speed and continued to make turns.

Caitlin could tell he was heading for the interstate. She considered not asking, but she couldn't help herself. "What's the alternative?"

Brendan sighed. "The oíche are getting backed by members of the Dusk Court. That would mean this civil war could be a lot bigger and a lot uglier."

"You mean an all-out war between the fae courts?"

"Aye, and with this world as the prize for whoever comes out on top. No more Oaths, no more hearth protections, no more limits on their influence in this world."

She swallowed. "What would that mean?"

Brendan licked his lips, obviously weighing what to tell her. "You really want to know?"

"Probably not." She looked out her window. "But go ahead and tell me anyway."

"You notice that no police came and no neighbors were peeking through windows?" he asked. "Not at your place, and not even at Edward's, after the explosion?"

Caitlin nodded.

"The fae have been involved with human kind for countless centuries. They've a natural glamour that hides them from most mortals. Either they appear as relatively normal people, or not at all. Mortals have learned to block out and explain away events that involve the fae. They excel at denial and self-delusion."

Caitlin was confused—and about to say so—when he continued.

"They'd probably write it off as you running out being late for work. Like as not, they didn't even see me or those I was tussling with."

"But Dante and his elves didn't look normal, not even close."

Brendan looked at her with genuine surprise. "You're saying you saw them as they were?"

"If you mean pointy ears and kind of luminescent eyes with no pupil or iris, then yes."

"What did the oíche look like to you?" he asked as he exited the highway to take another east, toward Vermont.

"Like Goth kids, really young, really beautiful, and creepy at the same time. Their faces were gaunt, more angular than seemed right. Their eyes were all black and their teeth were all pointed."

Brendan chewed on his lower lip.

"What is it?"

"Well," he said, "either the stories your Nan told you made you able to accept what was around you, or . . ."

"Or?" She waited for a response, but none came. "Brendan, what's the other possibility?"

"Let's find out, then." He turned down a rural highway, then onto a dirt road.

Caitlin waited, and waited, and then waited some more. She tried to keep patient, but it was taking all of her focus. Soon she began to fidget. After everything else that had happened, what could be so bad that he wouldn't just tell her?

Needing to fill the silence with something, she decided to change the subject. "What does all this have to do with Fiona?"

"Afraid I still don't know." Brendan's face scrunched up. "And that's the part that has me scratching me head. If the Dusk Court is involved, it doesn't make a bit of sense for the wizard to be. I mean, they wouldn't need him, would they?"

"Is that rhetorical, or are you actually asking me?"

Brendan stopped the truck. "Come on, love."

The road they were on bisected a large meadow. The wildflowers painted the clover and grass with patches of vivid colors, a last stand against the approaching end of autumn and start of winter.

"All right, then." Brendan pointed to the meadow. "Find me a four-leaf clover."

"What?" Caitlin couldn't help but laugh at the question.

"Go into that meadow, there." He pointed again. "And see if you can find me a four-leaf clover."

"You're joking, right? What does that have to do—?"

"Just humor me, love. I'll explain it all to you, I promise."

Caitlin shrugged and walked into the meadow. Her eyes went back and forth over the ground as she went. This was ridiculous. People go their whole lives without ever coming across a—

There at her feet, plain as day, was a four-leaf clover.

A cold feeling began to creep its way into her body. She plucked the clover from the ground.

"Well?" Brendan said.

She held it out to him and swallowed. "I've never even heard of someone finding—"

"Find me another," he said.

Caitlin didn't know what else to do. She turned around and walked back into the meadow. Her feet felt like they were filled with lead, and each step seemed to add more weight. The worst part was that she didn't know why.

Caitlin hadn't covered five feet when she saw another four-leaf clover standing out amidst the thousands of three-leaf ones. Her breathing went shallow as she reached down with a shaking hand and pulled the second one from the ground. As she did, she spotted another off to her right. Turning to pluck that one, she saw another, then another, and another. Though not clustered together, it seemed that everywhere she turned her eyes, amidst the normal-looking shamrocks was a four-leaf clover.

Brendan now stood in front of her. Unable to speak, she just dropped the collection into his hand.

He must've seen her worry, because the stern look on his face melted. He opened his arms and drew her in, holding her close.

"Brendan," she said, "how does someone just find a four-leaf clover every time they look for one?"

She felt him draw in a breath, causing his broad chest to expand.

"It's a common enough thing," he said. "For those what got fae blood in them, anyway."

CHAPTER NINETEEN

"Good. When you're done, lock everything down," Dante said into his cell phone as he paced back and forth in Edward's study. "Notify the Cruinnigh about that, too. Oh, and we need wardens and marshals watching every gateway in a hundred-mile radius. I don't want them slipping by us. We've been waiting for a chance like this for too long. It's time to finish it."

Dante listened. "Good. I also want anyone not fighting to go to ground and stay there till the dust settles." After a pause, he nodded. "That's right, and make sure the mortal involvement is as limited as possible. I don't want the police, or anyone else, involved." He ended the call.

"I'm almost done," Edward said without looking away from the bookshelves. Finding a book that looked useful, he shoved it into a bag with the others he'd pulled. When Dante didn't answer, he glanced up. "How bad is this?"

Dante gave him a sideways glance. "Pretty bad."

A noise outside caused them both to look up.

"I think the wardens have arrived," Dante said. "Stay here and finish, quickly."

"Do I need to—?"

"No door, no hearth protections," Dante said as he walked out.

Edward returned to his books.

"They're here," Dante said from the living room. "It's time to go."

Edward scanned faster to see if there were any other books he might need. "Too bad I can't take the whole thi—"

"Now, Edward."

Edward dashed into the living room. When he looked up from latching his bag on the run, he stopped so quickly he nearly toppled over.

Eight tall, handsome men—other elves he presumed—dressed in dark green tactical gear were standing in his living room. Five were holding submachine guns, the likes of which Edward had never seen. The other three were holding pale green pistols, and they all had two swords on their belts, one on each hip.

He blinked at the sidhe SWAT team, then at Dante, who somehow had managed a quick change into green fatigues. "Well, that's not going to draw any attention at all."

"Don't worry about it," Dante said. "It won't be a problem."

"Incoming!" one of the elves shouted. Edward was

tackled by one of the wardens and knocked away from the empty doorframe just before several black arrows passed through the air.

"Ah, damn it to hell!" Dante shouted.

"What?" Edward asked. Shouldn't they be happy? Arrows against guns didn't seem like much of a fight.

As if in response to his thoughts, automatic gunfire chattered outside and bullets struck the floor and wall opposite the doorway.

"How many, Arlen?" Dante asked from a crouch to one side of the doorway.

"Not sure." Arlen chanced a glance around the doorframe. "Two score, maybe. All oíche."

"Those arrows didn't come from oíche." Dante cocked a pistol.

Arlen snapped his head back just in time to avoid an arrow. "You're right. I see goblins, too."

Edward lost track of the commands given. The elves worked like a SEAL team. They shot and moved just before the return fire reached them. His mind was a jumble. He tried to grab lucid thoughts, but they slipped away. He flinched and cowered as more bullets peppered the floor and sent a spray of splinters into the air. The oíche and goblins had them pinned down. It was all just a matter of time. Edward might not be a soldier, but even he could see that.

"Do you have a back door?" Dante asked.

Edward snapped out of his daze and pointed down the hall.

"Faolan."

"On it." An elf bolted down the hall.

Moments later, more gunfire came from that direction and Faolan returned.

"No good," he said. "They've surrounded the place."

Everything around Edward seemed to slow. The sounds were faint, little more than a whisper. He felt like he was watching a movie, the bullets hitting the floor and wall, clouds of plaster hanging in the air like powder smoke, even the silent shouts from one soldier to another.

Then, like a trap springing, his mind locked into gear. Spells organized themselves in his head like a menu on a computer screen, just waiting for him to choose one.

"I think the wizard's lost it," one of the elves said, then fired out the door.

"No, I haven't." Edward got to his feet. Somehow he'd never seen it before, the magic all around him, just waiting for his command. Power was right at his fingertips. He lifted his hand as he walked to the doorway.

"Edward!" Dante shouted.

"*Aer.*" Edward's voice was calm and even as he reached out for the magic and seized it. Outside, pale-skinned, dark-haired children leveled their guns at him. Then the magic slipped away.

"Oh—"

Dante tackled him and they slid across the floor, just before bullets riddled it and the doorframe.

"What are you thinking?" Dante said.

"Focus, I have to stay focused."

"What?"

Dante looked at Edward as if he was insane. Maybe he was, but he wasn't going to just wait to get shot. He got to his feet and reached for the magic again. He found more of it there than he'd realized. He gripped it in his will and shouted, "*Aer!*"

A rush of wind roared past him. It carried splinters and debris up and out the door. A volley of arrows hit the gale and were scattered like leaves.

Gunfire erupted, but even the bullets were knocked aside by the torrent.

"Okay," Dante said. "Um, wow?"

Oíche and creatures Edward presumed were the goblins looked at him in surprise. Large red eyes and solid black ones blinked and stared.

Edward felt a smile cross his lips as his confidence grew.

I CAN do this. Pathetic little insects!

"Are the trails clear?" Dante asked one of the elves.

"Near as we can tell."

"We don't have a choice," Dante said. "Faolan, use the oak in the front yard."

"We'll cover you," Arlen said.

"No," Edward said with a voice still calm and even as he stared at the fireplace. "You'll want to duck first."

Dante threw himself prone on the floor. The other elves followed his lead.

Once more, Edward focused his will around the

magic and seized it. Again, he found more power than he expected, and it was easy to hold onto now. He finally understood. This was the power he'd touched on. It was incredible, and it was good.

"Let's see how you like the taste of this," he whispered. He waved his hand at the fireplace, then forward, as if throwing air out the door. "*Haearn.*"

The fireplace tools leapt from their holder and flew past Edward, out the doorway. He watched in glee as the iron implements struck home. They went clean through oíche and goblin alike. One even went through a car and impaled an oíche on the other side.

Screams, high and shrill, filled the air, along with low howls of pain. Clouds of darkness tinged with lights drifted around the yard. The fae's cries were like a symphony to Edward. He could nearly taste the torment, and it was sweet.

"Go, Faolan!" Dante ordered. "Now, open the trail!"

Faolan ran for the large oak in the front yard as the dark creatures flopped and writhed. Those not injured dove for cover, both from fear of Edward and from the covering fire the elves opened up on them.

"So this is what it's like to be feared," Edward said. Then his smile faded as understanding came to him. "Oh no."

There was a thrum of power, and Faolan gestured toward the tree. The trunk of it grew and stretched until it was a large archway covered by a swirl of white mist.

The elves ran for the tree, firing at the oíche and goblins on the way.

Edward tried to follow, but his legs didn't seem to work anymore. He felt himself falling to the floor.

"Gotcha," Dante said as he caught him. "Come on, time to go."

As Dante wrapped an arm around Edward and lifted the wizard until his shoes barely touched the ground, Edward figured he knew how Paddy Bear must feel being carried around by Fiona.

Edward noticed muzzle flashes and arrows zip past, but his brain didn't register them as anything important. "I don't think my head is right." He noticed the detail of an arrowhead as it passed within inches of his face. "Yep, something isn't right."

Then he was passing through the mist and his body seemed weightless.

No, that wasn't it. He was passing out, that's what it was.

CHAPTER TWENTY

"He's alive," said a voice in the black.

Edward opened his eyes and found a smiling face looking down at him. He was flat on his back, looking up at trees tall enough to make redwoods feel mediocre. They were so tall, in fact, that Edward couldn't see the canopy of the forest. The trees just vanished into a white haze.

"Gave us quite a scare," Dante said.

The way he said the word *scare* gave Edward pause, and he looked into Dante's eyes for a long moment. He felt completely transparent.

"Feeling better?" Dante offered his hand.

Edward took the offered hand, and Dante lifted him to his feet. Edward was happy to find his legs now seemed to be working. All of the elves were eyeing him.

"Give it a minute," Dante said.

Edward did a double take. How was it he hadn't

noticed the pointed ears before? Or that Dante's eyes had no pupil or whites and seemed to be lit from inside his skull? The eight other faces also had pointed ears and, though their eyes were varying shades of green, blue, and even purple, they were all solid colors with the same radiant quality.

"I love the look when a mortal sees through the glamour for the first time," one of the elves said with a laugh.

He was joined by his compatriots, including Dante, in a chuckle at Edward's expense.

"Oh, right. The glamour," Edward said.

"I put a simple charm on you to let you see past it," Dante said. "I'd planned on doing it in the car, but . . ."

"Thanks." Edward swallowed.

Get a grip, something inside him said. *They don't know about the power you tapped into. You didn't mean to, it just sort of happened. It wasn't you. Besides, you didn't have much—*

"That was quite the show back there," Dante said and crouched down on his haunches. He motioned to a tree stump for Edward to sit on. "You okay?"

"Yeah, I'm fine." Edward sat down.

Oh, hell, they know, he said to himself.

They will if you don't settle down, he retorted.

Dante narrowed his eyes. "You don't look so good."

"It was strange," Edward said. "I've never used those spells before. Not that I've used many. I guess I'm what you'd call a theoretical wizard. Not much experience in the actual practice."

"You've got good instincts," Faolan said. "Not many mortals with natural talent like that."

"No," Dante said. "Not many."

"Unfortunately"—Edward cleared his throat before continuing—"I'm not used to using the magic. I think it took more out of me than I was prepared for." And stop looking at me like that.

"Don't be so critical of yourself," Dante said. "You'll get stronger."

Edward put his face in his hands and took several long breaths. Magic had its costs, he knew that. Fatigue was to be expected, but it was mental more than physical. When he finally started to calm down and got a grip on the irrational paranoia, he looked up.

"Where are we?" he asked. "I heard you say something about trails?"

This was a bizarre version of a forest. The ground had no growth, no grass, no ferns, nothing. There was nothing but massive trees in every direction. It almost had the appearance of a manicured orchard, where everywhere you looked there was a clear path.

"The far trails," Dante said. "It's hard to explain in terms you'll understand." He considered for a moment. "Think of it like hyperspace."

"Hyperspace?"

"Haven't you ever seen *Star Wars*?" Dante laughed, and again the others joined.

Edward laughed too, but his wasn't as jovial. "So it's like a portal between points, outside of the mortal realm? Like Tír na nÓg?"

"Yes and no," Arlen said.

"It's like the Tír," Dante said. "But it isn't. Think of it as the space between spaces. We can use it to travel to specific points. Time flows differently here. In the mortal world, time is moving slowly. In fact, for all practical purposes, it's stopped."

"Interesting," Edward said.

"Indeed." Dante laughed again.

"What's keeping the oíche from following us?" Edward asked. The elves were relaxed, so he decided he didn't need to panic, not yet anyway.

"They might," Dante said. "But like I said, time is different here. If they came seconds after us, it would be days before they appeared, maybe weeks."

"So how long did you wait for me?" Edward asked Faolan.

"Just a couple days or—"

As if to dispute what had just been explained, there was a shimmer, and a creature that was vaguely wolf shaped, but much larger, leapt through the air. It hit one of the elves and drove him to the ground.

The elf brought his legs up as he fell backwards, kicked the creature up and over his head, then used the momentum to roll back to his feet.

"Shadow-Beast!" Dante yelled.

The elves all drew their swords as the creature landed on its back, then rolled to its feet.

Edward stared as it lowered its head and looked at them with smoldering, dark purple eyes. A low rumble came from it as it bared inky black teeth in a snarl.

"Stay behind us," Dante said as the elves formed a line between Edward and the beast.

It leapt at Arlen, but he spun and cut across it with his sword as it flew by. It landed silently and bounded right at Edward.

He raised his hands and reached desperately for power, but he found none.

Dante drove his shoulder into the thing, knocking it clear of Edward and into the ground. As it landed, the beast yelped. Dante pulled a sword out of its belly, then rolled away.

The thing got to its feet, but the elves had surrounded it. One by one, each lunged forward, drove a sword into the beast and withdrew the blade as it snapped its jaws, then an elf on the opposite side would attack.

Dark purple blood soaked the monster's flanks as attackers who kept just out of reach struck it repeatedly. When it began to stumble, Dante leapt in and drove his sword down through its neck.

The beast fell to the ground with a thump and slowly dissolved.

"You okay?" Dante asked once the shadow was gone.

Edward nodded. "I thought you said nothing could follow us."

"Shadow-Beast," Dante said as he flicked his blade clean of inky gore. "It moves at the speed of light, that's why it only took a few minutes to show up."

"Oh," was all Edward could say.

"The question is, how did the oíche get a Shadow-Beast?" Faolan asked.

"I don't know," Dante said, "but I'll damn sure find out." He turned to Edward. "You ready to move?"

"Oh, I think so." Edward said.

"Let's go, then," Dante said. "Faolan, you have the lead."

Faolan headed off down the trail, and the others clustered around Dante and Edward.

"Keep your eyes open, just in case they have another," Dante said.

Edward glanced at each member of the group, then at the forest around them. "Where are we going?"

"Somerville," Dante said.

"Outside Boston? Why?"

"It's easier to operate safe houses outside the city. Fewer people mean fewer eyes," Dante said.

Edward nodded. "That makes sense, but doesn't that complicate things if you have to get into the city?"

"How so?" Dante asked.

"Well, Boston is famous for its horrible traffic—"

Everyone but Edward started laughing.

Dante smiled at him. "It's not an issue."

They walked in silence for several minutes before Dante returned to their earlier conversation as if nothing had happened. "Faolan's our guide."

Edward nodded as though he knew what that meant and nodded again as Dante introduced each member of the group.

"I'm Edward Hunti—"

Everyone stopped and stared at him.

"He's going to give us his name?" Arlen asked.

Edward closed his eyes and shook his head. "Sorry, still not used to this, you know?"

"'Edward' will do just fine," Dante said as he motioned for the party to continue. "You might consider taking another name for use in this line of work."

"Good advice," Edward said. "If it helps, I do have a middle name I wasn't going to share." He laughed and felt better when they laughed with him, rather than at him.

The group walked on, and Edward saw Dante eye him. Edward's paranoia was becoming less irrational-seeming with each passing moment.

"If we're outside of time here, so to speak," Edward said, "can I ask a stupid question?"

Dante lifted an eyebrow.

"I mean, I wouldn't want to diminish your opinion of me or anything," Edward added with a slight smile.

"I like him," Quinn said. "Not many mortals have that kind of wit."

"Go ahead," Dante said.

"How far-reaching are the fae courts?" As they walked, the landscape never seemed to change. The idea of a guide started to make sense to Edward. "I notice your names are Irish, except, of course, for you, Dante."

"Not my true name, but considering the situation, that's about as far from a stupid question as you can get."

Edward laughed, but it was forced. "Really? I'll try harder next time."

"Without going into too much," Dante said, "the fae populate areas where they can exert the most influence. Ireland, Scotland, the Isle of Mann, Britain, and, by proxy, the United States, all of which have long histories of interaction with the fae. But the courts don't really have any boundaries as you think of them."

"That's why most of the stories come from those places," Edward said. "So, that would mean this war could be pretty far-reaching?"

No one answered right away.

"Global," Dante finally said.

"So," Riley said, "you think you can find the wizard helping the oíche?"

"I think so."

"Are you prepared for what that means?" Sean asked.

"Find him? You'll rip him to pieces," something in Edward said.

Edward faltered a step, and Dante caught his arm.

"You all right?" Dante asked.

"I think—"

"Give us a moment," Dante said to the other elves without looking away from Edward's eyes.

Edward felt the elves walk several paces away. His eyes were locked on Dante's penetrating stare.

Dante leaned in close. "Listen carefully," he said. "There is evil, and there is darkness."

Edward swallowed.

"It isn't always ugly and twisted. Oftentimes it's alluring and beautiful. The oíche and the Dusk Court are part of that evil and darkness." Dante drew in a breath but never looked away from Edward. "Now, some wizards manage to use the darkness without it consuming them."

Edward felt a rush of exhilaration flood through him.

"But they are exceedingly rare."

The rush vanished.

"I like you, Edward," Dante said, "but make no mistake. If I think for one instant you'll betray us, or jeopardize this mission—"

Edward reminded himself to breathe.

"I'll kill you without a thought." Dante's tone was calm and matter-of-fact, as if he were reading a shopping list. He drew back. "Do we understand each other?"

Edward just stared. The enormity of how stupid it was to use that dark power was suddenly apparent. He licked his dry lips and finally got his eyelids to blink.

"Well?" Dante asked, hand resting on the pommel of one of his swords.

"We do," Edward said.

"Good."

"I just want to help Caitlin," he said. "I just—"

Dante's look told him the conversation was over.

"Let's get moving," Dante said to the elves, and his tone was back to normal.

They walked in total silence after that. Apparently

the other elves knew not to ask any questions. Edward chewed on his thoughts, marinating in his stupidity and arrogance.

Time was indeed warped on the trails. Edward had no idea how much time passed. Of course, he had a sense of time passing, but he had no feeling of time as a whole. He could honestly say it might've been hours, or just minutes. It was an unsettling feeling. He'd never realized how much he relied on time for comfort and stability.

Faolan pointed to a tree off to the right. "Here it is."

Edward looked at the tree closely, then at the others. He had no idea how someone could tell one from another.

"Right," Dante said. "Quinn, you and Riley go first, then Nollaig and Arlen. Edward and I will be next, followed by Padraig and Daire. Sean, you come with Faolan when he starts closing the trail. You ready for this?" he asked Edward.

The hard look in his eyes was gone, which Edward was glad to see. Dante apparently wasn't the sort to beleaguer a point that had been made.

"I am, but what's the problem?" Edward asked.

"We don't know what's on the other side," Faolan said. "We could be stepping into an ambush."

"Oh," Edward said. "Well, that would be par for the course."

All the elves drew their short swords, one in each hand. The blades had the faintest hint of a purple stain. Faolan held his in a reverse grip, with the blades facing back.

"Here." Dante offered Edward a long knife. "You know how to use it?"

"Sure," Edward said, grinning a bit as he pointed at the handle. "I bash them with this part, right?"

Dante smiled. "That's it."

"I just don't know how to use it well." Edward turned the knife in his hand. It was amazing how light it was. It felt like it was made of glass. The blade was almost liquid silver and was decorated with symbols down its length. Edward looked at the others, then without thinking asked, "I don't get a gun?"

Dante cocked an eyebrow. "So you can club them with the butt?"

"Well, I was thinking I could shoot them, too."

"Guns are fine when you're fighting at a distance," Dante said, "but up close, a blade is the best way to go."

"In other words," Edward said, "let you worry about the guns."

Dante chuckled and patted Edward on the shoulder. "Here's hoping you don't even need the knife." He nodded to Faolan. "All right, open it."

"Wait," Edward said. "How is it we won't come out the other side on top of each other? I mean, if time is distorted."

"He's quick," Faolan said.

"It's hard to explain," Dante said, "but the simple version is when you open a portal on this side, it makes a bubble of time around us that closely matches the regular world without diverging from the flow of time here."

Edward nodded. "Since I don't have a degree in quantum mechanics, I'll just let it go, then."

The elves laughed.

"Go ahead," Dante said to Faolan.

This time Edward heard the words that went with the gesture. He wasn't familiar with the language, but it was definitely Celtic.

Like the tree at his house, this one swelled and became distorted until its trunk opened into a doorway. Once again, all that was visible was swirling white mist. Quinn and Riley tapped blades and stepped into the portal. Nollaig and Arlen stepped through next after a pause.

Dante turned to Edward. "You sure you're ready?"

"Let's go."

"After you."

Edward drew in a deep breath, held it, then stepped into the mist.

CHAPTER TWENTY-ONE

Being nearly unconscious the first time he went through the mist had spared Edward the interesting sensation he was now experiencing. Interesting, in the same way falling into a black hole would be interesting. Not comfortable, but interesting. Before he could consider it fully, Edward was standing in an alleyway, and the scents and sounds shared by all large urban areas bombarded his senses.

Then Dante was shoving him.

Edward fell to the ground as a long and strangely curved blade sliced through the air where he'd just been standing.

"Kill the wizard!" someone shouted.

That caught Edward's attention. He rolled, and kept rolling, until he hit something. Getting to his feet, he tried to assess what was happening.

Dante and the other elves were fighting a group of

oíche and humanoid creatures straight from a nightmare. They weren't much more than two feet tall, and they were covered in black fur. They had long, sharp claws and gold almond-shaped eyes.

Faolan and Sean stepped from the portal and joined the fray.

The gateway closed and once more became a brick wall painted with a realistic image of a tree. An oíche leaping over the elves in Edward's direction interrupted his clinical review of the scene. He drew back his hand and focused his will.

"*Tân!*" A ball of fire manifested in his hand, and he hurled it at the oíche.

Fae and fire connected in midair, the flames engulfing the small faerie. It dropped to the ground and rolled, trying to put itself out.

The dark power welled up inside Edward again, and he pushed it back. He had to do this without the darkness.

He concentrated and waved his hand. "*Fwy!*"

The flames erupted into a massive pyre. Screams stopped as clouds of darkness and smoke drifted from the inferno.

The magic was coursing through him, and Edward knew it was his magic. Wind rushed past, sucked into the maw of the blaze. The mental fatigue began to gnaw at him, but for now, it was still manageable.

The magic, and therefore the fire, was not.

Edward panicked as it continued to grow beyond his control. He struggled to pull the magic back, but his growing alarm and weariness prevented him from keeping hold of it. The magic-fed fire spread to the walls and finally to a Dumpster.

"No," Edward said through gritted teeth.

A high-pitched, guttural cry came from the other side of the conflagration, and one of the small, furry creatures jumped through the flames at Edward. Its fur ignited as it passed through the wall of fire, but that didn't even slow it.

Edward didn't have time to react. The creature hit him full in the chest and knocked him to the ground. Edward's head smacked the asphalt and bounced. A ringing filled his ears and his hands began to burn as he struggled to get the flaming whatever it was off him.

Snapping jaws were inches from his face. Spittle landed on his cheek as Edward struggled with arms and claws. His clothes started to burn, and the air drawn into his lungs grew hotter with each breath.

Suddenly Edward remembered. The knife! He'd dropped it when he'd fallen.

Letting go of one of the furry arms, Edward reached for the weapon. Searing, blinding pain shot through him as the creature tore into his flesh with its claw. He screamed and tried to kick the thing off, but it wouldn't budge. It was small, but incredibly strong.

At last, Edward's fingers touched cold metal. He gripped the knife and drove it repeatedly into his attacker.

The thing shrieked but only seemed to become further enraged.

Edward screamed and waited to die. Blood was soaking his clothes, and blisters emerged on his hands. There was a sickly sweet smell in the air, and it took him a minute to recognize it as burning human flesh. He'd smelled it before, on burn victims in the hospital.

Edward tried to scream again but couldn't.

He heard a series of pops and the creature convulsed, then went limp.

Edward tossed it to one side, suddenly aware he might survive, and sucked in cool air. The creature was motionless and charred as black blood pooled around it. A dozen paces away, Riley stood, holding his pistol. Between them, the fire was finally diminishing, now simply consuming the mundane fuels.

"You've got to get up," Faolan said. He and Riley each took an arm and pulled Edward to his feet.

Pain unlike any he'd felt or even imagined possible brought forth the screams that he'd been unable to release moments before. After a few agonizing seconds, the pain subsided to merely excruciating, and at the far edges of his consciousness, he noted that the fight was over. He only hoped that meant they'd won.

Edward had to focus so hard on keeping the pain back that it was hard to breathe. Around him, the urban setting seemed unaware of the battle that had just taken place.

Dante ran over. "Come on, we've got to get out of here. There's a *tearmann* nearby."

Edward felt himself being urged along and he moved as quickly as he could, gritting his teeth so hard he could feel them grinding. Tears ran down his face, leaving a trail of stinging flesh. With effort, he opened his eyes, and in the distance, he could just see the buildings of Boston's skyline.

"Hang in there," Dante said near his ear. "We'll help you. We can take the pain away, but you have to move."

Edward wanted nothing more than to just lie down and die. Let the darkness come. Let it swallow him and take away the hurt. Then he thought of Caitlin and Fiona. He'd made a promise to them. Whatever he could do, he would. He could do this. He had to do this.

Holding the image of Caitlin in his mind so tightly he could almost smell her perfume, he increased his speed.

Mercifully, the group slowed and led Edward down a series of stairs. A door opened and he was pushed inside. Scraping for a bit of spare concentration, he gestured his hand at the door.

"*Atgyfnerthu.*" With that final exertion, everything went black.

CHAPTER TWENTY-TWO

Edward considered how strange the human body and mind were. While in pain, there is only the memory of how sublime not being in pain feels. Then, when the pain finally subsides, the sufferer remembers that it hurt, but the pain itself is vague and distant. There was no pain in this darkness, this void where he now found himself. He was hesitant to respond to the distant voices calling to him. He knew answering them meant a return to pain.

Edward didn't think he was dead. Having worked in a hospital, he'd encountered his share of death even though he was not a practicing medical doctor. Sometimes people who had been revived had memories of death, and this didn't match what they'd said. There was no light, no tunnel, and no loved ones waiting for him. There was only darkness and a lack of pain. He wasn't sure what that said about him.

He didn't know what to do, but he knew it was his doing, his failure, that brought him here; burned, bleeding, and unconscious.

I tried, I tried to do it without the darkness, he said to himself, *but I wasn't good enough. I'm not a wizard, no matter how badly I wish otherwise.*

This was already a dangerous game, and he'd only made it worse. The dark power he'd touched had easily influenced him. Worse, without it, he was completely incompetent.

But what about the summoning?

No, that had only been with Dante right behind him, guiding his every step. When it had mattered, when the other wizard had lashed out, Edward had failed, and because of that, Justin had escaped the circle. Now he'd stumbled again, and this vast darkness was where it got him.

I should just stay here, he thought. *Away from the pain. Let those who know what they're doing deal with it.*

He thought of the heirloom bracelet that was on his wrist, or had been before he'd been fricasseed. He hoped it was intact. It was one of the few pieces of his Taid that he had. The quiet spoke to him then, much as it often did when he was in the library or, occasionally, in his office. However, unlike those times, this wasn't Nghalon; this was his grandfather's voice.

"Don't listen to it, Edward," the voice said. "It isn't you thinking these things."

What? That doesn't make sense. Of course it's me thinking this. Who else would it be?

"No one is ever prepared, but that doesn't give you leave to stand aside. You must rise and be counted amongst those who will fight against darkness. If you can act and do not, then you're giving your consent to the evil. You must not give in to it. Stand apart from the darkness, not just against it."

But I failed. I tried, but I couldn't— Wait, why am I listening to this? It's just some kind of delusion. It's trying to trick me by using my grandfather's voice. Even if it is Taid, what does that crazy old man know?

No, that wasn't right. His Taid wasn't a crazy old man. That's when it dawned on him that he wasn't alone in his own head.

"Just stay here, stay in the quiet and peace—"

Anger filled him at the very idea of this intrusion.

The thoughts changed, and the voice was different now, not even trying to hide. *"Why fight it? You felt that power. You destroyed those creatures with hardly an effort."*

Edward remembered the twisted delight he'd taken in their pain, and it didn't turn his stomach. That was unsettling. But Dante said—

"That sad little sidhe can't stand against you," the voice said. *"You don't need him. You can do this alone. You can save her and the child."*

He thought of how happy, how impressed Caitlin would be. She'd love him then.

"Yes, she'll see your strength and want to be close to it.

Just let the power in. Take it for your own, use it as you want. You can be the master of it!"

With that kind of power, he could take whatever he wanted. No one could stop him, not Dante, not Brendan, no one. Why should he struggle with these meager pieces of magic, these scraps from the table? He was no dog!

"That's why she's never seen you before. Your weakness distracted her."

He thought of how sad and small, how weak he'd been. No, he'd been pathetic!

"Take the power! You can become a god!"

Edward sensed movement and opened his eyes to find himself seated at the front of a grand hall. Wizards sat before him; scores of robed and cloaked figures were watching him, waiting for their lord to issue his edict.

As Edward looked around the chamber, he knew that beyond these walls, world leaders waited for his wisdom and guidance. The most powerful nations would answer his summons and obey his command.

Caitlin, seated to his left and lovely as ever, stared at him with adoring eyes. She smiled, rose, and walked to him. Slowly, she straddled him and wrapped her arms around his neck.

He could feel her press against him.

Her lips touched his, and their softness was intoxicating. Her delicate tongue reached into his mouth and found his, dancing with it in an erotic waltz. Her flesh was warm and soft as his hands caressed her sides. Her body pressed into his as she moaned in delight.

Her kisses moved along his neck and to his ear. "What do you wish of me, my lord?" she asked. "I am yours, take me as you like."

"*All this can be yours,*" a disembodied voice said, and the scene was gone.

Edward was back in the darkness, though his heart still pounded and he could feel the lingering touch of Caitlin's body and lips. He drew in a shuddering breath.

"*Take it, you deserve it.*"

There was another voice, barely more than a whisper. It was Caitlin's. Not the husky seductress from the moment before; this was the real Caitlin, the one he loved. He could see her smile and smell her perfume.

"Thanks, Eddy, you're a good friend. The best, actually," her voice said.

No, it wouldn't be me she loved—

Again, the darkness changed, but this time he saw Caitlin and Brendan lying together, their nude bodies tangled. Caitlin flung her head back and she moaned in ecstasy, then she threw her arms around Brendan's neck and kissed him.

Jealousy tore at Edward's insides. It churned, a vast and rancid ocean of hate that threatened to drown him. His hands tensed, wanting nothing less than to tear Caitlin away.

"*This is what awaits you should you refuse,*" the darkness said.

Pain and anguish ate its way through Edward's heart, leaving behind only nothingness. It should be him, not Brendan.

"Even now—"

"NO!" he screamed into the nothingness.

The scene shattered and evaporated into darkness.

There was a dampness of tears in his eyes, though Edward wasn't sure if it was his actual body. He drew in a breath and resolved himself. He knew the truth: all he could do was love her, and that's what he would do, whether or not she loved him in return. Love didn't work that way.

"You'll fail without it!" the voice said. *"She and the child will be lost forever! Their blood, their deaths, will be on your hands!"*

Edward laughed, actually laughed. How many times had he heard that argument from patients? Victims of assault, rapes, or molestations, they all thought they were the reason it had happened to them. But it was the rapist, the molester, or the murderer who was to blame.

"They'll die—"

"Then I'll spend the rest of my life searching out those who did it, and kill them myself." Edward said. "You're right, neither of them may come home, but now that's not something I can control. I'll do my part to help, and I can only hope."

He felt the frustration of this intruder as Edward fought back the fear and dread growing inside him. Then it all became clear.

"You're not offering me power," he said. "You're asking for it. That wasn't me at all, it was you."

Edward's anger flared. Whoever this was had used

him, and he'd nearly fallen for it. No, he had fallen for it! Edward reached out, using the rage as fuel for his own power. His magic drove out into the darkness, and he felt something. No, someone.

"What are you doing?" The voice was tinged with fear now.

Edward seized the intruder, this violator of his mind. Edward dug his magic into the essence of this trespasser, like claws, holding him fast.

"Let's see how you like it, *anghenfil*."

Edward pushed deeper and drove his magic into the interloper's mind. There was no doubt now—it was the other wizard.

"This will end badly for you, Edward Hunt—"

Edward used all his anger, his fear and pain, to drive his power deeper until he found what he was looking for. It was soft and seemed to pulse with an inner life. His first instinct was to withdraw in disgust, but he fought the urge.

It was so cold that it burned and seemed to draw the heat from Edward. Hardening his resolve, he tightened his magic around it and pulled. Edward's prize held fast, but he felt it begin to tear loose.

The intruder's scream filled Edward's head, but that only drove him on. With a final pull of his will, the piece ripped free.

Edward drew it close and felt something warm seep from it. Then, after a moment, he withdrew from the darkness, returning to the world.

CHAPTER TWENTY-THREE

"Faerie blood?" The world was spinning around Caitlin, and she clung to the only thing that seemed real: Brendan.

"Aye," Brendan said. "I sme— sensed it on you earlier, but I just passed it off as lingering fae magic from the oíche."

Closing her eyes, Caitlin focused and the spinning slowed. "So, what does that mean? I'm not—" She stumbled, as if her mouth didn't want to say the words. "I'm not human?"

"Not mortal is a truer way of saying it. But even that's not entirely true."

Caitlin opened her eyes as she felt Brendan pull back. She searched his blue eyes for comfort or something to make her life normal again. It wasn't there.

"You're still you." His words were soft. "You're still the same person you was before. This doesn't change nothing."

"Doesn't change—" She stared at him. "Are you kidding me? How can this not change everything?"

"I mean, it doesn't change who you are. You're still—"

"Could that be why they took Fiona? I mean, if I'm a—" Again, her mouth struggled with the words. "Changeling. If I'm a changeling, she is too, right?"

"It might at that," Brendan said. "She might be, and if she is, like as not that was the reason they picked her."

While there was some sick sense of comfort in finally knowing why, she still felt the rancid touch of guilt. "Does that mean I'm not Caitlin Brady?"

"What?"

"Was I left behind when the real one was taken?" Caitlin's heart stuttered.

"No."

The reply brought truckloads of relief, but then she considered the alternative and felt cold again. She wracked her brain, thinking who in her family could've been fae. The problem, of course, was that she didn't know much of her family.

"Come on." Brendan led her back to the truck. "Let's get you sat down."

Question upon question unfolded in her mind. Did Nana know? Was that why she'd told her all those stories?

Brendan helped Caitlin into the passenger seat and closed the door. She was only dimly aware of him getting in the other side. The engine started, and soon they were moving again.

Caitlin let the gentle breeze blow over her face as her breathing returned to normal.

"You still with me, love?"

Brendan's voice seemed to be more real now, as if her whole life up until now had been some kind of dream and she was just now waking up. "I'm just trying to get a handle on all the thoughts in my head."

"I shouldn't have reacted the way I did. I didn't mean to scare you. It's really not as important as all that."

She knew he was lying, but she decided to take refuge in the lie rather than calling him on it. "How many are there?"

"Changelings, you mean?" Brendan considered the question for a moment. "Well, it's not that they'd make a large collection, but it actually isn't that uncommon. I'd say odds are anyone with Irish, Scots, Manx, or even Welsh blood has some fae mixed in there as well. Even the Nordics dealt with the fae."

"Really?" Caitlin asked. It sounded like he was telling the truth, but something didn't mesh. "You're leaving something out."

His expression told her that her instinct was right.

"*Damnú air!*" He punched the steering wheel. "Never any use at cards either," he muttered.

"Just tell me. I can handle it." She braced for the worst.

"Oh, aye, I can see that. Sound job you're doing so far." He glanced at her, but her glare made him turn away. "I'm just saying you'll take it arseways."

"Brendan, please, tell me."

He sighed. "It's true plenty out there have fae some-where in their family tree. But the blood loses its po-tency after a generation or two."

He looked at her, probably judging her reaction. She could see where this was going.

"After that, they wouldn't have no sign."

"Like being able to find four-leaf clovers like they were grains of sand?" She didn't need to see him nod.

"Those are few and far between."

She swallowed. That meant it was one of six people; her mother, her father, or one of her grandparents.

"Jesus, love, it ain't cancer." Brendan laughed. "You'd like as not never have known if I hadn't just done that."

"I just need to get my head around this. Okay?"

"Aye." He shrugged. "But it's really not as bad as all that."

"Even so," she said. "It's kind of a lot to take all in one day."

"Aye, fair play that, I suppose." He paused for moment. "But there is something you should know. A changeling has to make a choice. Either they choose the fae side, or they choose the mortal."

"What's that mean?"

"They have to decide which they want to be. If they choose the fae, then they show signs. They stop aging around adulthood, or younger. They might get points to their ears, things like that."

"And if they choose mortal?"

"They grow up like anyone else. You get little hints of it, like finding four-leaf clovers and seeing through glamours."

"And seeing faeries," she said.

"Aye, that as well."

"But I didn't choose."

"You weren't aware of the choice," he said. "You thought you were mortal and grew up as one. You made your decision without ever being aware of it." He gave her a quick glance.

"What?"

He let out a breath. "Well, crossing into the Tír might affect you strangely."

She sighed. "Of course it could."

"I can't say how, because I don't know. It'll work to our favor though. I was worried how we'd handle crossing with you as a mortal. It's not a place friendly to such, but that's not a problem now."

She answered mechanically as her mind began to work. "That's something, I suppose."

So Brendan, you're not mortal? What are you then? she thought.

They drove in silence, and Caitlin was left to wonder about how all this would affect Fiona if—no, when—Caitlin got her back. She would find a way to use it to Fiona's advantage. A thought came to her, and instead of considering it, she pushed it aside . . . well, she tried.

What if her faerie blood was Dusk Court?

The minutes crawled by, and the road unfolded before them at the same lagging pace. They drove, winding back and forth between trees nearing the peak of their change. The approaching sunset turned the sky to painted flames, almost as if it was trying to outdo the trees. Caitlin's whole world had changed, yet the rest of the world was exactly the same.

Anger flared in her heart. How dare she spend a moment wallowing in this when her child was out there? And how much farther did they have to go?

Brendan apparently read her mind. "About an hour or so to go still, I'm afraid. And we have to make a quick detour as well."

Caitlin mumbled a complaint under her breath.

Brendan turned off the country highway and down a local road.

"Where are we?" Caitlin asked. It was clear they were well off the beaten path.

"The detour." Brendan turned into the dirt parking lot of a small general store. "Look, love. I didn't mean to downplay it all to you back there."

Caitlin didn't look at him. She didn't want to think on it anymore. Why couldn't he just let her be?

"Is it the realization, or the fact that someone in your family was untrue to you, that's nibbling at you?"

She gave him a withering glare but didn't answer.

"If it's the second, there's something you should be considering. The one you get your blood from might've been trying to spare you. Or maybe they just never got the chance to tell you."

Her eyes went wide in realization.

"What is it?"

Closing her eyes, she focused on the few memories she had of her father and tried to picture him in her head.

One by one, the pieces fell together.

How could she not have seen it before? That was why her mother had always looked so heartbroken when Caitlin had asked about him or about his illness, and why her mother had never wanted her to hear Nana's stories.

"I think it was my father."

"What happened to him, then?"

"When I was really little, he got sick." The scent of the hospital came back to her. She still hated that smell and questioned the psychology of tormenting herself with it every day.

"He died. That's why I became a nurse." She shook her head. "Wait, can faeries even get sick?"

"Not in the sense you think of, no. But if he was called by one of the courts and didn't answer? Well, the longer he resisted the call, the weaker he'd get. That'd be easy to mistake for sickness."

"He didn't want to leave Mom." Caitlin could see her mother sitting at her father's bedside, his hand in hers. A couple of tears rolled down Caitlin's cheek, and she wiped them away.

Brendan sat in silence.

"Nana's stories must've been too painful for Mom to hear. They reminded her of Dad. Which means they all knew." Caitlin closed her eyes and had clear memories of her father for the first time in a very long time. Sitting in his lap and looking into his radiant blue eyes, eyes just like Dante's.

"I can remember him." Caitlin smiled as tears continued to roll down her cheeks. "He'd sing to me." A sob escaped as the sound of his voice came back to her. "I remember he was almost enchanting in the way—" Her smile vanished.

"*Mo mhallacht ort.*" Brendan looked away from her.

"He'd enchant you with his music. Never a whole gallery full of people, but—"

"I know where your mind's leading you, and it's the wrong path, love."

"What are you?" she asked. "Not mortal. That would cause problems crossing into Tír na nÓg. That's what you said, right?"

Brendan opened his mouth, then closed it and clenched his jaw.

"What's a *díbeartach*?"

Brendan flinched. When he spoke, it was softly, through gritted teeth. "Listen carefully. There's a power behind words, and that's not the kind of word to bandy about."

"I—"

He looked at her, anger flashing in his smoldering eyes. "I wouldn't say it again."

Caitlin felt a rush of fear, and she pressed herself

against the passenger door, her hand reaching for the handle.

Brendan blinked and looked away. He got out of the truck and slammed the door.

Caitlin's stomach twisted as a fresh dose of guilt and panic took hold. She got out and walked around the truck.

Brendan was a few feet away, smoking a cigarette and pacing back and forth.

She watched him for a long time, trying to figure out what to say. Nothing came to her.

Brendan looked at her, then away. He took another drag, then blew out the smoke.

"Brendan."

He didn't look at her.

"You shouldn't smoke." As soon as the words got out, she winced. "And I can't believe I just said that."

"You're right." He looked at the cigarette. "It wasn't always like that, you know? They used to say they was good for you." He dropped the butt on the ground and crushed it out. "I suppose it's past time I gave it up." He dropped the pack of cigarettes into a trashcan.

"Wait." Caitlin grabbed his shoulder.

He turned, and when his eyes met hers, she took a step back. He wasn't mad. He was hurt. Whether it was the word that had cut him, the fact that she'd been the one to say it, or both, she didn't know. But it didn't matter; the results were the same. She ran a shaking hand through her hair.

He spoke quietly, never looking at her. "If you're

thinking I'm going to back out, you needn't worry. I promised I'd get her, and I will."

Caitlin opened her mouth.

"It means 'outcast' or 'exile,'" he said so quietly that Caitlin barely heard him.

"What?"

Brendan swallowed with effort and his face twisted. "*Díbeartach*, it's a curse that means 'outcast.'"

Caitlin lowered her eyes.

"It weren't your doing. You didn't know, but you have to be careful with words. This is a massive ball of shite, but you're handling it better than anyone could expect."

A subtle tinge of grateful relief whispered over her.

Brendan looked at the sky, then at the store's door. "We need to pick some things up before the place closes. If you're needing the jacks, you should do it now." He shook his head. "I mean the toilet, bathroom, loo, whatever."

"I know what you meant." Not knowing what else to do, Caitlin hugged him and let out a deep sigh when she felt one arm wrap around her and give her a small squeeze.

He opened the door for her. "Go on with you, then. They're at the back of the shop."

Caitlin went down the small aisles of the store. It looked as though it hadn't changed since the 1950's. Glancing over her shoulder, she saw Brendan nod to an old man behind the counter.

Caitlin stood in front of the restroom sink, washing

her hands and looking at herself in the mirror. "Get it together." She splashed some water on her face and went back into the store that time forgot.

Brendan was standing at the register. On the counter sat a loaf of homemade bread, wrapped in white paper. There was also a quart of milk, a jar of local honey, a small bottle of whiskey, four bottles of water, a bag of trail mix, and some fruit.

"That'll be twenty-nine, forty-seven," the old man said after the ancient register spun and lifted the numbered tiles into view.

Brendan opened his pouch.

"At least let me pay for this," Caitlin said.

"It's fine—"

"Please, it's the least I can do." She realized then that she didn't have her wallet. Reaching into her pocket, she fished out a couple of bills and set them on the counter, glad she often forgot to check before doing laundry.

The shopkeeper made change and bagged the food.

Brendan picked up the bag. "See you around, Gordon, me best to Muriel."

"See you, Brendan," Gordon said, waving.

Caitlin opened the door. "So what is all this stuff, dinner?"

"The fruit and trail mix is. Not much of a selection, I know. Normally, Gordon has sandwiches, but he was out just now." Brendan pulled a backpack out from behind the driver's seat.

"It's fine." Caitlin accepted an apple, the bag of trail

mix, and a bottle of water as he began putting things in the pack. "What's the rest for?"

"The bread, milk, and honey are for payment."

"Payment?"

"Aye. We'll be needing us a guide when we cross."

"What about the whiskey?"

He gave her a sideways glance. "That's for me." He tossed the whiskey and a bag of beef jerky onto the seat.

"Drinking and driving?"

"Oh, don't go there, love. We're nearly there, and I could use me a bit."

"You're not the only one."

"As a good and proper Irish girl, you should know better than to ask a fella to share his whiskey." Brendan took a drink and sighed. "Oh, that's not half bad, there."

He smiled at her, and she felt a weight lift from her shoulders. The last thing she needed was to distract him with her idiocy.

A wry smile crossed Caitlin's lips. "You know, you're right. I'll just help myself." She reached over, grabbed the bottle, and took a small drink.

"Aye." Brendan started the truck. "That's more like it, then."

The mood only grew solemn after that.

Soon they were deep in the back woods. They'd been on a dirt road for what seemed quite a while, and now the trees loomed around them in the twilight. In the depths of the forests on either side, it seemed shadows were lurking and watching them. However, the shadows didn't make her afraid now.

This time, the shadows should be afraid of them.

Brendan turned down what could just barely be called a road. He shifted his truck into four-wheel drive and crawled over the rocks, through the mud, and across the ruts.

The woods were deeper here, and the darkness was growing. Brendan reached down and flipped a couple switches. Lights on the bumper and a bar on the roof came to life. The trail in front of them was washed clean of darkness and shadows by bright, white light.

Caitlin's head snapped around when she saw movement in the shadows from the corner of her eye. "Could there be something in the woods watching us?"

Brendan sniffed the air. "If there is, it's not close by. It's possible though that we might run into trouble at the sidhe mound."

"That's comforting."

The trail ended at a clearing several hundred feet across. At the far end was a large earthen mound covered in grass and wildflowers. Something about it was oddly familiar.

As Brendan pulled into the glade, the truck's lights swept over the expanse of it. "Well, that's something in our favor, then." He put the truck in park.

"What is?"

"Either the oíche don't know that Justin told us Fiona was taken to the Tír, they don't think we'll come after her, or they don't care if we do."

"Or they're waiting to ambush us."

"Aye, there's that as well, I suppose. If they are though, it isn't on this side. You're sure you're ready for this? No one, meself included, would think less of you if you waited here for me to bring her back to you."

Caitlin took a deep breath and tried not to think about the whole of the situation. "I'm sure I'm not ready, but I'm still going."

"Well then, you'll never plough a field by turning it over in your head."

Caitlin didn't have an answer to that.

Brendan turned off the engine and killed the lights. Darkness swallowed the clearing, leaving only the silvery glow of the moon upon the grass. They opened their doors and got out.

Brendan pulled the backpack from behind the seats and dropped it on the ground. "Give me a minute, love." He pulled something else out and draped it over the side of the truck.

Caitlin's eyes were still adjusting to the darkness, so she couldn't tell what it was.

As Brendan moved about on the far side of the truck, her eyebrows went up. Was he taking off his belt? There was the sound of rustling fabric, and it looked as though he'd just pulled his kilt off, folded it, and put it behind the seats.

She cleared her throat and looked away. "Um, what, what are you doing?" She felt her face flush.

"Putting on something a bit better suited to the task."

She glanced back just in time to see him take a different kilt from the side of the truck and wrap it around himself. He put something on each of his wrists. Finally, he pulled a long-sleeved shirt over his head, opened a box in the bed of the truck, and pulled out a duffel bag.

"All right, all's well." He dropped the tailgate of the pickup and set the duffel bag on it. "Come on."

Caitlin noticed that this kilt was similar to the other, but this one had leather straps on either side holding it closed, and it was a dull mustard color. Her mind clicked; it was saffron. Didn't the Irish military wear saffron kilts? Well, at least her eyes had adjusted to the darkness.

Something inside the bag glinted in the moonlight. He pulled out a wide leather belt that had two large sheaths built into it at the center. He wrapped it around his waist and secured it. Next, he slid two curved knives into the sheaths.

She saw then that it had been leather bands he'd put on his wrists. On each, she could just make out some kind of symbol. Caitlin had to admit, it was quite a sight. She'd never seen a warrior preparing for battle before. If it was possible, he looked even more like he was in the wrong time.

He pulled out what was either a long knife or a short sword. "You know how to use this?"

"I took a self-defense class once." She took the blade. "We learned how to disarm someone with a knife and use it against them."

"Well, as weapons go, they don't get much simpler. No need to worry about being fancy when it comes to it."

"When?"

"Fine, if it comes to it, just do what you need to do."

She gripped the weapon. Things were certainly real now.

He set a small jar on the tailgate. "Best to keep it tucked away out of clear sight . . . until you need it, anyway."

Caitlin undid her belt and fed it through the loop of the scabbard. After securing it to her satisfaction, she tried twisting the sheath so it would go horizontal to her waist, only to find it had some kind of swivel for doing just that.

Brendan pulled a necklace, a piece of carved wood hanging by a leather cord, from the bag and put it over his head. He rolled his sleeves up to his elbows.

"Your fae blood should let you see through the glamours." He opened the jar and released a rather unpleasant odor. "But just to be safe . . ." He dipped his finger into the jar.

Caitlin tried not to breathe through her nose as he applied the jar's contents to her forehead. It felt like he was drawing something. "Please tell me the smell goes away."

"Aye." He chuckled. "In a minute or so it'll soak into your skin and the smell will go."

"I don't want to know what's in it, do I?"

"No."

He returned the jar to the duffel bag, put the bag

back in the box, and pulled on the backpack. "All right then, time to go over the ground rules."

"Okay."

"I know you heard the old stories from your Nan, but you've also learned they weren't all accurate. So, I'm going to cover everything. First thing, you do what I tell you, when I tell you."

Caitlin looked away as her cheeks flushed again.

"No food or drink, at all. That's why we're bringing our own. Fae blood or no, you could still get bound if you partake. And for God's sake, don't make any fec—any bargains with anyone. I don't care how innocent they seem, or how helpful. These are clever ones. They'll be masters of turning the deal so you wind up the worse for it."

"Right."

"Don't be offering nothing to no one, and let me do all the talking as well."

"Understood." Caitlin swallowed. "You're in charge." The knot that had periodically taken up residence in her stomach began to return.

"All right, then. Let's go."

Brendan dropped the keys to the truck in the box and led her to the base of the hill. As they got closer, she could see it was oval shaped and they were approaching a long side. It was fifty or sixty feet long, fifteen or twenty feet wide, and just as tall.

They reached the base of the hill, and Brendan produced a strip of cloth. "I've got to blindfold you." He stepped close to her.

She felt the cloth cover her eyes and him tie it at the back of her head. His strong hands were on her shoulders as he stood behind her.

"We're going to walk anti-clockwise about the hill nine times, but we have to do it facing backward."

"Nine times?"

"Aye, three sets of three. Now, we're not in a race, so go slow. I don't want you twisting your ankle or the like. I'll be right here guiding you the whole way. You ready?"

Caitlin took a series of deep breaths, then nodded.

"Here we go, then."

Brendan's hands steered her, and she found them a comfort amid the blindness. After she stumbled a couple times, she decided to start taking high steps, placing her feet down slowly to measure the terrain first. Thankfully, Brendan matched her pace.

Before long, the steps became part of a seemingly never-ending chain. The sounds and scents seemed to become more vivid. She could smell the damp earth, even each of the different trees. She could hear the leaves rattling in the wind and the fluttering of birds in the branches.

Just as she was beginning to wonder how much longer it would be, her stomach lurched, her head spun, and she nearly fell over.

Brendan's hands gripped her, and she only went to her knees.

"I think I'm going to be sick."

"Give it a moment." He stroked her back. "The sick

feeling, dizziness and the like, it'll pass in a bit. Your first time crossing can be a rough one."

"Did it work?" She took slow, deliberate, deep breaths, trying to push the nausea back.

"Aye." Brendan untied and removed the blindfold. "Welcome to Tír na nÓg, love."

CHAPTER TWENTY-FOUR

Caitlin felt like she had drunk too much, and, as a consequence, every time she tried to open her eyes, all she saw was a whirling blur of green and blue, which only served to make her feel worse. Thankfully, after a few more deep breaths, the spinning world started to slow and the dizziness and nausea began to fade.

She opened her eyes and found herself kneeling on grass the color of a child's crayon drawing—beautiful, but unnatural. She saw Brendan's silhouette against a blue sky. A warm breeze brushed over her, bringing the smell of grass and flowers in bloom. Memories of childhood summers came to her in a rush, of playing in meadows and fields with no cares or concerns. That's what she smelled more than anything: the summers of her youth.

"Can you stand, love?" Brendan crouched down

and looked her over. "Well, you look as well as can be expected. Come on. Let's get you to your feet."

Caitlin stared at him. It was still Brendan, but there were definite, if subtle, changes. His scars were not so prominent. His shoulders looked broader, which was saying something. His jawline was strong, and his eyes had taken an almost shifting, electric blue color. Just beneath their surface, she could see something burning. It was a fire that, she knew, if let loose, could burn this whole land to ash.

Brendan must've noticed her reaction—not that she was trying to hide it.

"Things can take a different look here," he said, "but you can't let yourself get pulled in or distracted by it."

Caitlin just nodded.

"Come on, then." He stood and offered her his hand.

She took it and he pulled her to her feet. Her legs were a little unsteady, but she was able to stand. Brendan's arm went around her waist and kept her from wobbling.

"I'm okay, just give me a second." Each passing moment eased the disorientation a little more.

They were standing in a clearing similar to the one they'd been in moments before, but there were a few differences. The first, and most obvious, was that it was now daytime, near noon from what she could tell. In addition, it was spring here, as opposed to the autumn they'd left behind. Like the green of the grass, every color appeared much more vivid. The leaves, the flowers, the trees, even the clouds and the sky were the right colors, but unnatural in their brightness and depth. This place appeared more real than the world they'd left behind. She felt a bit like Dorothy leaving the black and white of Kansas for the Technicolor of Oz.

"It's quite a thing, isn't it?" Brendan asked.

"Quite a thing," was all Caitlin could manage for a reply. She was actually here, in Tír na nÓg, the land of eternal youth, the place between shadow and light. In a real sense she was also home, or a piece of her was, anyway.

"Let's get moving. It'll help." Brendan used the arm that was still around her waist to urge her along.

She complied, and they crossed the meadow. Behind them, as she suspected, was a large hill, the twin to the one they used to get here. Sounds and flashes of movement came from the woods around them. Caitlin scanned the area and realized her senses were improved. Her eyesight, which had been average, was now picking out minute details from a great distance. The sounds were clear and easy to distinguish. However, it all just served to feed a sense of paranoia.

"Plenty of eyes watching us now," Brendan said as he led the way down a well-worn path away from the mound. "Stay on the trail. We're in the noon lands now, but don't let that fool you."

Before long, Caitlin was walking on her own, following behind Brendan.

"So, where are we going?" She followed him up and over another rise.

He didn't turn around. "Like I said, we're going to need us a guide. For that we need to go to the faire and see if we can bargain us one."

"Fair?"

"It's the faerie marketplace. We shouldn't have any trouble finding someone who knows something and can take us where we need to go. Likely as not, it'll be a leprechaun."

Caitlin opened her mouth.

"No, they don't have any gold. Fecking Disney, they did a number on them with that damned movie. Darby O'Gill, my arse."

"Oh." Caitlin tried to bite back a chuckle. "So, if there's no truth to it, where'd the idea come from?"

"Leprechauns are cobblers and keepers of treasure." Brendan raised his hand, and Caitlin stayed silent. "To the fae, gold is pretty, but information and secrets, that's the real currency of the fae."

"So, if anyone knows anything, it'll be the faerie information brokers and busybodies."

"That's the idea," Brendan said. "You should know though, they hate being called faeries. It's like calling you an ape. They prefer fae."

Caitlin considered that. Political correctness even in Tír na nÓg.

Tiny shadows leapt from branch to branch in the trees around them, and things scurried around in the ground growth. That's when she noticed that the trees seemed to have faces on their trunks. Each bore a serene expression formed of knots and irregularities in the bark.

She stopped in her tracks.

Brendan halted midstep and turned around to look at her.

"You said I shouldn't eat or drink anything." She fought back the panic that was trying to claw its way up her spine. "Fiona's been here almost a day, she'd be hungry—"

"Aye, I thought about that as well."

"You did? When did you plan on telling me?"

He lifted his hands. "Easy, love. If the oíche planned on giving her over to someone, they wouldn't be giving her any of the local stuff."

She considered his words.

"They wouldn't want to risk her being bound here, would they? But, if they did, we'll get something at the faire to break the binding." He put a hand on her shoulder. "Of course, it may not matter. The fae blood you passed on to her might protect her anyway."

"You promise?"

Brendan's face went serious. "Aye, I promise."

"Okay. I trust you," she said, then thought, Don't make me regret it.

Brendan opened his mouth as if he was going to say something. Then, thinking better of it, he turned back around and continued walking.

Caitlin shook her head and followed.

They walked in silence, the trail leading them up

and down several more hills. Caitlin became aware of how out of shape she was. Occasionally, she considered taking off her jacket, but each time, a breeze of cool air made her reconsider.

"Brendan," Caitlin said between breaths. "Do you get the feeling we're being followed?"

He didn't answer or even look back.

"Brendan?"

Again, no response. Caitlin increased her pace and reached out a hand to grab his shoulder, but as she touched him, he sprinted into the trees and vanished into the shadows.

Caitlin stopped, frozen in place, her arm still extended. She heard no sound, only the rustling leaves on the cool breeze. She couldn't believe he'd abandon her, not now. Slowly, she looked around. She touched the handle of the knife at her back in what she hoped was a casual movement.

After several long seconds, she started to wonder if he really had left her.

"Let me go!" shouted someone from the woods.

The voice sounded like a young girl. Caitlin remembered the oíche and gripped the knife.

Brendan emerged from the woods holding a girl, perhaps eight years old at most, by the back of a coppery sundress. The girl was kicking and protesting, but Brendan held her tight.

"Sorry, love," Brendan said. "I had to move, brownies are fast things."

"Let me go! I didn't do anything!" the brownie protested. She had a mess of blond hair, and her eyes were large and all green. Her ears grew into long, pointed tips, vanishing into her hair and emerging at the back of her head. She tried to kick Brendan with dirty bare feet.

"Brendan, what are you doing?" Caitlin asked.

"She was following us," Brendan said. "Weren't you?"

The brownie's mouth moved as she was going to say no, but nothing came out.

"Aye, as I thought." Brendan looked at Caitlin. "Fae can mislead you, but they can't say something outright false."

The brownie's huge green eyes were wet, and they pleaded with Caitlin. She could see trails where tears had washed dirt from the brownie's face.

"Why were you following us?" Brendan shook the girl. "Did the oíche put you up to it?"

The brownie started crying.

"Brendan, you're scaring her," Caitlin said. "Put her down."

"Are you daft? You don't know what a chore it was to catch her in the first—"

"I said, put her down."

Brendan and Caitlin stared at each other. Finally, his eyes still on Caitlin, Brendan set the brownie down.

The brownie made to run, but Brendan hadn't let go of her dress.

"No, you don't," he said.

"Please, don't hurt me," the brownie said between quiet sobs.

Caitlin knelt down and wiped the tears from the brownie's face. "We're not going to hurt you."

Brendan was about to say something, but Caitlin gave him a look and he stayed silent.

The brownie sniffled and wiped her nose with a hand. "I wasn't doing nothing, I just saw you and wondered what you were doing. That's all."

Caitlin smiled. "We believe you."

The brownie's eyes went toward Brendan, but she didn't look at him. "He doesn't."

"Sure he does," Caitlin said. "Don't you, Brendan?"

"Oh, aye." He didn't even try to sound sincere.

Caitlin slowly reached out to brush aside some of the brownie's tangled blond hair. Something glinted in the girl's hair, and Caitlin's stomach lurched when she saw the shining silver barrette with a bright green clover of cut glass.

"Where did you get that?" Caitlin asked.

"It's mine!" The brownie's hand went to her hair. She tried to back up, but Brendan held tight.

"What is it?" Brendan asked.

"That's Fiona's barrette."

"I found it!" The brownie struggled uselessly against Brendan's grip. "That makes it mine, squares and fair! You can't have it!"

"You're sure?" Brendan asked Caitlin.

Caitlin nodded. "Nana gave it to me when I was little, and I gave it to Fiona on her last birthday."

Now Brendan knelt down, looked the faerie straight on, and spoke, his voice low and gentle. "We know you didn't you take it, love. Just tell us where you found that shiny."

The brownie eyed Brendan, then looked to Caitlin.

"Please," Caitlin said.

"She was sleeping." The brownie's face became a little pinched. "The bad ones were carrying her, and I saw it fall."

Brendan and Caitlin shared a look, then Brendan scanned the area.

"They're gone now," the brownie said.

"Could she be helping them?" Caitlin asked in a whisper.

"I don't help the bad ones!" The brownie stomped her foot.

"Please, that was my little girl you saw." Caitlin struggled to keep her voice calm. "The bad ones took her, and we're here to take her home."

The brownie eyed Caitlin and raised a protective hand to the barrette.

"Can I please have that—?"

"Caitlin!" Brendan's voice caused both Caitlin and the brownie to jump. "Remember what I said."

The brownie scowled at Brendan. "I don't like him." She smiled at Caitlin. "But you're nice, so I'll trade you for it."

Caitlin felt a surge of elation, and she reached into her jeans pocket. "Thank you, I don't have much with me, but—"

"I like your hair," the brownie said. "It's very pretty, and almost the same color as my dress."

"Caitlin," Brendan growled.

"Give me a knife," Caitlin said without looking from the brownie.

"You don't know what you're—"

"Never mind." Caitlin drew out the knife he'd given her.

"Bane!" the brownie screamed and cowered. "That's bad, you can't have that here!"

Caitlin tucked the knife back out of sight and showed her hands. "I'm sorry, it's okay. See, I put it away." She leaned close to Brendan and spoke in a whisper. "Can you cut some and keep your knife out of sight?"

Brendan didn't answer; his eyes were burning and his jaw was clenched.

"Brendan, please."

After a moment, Brendan cursed under his breath, but then a moment later there was the sound of hair being cut. He held out Caitlin's hair to the brownie. "You agreed to the trade. That shiny there, for this hair."

The brownie held a hand out.

"But you must also promise that you'll keep it as a treasured possession," Brendan said.

The brownie didn't move. "And you'll let me go?"

"Aye," Brendan said.

Caitlin didn't dare to breathe.

The brownie pulled the barrette free, set it in Brendan's hand, and took the hair.

Brendan let go of the brownie's dress.

There was a blur of movement, a rush of air, and the brownie was gone.

Caitlin grabbed the barrette from Brendan. "Thank you, I—"

Brendan wheeled on Caitlin. "Are you out of your fecking mind? What did I say? No bloody bargains!"

"I couldn't let—"

"You should've let me deal with it! Now there's a fae with a piece of you wandering about, isn't there?"

Caitlin could feel the heat of his anger and see the fury in his eyes, but she didn't back down. "You don't understand."

"No, you don't understand." He pointed at the barrette. "You think it were just happenstance that the oíche didn't notice it fall? Or that it just happened to be where a curious brownie would see it?"

Caitlin felt her stomach drop. "But—"

"This isn't a fecking game or a pretty story. This is as alien a place as you'll ever see."

"Brendan, please, I'm trying to explain—"

"No! You don't get to explain," Brendan said. "Now, she agreed to keep it as a treasured possession, which binds her from giving it away, and if she loses it, or it's stolen, then it's destroyed. So if the oíche had plans to use it against you, and likely they did, now at least they won't be able to."

Caitlin felt a wave of relief.

"But the brownie still could."

She swallowed.

"Mind, she's a noon fae, a young one at that, and

likely just looking for something pretty, but that's not a complication we need." Brendan turned his back on Caitlin and took several breaths. "You have to trust me, love."

When Brendan turned back around, the fire in his eyes had cooled, and the last remnants of anger faded when he saw the tears rolling down Caitlin's face.

"I can't leave her here," Caitlin said. "Not even a piece of her. This isn't about me, do you understand that?"

"I don't claim to know what you're feeling, or what an ordeal this is for you. Next time, just let me handle it."

Caitlin wiped her tears away. "Okay."

"Good, now let it go. It's done and it ended well enough. We outschemed the schemers." Brendan looked over his shoulder. "Now, we're almost there. Let's go and finish this." He continued down the trail and Caitlin followed. Neither of them spoke.

Caitlin plodded up yet another rise. At the top, Brendan was waiting for her.

"Here it is," he said.

Caitlin increased her pace. The destination being so near gave her a second wind. When she crested the hill, Brendan offered her a banana and a bottle of water.

"Here, a peace offering," he said. "You should eat before we go down. That was quite a hike, and I'm sure you're thirsty."

"Thanks, I am." A thin smile emerged on Caitlin's face as she accepted the items. She opened the sports bottle with her teeth and squeezed cool water into her mouth. After several swallows, she passed the bottle to Brendan and ate the banana. She didn't see a faire; all she saw were trees and—

"Wow."

Nestled in the valley was what at first appeared to be a thick forest. A closer look revealed a huge market, not unlike the state fairs she went to as a child. In size, it would rival most shopping malls. What made it hard to see was that there were no shops. Instead, bushes grew into a shape that made stalls and provided shade. The trees varied in size, from average to massive. Several were topped by brightly colored banners that flapped in the wind.

Her body froze as images flashed in her head: vicious sneers, twisted trees, writhing shadows, an overwhelming sense of dread, and a face distorted in absolute terror. The brownie? The image was so brief she wasn't sure. Her mouth went dry as Brendan's warning rang in her ears.

"We'll find a guide there, don't you worry," Brendan said from behind her.

Caitlin jerked and snapped back.

Brendan put the empty water bottle into the pack and looked at the banana peel in her hand, a wry smile on his face. "You want to see something?"

"Okay."

Using his heel, he dug out a small spot in the

ground. He dropped the peel in the hole and covered it with the dirt he'd pushed aside.

Caitlin licked her dry lips. "I don't get—" She saw movement in the freshly covered spot, and in moments, a small green plant emerged from the soil. The sprout grew, and in just a handful of seconds, a full-grown banana tree, complete with large bunches of bananas, stood before her.

"That's the business, aye?" Brendan asked.

"That's what I call recycling. Can we eat them?"

"No." Brendan pulled on the pack. "It's the magic of the land what caused it to grow, so it's no longer mortal fare."

Caitlin stared at the tree.

"There's a lesson in this."

Caitlin bit her lower lip.

"To show you the power that's in the very soil of the place. You can't afford any more slips, not of any kind." He stepped around her and pulled the back of her jacket down so it covered the knife. "Best keep this out of sight."

Caitlin swallowed and wiped her sweaty hands on her pants. "You, um, you don't think that brownie was working with the oíche, do you?"

"No, she's a noon fae of the Tír. They don't like to consort with the oíche."

"Oh, good."

Brendan put a hand on her shoulder. "Let it go. I told you the hair was useless to the oíche. Just make sure you learned the lesson, aye?"

Caitlin licked her dry lips and nodded.

Brendan looked down at the faire. "Even if she spread word of the iron, it'll take some time. Sure, some in the market may smell it on us, but hopefully we'll be in and out before anyone does anything about it."

"What if we're not?" Caitlin asked.

Brendan pulled the pack tight. "Just follow me lead." He started down the hill and into the valley.

Caitlin followed close behind.

CHAPTER TWENTY-FIVE

The soul-wrenching pain Edward had been expecting wasn't waiting for him. It still hurt really, really badly, but compared to what he'd felt before, it was nearly euphoric. Still, he didn't dare to move, out of fear of disturbing the relative comfort he'd found.

Opening his eyes, he found himself on his back once more. All he saw at first was a white blur. After blinking a few times, the images became discernible.

At least blinking didn't hurt.

He was staring at a white plaster ceiling. Around him, the elves were talking in quiet tones.

"What do we do if he doesn't come around?" Quinn asked.

"We do what we need to do," Dante said.

"And what if he gives in—" Arlen started to ask.

"We do what we need to do," Dante said again.

Edward stifled a tinge of fear. He swallowed and

felt a stab of pain, but he focused hard and got a hold of it. At least now he had an edge on the wizard.

"Help me up." His voice was parched and dry.

The elves looked at him, and soon he was surrounded by pointed ears, radiant eyes, and somber faces.

"You really shouldn't move," Dante said. "We've done what we can to ease the pain and heal you, but—"

"How bad is it?" Not that any answer would change things, but Edward needed to know. He'd have to account for that when figuring out his next move.

The elves all looked away.

"That bad, huh?"

"Well," Dante said, "the pùca got quite a piece of you. We've bound that wound and stopped the bleeding—"

"But?" Edward was pretty sure he knew what was coming; it was written on every face.

"The fire," Dante said. "That's what caused the worst damage." He lowered his head. "Fire is dangerous, even for the fae. You don't need to worry about infection, we've taken care of that, but there's—" He drew a breath.

"Just tell me."

"There's going to be a lot of scarring. In time we might be able—"

"Help me up."

Everyone stopped and looked at him.

"I said, help me up!" Edward repeated louder. "We've got work to do, and I won't get it done lying here. I'm hurt, not dead. I can still help."

After a moment of indecision, the elves sat him up. Edward gritted his teeth as the pain flared. He was sitting the edge of a heavy wooden table. The room had brick walls, and the small windows near the ceiling told him they were at least partially below ground.

"Where are we?"

"A *tearmann*," Dante said. "A sanctuary. It's a safe house, to use your parlance. Of course, you made it even safer."

Edward furrowed his brow.

"Before you passed out, you cast one last spell," Dante said. "There's some kind of shield surrounding the door. No one can get in or out."

"Oh," Edward said. "Sorry. I just wanted to make sure the place was secure. I didn't know where we were."

"We're all curious why it didn't drop when you went unconscious," Arlen said. "Without you holding the magic in place, it should've collapsed."

"Arlen, now's not the time," Dante said.

"No," Edward said. "It's okay. Wards are the one thing I've got any skill with. It wasn't the dark power."

The elves' reactions were so subtle they were hard to see, but there was relief in their eyes.

"Several months ago," Edward said, "I figured out how to invest wards with a way to draw their own magic."

The elves shared a look of surprise, and several nodded in approval.

Edward eased himself down from the table, wincing as he did. His shirt had been removed, and one of the elfin bandages now covered his entire midsection. Others crisscrossed his chest and covered his left shoulder. The pain seemed worst there, and he figured that was where the burns were.

"The herbs will speed the healing," Dante said. "Like mortal healers though, there isn't much we can do for the scarring from burns."

Lifting his hands, Edward saw his left arm was bandaged down to his elbow. His right was unbandaged, but red and tender, and thankfully his Taid's silver bracelet was unscathed. Going for the knife must've spared it some. He wiggled his left hand and noted his fingers were all there. Lucky. He seemed to remember fingers were often lost in bad burns.

Then he remembered the heat on his face. "Is there a mirror?"

"No," Dante said. "They can be used as gateways, so we don't keep any."

"I have this." Quinn offered his sword. The metal of the blade was polished to a high sheen.

Edward raised the sword up to his face, not sure he wanted to see. The first thing he noticed was that his eyebrows were intact, as was his hair. This surprised him.

"The herbs," Dante explained. "They speed normal healing, and hair regrows quickly."

Edward looked again into the blade. His ears had survived with only slight burning, but the tips were bright red. He turned the blade and saw that the left side of his face seemed to have taken the brunt of it.

He'd always liked his long, lean features. He had

the kind of face you expected to see buried in a book. Now a large patch of red ran from just below his hairline, down the side of his face, to just below his cheekbone. His goatee was likewise intact. It wouldn't heal pretty, but it could've been a lot worse.

This'll be fun to explain to everyone at the hospital, he thought.

Edward knew, all things considered, that he was lucky, but that didn't stop him from berating himself for his stupidity. This was his fault, and it was a hard lesson learned. He should probably be thankful he was the only one hurt.

Handing the blade back, Edward closed his eyes and sighed. He was done with self-pity. "I can find the wizard," he said.

No one said anything.

"He got into my head. I mean, I allowed him into my head, unintentionally. I was stupid, but he's gone now, but I got a piece of him during the eviction. I can use it to find him."

"You've got the wizard's thread?" Dante said. "Okay. What do you need?"

"A circle," Edward said.

Under his careful instructions, the elves drew the circle in an adjoining room. Edward recounted every detail from the circle in his basement and analyzed each part as it was drawn.

"I seem to have underestimated you on a number of

levels," Dante said. "These aren't easy, even for those well practiced in magic."

"Eidetic memory." Edward shrugged, and the pain made him wince. "I've always been able to remember things. Seeing it, hearing it, doesn't matter."

"Quite a skill for a wizard to have," Padraig said.

Edward had to stifle a laugh. He appreciated they were trying to boost his confidence, but it might've worked better had he not been burned to a crisp by his own incompetence.

"It's good," Dante said, "but you know with you inside that thing, we won't be able to help you if something goes wrong."

"You can't cross the circle once it's closed."

Dante nodded.

"Well, then, I'll just make sure nothing goes wrong this time."

The elves cleared the circle, and Edward stepped into its center.

Dante stepped close. "Are you good?" he asked in a whisper.

Edward looked him in the eye. "I am. I was stupid, but I see that now."

Dante scrutinized him for a long moment. Finally, he nodded, helped Edward sit, and then left the circle.

Edward closed his eyes and reached inside to the place where he'd stored the wizard's thread. He touched the circle and pushed power into it. The instant before it closed, he pushed the wizard's thread in as well. Edward's pain eased as the circle closed and sealed him off from the world.

"Agor y ffordd." His senses reached through a portal connecting him to the other wizard. In moments, Edward found what he sought. Channeling his anger and pain, he grabbed hold of the wizard and heard a name in his head. Akhen.

Then a wall came up, cutting him off from the wizard.

The duel, it seemed, had begun.

Edward pressed against the barrier and felt like he was trying to push through steel with only his fingers. He reached for the wizard's thread and took a fragment from it. He focused his will and tried to shape the fragment into a point. It resisted him, remaining unchanged.

Redoubling his efforts, he tried again, struggling against the fragment's rigidity.

It wasn't working.

"Come on, focus harder. I can do this. I have to do this," he thought.

He couldn't think of anything. How could he sharpen a sword with a cloth?

Then it dawned on him. He was spreading his focus too wide, working too big. He tried again, concentrating on just a small piece at the very edge.

It began to give.

He worked his way around the edge, feeling it soften more and more. Before long, the thread fragment had a sharp point and keen edge. It was a weapon now, forged from the very essence of the wizard he meant to use it against. He focused his power into it, hardening it. Then he drove it into the barricade.

Screams filled his mind as the spell blade bit into the wall, piercing past the surface.

Cold swept over Edward, and he felt hands grip his neck. The force of it was such that if he'd been in his body, his windpipe would've been crushed. As it was, he was still finding breath hard to come by, and he started to sink into unconsciousness.

The image of Caitlin smiling at him appeared in his head and warmed his heart. The memory of her lips, soft and sweet, pressed to his cheek, filling him with heat and driving out the cold. That was the real Caitlin he knew, not the other wizard's twisted imitation. Edward's resolve hardened beyond that of the wall.

Focusing his will, he drove the spell blade deeper, and cries of pain filled his mind. This time it wasn't just a single scream, it was two. One was certainly human. The other most certainly was not.

The grip on Edward's throat weakened, and he pushed, leaning into the blade with all he had.

The wall shattered and he lurched into the wizard.

Emotions flooded him, and each was as tangible as a change in climate: ice-cold fear, burning rage, vast and empty indifference. Edward felt himself hurtled forward, racing through Akhen's mind. Then the motion stopped abruptly and he found himself looking through Akhen's eyes. Surrounding him were oíche and other dark creatures he couldn't name.

One of the oíche held up a large, dark purple crystal. "This is the vessel. Destroy it, and our bargain is complete."

Before Edward could react, a voice in his head spoke to him. Its tone was deep, guttural, and bore an accent that he'd never heard.

"Give up, wizard," the voice said. *"All that awaits you here is pain. More pain than your sad little mind can possibly conceive. You will beg for a death that will not come for centuries."*

Edward made a decision then, the effects of which he found quite liberating. "That may be," he said, and found his words came out of the wizard's mouth. "I don't have to survive to succeed. I only need to stop you."

The oíche and other creatures looked on with uneasiness. The one closest drew back the crystal.

A violent pull caused Edward's vision to blur and he was yanked out of the wizard, past the oíche, and out of the building. He saw the old warehouse from the outside and the Boston skyline in the distance. He searched for a street sign, hoping it would tell him his location, but he only caught a quick glimpse before he was pulled away again.

After that, there was only a blur.

Red lightning leapt from the warehouse to chase him.

Soaring past the buildings of downtown, Edward moved so quickly that the cars and streetlights were reduced to streaks of green, yellow, and red. He saw the magic in pursuit, matching his every turn and gaining on him.

It was trying to track him back to the safe house.

Straining with the effort, Edward reached out to the force pulling him, willing it faster and faster. He pushed energy into it and the lightning fell back until, at last, Edward slammed into his body so hard that it knocked him over and slid him to the edge of the circle. Even before his senses had fully returned, he touched the circle.

"*Diwedd!*" he said, and opened the circle, breaking the connection.

Edward lay on his back, gasping for breath against the pain that surged through him with renewed vigor. Luckily, his back had been spared any burns, but the pain in the rest of his body flared. Each tender part of his skin screamed at being moved and stretched.

Dante knelt over him. "Are you okay?"

"I found him," Edward said. "I know where they are."

"Well done, wizard!" Quinn said. "I'll make sure everyone is ready to move out as soon as you are."

"Wait," Edward said. "There's a problem."

"Isn't there always?" Dante asked. "What's this one?"

"There was something else in there." Edward pushed himself up to a sitting position. "I felt fear in him, but it wasn't toward me. And the hatred—" He shook his head. "It was almost inconceivable in its magnitude and scope. There was so much rage. He was consumed by it." He looked at Dante. "Are possessions real?"

"Not possession by the fae," Dante said.

Faolan cursed and spit on the floor. "I can't believe they actually went that far!"

"What?" Edward asked.

Dante cleared his throat. "The oíche are the only fae who are, shall we say, cordial with Hell-Spawned."

"Demons?" Edward's voice came out a little higher than normal.

"For lack of a better term, yes," Dante said. "Even the Dusk Court doesn't deal with their ilk. Bargains with them never go well and are costly at best, even for fae."

"Why would they do that?" Edward asked. "Why risk it?"

"Because they're oíche," Riley said. "They don't think about the consequences of anything. They only think of advancing their own desires."

"Or," Dante said, "the wizard outsmarted them. Maybe he found a loophole in their bargain and was able to get out of it ahead." He chuckled. "The oíche wouldn't like that. So maybe they enlisted a Hell-Spawned to possess him and finish the job. They could even use the wizard as payment when it was done."

"What would that mean for Fiona?"

Dante didn't answer. He didn't have to. Edward could read the answer in his eyes.

"We're going to need the gold weapons," Arlen said. "Go to the cache and make sure everyone has at least one gold blade in addition to their regular armament," Dante said. "And ammunition. Lots of ammunition."

"Gold?" Edward asked. "Is that to demons what iron is to fae?"

"Silver works, too," Dante said. "But gold is best."

"There might be something else," Edward said. "Help me up."

"It never rains," Dante said. "It only pours."

He and Quinn helped Edward stand, careful not to put too much pressure on his wounds. Once he was standing, Edward explained what he'd seen with the crystal, and what the oíche had said.

Dante and Quinn shared a look that made Edward's heart skip a beat.

"You don't think—?" Quinn asked.

"We need to find out," Dante said. "We still have that informant?"

Quinn nodded.

"Have Arlen get in touch with him, now."

Quinn left the room.

"Bad, huh?" Edward asked.

Dante looked at Edward. "You sure you're up to this?"

"I'm going," Edward said.

CHAPTER TWENTY-SIX

As the trail into the faire widened to a dirt road, Brendan stopped. "All right, love. As I said before, don't speak to no one, and don't touch nothing."

Caitlin set her jaw. "I won't make the same mistake again. I know—"

"You know now. In two minutes, when we're walking amongst the fae and their wares, well, then you might not remember, yeah?"

Caitlin blinked. She hadn't thought of that. It might take just a glance at something to become enchanted by it. The faeries probably had enchantments practically falling off them. "You're right."

"Keep your wits about you. This is serious business here."

Caitlin followed close behind Brendan. When they entered the market, she stopped and stared with wide eyes and a slack jaw. The market was also a village, but instead of houses, there were trees with doors set in the trunks at ground level. They also had windows, most of which were open. Along either side of the path, and between the trees, shrubs had been grown into odd shapes to form the stalls where goods were offered for sale. But it was the shoppers and sellers of this market that truly caught her off guard. She saw small, winged pixies, little more than balls of light, flitting about. There were stocky, bearded dwarves working the stalls, and tall, elegant elves perusing the various goods. She even saw a dryad leaning out the window of a large oak tree and flirting with a satyr. In fact, every kind of faerie Caitlin could remember hearing about seemed present. There were also several creatures totally unfamiliar to her.

When Caitlin spotted a goblin, she stared. It had the same huge red eyes and dark green skin as the one who'd attacked them at her house.

"Brendan?" She tried to look away and fight back her fear.

"Not all goblins are Dusk Court," he whispered. "They do make up some of the noon fae. Keep moving—we'll draw enough attention to ourselves without you gawking at everyone." He tugged at her arm.

"Right." Caitlin tore her gaze from the goblin and looked at the other inhabitants, only partially aware of the larger world around her. She shook her head and blinked. It was kind of like visiting a Disney movie set and seeing all the animated characters walking around as flesh and blood.

As they walked down the dirt road that bisected the market, Caitlin glanced into the stalls. Fabrics of bright colors rippled like liquid, and plants grew in every kind of strange shape, color, and size she could imagine. In one stall, she saw clear glass jars filled with swirling mist and tiny blinking lights. She swallowed as the memory of the strange darkness that escaped the oíche's wounds came to her. Yet another stall sold wands, charms, necklaces, and other jewelry fashioned with stones of every color, some of which were glowing.

The sounds of haggling and friendly chatter stopped. All eyes were now on Caitlin and Brendan, or, more correctly, on Brendan. Windows and shutters were drawn tight. People shut their doors and vanished in all manner of ways, some literally. Those who remained wore looks of fear or contempt. But a few appeared almost respectful. The word *Fian* was whispered more than a few times. Everyone gave Caitlin and Brendan a wide birth. Brendan had called it right.

Out of the corner of her eye, Caitlin saw something else that made her look again. A stall was filled with stacked ceramic jars, each of which bore a label. However, the labels read things like A Baby's Laugh, Summer's First Morning Light, Winter's Breath, Spring Rainbow (all colors), Lover's Longing, and Cat's Purr.

"Brendan," she said and gestured to the stall. "Do they really?"

"Aye. They hold what they say, and every bit is useful in causing mischief. Now come along, we're almost there."

"Where are we going?"

"Just up ahead. Our man will be at the pub." Brendan nodded at a monstrously huge oak tree ahead of them.

Caitlin was about to ask him to repeat himself when she saw that this tree also had a door at its base. Windows were scattered across the tall trunk at different levels, which she deduced meant it had several floors. Above the door was a sign that bore the picture of a mug with froth on top.

"Right." Maybe this should have surprised her more, but compared to everything else, a tree pub didn't rate much. "Of course. The pub, where else would he be?"

Brendan chuckled under his breath. "Aye, that's right. Come on, then, love."

She followed him inside.

The pub was . . . well . . . it was about like she'd expect a Tír na nÓg pub inside a giant tree to look. At this point, she began to wonder if maybe her mind was just overloaded and that was why she wasn't reacting more strongly. What the final straw was, she didn't know. Maybe it was the Tinker Bell-like pixie flitting through the air holding a mug that was easily ten times her size, one-handed no less, or it could've been the centaur at the bar resting a hoof on the rail and drinking from his own large mug. It could've been the gnomes that were arm wrestling, or the elf playing darts with a nixie.

No, it was almost definitely the arm-wrestling gnomes.

The entire pub was part of the tree, alive and well, no less. The tables grew up out of the floor, as did the bar and benches that were set against the wall. Once more, everyone went quiet and all eyes turned to Brendan, but he seemed unconcerned. Caitlin felt a bit like she was walking with a quarterback through a comic book convention.

Brendan nodded to a table in front of a bench in the corner. "That's our man there."

Resting or, more correctly, passed out on the table was a small head of frizzy red hair. Attached to it, sitting on the bench, was a little man dressed in green. Caitlin could just hear the faint sound of his snoring from across the room.

"That's our guide?"

"Easy, love." Brendan chuckled and led her to the booth. "Seamus is a good sort. Don't you worry none, he's not as mangled as all that."

Caitlin knew she was out of her depth, so she just followed Brendan.

"Seamus!" Brendan banged on the table. "Wake up, lad. Got some work for you."

Seamus's head shot up to reveal a round face, red cheeks, and a beard of the same frizzy hair that was on top of his head. He cast a bleary-eyed glare around the room. "Bogs, man! You trying to wake the bleeding dead in here?" There was a slight slur to his speech. Blinking again, his eyes opened wide, and he smiled even wider. "Brendan! Well, I was thinking you'd forgotten about old Seamus, you had."

Brendan sat in a chair opposite the leprechaun and nodded for Caitlin to sit as well. She pulled a chair over.

"So, what brings you back to the Tír?" Seamus asked. When he saw others in the pub eyeing his table and whispering, he shouted across the room. "Mind your own, or I'll mind it for you! Can't a fella just have a word with a Fian without you clucking like a pack of hens?"

Brendan leaned in close. "We need us some information about a *girseach*. She would've been brought here by the oíche, and not long ago."

"Bleeding oíche, bah." Seamus picked up a pipe from the table and poked it with the tip of his finger. There was a little explosion of sparks, and it started smoking. He took several puffs on it and leaned back.

"Seamus." Brendan's voice was straining to remain calm. "We've not got time for your usual games. We need to know where they've taken her." Seamus was about to speak, but Brendan cut him off. "No bollocks about not knowing nothing either. If anyone knows something, it's you."

Seamus laughed. "Easy there, lad." He looked at Caitlin, and his smile faded. "I'm guessing you'd be the mother, then?"

Caitlin nodded.

Seamus drew in a breath. "Then some free advice for you, love." He hesitated, then his look became serious. "Go home. Have another child, and forget about this one."

The floor seemed to drop out from under Caitlin. She had to concentrate to take a breath.

Brendan backhanded Seamus. The blow knocked the leprechaun into the wall and down onto the floor. It happened so fast that it was hardly visible.

Caitlin looked at Brendan in shock.

"Now, Seamus," Brendan said calmly, ignoring Caitlin. "You know better than to speak to a lady like that. I suggest you apologize, mate."

"Bogs, man!" Seamus cried out from the floor. "I'd forgotten what a punch you pack. Rivers and stones!" He picked himself up from the floor and took his seat once more, giving Brendan a wary look as he rubbed the side of his face.

"That wasn't a punch, bucko," Brendan said. "Would you like to see one of those instead?"

"Easy there, son," Seamus said. "No need to get your hackles raised. I wasn't playing at nothing." He recovered his pipe, took a puff, then looked around and leaned in. "There're factors in all this you obviously don't know."

"Well that's why we came to you now, isn't it?" Brendan reached into the backpack, drew out the jug of milk, and set it on the table. "Can we bargain, then?"

"Oh, lad," Seamus said, nearly drooling as he eyed the jug. "Aye, we can at that."

"Fine," Brendan said. "You tell us everything we want to know in regards to the girl—"

"Everything I know," Seamus said, correcting him. "You'll not bind me into a bargain that has me scouring the whole of Tír na nÓg for an answer. I've affairs of me own to attend to, you know."

"Fair play," Brendan said. "You tell us everything you know in regards to the girl. In return, you get the fresh, delicious, sweet milk."

"Deal." Seamus eyed the jug and licked his lips. "Can I get a wee taste now? In good faith, you know?"

"Talk first, then you get your milk. You know how it works."

"Can't blame a fella for trying, now, can you?" Seamus drew in a breath. "All right, then. It just so happens that I do know about your *girseach*. She and her escorts passed through the market not long ago."

"You're supposed to be telling us what we want to know," Caitlin said. "Not what we already know."

"Oh, I like that one, there," Seamus said. "Fiery spirit, she has. Reminds me of Á—"

"Seamus!" Brendan said. "The *girseach*."

"Right." Seamus cleared his throat. "Sorry. Well, I do know where she is, but trust me, lad, you don't want to be going after her."

"I'm not worried about a pack of oíche, now, am I?" Brendan said. "I'll tear the Tír apart if it's needed to get her back, and you know that's the truth."

"Aye, that I do," Seamus said. "But it isn't the oíche what have her no more."

"What?" Caitlin asked, unable to stop herself.

Brendan squeezed her hand under the table. "They took her out of the Tír, then?"

"No, they're still here," Seamus said. "And from what I hear, they're not at all happy about it, neither."

"Don't be lying to me now. Did the wizard come here to claim her?"

"Wizard?" A look of genuine confusion came to Seamus's face. "I don't know nothing about no wizard."

Caitlin blinked at Brendan. "But you and Dante—"

"I'd say we was wrong," Brendan said to Caitlin. He turned back to Seamus. "All right, who'd they grab her for, then?"

"Well." Seamus lowered his voice even more. "That's a fair piece of information you're asking for there, not the usual bit. This is prime—"

"Seamus," Brendan growled. "We made us a bargain. You really want word to spread that you backed out of an agreement?" He stared hard, then spoke quietly and calmly. "You really want to back out of a deal with me?"

"No need to be threatening me there, lad," Seamus said.

"Oh, I'll do worse than threaten you if you don't—"

"All right." Seamus took a deep breath. "It'll be the Dark King himself you'll be wanting to visit." His eyes darted around the room. "That's who they turned her over to."

Brendan's eyes went wide. "Fergus? Go on with you now!"

Caitlin saw the disbelief in Brendan's eyes, but there was a flicker of something else. She wasn't sure if it was worry, fear, or shock. None of them boded well.

"As you say, we're in a bargain. Besides, I can't be lying to you, now, can I?" Seamus asked. "They went off into the Dusk Lands."

"That don't mean it was—"

"I heard it from a very good source," Seamus said. "It was Fergus himself they handed her over to."

Caitlin looked at Brendan. His brow was furrowed, and he was looking down.

Her head was spinning and her heart was pounding. The King of the Dusk Court had Fiona? Why would he want her? What did this mean for getting her back?

"This don't change nothing," Brendan said to Caitlin. "We'll still get her back, if I have to pull her from Fergus's hands meself."

Caitlin tried to find some comfort in his words and the look in his eyes, but she couldn't. It wasn't there. Still, though his eyes held uncertainty, she understood the commitment he was making to her with those words. It touched her deeply and filled her with gratitude, but it didn't ease her fear.

"Don't change nothing?" Seamus laughed. "I do admire your courage, lad. A fine example of a Fian you are, even if you got bollocks bigger than your brains."

"So what does Fergus want with a mortal—" Brendan stopped midsentence and cast a quick glance at Caitlin. "What's he want with a child?"

"That I don't know, lad," Seamus said. "Wish I did. That'd be a fair bit of currency to bargain with."

Brendan got to his feet. "Right, we're done, then. Come on, love. Time to go."

"Hold on there, lad," Seamus said, his tone hesitant. "I do know one other thing."

Brendan's jaw clenched. "Forgot something, did you?"

Seamus didn't say anything.

"Come on, out with it, then."

"I know what it was that Fergus paid the oíche," Seamus said.

"Aye? Well, go on, then."

"He's offered them a chance for release." Seamus leaned back and began puffing his pipe with a shaking hand, his eyes darting around the room.

"Seamus," Brendan said, "can you smell what you're shoveling, mate? They was released when the Rogue Court formed, weren't they? In fact, right now they're fighting a war to take control of it."

"I didn't say release them from his court," Seamus said between puffs.

Brendan's face fell. "*Dar fia*, is that even possible?"

Seamus nodded. "Oh, sure it is, lad. Not something that happens often, and it does come with all kinds of strings, mind, but it can be done. They have themselves one full day to pull it off, and they don't have the means to do it themselves."

"That's why they needed the bloody wizard," Brendan said.

"Aye. That'd be one way to do it, to be sure."

"Brendan?" Caitlin had no idea what this meant, but clearly it wasn't good.

Brendan looked at her, then back to Seamus. "Anything else you're forgetting to tell us?"

Seamus didn't answer. He just puffed on his pipe.

"Right, then." Brendan took Caitlin's hand and pulled her along behind him as he went to the door.

CHAPTER TWENTY-SEVEN

"**B**rendan," Caitlin said as soon as they walked out the door of the pub, "why would the King of the Dusk Court want Fiona? Is it because she's a changeling?"

"It'd have to be, but it doesn't make any bleeding sense."

"Why?"

"Cause your blood line isn't of his court," Brendan said.

Caitlin felt a surge of relief, though it was tempered with caution. "How do you know that?"

"Well, your da stuck around, didn't he? Well, as long as he could anyway. If he'd been one of Fergus's, he wouldn't have been so kind. That means he was either Dawn Court or a noon fae that were connected with the Dawn Court." He looked away and let out a breath. "Why the bloody hell would he want a changeling child that weren't of his own court?"

Caitlin's hand went to her pocket and caressed the little stuffed bear.

"No use trying to figure that one out," he said. "We need to focus on getting her back, is all."

"What?"

Brendan looked her in the eye. "Look, love. I don't know what he'd want her for, but it's not going to be anything good. We can either sit here trying to reason it out, which will be for nothing, or we can just go and get her back. You tell me, which do you prefer?"

"Okay. What's a chance for release mean?"

"That's another ball of shite." Brendan began pacing. "It means the oíche wouldn't be fae anymore."

"So, what, they'd be mortal?"

"No." Brendan took her hand and led her around the pub, out of sight. "They'd have their strength, their speed, probably even their magic. What they wouldn't have is anyone to answer to. There wouldn't be nothing stopping them from doing as they please. No hearth protections, no Oaths, no nothing. Hell, even iron might not bite them anymore."

"Monsters free to roam the countryside."

Brendan nodded.

Caitlin shivered. "Edward. We have to warn Edward and Dante."

"Aye, but we got no way to get word to them."

Caitlin's knees felt weak. She thought of Eddy and Dante walking into something very different from what they expected. Eddy was the smartest person she'd ever known. Maybe he and Dante together would figure it out. She held tight to that hope, then refocused on Fiona and getting her back.

She looked up at Brendan. "Okay, what's next?"

"Well, considering where we need to be going," he said as he led her back around the tree, "we need to pick us up a charm."

Caitlin followed him back into the market. Again, the chattering went silent as they walked down the street to the stall selling the wands and jewelry. A goblin stood behind the table, watching them warily.

Brendan stared back in silence.

"Are you . . . um . . . ," the goblin said with a shaking voice, then cleared his throat. "Are you looking for something specific?"

"Aye." Brendan examined the necklaces hanging from a stick. "We need us a seeking stone."

The goblin's eyes widened, and a smile came to his face that made Caitlin uneasy. She could almost see the cartoon dollar signs pop into his eyes.

"I take it you have payment?" the goblin asked.

Caitlin saw the goblin look at her, and she shuddered.

"We can bargain," Brendan said, locking eyes with the goblin. "If you have one, that is."

"Oh, I do happen to have one left." The goblin drew a necklace out from under the table. From a leather cord hung a dark blue crystal. It was flat and smooth, with a hole in the center through which the cord was tied.

"One left?" Brendan laughed. "Oh, aren't we just lucky, then."

"Indeed you are, Fian." The goblin nodded several times. "In fact, a nixie was just inquiring about it." He held up the necklace. Light glittered and danced inside the stone. "Finest goblin craftsmanship you'll find. A dreaming stone, polished with silk that was woven by a traveler longing for home."

Brendan reached to grab and examine it, but the goblin pulled it back.

"Payment?"

Brendan eyed him. "You wouldn't be stupid enough to try and pawn me something false, would you?"

The goblin's mouth dropped open and his eyes went wide. It was hard to tell, but he looked genuinely insulted. If she hadn't seen it, Caitlin wouldn't have believed his face was capable of it.

"Of course not!" the goblin said. "I don't sell imitations."

"Fair enough," Brendan said. "How much?"

The goblin smiled at Caitlin. "I like her eyes."

"My . . . my eyes?" She gulped. Cold ran down her spine as she remembered the kind of payments that faeries took. She had a brief flash of a ceramic jar with a new label. Changeling's Eyes (Green).

Brendan crossed his arms. "No."

The goblin scowled. "Then, how about—"

"No memories either, no names, none of that."

The goblin gritted his teeth. "Well, it isn't free, Fian!"

Brendan set the backpack on the table, and the goblin eyed him with interest. "How'll this do, then?" Brendan pulled the bread out and set it on the table.

The goblin snatched up the bread and sniffed it. "It's a start, but I'll need something else as well."

"Fine." Brendan reached back in and set the honey on the table. "This as well, then."

The goblin licked his lips. "My good Fian, you must understand, this is a fine example—"

"And this." Brendan pulled the half-full whiskey bottle from the pack. "Final offer, or we take our—"

"Done." The goblin snatched up the honey and whiskey, then handed the necklace to Brendan.

"Pleasure." Brendan took the stone and pulled his pack back on. "We're done here."

Caitlin followed Brendan out of the market. She couldn't help but think they'd forgotten something.

When they were well away from the market, Brendan knelt down and picked up a small stone from the ground.

"What's that for?" Caitlin asked.

"Well," Brendan said as he pressed the stone from the ground against the blue crystal. "Odds are we won't be able to just walk out of the Dusk Lands." The stone melded into the crystal and filled the hole in the middle. "This will bring you—"

Caitlin flashed him a look.

"—us back to this spot." He stood up.

She tried to ignore the fact that he wasn't looking her in the eye anymore.

"It seeks the place it were joined." He slipped the necklace over her head. "Make a note of the land. If something should happen to me, make a flat run for the sidhe mound. Don't stop for nothing, or no one."

Caitlin looked at the necklace and back to Brendan, who still wasn't looking at her.

Whatever it takes, right?

He started back to the trail leading away from the market. "I suppose there's one good thing to come of the turn of events."

"And what's that?"

"The Dusk Lands are easy to find. Just walk away from the light."

The sun was hanging in the sky above them, but slightly behind. The implications of Brendan's words weighed heavy on her heart, but there was something else.

What were they forgetting?

Caitlin opened her mouth to ask Brendan, but she closed it again. He would've remembered whatever it was; it was just her mind playing games with her.

CHAPTER TWENTY-EIGHT

"**A**re you sure?" Edward asked, eyeing the table.

"We treated you quickly," Quinn said. "It was to keep out infection and treat the pain. We didn't do it with the intention you'd be going into combat."

Edward climbed, slowly, back onto the table.

Faolan and Quinn helped him lie back down. Edward closed his eyes against the encroaching headache and the anticipated pain.

"Breathe," Quinn said. "Just relax. Everything will be okay." He gave Edward a minute, then asked, "Are you ready?"

"Just work as quickly as possible."

Edward clenched his already aching jaw and sucked in a breath as the bandages were pulled away. While they didn't stick, for which he was incredibly grateful, they still sent waves of pain through him. He took long, deep breaths and the pain began to subside, but he could feel tears running down the sides of his face.

Caitlin and Fiona, just think about them. This too will pass.

The air was cold on his skin, and Edward dared a glance down. Only his shoulder was clearly visible, and it wasn't an encouraging sight. A large patch of bright red skin glistened with moisture, typical of a bad burn. He could see remnants of blackened skin that had been sloughed off at the edges of the pink swath. As his stomach lurched, he dropped his head down on the table and fought back more tears.

"All right," Faolan said. "We're going to apply more ointment now. It'll ease the pain, but the initial contact will hurt. And since you're going outside, we're going to bandage both hands and the side of your face."

Edward steeled himself. "Go ahead."

Something cold touched his stomach and pain tore through him, but it was minor in comparison to what he had already suffered and quickly faded to a dull burn.

The process was repeated on his various injuries; deep breath, grit through a moment of pain, then, finally, relief. His face was last, and one of the elves had to wipe some tears away. As the salve was applied, he noticed a musty, earthy smell to it.

"That's the last of the ointment," Quinn said. "Now we're going to place the bandages. This part shouldn't hurt at all."

There was a cool sensation, then a gentle tightness

on his stomach. Next was his chest, and it became hard to draw a deep breath. Edward had no idea how much time passed, but eventually he felt something cool on his face.

"That's it," Quinn said. "We're done."

Edward gave himself a moment to take stock. He drew in a breath and felt a twinge, but it was manageable. He wiggled his fingers and bent his arm. It felt like he was wearing tight leather gloves, but he could move with only a slight hindrance. The pain was much reduced, which was like being hit by a bus, then saying that a sixteen-pound sledgehammer wasn't a big deal.

"Help me up, please."

Faolan and Quinn went to opposite sides and lifted him up to a sitting position.

Edward eased himself around so that his legs hung off the table. "So far, so good," he said, more to himself than anyone else.

He slid off the table and stood. With a slight hesitation, he moved his arms and fingers, then turned his body. When pain didn't lance through him, he risked a little more movement, then a little more. He found that it was the bandages, not the pain, that limited his movement.

"How do you feel?" Faolan asked.

"Good." Flesh-colored bandages clung to Edward's body. As far as his torso went, it seemed he had more bandage than skin. "You could make a fortune off these, you know?"

There was a wave of tense laughter, and Edward

smiled despite himself. When satisfied he was in good shape, Faolan and Quinn joined the others at a large wardrobe against the wall. Edward watched them pull out armor plates made of a faintly greenish metal and affix them to their wrists, shoulders, and shins. Each had some kind of sigil or rune on them.

So, the tactical gear was the light stuff?

"I've got something for you," Dante said. He was dressed like the others; dark green military-style pants, black boots, and what Edward presumed was a bullet-proof vest. The outfit looked like the kind soldiers or SWAT teams wore, as opposed to the lighter police issue. He already had on his armor plates, and it was a very strange look—old world meets new. He also had a belt around his waist with two scabbards hanging from it, one on each hip. A third sword, much shorter than the other two, went across the back of the belt horizontally, and Edward could see a gold blade. There were knives on his wrists and calves, and one of the elfin submachine guns hung from his shoulder.

"That's some outfit," Edward said.

"About that. We can't have you going into battle half naked." Dante handed Edward a bundle of black cloth.

"What's this?" The fabric was light, like silk, but without the sheen.

"Open it and look."

Edward unfolded the bundle. He found a long-sleeved black shirt of the softest cotton he'd ever en-countered. He slipped it on over his head and found it fit him perfectly. It was so light that it hardly felt like wearing anything.

"There's more," Dante said.

Edward unfolded a long, black coat similar to a trench coat, but sans the lapels. It was also incredibly light and a black so flat it seemed to absorb light. As the fabric moved, symbols that were either painted or drawn on became visible. While the coat was dull, the symbols had a patina that was almost liquid in appearance. He couldn't help but smile as he slipped it on. Again, it fit perfectly and hung to midcalf.

"What do you think?" Dante asked.

"Amazing," Edward said. "Look the part, act the part?"

"Something like that."

"What's with all black? Aren't elves supposed to be light and all about greens and such?"

"Usually, but black is just so stylish." Dante laughed.

"So, what are these symbols?" Edward asked.

"They'll provide you protection and help you focus your magic," Dante said.

Edward picked up the subtle emphasis on the word *your*.

"They're called Asarlaí robes, used primarily by the high sidhe conjurers." Dante gave him a wry smile. "Wizards have been offering their first born to the fae in hopes of getting one for centuries. Normally, they don't look like that, but I thought a coat suited you better than literal robes."

Edward noticed for the first time that the buzzing in his head was gone. "I don't know what to say. 'Thank you' seems a little lacking."

"You earned it."

Edward didn't answer.

"You've proven yourself a friend, and you'll need it." Dante handed him another bundle of black, then motioned with his head to the room with the circle. "You might also want to change out of your scorched pants."

"Right," Edward said. "I appreciate it."

"Don't go getting sentimental on me. We don't just give those robes away—you have to earn one."

Faolan turned. "And you have."

There was a murmur of agreement amongst the others, and Dante joined the elves in checking each other's armor. With a sizeable boost to his confidence, Edward went into the other room to change.

When he was done, he stood there for a long moment, alone in the darkness. The effect of the coat was noticeable now. His mind felt focused and in control. All signs of fatigue, both mental and physical, had melted away.

Letting out a deep sigh, Edward considered the situation and everything that was at stake. He prepared as best he could, mostly just calming himself. As he reached for the door, a voice spoke to him from the darkness.

"I'm very proud of you."

Edward froze. The last time he'd heard that voice, it had been an attempt to fool him. Of course, it hadn't been aloud, and he hadn't been conscious.

"Believe in yourself, Edward," the voice said. "Know yourself and your own power."

Edward's mouth felt as if it were filled with cotton.

"Remember that magic is an expression of who you are. Understanding of yourself is needed to understand magic. It's part of being a *dewin*."

"Taid?"

Edward waited for several long seconds, his hand absently touching his Taid's bracelet, but no other sound came.

"No, that's not creepy at all."

"What isn't?" Dante asked.

"Jesus!"

"No, but people confuse us all the time," Dante said through a smile. "Sorry, didn't mean to scare you."

"I know cats that make more noise than you."

Dante's smile melted away.

"What is it?"

"The situation has changed," Dante said.

Edward sucked in a breath. "Caitlin?"

"No, it's not about her. Arlen got in touch with our informant."

"So this is about the crystal I saw?" Edward asked.

"Time is short, so listen closely."

Edward nodded.

"The oíche took Fiona to Fergus," Dante said. "Our informant couldn't tell us why, because the oíche have been tight lipped. What we do know is that in return for the girl, Fergus is giving the oíche a chance to be released from every fae court. The catch is they can't do it themselves. What you saw was, for lack of a better term, a vessel that holds their essence, bound into a Tír-ian crystal. If the wizard succeeds in destroying it, wherever it's destroyed becomes their new homeland. If it happens here, they're free. They could run loose over this world with impunity."

"Dear God," Edward said.

"My reaction was similar, if somewhat more colorful," Dante said.

"You're sure this informant wasn't lying?"

"Fae can't lie, not even to each other. The informant didn't even try to dance around the subject. He told Arlen everything almost before he could ask."

"Can we get to Brendan and Caitlin? They'll need our help," Edward said.

"There's no way to reach them now," Dante said. "The noon fae have been touchy about installing cell towers. Listen, this end of the fight has nothing to do with you, Caitlin, or Fiona anymore. If you want out, I'll understand."

"Can you stop the ritual without me?" Edward asked.

Dante hesitated. "I'm not sure."

"If you need me, I'm with you."

"Glad to hear it," Dante said and smiled.

"You know, you could've kept this from me, at least until after it was done. I'd have gone along and, all things considered, I would've understood."

"I considered that, but I decided to trust in you, again." Dante patted Edward's back, careful to avoid his burned shoulder, then stepped into the main room. "Don't worry, my friend. You're not going into this alone."

There was a chorus of agreement amongst the elves.

"So, where is this place?" Dante motioned to Quinn, who was working on a laptop. After a few moments, he found the building on, of all things, Google Maps.

"You sure that's the place?" Dante asked, looking at the screen in street view.

"Positive," Edward said.

"All right, Quinn, upload it to the GPS units," Dante said.

Quinn began hitting keys.

"Listen up, everyone," Dante said. "The horses will be here soon."

Edward quirked a smile, but after a moment of no one laughing, it disappeared.

Dante addressed the troops. "Quinn told you the situation. Be smart and be quick. The consequences of failure are higher than we expected, but we've known something like this was going to happen. Fergus won't give the oíche more than one chance. If we can disrupt the ritual, the vessel with their essence will return to Fergus and the oíche will be forced back into the Dusk Court." He looked from one face to another. "Is everyone ready?"

The elves put their fists to their hearts in what Edward presumed was a salute.

Dante turned to him and motioned to the door. "Now, if you'd be so kind as to let us out."

Edward focused his will. Power flowed through him as he reached out to the barrier he had raised. He felt the weaving of magic that it was built upon. It was crude, but effective. He pulled the magic apart and the barrier evaporated.

"Are the horses here?" Dante asked.

"Just waiting for our signal," Riley said.

"Good. Edward's with me in the lead, the rest of you take positions around us. I want one driving and the other keeping a look out at all times. Odds are good we'll get hit en route."

Before Edward could ask about how sharing a horse would work, Faolan and Quinn opened the door and ran up a short set of stairs. A moment later they shouted an all-clear, then Padraig and Daire went out next. Edward's heart pounded. Dante nodded at him, and Edward climbed the stairs as quickly as he could. Thankfully, his pain was almost nonexistent now.

When he reached street level, Edward looked around. The sun was long since set. The elfin Delta Force took up positions in a circle around Edward and Dante, weapons leveled in all directions.

Edward didn't see any horses. He was about to ask Dante about it when Faolan whistled.

There was the roar of several engines starting, then a shimmer in the street, and Edward found himself looking at five brand-new black Ford Mustangs.

A crooked smile crossed Edward's lips.

Each of the cars had two racing stripes running up the hood, over the roof, and down the back. The doors opened, and Dante urged Edward into the passenger seat of the lead car, then sprinted around to the other side and climbed in.

"Buckle up."

Edward had just started to reach for the seat belt when Dante put the accelerator to the floor. Edward was pushed back into his seat as the car sped off.

"You know," Edward said, after finally fastening the belt, "traffic through Boston at this time of night is going to be—"

"Don't worry. Traffic won't be an issue." Dante made a gesture and said something too quiet to make out.

The hood shimmered and the racing stripes now glowed with symbols Edward didn't recognize. Magic came off the stripes and surrounded the car. Looking behind him, Edward saw the other cars in close pursuit, all of them with the same glowing writing in the stripes.

Edward turned back around and flinched when he saw a car just ahead of them, right in their path. "Ah!"

The car moved to the side, allowing them all to pass.

"You okay?" Dante asked without looking over.

"Couldn't you have warned me first?"

Dante chuckled a little, glanced at the GPS unit mounted on the dash, and turned onto the interstate. There, like on the city street, cars just moved aside for them.

"Some kind of car glamour?" Edward asked. "I mean, Boston drivers don't even move over for cops."

Dante shrugged. "We live here. Don't you think we'd find a quick way to get around?"

Edward eased his death grip on the armrest. Despite knowing it was a bad idea, he glanced over at the speedometer. It was bouncing between 110 and 120. When a state trooper pulled aside and let them pass, he wondered if anyone had ever gone that fast through Boston, and if he could get one of these cars when this was done.

CHAPTER TWENTY-NINE

Edward watched, more exhilarated than scared, as they approached downtown. His excitement ended, however, as they crossed the Bunker Hill bridge. He heard automatic gunfire erupt from behind them. He ducked down and then looked back.

Faolan was standing up through a hatch in the roof of his car and was firing up at something that Edward couldn't see. As they entered the tunnel under the city, two of the enchanted Mustangs pulled up on either side of Faolan's car; Quinn was firing from one, Riley from the other. Edward struggled to see what they were shooting at when something black with wings came out of nowhere. Quinn and Riley turned their stream of fire on it.

"Banshees," Dante said. "Cover your ears." He swerved sharply, avoiding one that came right at the windshield. He rolled down his window and drew a pistol.

Edward put his hands to his ears and saw more of them encircling the group of cars. The banshees seemed to be coming out of the darkness itself. Somehow, the other cars on the road didn't react any differently. They just kept moving aside as the elves darted back and forth, dodging and firing.

Dante fired off several shots and took an exit. In moments, they were out of the tunnel and back on city streets. The GPS said they were closing on their destination.

Edward's heart felt as if it was going to explode when the air was torn apart by a high, shrill scream. His stomach dropped as a complete and devastating fear took hold of him, shutting down his brain. He vaguely heard windows breaking around him as he began to shake uncontrollably. He barely noticed that everyone kept firing as they tore down the streets and flew around corners with tires squealing.

"Hold on!" Dante threw the wheel to the left and the car slid sideways before coming to a stop.

Edward slammed against the inside of the door, shaking and still unable to move or think. The other cars slid to a stop around them, creating a circle of steel.

One of the banshees reached for Edward through the window, its hand passing through the glass as if it didn't exist.

He screamed as he saw the face of an old woman who'd been tortured for decades and dead for years. Her eyes were red, and the mouth stretched in a shriek, exposing twisted yellow teeth. On her back were incorporeal wings.

Dante fired his submachine gun. Edward pulled himself into a fetal ball, trying to squirm away as glass rained down on him. The bullets struck the banshee and her wings. Puffs of darkness burst from her wounds, and she fell to the ground.

"No, no, no!" Edward closed his eyes tight and pressed his hands harder to his ears, trying to block out the wailing. His heart pounded so hard he thought it might burst. "It's hopeless, all hopeless," he whispered.

Dante opened his door, rolled out, and began shooting.

Edward sat there, alone and terrified, until somewhere deep inside him, in a place the fear hadn't gotten to, something stirred. At first, it was anger, but he soon realized the anger was just at the surface. Deeper and stronger was love. It surprised Edward. He wasn't thinking of those who'd taken Fiona, but of Fiona and Caitlin themselves. It was a warmth that melted away the fear. The warmth was powerful and persistent, not like that flash of anger. And, unlike the anger, this calmed his mind and heart.

Edward opened his eyes, then his door, and stepped out. Everything was moving in slow motion. He noticed there was no sound at all, but maybe going deaf was for the best.

He watched the silent pandemonium around him with detached horror. A banshee came from behind Nollaig and lifted him from the ground. It twisted his head and tossed him through the air, where he vanished from sight.

Riley's gun clicked empty. He jumped onto the hood of his car and then through the air, toward the banshee that had taken Nollaig. In midleap, he drew his swords and cut. The banshee dropped like a stone, and Riley tucked into a ball, rolling as he hit the ground. He came to his feet with both swords ready, and in moments, oíche and small, stunted creatures with bright red stocking hats were on him.

Daire fired into another banshee that was coming straight at him. Her face erupted in bursts of darkness, but her speed carried too much momentum. She hit Daire and drove him over the hood of the car and into the asphalt, where they both slid for several feet, then neither moved.

Edward reached into the warmth that had now spread through his whole body and gathered it to him. He raised his hand and spoke softly. *"Aer!"* He heard nothing, but a blast of wind struck a banshee from above and drove her down until she hit a parked car, which crumpled. Clouds of darkness filled with tiny red lights exploded from the dozens of wounds where the car's bare steel had cut her. In seconds, the banshee vanished.

Dante was shouting at Edward. Faint sounds began to grow at the edge of his perception.

"Can you hear me?" Dante screamed.

The noise of the battle abruptly returned. "Yes," Edward said.

"We can't stay here," Dante said. "We have to get to the warehouse."

Edward saw the others closing in, trying to defend them. The other elves leapt over cars and evaporating banshee corpses. At the edge of his mind, Edward felt a slight buzzing. He tried to push it back. He was going too big. He had to keep his magic small and focused.

"Go, now!" Dante drew his swords, ran up and across a car, and leapt. In a move that any kung-fu star would envy, he spun in midair, cut through two banshees, and landed in a roll. He cut down an oíche as he sprang to his feet.

Edward drew up his courage and climbed over the car. There was a flash in the corner of his eye and the bark of gunfire. He dove for cover as several oíche began shooting at them. Everyone huddled on the far side of the car.

Padraig popped up and fired, dropping two oíche before his gun clicked empty. He replaced the magazine and turned to Dante. "We're getting overrun."

"Keep moving, and protect the wizard." Dante sprang to his feet and charged the oíche.

Faolan, Arlen, Quinn, and Sean moved between the cars as they fired, but soon they were pinned down. The elves circled around Edward as best they could, continuing to fire at the banshees and countless other dark creatures. Over and over, they emptied magazines, replaced them, and then emptied those, but more creatures kept coming. However, less and less return gunfire could be heard. Edward hoped that meant the oíche were running low on ammunition as well.

One oíche bounded over a car at them, no gun, but with teeth and claws bared.

Quinn drew and swung his swords at it.

The oíche twisted, barely missing the blade, and landed on the far side from Quinn. Then it came at Edward.

Edward focused his will on the hood of the car. "*Denu haearn!*" Magic leapt from him and the hood flipped open, hitting the oíche square in the face. It was knocked back into the roof and through the windshield. Edward could just hear the shrill, dying scream as light-tinged darkness seeped from around the edge of the bent hood.

Steel, use the steel! Steel has iron in it!

There was a pop and Quinn looked confused, then saw a growing golden spot on his chest. He touched it and tendrils of white light, filled with tiny blue motes, drifted away from a small hole in his vest. There were several more pops and Quinn jerked, then fell to the ground, revealing an oíche standing on another car's roof behind him. It had some kind of high-powered rifle leveled right at Edward.

He focused again. "*Denu haearn!*"

Again, the hood popped up. This time, there was a crashing sound, then the oíche tore the hood from its hinges and tossed it aside. Edward's stomach dropped as the oíche grinned, raising the middle finger of a gloved hand at him.

"Gloves? Are you kidding me?" Edward asked.

The oíche smiled as it took aim with the rifle.

In that moment of panic, Edward had an idea. He focused his attention. "*Tân.*"

For a brief moment, nothing happened. Then there was an earth-shattering boom as the fuel tank of the car ignited and exploded. The oíche flew through the air like a comet, and satisfaction coursed through Edward. Until, that is, other cars caught fire and began exploding, and flaming debris began raining down.

"Move, now!" Dante shouted.

The elves dodged falling wreckage and hurried Edward toward the warehouse at the end of the block. He stumbled as a large melted piece of, well, something, crashed into the ground, inches away. A firm hand grabbed his shoulder and yanked him several feet back.

Dante stared at him. "Don't do that again, please," he said in a calm tone.

Edward didn't have time to apologize. Dante pulled him to the ground just before a series of bullets hit the car.

"The steel is exposed on these," Faolan said. "Keep your distance."

Dante popped his head up and looked around. "We can't stay here. Get everyone inside!"

They made their way toward the front of the warehouse.

As they moved, Edward saw a couple more oíche leap over a car, each holding a chrome pistol pointed at him.

"*I mi!*" Magic surged from him.

The pistols leapt from the oíche's hands, and they watched with wide eyes and opened mouths as the pistols flew through the air to Edward.

They struck his chest, sending a wave of pain through him, and he fumbled not to drop them. "Here!" he shouted and held them out to Dante.

Dante took the offered weapons and, with a pistol in each hand, began firing at the oíche and their allies.

They reached the door, and the elves closed in around Edward. Oíche, goblins, pùcas, banshees, the red-capped things, and other dark creatures emerged from the shadows every time they turned. There wasn't an army of them, but they seemed to be everywhere.

"Get that door open," Dante said. "Now!"

"What I wouldn't give to have the Fian here." Sean began trying to kick the door down.

"They're regrouping. We can't hold this position, it's too open," Faolan said.

Sean continued to kick at the door, but it wasn't budging.

"Can't you shoot out the lock or something?" Edward asked.

"Only if we were in a movie," Dante said.

The elves around Edward were firing the last of their bullets. This was going to go hand-to-hand soon. There was a pulling feeling in his stomach, and Edward thought he was going to vomit. Someone was drawing a ton of power. Panic ran up his spine, but he closed his eyes tight. He couldn't be out of the fight, not yet. He still had a job to do.

They needed cover and time to get the door open. Edward looked around but didn't see anything useful. They were crouched in a semicircle, with only an awning above them. There were, of course, several flaming and smoking remnants of cars around them, but—

It was risky, but they didn't have much of a choice.

"Watch out." Edward drew as much power into him as he could manage. "*Tymestl!*"

When he let the magic loose, a small tornado rose up around them, flinging dirt, rocks, debris, and anything the size of, say, a prepubescent-sized dark faerie in all directions. Several oíche were blown off their feet and hurled through the air. They smashed into buildings, the ground, and anything else that got in their way, including their larger allies.

Edward focused as hard as he could against a pounding headache, trying to direct and channel the focal point of the spinning wind while the elves around him huddled down, shielding their eyes. The effort of holding the magic cyclone was actually starting to make his hands ache. Then, finally, a few cars began to tumble and roll down the street toward the elves. Several stacked around them in a haphazard shelter, their fires blown out by the wind.

The torrent died as Edward staggered and began to fall. Someone caught him and lowered him to the ground as the ice pick drove deeper into his temples. "I think I blew a fuse," Edward said.

"You still with us?" Dante asked.

Edward sucked in a breath and nodded. "I think it's starting."

"Sean?" Dante asked.

"It's a no go, the door is solid. We should've brought explosives."

Looking at the door, Edward was surprised it hadn't rusted off its—

He smiled. "Let me try something." He pushed himself up to his wobbly legs and focused his intent, ignoring the throbbing in his head.

"*Cyrydu.*" The door shook, and a crashing sound came from inside the building. He focused harder, and soon a dirty red color flooded over the hinges. In seconds, they crumbled to rust, and the door toppled over, falling into the street.

"Magister, go," Arlen said. "We'll hold them here. Get the wizard inside and stop it."

Dante shoved Edward toward the doorway as the world around him spun faster.

CHAPTER THIRTY

Edward managed to hold onto consciousness as Dante pulled him along.

"You're looking a little green," Dante said once they were well inside.

Edward put his hand to his head and took slow breaths. "I may have overdone it." He leaned against the wall as he wrestled with the pain. In the distance he could just hear the faint sounds of the battle. They were inside some kind of office area that had long been abandoned.

"Don't mean to rush you, but time is sort of pressing," Dante said.

Edward drew in another series of slow breaths. The buzzing sound in his ears faded, and the pain at last began to ease up. "I'm okay, let's go."

He followed Dante through the ruins of cubicles as the sounds outside faded.

"It's quiet," Dante said, looking around. "Too—"

"I really hate movie quotes."

Dante chuckled.

"And elves who laugh and make jokes in the face of death."

Edward matched Dante's steps as quietly as he could, which, compared to the elf, was like a herd of stampeding elephants wearing tap shoes. The farther they ran, the more severe the darkness grew. When they came to a door and Dante raised a finger to his lips, Edward could hardly see it, but he complied.

Dante put his ear to the door for about a week.

"I think it's clear on the other side," he finally whispered.

"You think? Is that supposed to fill me with confidence?"

Dante shrugged and eased open the door. As all doors in these situations are wont to do, it creaked at about a hundred decibels. Dante stepped through first and Edward followed.

On the other side, the darkness became complete. Even the little light that leaked in from the office area windows didn't reach here. The door creaked shut, and they were swallowed in blackness.

Since he was completely blind at this point, Edward stopped moving. He knew that the fear of darkness was just instinct and ancient in nature. It came from the time when animals that found humans quite tasty waited in the night. He also knew, practically speaking, that humans as a species weren't far removed from those times. Sure, he understood the psychology behind it. However, knowing his fears were purely evolutionary didn't remove the desire to wet his pants.

Once more, he thought of Caitlin and Fiona and reached deep inside to the warm and comforting feelings. He allowed it to wrap him in a cloak against the fear. His mind calmed, his breathing eased, and the pain from his injuries was pushed back to the periphery of his senses.

There weren't many options, so he focused. *"Tân."* Flame enveloped his hands, and light was cast in an impotent circle around him.

It did help, a little. After all, for nearly as long as bad things wanted to eat humans, humans knew fire could keep those things away. He couldn't help but wonder if any of those primordial fears were because of faeries.

With another exertion of will, careful to keep it under control, he pushed more power into the flames. They answered by growing brighter, and the circle of light around him grew.

"Well, so much for the element of surprise." Dante stepped into the light.

"I kind of thought the war raging on the curb took care of that."

"Fair enough, I suppose. Get behind me and watch the rear."

Edward turned and backed up until he felt Dante against him. He surveyed the area as best he could. The only sounds were their breathing and the crackling flames on Edward's hands. Slowly, Dante moved forward, and Edward matched him step for step.

"Look out!" Dante shouted and twisted to one side, bringing his sword up as he did.

Edward dove to the ground, and as he tumbled to his back, he saw an oíche leap into the light. The oíche barely avoided Dante's sword, but missed with her own. The oíche landed in a roll, sprang to her feet, and ran back into the darkness.

"I don't know about you," Dante said, "but I'm already sick of this game."

"Agreed," Edward said, getting to his feet. "At least they're not just shooting us, though."

"Great, give them ideas."

"You think that hasn't occurred to them?" Edward concentrated on his left hand, whispering a word of power. Fire swirled from his palm and gathered into a ball, which he hurled into the darkness. It exploded a moment later, lighting a large section of the massive room for a split second. It was devoid of anything except oíche, who had them surrounded.

Dante let out a sigh and shook his head. "Well, shit. Bet my stocks are down, too."

"Ever the eloquent Magister," a feminine voice said from the darkness.

"What can I say? I'm witty like that," Dante replied. "If you want to come here, we can trade banter."

"Can I get in on that?" Edward asked.

"Sure, why not?" Dante said. "That'll be fun, we can get everyone—"

"Shut up!" the voice shouted. "Just kill them both, it's almost done. Then we'll deal with the ones outside."

"If you've got a magical ace up your sleeve," Dante said, "this would be a good time."

Sweat began to run down Edward's face. He was running on empty, but at this point, what was the risk? They were going to die if he didn't do something.

"*Lluosi tân,*" he whispered. Flame engulfed his hands once more. Several small globes of fire lifted from the dancing flames and began circling Edward and Dante in a rapid orbit. He concentrated and tried to empower the globes like the wards, letting magic flow directly into the globes instead of through him.

He gave it a little nudge. "*Ymdeithio.*" A trace of magic drifted from him to the globes, which then began splitting, like a presentation on mitosis done in fire.

"That's not bad," Dante said.

Soon hundreds of little comets were circling them and spreading out, casting nearly the entire room in light. Though Edward wasn't feeding them magic, he was holding them in orbit, and even that small effort was causing him to struggle. He was just too weak. He'd used too much, too fast, and he could almost sense the oíche waiting for him to tire. He had to assume they were out of bullets. After all, they hadn't shot them.

"Well," Edward said through gritted teeth. "Are we going to spend all day here?"

In answer, several oíche dropped from the ceiling inside the circling wall of flame.

Dante went after the one nearest Edward. He spun, and his blade severed the oíche's arm.

That distracted the oíche long enough for Edward to smack his face with a flaming hand. The oíche gave a look of surprise before being consumed in fire. The faerie fell back, and both the oíche and the fire vanished in a cloud of darkness.

Dante had already turned on the others that had dropped when more figured out the trick.

Edward's hands were shaking now. "Get down."

Dante dropped to the floor.

Edward brought his hands together, and the circling wall followed his command. The spheres began launching themselves at right angles, streaking straight across the circle instead of orbiting it.

Oíche dove in all directions. Some were hit in midair by the flaming globes, which splashed like napalm and stuck. Others were hit by the spatter, and while it didn't consume them, it did stick, it did burn, and, going by the screams, it did hurt.

In moments, oíche were flailing with arms and legs ablaze, shrieking and trying to put out the fires. Some slapped at their faces, trying in vain to extinguish the flames. A few were truly determined and charged at Dante and Edward in spite of the fire.

Dante moved with the kind of grace and skill that would make a prima ballerina hang up her slippers. His silver blades glinted as he cut down oíche, avoided their attacks, and dodged the flaming orbs that were flying back and forth.

Edward, meanwhile, was doing his best not to pass out, trip, or be burned by his own fire again. He did get a lucky hit with his hand-fire on an oíche that had backed away from Dante, though.

As the last one close to him vanished in a cloud of darkness, Edward noticed the rest of the oíche were keeping their distance.

"They're stalling us, it's a distraction!" he said.

"Well, it's a good one." Dante dodged swipes and grunted in pain as a claw raked over his face. He scowled and, in a flash of steel, felled the oíche.

"We need to find the wizard," Edward said. "Time is running out."

"I'm open for suggestions."

The oíche were keeping them at arm's length, not risking a full-out mob attack but rather dragging out the fight. Edward needed to clear the oíche out of the way so he and Dante could make a break for it. He looked around for something to give him an idea, but it was just a large warehouse with occasional I beam columns. It was empty.

He looked back at the closest I beam. "I have an idea, but it's risky."

"Well, don't do it, then," Dante said. "We're much better off here."

Hoping that was sarcasm, Edward hurled the flame from his hands at one of the I beams. The fire stuck and began to heat the metal. He waited a few seconds and hoped that was enough to soften the beam. Then he extended his hand, scraped together the meager power he had left, and focused it.

"*Haearn!*"

Rivets tore from the I beam supports and shot across the room like bullets, striking the oíche. There was a series of surprised, pain-riddled shrieks from the darkness. This time, only the tiny lights could be seen, but it was still satisfying.

"Um, I'd run." Edward broke into a sprint for the far end of the warehouse.

Dante was right behind him, and then ahead of him as the building began to groan.

First one I beam collapsed, and a section of roof fell in. That stressed another I beam, and a chain reaction started. Dante and Edward ran, trying to keep ahead of the wave of destruction. The oíche fled, desperate to avoid the falling debris. When the collapsing stopped, both Edward and Dante turned around. There was a massive hole in the ceiling, and night sky shone through, moon and starlight illuminating the heap of broken and torn metal.

Edward let out a breath of relief.

The wretched sound of pained groans came from the pile of debris. It shifted and hands appeared, most trailing motes of light from dozens of wounds. The oíche began pulling themselves from the rubble, faces and bodies black and charred where the iron had burned them. They turned hate-filled eyes onto Edward and Dante.

"Go. Stop the wizard," Dante said. "I'll keep them off your back." He drew the gold sword from his belt and handed it to Edward.

Edward just looked at him.

"I said go!"

Edward took the sword, but he didn't know where to go. They'd reached the far end of the warehouse. He looked around and saw an elevated office at the corner. Letting down his guard for just a moment, he felt the pull of magic being drawn into it. He climbed the stairs as quickly as he could. When he reached the top, he was gasping for air, but he used his forward momentum to bash into the door with his good shoulder. Thankfully, it gave and flew inward.

He stumbled into the small room. All the furniture had been pushed clear of the center, where a huge circle was drawn in what he hoped was red paint. The metallic taste in the air told him it was probably blood. In the center of the circle was the crystal. On the opposite side of the circle from Edward, a man was getting to his feet. He had thick red dreadlocks that went to his shoulders. His skin was deep brown, and when he looked up, Edward could see that his eyes were two different colors, one blue and the other green.

"You're too late, wizard," Akhen said. "In moments, the ritual will be complete and the oíche will be free. I will have my payment, and this one will be mine." The voice was deep, but it had a strange tone, as if he were speaking while breathing in instead of out.

"*Tân!*" A pathetic ball of fire coughed from Edward's hand at the crystal. Pain lanced through his head, and he fell to his knees. The fire struck the circle's invisible barrier and fizzled into nothingness. Edward cursed his stupidity, swallowed down the rising pain, and slowly got to his feet.

Akhen laughed. "You'll hardly be worth the time it will take to kill you. *Tenebrae!*" Darkness swirled in the air and large black tentacles stretched out from it, reaching for Edward.

He dodged one and cut it down with the golden blade, which went through the tentacle and dropped it to the floor. Nothing but black goo remained. This minor victory, however, was short lived as the remaining tentacles reached for him. Moving first one way, then the other, Edward was able to avoid them. He slashed with the blade when he could, which wasn't often. Leaping out of the way didn't lend him many chances to strike back, and his strength was fading fast.

Akhen laughed, turned his attention back to the circle, and began chanting.

Inside the crystal, small orbs of light swirled faster and faster. It began to shake and melt away as if it was a candle.

Edward was drained, and even the coat wasn't helping anymore. To top it off, the ointment was wearing off, allowing his pain to grow a little more intense each time he twisted, leapt, or moved too fast. He was running out of time, and his options were limited. Not to mention the fact that dodging black tentacles didn't allow much time to think of an option. When the solution came to him, he wanted to kick himself for not doing it first. He waited, and when a tentacle shot forward to grab him, he spun and jumped toward the circle, blade extended to the crystal.

Pain so intense that everything went white ripped through his body as another tentacle, one he hadn't seen, grabbed him around the torso. It squeezed his burned and torn flesh in a viselike grip. He screamed as his muscles convulsed, torment shattering the last of the ointment's dulling effects. His vision began to fade from white to black, the iron grip on his stomach and chest mixing with the agony that kept him from drawing a breath.

"It looks as though I will have two wizards to dine upon this night," Akhen said.

It dawned on Edward at that moment that his clenching muscles had kept him from dropping the sword. Clawing through the pain, he tried to seize control of his failing body. He forced his vision to clear. The room was a shadowy haze and dimming fast, but the circle was only a foot away, the crystal another two feet from that. He had only one chance.

Ignoring the pain, he drove the blade into the tentacle gripping him.

The sword passed through without resistance and the tentacle fell apart, releasing him. Edward sucked in a breath as he fell but was unable to move his hand. He landed on the blade, and half its length sank into him. A gasp escaped his lips as he felt warm fluid begin to spread over his chest and down his stomach.

Using nothing but willpower, he drew the sword out of himself and got to his knees. Sucking one last breath, he launched himself at the crystal, sword extended. Dante had told him that a circle protected against magic, but a mortal crossing over it would shatter it. He could feel it as he passed the edge, a soft but tangible tension that gave easily, like leaping through plastic wrap. The protections collapsed and the magic rushed out and dissipated.

Distantly, Edward heard Akhen scream in fury.

"Take that," he said, or thought, he wasn't sure which, and renewed hurt tore at him as he swung the blade at the crystal. The end of the sword made contact, knocking the crystal hard to one side. It flew from the circle. He cringed when it smacked against the wall, but it didn't even crack.

Edward collapsed and struggled to draw in a breath that wouldn't come. His shirt was soaked with his blood, and it was getting worse, fast. The pounding of his heart was so loud it drowned out all the other sounds, and it was slowing. His head rolled to one side, and he saw the crystal restore itself, the melting reversing until it was whole once more. The lights moving inside the crystal slowed and dimmed.

"Insolent worm!" a new voice said from Akhen's

mouth. "I will not be denied what was promised me!" Akhen threw his head back, and black smoke poured from his open mouth. The body collapsed to the ground, and the smoke coalesced into a massive form that was only remotely humanoid. Two familiar, burning red orbs floated in the smoke and shadow, staring at Edward. One massive hand of darkness reached over and grabbed him.

The sword slipped from Edward's grip as torment ripped through him anew. He could only weep from the overwhelming torture, and pray for it to end soon. The last things he saw were dried and twisted vines growing up and over the crystal. There was a strong odor of damp earth as both the vines and the crystal vanished in a flash of black flame. It had worked. It was done.

There was only darkness and a sense of weightlessness as Edward was hurled through the air. Glass and metal smashed into his back and gave way as he fell through it. For a second, he found peace and comfort, but the tranquility shattered as his back hit concrete. His head bounced as he rolled across the floor, and somewhere distant, he felt something break.

Then all was quiet, except for his fading heartbeat and a ringing in his ears. The darkness reached out for him, but it didn't matter, not anymore. He didn't fight it this time.

It's okay. I didn't tell her how I feel, but she knows. No regrets.

He smiled as he thought of Caitlin at last knowing his true feelings for her. "I love you, Caitlin," he said, and allowed himself to sink into darkness.

"Edward!" Dante shouted, but his voice was very far away. "Hang in there, don't—"

All was silent and black.

CHAPTER THIRTY-ONE

After some time of struggling to follow Brendan down the trail, Caitlin realized the sun had never changed position in the sky. After noticing her trouble keeping up, Brendan shortened his long strides. That made it easier for her to keep pace, but she was still gasping for air.

"Here we are," Brendan said, pointing to the side of a hill several hundred feet away.

Caitlin sighed in relief. As they approached, she was able to make out exactly what Brendan had been pointing at. A door was set into a large boulder in the hillside. The rock looked like black granite, and the door was made of a wood that hadn't aged well. Spiderwebs clung to the corner of the doorframe, and the metal ring used for a handle was a copper that had tarnished to green. The wood itself was warped and split.

"Rest for a bit before we go in," Brendan said and sat down on a rock.

"Is it safe here?" Caitlin asked between breaths. "Isn't this Fergus's front door?"

"More like his front gate." Brendan took off the pack. "He wouldn't set foot in the noon lands without good cause. Queen Teagan herself would have to make an appearance then."

"She would?" Caitlin sat down on another rock and caught her breath.

"Aye, it's all about balance with fae." He handed the last apple and half-empty bag of trail mix to Caitlin. "You should eat. We won't have a chance once we're in the Dusk Lands." He took out the last two bottles of water and handed one to her.

They ate in silence, Caitlin her apple and trail mix, Brendan his beef jerky. She glanced at him as she drank her water. The change in his demeanor had been subtle at first, but it was obvious now. He was nervous, clearly, but deeper inside she could tell he'd resolved something. She just hoped she was wrong about what it was. She couldn't let him give up hope.

"I do have reasons for not telling you about meself," he said without looking at her.

"I'm sure. And it's none of my business."

"You've no doubt figured that I'm not just another mortal."

Caitlin could tell he was struggling with the words. "You don't owe me any explanations," she said, her eyes focused on the ground. "After all you've done, I've no business asking anything else of you."

"I'm just no use with people, you see?"

Caitlin felt her heart pound faster. She didn't want him to make a confession to her. If he did that, it would mean her suspicions were right and make his decision real.

"I wasn't cast out of the Fianna. It was an exile. I had to leave Ireland."

A pang struck her. "Brendan, you can tell me this later, when all this is done."

Brendan ignored her. "The fae were becoming more active in America, so I boarded a ship."

"What about your family?"

"Me ma died in childbirth."

The pain in his eyes was a familiar one.

"Me da," he said. "Well, he was killed a long time ago, when I was just a lad."

"Who raised you?"

"The other Fian," he said. "They took me in. But when I got older, they saw that me ma and da had done something to make me, well, different. Special, they thought." He sighed. "The Fianna didn't see it that way, so they sent me packing. Truth of it is, I don't know what I am."

His voice was calm, and he said it all so matter-of-factly that her heart twisted even more. She must not have masked her reaction as well as she'd hoped, because he forced a slight smile to his face before continuing.

"It's not so bad, yeah. I met up with Dante not long after I got to Boston. He's annoying, to be sure, but a good sort through and through." He chuckled, and a genuine smile came to his face. "He watched out for me like a brother."

Caitlin's heart ached for him, and she wanted nothing more than to hold him, to give him the comfort he clearly hadn't had for a very long time. Comfort he probably denied himself intentionally. She wanted to but knew she couldn't. He probably wouldn't let her.

"The reason I'm telling you this," he said, "is that things are like to get nasty in there. If it comes to it, getting Fiona out is all that matters."

Caitlin swallowed and fought back tears as she nodded, hating that he'd actually said it out loud.

"If I tell you to go, you need to grab her and get the hell out. Right then, no questions, no arguments, and no hesitation."

"But—"

"You can't be worrying about me, love. You need to get Fiona and use that seeking stone." He pointed at it. "Use it and don't look back. I'll do me best to give you a clear path."

"Brendan, I—"

"Damn it, Caitlin, would you just listen to what I'm saying for once? This isn't a fecking story. It's a lethal business we're getting into. I'm prepared to do what it takes, and you need to be as well. Your daughter is what matters. I can take care of meself."

The lump in her throat prevented her from saying anything. Up until now, she'd managed to put off thinking about what this might cost. She'd planned to deal with that cost, whatever it was, once she got Fiona back, but now—

"Look, love," Brendan said, his voice softer. "I'm

not eager for things to go *wojus,* but if they do, I need to know you'll get well clear. Aye?"

She didn't answer.

"Caitlin? Did you not hear me?"

"I heard you," she whispered.

"You got it, then?"

She took a deep breath and nodded once.

"Say it. You need to say it."

"I got it," she said, the hint of a sob leaking through.

"Good."

They sat in silence for several long, quiet moments.

Brendan stood up, put the empty bottle into the backpack, and pulled it on. "We need to get moving, then. We're almost done."

"Wait."

She threw her arms around him and held him tightly.

For a moment, he just stood there. She didn't care, she just held him: someone sure as hell should. At last, she felt his arms wrap around her and his chest move as he drew in a shuddering breath. A moment of peace, of comfort—that was the least she could give him.

As she expected, he pulled away first, and this time she let him. His eyes told her all she needed to know.

"Let's just get going," she said.

"Aye." He cleared his throat. "Keep your wits about you. There isn't going to be a welcome mat there waiting for us."

"I'm ready," Caitlin said. "Let's get Fiona back and go home."

Brendan pulled the door open. On the other side was impenetrable darkness. Brendan gave her a look over his shoulder, then stepped through and vanished into the black.

For that split second, she felt even more alone and more afraid than when he'd gone after the brownie. The idea of going through that door was terrifying, but leaving Fiona alone for one moment more was even scarier.

She made to step through when the images returned, clearer now, but very different. The onslaught sent her to her knees, her hands to her head. Whereas Caitlin had been an observer before, now she was the target of the torment. Beautiful and terrifying creatures danced around her, taunting and tormenting her. She could almost feel their disdainful touch as they brushed long, graceful fingers over her face.

"No!" Caitlin yelled.

The images more insistent, the creatures were laughing, and some leaned in with sharp teeth. As she felt them, or the chill ghosts of them, begin to devour her, Caitlin could feel someone watching her. When she looked up, not ten feet away stood the brownie. Only now, the brownie's child-like face was swollen and bruised. Pink blood seeped from a split lip. Red hairs were held tight in the brownie's shaking hand. The images stuttered, but persisted.

"I'm sorry," the brownie said as tears ran down her cheeks, glittering like tiny jewels. "They hurt me. They made me do it."

Caitlin's brain fought back the images and phantom sensations, clinging to a sudden realization: it was a loophole, one Brendan hadn't considered. The brownie couldn't give the hair to the oíche, and they couldn't take it from her, but they could beat the little faerie until she used it against Caitlin.

"Please," Caitlin said between gasps. "You can stop this." She had the sense of cold fingers reaching into her stomach, passing through her flesh like it wasn't there.

"I can't," the brownie said. "They made me promise. I'll go away if I break it."

Caitlin winced. "You mean you'll die."

The brownie nodded.

Caitlin struggled to keep her mind focused, but she was getting to her limit. She could feel her sanity slipping away. That's when she had an idea. It made her sick. Her very soul felt dirty, but she knew there was no other choice.

Caitlin swallowed the bile back. "If you let me see the hair, I can make it not work."

The brownie looked confused. "Magic?"

"That's right," Caitlin lied. "And it's a magic that the bad ones won't be able to sense, so they won't know."

Tears rolled down the brownie's cheeks. "They'll be mad. They'll hurt me more."

Caitlin forced sincerity into her words. "No, they won't. When they find out it doesn't work, they'll think Brendan or I did something. You won't be any use to them, and they'll let you go."

The brownie considered it for several long seconds. "You promise?"

Caitlin smiled, working hard to make it genteel and not insane. "I promise." She held out her hand. "Give me the hair."

The brownie smiled. "Thank you." She dropped the hair into Caitlin's hand.

The hair vanished in a flash of flame.

The images and sensations stopped instantly. It was nearly as jarring as when they'd started.

"No!" Convulsions started to wrack the brownie's tiny frame. "You lied."

"I'm sorry," Caitlin said through tears.

A blackness that reminded Caitlin of severe gangrene spread over the brownie's flesh, and she fell to the ground.

"Hurts, it hurts," the little faerie said between sobs.

Caitlin couldn't speak. She reached to take the child-like faerie into her arms. The brownie resisted, but Caitlin held her close, trying to offer comfort against the pain her lie had wrought.

After what seemed like an eternity, the faerie girl stopped moving and the little body vanished in a mist of gray filled with tiny yellow lights.

Once more, Caitlin was alone. She stared where the body had been and wiped tears away. "I'm sorry," she whispered. She took a deep breath, letting the grief and guilt turn to rage. Those dark bastards had put her in this situation. They'd set her up and used an innocent fae to attack her. Caitlin rose and turned to the still open door.

"I'm done fumbling about in the darkness."

Facing the blackness, Caitlin found she wasn't afraid of it anymore. She clenched her hands into fists and stepped through.

CHAPTER THIRTY-TWO

Strong hands seized Caitlin's shoulders and pulled her to one side. Instinctively, she lashed out with a fist, but whoever had grabbed her was too close to allow a decent swing.

"Easy, love," Brendan said in a hushed tone. "It's me." His eyes were bright and wide. "What took you so long? Are you all right?"

"I'm pretty far from all right," she said. "I'm ready to get Fiona and go home."

He didn't say anything; he just nodded and released his hold on her.

After a few slow breaths, Caitlin calmed the fury in her heart.

She looked around, and what she saw wasn't what she'd expected. Passing through the door, she'd naturally assumed the Dusk Lands were underground. Instead, it looked as though they'd stepped back through door the other way. The terrain was exactly as it was on the other side, except it was night and a large orange moon hung in a clear spot of an otherwise cloudy sky.

"Best not to speak unless you have to," Brendan whispered. "Keep your eyes open and your mind sharp."

When he looked at her, Caitlin felt completely transparent, but she pushed her turbulent emotions into her gut. Later, she reminded herself, deal with the costs later.

She followed him away from the door. As they walked, fear began to tickle the back of her neck. The whole place had a sense of foreboding. Though the terrain was the same as the noon lands, the same hills and even trees in the same places, this was clearly a dark place. Where the grass had been thick and green before, now it was dried and dead, crunching underfoot, with large patches of bare earth showing through.

The trees were perhaps the most frightening part. In the noon lands they'd been massive, full of leaves, with almost serene faces hidden in the bark. Here, they were barren and twisted, the placid faces replaced with sneers and scowls. It was as if someone had plucked the worst trees from every child's nightmares and planted them all here.

After a few minutes, they stood at the top of a hill, and Caitlin saw a thick forest ahead of them. Hundreds, thousands, of those dead, twisted trees were grouped close together. Branches swayed in the wind, threatening to grab anyone who came too close.

"We're not going in there, are we?" Caitlin asked in a whisper. She found herself overcome with a fear normally reserved for children on Halloween, visiting strange old houses or graveyards at midnight.

"Aye. It's the only way to get to Fergus's court, I'm afraid." Brendan put his hand on her shoulder. "I'll be right with you the whole way."

Caitlin hardened her resolve, focused on Fiona, and began walking forward. Brendan took up step beside her.

Fifty feet from the edge of the forest, Brendan put his arm out and stopped her. "Wait."

She didn't see anything, but she knew something was out there. It was the parking garage all over again.

Dread danced up her spine and her muscles tensed as an armored figure on horseback emerged from the shadows. It wasn't that the shadows had kept him hidden. He literally stepped out of the darkness like it was a pool of black water and he'd been waiting beneath its surface.

As the figure approached, Caitlin could see his armor was made of scales and had a sheen that continuously shifted from dark silver to deep blue to blackish purple and back again. His face was hidden beneath an ornate great helm. It was the kind knights would've worn centuries ago, and on his hip hung a long, thin-bladed sword. The horse was even more disturbing. It was all black except its hooves, which were gleaming silver, and blemished with flecks of what looked like dried blood. The eyes were glowing red, and smoke blew from its nostrils. It would've been less disturbing had the rider been headless, holding a jack-o'-lantern under one arm. Vague shadows seemed to move in Caitlin's peripheral vision.

"Ready yourself," Brendan whispered as the horseman approached. "I'm going to try and be diplomatic, but I'm not hopeful."

He stepped in front of Caitlin and raised his hands. The horseman stopped several feet away, drew his sword, and pointed the tip at Brendan. When the horseman spoke, it was with a deep, echoing voice in a language Caitlin couldn't understand but was somehow oddly familiar. Not quite Irish, not quite Welsh, but something in between.

Brendan said something in return and lowered his hands. With each spoken word, the next sounded more familiar to Caitlin, until, inexplicably, she could understand them perfectly.

"Yes, Fian, we do honor the old agreements, but you've no claim to that treaty. Your clan welcomes you no more, and so neither shall we." A strange accent tinged the horseman's voice, which was soaked with contempt.

"This one's daughter," Brendan said, motioning to Caitlin, "was taken by oíche-sidhe this evening past. We come only to retrieve her, nothing more. As a member of the Fianna, I demand that you stand aside."

"If you've a grievance with the oíche-sidhe, you should speak to the Rogue Court," the horseman answered. "His Dark Majesty will not see you. You are an outcast of the Fianna, and you've no claim to the treaties. Be gone from these lands, *dibeartach*. You are not welcome here. Your very presence is an insult to His Dark Highness."

Brendan drew in a slow breath before he spoke. "I wouldn't toss that word about so—"

"Silence, scum!" the rider said. "You have no standing to speak to me. I say again, be gone, *dibeartach*!"

Brendan drew in another slow breath and flexed his hands.

Caitlin could almost feel the heat of his anger radiating from him.

"I gave you fair warning, faerie," Brendan said, the last word clearly meant to insult. His hands went to his back and drew the knives.

"You have the impudence to claim the rights granted to those who cast you out, then dare to bring the bane into these lands?" The horseman's voice was full of rage. "His Dark Majesty shall hear of this offense! I will present him your head, *dibeartach*!"

The horseman drew back his sword, but before the blade began its return swing, Brendan howled and leapt at him. He crashed into the horseman, knives biting into the strange armor, and knocked the fae knight off his mount.

Brendan landed on top of him, but the armor didn't slow the knight. He brought his sword up and drove the pommel into Brendan's head. The big Irishman grunted and fell to one side.

The shadows that had been hovering at the edge

of Caitlin's vision surged forward and joined the fray. The shapes were obscure, and Caitlin wasn't sure how many of them there were, but they seized Brendan and pulled him away. The fallen horseman got to his feet.

Panic, followed by fury, rose in Caitlin, and her body acted on its own. She drew her knife and charged forward, sinking the blade into the closest shadow and then slashing out. Darkness and purple lights erupted from the wound, and a shrill howl filled the air as the creature released Brendan.

Brendan roared and spun, cutting through another shade holding him. Once free, he pounced on the knight again.

Caitlin hacked into the living shadow again, eliciting more shrieks of pain. What felt like a block of ice struck the side of her face and sent her reeling. She landed hard several feet away and looked up in time to see the deep purple, glowing eyes of the shade closing in.

She tried to roll and scramble away, but the creature moved fast. In moments, ethereal hands, so cold they burned, gripped Caitlin's neck and lifted her from the ground. The knife fell from her hand, and her throat began to freeze beneath the crushing grip.

She tried to pry the creature's hands loose, but they held tight. As blackness rose up to take her, she thought of Fiona, scared and alone. She gripped the freezing arms of solid darkness, swung her body forward, and planted her boots into the thing's chest. When it stumbled, she twisted and kicked at where a human's delicate floating ribs would be.

The kick didn't seem to hurt the shadow, but it did cause it to lose balance. Caitlin and the shade tumbled to the ground, and the frozen grip eased just enough for her to reach for the dropped knife.

Her fingers found the blade. Ignoring the pain of the keen edge cutting into her hand, Caitlin brought the handle up and, using it as a club, smashed it into the shadow's head.

The monster howled and released its hold on her.

Caitlin flipped the knife, caught the handle, and lunged forward. With her whole body weight behind her, she drove the blade into the creature's chest over and over until the thing evaporated amid a cloud of darkness and purple lights.

Gasping for air, Caitlin saw Brendan cut down a final shade then sidestep, barely avoiding the knight's thin sword.

"You fight well, *díbeartach*," the horseman said, "but your rage blinds you."

The armored warrior lunged and Brendan moved to block the blade with a knife. However, this was apparently what the knight intended. Before Brendan's knife connected, the horseman twisted his wrist, brought the sword up, and slashed across Brendan's chest.

"You make my point," the fae knight said.

Brendan didn't respond. He flung the knife in his left hand into the ground and took a ready stance.

The gleaming sword flashed in the moonlight. Brendan stepped to one side. The knight reversed his turn and drove an elbow toward Brendan's face. At the same time, he brought his sword around to drive it into Brendan's stomach.

At the last moment, Brendan twisted and drove his knife into the armored warrior's elbow. His free hand seized the blade of the sword; carefully holding the flat of it tight between fingertips and palm, he spun in place. Using the sword as a fulcrum, he hurled the knight through the air. He landed with a sound akin to a car wreck.

Brendan leapt and landed on the prone fae. He drove his knife into the horseman over and over again, striking so fast that the knife was only a silver blur.

An echoing shriek filled the air as darkness and swirling blue lights escaped from the holes in the armor, the seams in the scales, and the eye slits in the helm. The horse bolted away with a whinny, and in moments, there was nothing but silence and stillness. Then came a clatter as the rider's suit of armor collapsed and fell into its individual pieces.

Brendan lifted his hands, threw back his head, and roared into the night.

Caitlin faltered and, without realizing, stepped away from him. Then, all she could hear was Brendan's labored breathing as he straddled the empty armor.

"Brendan?" she whispered, as she forced herself to stop retreating.

His shoulders rose and fell as he took quick, deep breaths, the muscles in his back and arms contracting in spasms.

Caitlin approached, slowly, and reached out with a

shaking hand. As she touched his shoulder, he flinched and looked at her over his shoulder, teeth bared.

She gasped and took a step back when she saw the look in his eyes. Some of the fire she'd seen earlier had gotten loose.

He blinked at her, then closed his eyes, took another deep breath, and shuddered once. When he opened his eyes, they were the eyes she knew, the fire restrained once more.

"I'm sorry, love," he said. He got to his feet and retrieved his knife from the ground. He sheathed them both before turning to her, eyes cast down. "We need to go. There'll be others coming soon, and they'll be none too pleased about this." He extended his hand to her and took a step forward.

She didn't take it. In fact, she took a step back.

"I didn't mean to scare you," he said. "I'm the same man I was before. There's an explanation for this, but now is not the time." He took another step forward. "You've trusted me this far, you need to still."

Caitlin didn't back away this time, but she still didn't take his hand.

"Please." His voice was shaky. "We've got to get out of here."

She looked at him, at the pleading in his eyes, and thought of everything Brendan had done up to now. She extended her hand and took his.

Together they ran into the dark forest. Brendan led the way down a path of worn marble tiles. They looked centuries old, pushed apart by earth and the dead grass that partially covered them. Most were broken, and all of them were uneven.

Caitlin tried to keep up, but between the pace and the uneven ground, it was too much. Soon, she was gasping for air as her legs and lungs began to burn.

When he saw her, Brendan stopped.

"I'm sorry," she said between gasps. "I can't run anymore. I just can't."

Brendan pointed to a tight group of trees just off the trail. "Come on." He half led, half dragged her behind the cover of the thicket. There, they found a small hollow where the roots had eroded the ground.

Brendan sat Caitlin down and pulled off the pack. He took out the remaining half-empty bottle of water and handed it to her as his eyes darted around. He pulled out a roll of gauze, then wrapped his cut hand and Caitlin's.

She took several gulps of the water and tried to catch her breath. Brendan's face was pale, and when he took a deep breath, he winced. She'd forgotten about his ribs.

"Get your breath back," he said. "We can't stay here long. We're out of sight, but in this forest, the trees keep no secrets."

"Are you okay?"

He followed her gaze down and saw that his bandaged hand now held his side. He dropped his hand. "I'll be fine."

Caitlin had to believe him. He knew what he could do better than she did, but she had her doubts. Besides, he was clearly struggling with something.

"What happened back there?"

He didn't answer.

"You didn't seem, well, yourself."

He stared at the ground. "Sorry if I scared you. I've got this—" He drew a breath. "This beast inside me."

"What's that mean?"

"It's a—" He looked around as if the word he wanted was hanging in the air. "A frenzy, a battle frenzy that takes me. The *deamhan buile*, it's called."

"No. You just got angry because of what he called you. I understand, I got mad—"

"There's more to it. Me parents did something to me. I don't know what. It made me faster and stronger, but it weren't free."

Caitlin fought back tendrils of fear nibbling at her stomach.

"I'd hoped it wouldn't be an issue. But now that Fergus himself is involved, you need to understand—"

"You're a good man," she said. Whether it was for him or for her, she couldn't say.

"Listen, the *buile* is something you should well be afraid of." He was looking right at her now, his gaze hard. "It's the embodiment of rage. I'm no longer meself. I'm blinded by it, and I can't control it." He swallowed. "That's why I told you that, if I tell you to run, you must."

Caitlin saw the pain and the fear in his eyes. It left her dumbfounded. "No, no one who's done what you have—"

"Damn it, would you listen? I can't have another—" He looked away.

"Another?" Then it all started to make sense.

She should've seen it before. How could she have missed it? It might have been her he was looking at, but she wasn't who he was seeing.

She lifted Brendan's face and forced him to look at her. As plainly as words on a page, she could read him and knew that she was right.

"What was her name?" she asked.

"Áine." His eyes were wet with tears, and he shuddered.

"Like the Irish goddess of love?"

Brendan smiled and sighed. "Aye. She was every bit the name, as well. Loveliest thing I ever saw, and tough as steel."

"From a man who spends so much time around faeries, that's quite a compliment." Caitlin swallowed. "Brendan, you don't have to tell me anything you don't want—"

"Dante's the only person what knows it all." Stray tears spilled out of his eyes and ran down his cheeks. Absently, he wiped them away.

Caitlin listened.

"One night, she was late meeting me, so I went to look for her. I found her, and the oíche that were set upon her."

Caitlin squeezed his hand and wiped an errant tear of her own away.

"I lost me head, and the *buile* took me, right there in the alley. I didn't know what was what, or who was who. I knew only rage. When it was done, I'd cut the dark *bastúin* down, all of them. But I'd done in a dozen innocents, and her as well. I killed them all with me own hands. It weren't till well after that I learned she was—" He swallowed, unable to finish.

"Brendan, you can't blame yourself—"

"It was me own fault, wasn't it? I shouldn't have let the beast out. I should've controlled it. I knew it was there. I'd used it before in little ways. When I saw what they was doing to her, well, that was all it needed to take control."

"You didn't mean to."

"Aye, but me intentions don't change things, do they? She's still in the ground, just the same." He let out a breath. "I'm sorry to be dumping this on you now, love."

He stared right into Caitlin's eyes, and it sent a shiver through her.

"You understand now?" he asked. "I'll not have the same happen to you or, God forbid, Fiona."

Caitlin saw it in his eyes. He was pleading with her. "I understand." She wiped some tears away. "Thank you."

"*Dar fia*, would you stop thanking me? I'm not a fecking saint. I'm about as far from it as you can get."

"You're not a saint," she said, then silently added, *You're much more than that.* "I just meant thank you for trusting me enough to tell me."

"Well, I had to, didn't I?"

"No, you didn't."

He leaned back against a tree. "I admit, it's nice to tell someone else about her." He smiled, but it was bittersweet. "She deserved to have others know about her. She was so kind. More full of love than any dozen others put together. And she was bloody well more than I deserved. I was lucky to have her in me life, even if only for a bit. Lord knows, she could've done better than me."

"Don't."

He looked at her again and Caitlin felt that same shiver run down her spine, but this time her heart beat a little faster as well. The last piece fell into place.

I remind him of her.

Caitlin closed her eyes. She truly understood the massive weight and torment he'd been carrying this whole time. She felt ashamed for how she'd been acting, so weak and small.

"We should get moving." He wiped his eyes. "We've been here too long as is. I'll try to keep a better pace for you." He offered her his hand.

She took it and he pulled her up. She could still feel the anguish, the guilt, and the dark clouds that loomed over him. "You can let it go," she said. "You can let it go without letting her go. She'd want you to hold onto the joy and happiness you shared, not the darkness . . ." Brendan drew a deep breath, and when he let it out, it seemed perhaps he stood a bit taller, carried less of a load. He smiled and nodded, just once.

Nothing else needed saying. He led the way back to the trail, and she followed.

They continued moving at a brisk, but much easier, pace through the woods. When she looked around at the barren trees, Caitlin noticed they didn't seem so intimidating anymore.

CHAPTER THIRTY-THREE

The winding path continued through the woods, and the utter silence bore down on Caitlin. Aside from their footsteps on the tiles, there was no sound at all. There were no birds, no rustling leaves, no insects buzzing, nothing. Woods were supposed to be full of life. These were devoid of it.

Brendan stopped and crouched down low.

Caitlin knelt behind him, hand going to her knife. "What is it?" she whispered.

Brendan sat perfectly still, scanning the area and sniffing the air.

Agonizing seconds ticked by.

"*Dia ár réiteach!*" he said and stood up. He yanked off his pack and tossed it into the woods. "He's done loosed the hounds of hell."

A loud horn sounded from behind them, shattering

the silence, and from ahead came a scurrying sound followed by barks and growls.

"Stay behind me," he said. "Get your knife out. I'll try to keep them off you, but one might get past me. Be ready."

Caitlin drew her blade.

Brendan unsheathed his knives and spun them so he was holding them in a reverse grip.

Caitlin's stomach tried to mimic the move.

"Don't hesitate," Brendan said. "Trust your instincts and think about Fiona." He looked over his shoulder at her, and this time his eyes brought her comfort instead of fear.

Two large black dogs came running down the trail. They looked like mastiffs, but their fur was as black as pitch and, like the horse before, they had smoldering red eyes.

The hounds stopped a dozen or so paces in front of Brendan. He put one foot back and gave a rumbling growl. The hounds bared their teeth, which were the color of slate, lowered their heads, and growled back.

The three stood there, staring each other down. Then, at the same moment, they leapt at each other. Brendan slashed one across the muzzle. The other avoided his blade and sank its teeth into his wrist, and the three fell to the ground.

Brendan drove a knife into the flank of the hound that gripped his arm. Darkness and orange lights seeped from around the blade. The hound let out a whimper and released him. The other licked its muzzle, and the seeping darkness from Brendan's slash stopped.

Caitlin watched, frozen. Her heart was pounding so hard that it felt like it could break her ribs. Somehow, these hounds' similarity to real dogs caused her more fear than the unreal shadow things from before. As if sensing her fear, one turned its gaze on her and bared its teeth.

She felt like a child, but she gripped the knife tighter in her white knuckled hand and thought about her lost child.

The hound looked at the blade, then at her. It was almost as if the dog knew what it was.

"No!" Brendan shouted and pounced on the beast.

The dog moved just in time. Brendan's blade missed, but his arm went around its neck. The other hound, now free, went after him again, and the three tumbled and rolled. Brendan kicked repeatedly at the one tearing at his boot before landing a blow to its head. The hound released him with a yelp as it was knocked several feet away. Brendan twisted and hurled the other into the woods. There was a thump as it struck a tree, followed by a whimper. Brendan was quick to his feet, as were the hounds. When he faced the one he'd kicked, the other leapt from the trees to stand behind him.

Slowly, they began circling him.

Every time one of them looked at Caitlin, Brendan lunged at it and slashed in the air, drawing its attention back to him.

Caitlin wanted to help, but she struggled to figure out how.

In concert, the two hounds attacked again.

Brendan met the first with the handle of one knife and swiped at the other with the blade of his second.

The hound at his front had faked. Brendan's knife passed through empty air, which allowed the hound to dart past him, heading straight for Caitlin. She gasped and jumped back. Her footing slipped and she nearly fell, thrusting out wildly with the knife.

It bit into flesh. There was a yelp, and the blade was wrenched from her hand.

She caught her balance and saw the hound eyeing her warily. The handle of her knife stuck out from its front shoulder, and the thing paced on its remaining three good legs, watching her. It lowered its head, pulled back its lips to expose sharp gray teeth, and growled, low and deep.

She took a breath to stifle her terror and stared at the blade. Wisps of darkness drifted from the wound each time the monster moved. She knew she had to get her weapon back.

The beast barked and lunged at her, snapping its powerful jaws.

She flinched and jumped back.

It repeated this maneuver several times, never closing, just driving her back, almost as if it were taunting her.

Caitlin just kept looking from the hound to the knife, waiting for a chance.

When next it lunged, she went forward instead of back, throwing herself past it. As she dove, less gracefully than intended, she reached out for the handle.

Her hand touched the carved wood and she grabbed it, holding on for all she could. The blade tore free, and the dog yelped as Caitlin hit the ground. The world turned as she tumbled, but she came up short when she smacked into a tree.

She rolled to her back and watched with wide eyes as the beast sprang at her throat with open jaws. She screamed and closed her eyes while gripping the knife in both hands and driving it forward. She felt an impact and heard a yelp of pain, then weight bore down on her arms so fast it threatened to break them.

She opened her eyes and was face-to-face with snapping jaws. The knife was buried in the creature's massive chest, and it was pushing hard against her. She grunted and pushed back with all the strength she could find.

Drool sprayed her face as the hound barked and snapped, struggling to get at the tender flesh of her neck, but its claws couldn't find purchase on the tiles. She pushed back against it, keeping it at bay. Her arms were burning and her strength was failing. She gritted her teeth, turned her face away, and twisted the knife hard to one side.

The hound let out a pathetic yelp and twitched.

A deep satisfaction filled her, and she twisted the knife back the other way. Again the beast convulsed and cried out. Finally, she felt the strength of the thing begin to fade. Anger mixed with the pleasure in her, and she twisted again and again. Each turn of the blade elicited another yelp.

"Would you die already?" she said through gnashed teeth. Her arms felt like they were going to come off, and her hands were shaking. She couldn't hold it much longer.

At that moment, the hound snapped its jaws one last time, let out a breath, and went limp. Its full weight came down on her as its legs gave out.

She blinked a few times, and the hound evaporated into a cloud of darkness and orange lights. Her arms dropped to the ground, and the fire in them at last began to subside. She gasped for breath, but a groan made her look up.

Brendan was grappling with the remaining hellhound. Caitlin rolled to her knees, got to her feet, and moved toward him, but he shook his head and she stopped. The hound twisted in his grasp, and all Caitlin could think of was Hercules wrestling the lion.

The muscles in his big arms flexed as he tightened his grip around the hound's neck, grabbed its maw, and pulled it back. The other hand dragged the knife across the now bared throat, and, in seconds, there was nothing left.

Caitlin ran over to Brendan and helped him stand. As he got to his feet, he sucked in a breath and gripped his side.

"Are you okay?" She could see scratches on his face, neck, and arms.

"Aye, I'm all right. Just smarts a bit, is all. And you?"

"I'm okay." The burning in her arms was fading, the adrenaline rush wasn't. "Let me look at your injuries."

"Don't bother." He sheathed his knives. "They aren't nothing serious." He used his shirt to wipe some of the blood from his face. "Besides, we don't have time. The hunt will be here soon."

"I'm sorry, did you say the hunt?"

"Aye."

"As in, the wild hunt?"

He nodded.

"I thought Fionn Mac Cumhaill was the leader of the hunt and that they chased only—"

"Afraid that's not quite right. Fionn and the Fianna defeated the hunt," he said. "As such, the hunt had to obey his command. He didn't lead them. He banished them back here. They're a nasty bunch, and they hold a grudge."

"Against the Fian—"

"Look out!" Brendan shoved her to the ground as an arrow zipped through the air and struck Brendan's shoulder.

They both tumbled and rolled as they hit the ground. When they finally stopped, Caitlin saw the arrow shaft had broken in half. "Are you—?"

"It's too late now," he said. Anger burned in his eyes. He tore the broken arrow shaft from his shoulder without so much as blinking and tossed it aside. He walked back to the middle of the trail, drew his knives, and again spun them into a reverse grip. "They're here."

Another horn sounded, this time so close Caitlin felt it reverberate through her. When it stopped, the air filled with the shouts and cheers of countless wild men.

She stood behind Brendan, and over his shoulder she saw a massive throng emerge from the shadows and haze. At the lead was a man over seven feet tall. His chest was bare, except for blue painted whirls and knots. He wore a wide leather belt and a blue battle skirt. A large helmet covered his face, but it allowed long blond hair to hang over his shoulders. Growing out of the sides of the helmet were antlers that should have belonged to a massive stag. The Hunt Master was flanked by two hounds identical to the ones they'd just dispatched. Behind him were warriors adorned in furs and animal hides, all carrying spears, swords, clubs, or other wicked-looking weapons. All of them were screaming and shouting.

The Hunt Master stepped forward. His left arm held a shield, and in his right hand was a spear. He raised his shielded hand, and the horde was silent.

Caitlin could feel him taking the measure of her and Brendan.

"Greetings, Fian." The Hunt Master inclined his head in a slight bow. "Lord Fergus told us prey could be found in these woods." His voice was deep, but clear, despite the helmet. "He did not say, however, that we would have our retribution this night."

Cheers and shouts erupted from the pack of warriors.

"Nothing for you here, Cernunnos," Brendan said. "Take your hunt and go back the way you came. Our quarrel is not with you."

"Your mate smells sweet," Cernunnos said.

Caitlin felt a chill run through her as the hunt began laughing and hooting. She could feel their eyes violating her.

"I've been promised flesh this night, Fian," Cernunnos continued. "If you stand aside, our quarrel with you can wait for another day."

Caitlin clenched her jaw, and images of Fiona filled her mind. Fury burned inside her and melted away the chill. She was tired of being afraid, tired of cowering, and, most of all, tired of obstacles keeping her from Fiona. She gripped the knife and took a step forward.

"Fergus has my daughter!" she said. "And so help me, if I have to, I'll cross through hell and back to get her."

"Well then, my lady," Cernunnos said, "you've achieved half your goal. You see, we are the hordes of hell."

Laughter and cheers erupted from the hunt once more.

"That's the Celtic fire in you talking now, love," Brendan said to her. "Stoke it."

Caitlin could hear the pride in his voice.

"Cernunnos, you've got yourself a problem, mate," Brendan said.

"And that would be?"

"You thought Fionn and the Fianna were a bad dose?" he asked, a chuckle escaping with the words. "You just stepped between a daughter of Erin and her child."

There was a moment of confused silence. Then

Brendan let out a battle cry and sprang forward, clearing more than twenty feet to tackle Cernunnos. Without losing a beat, he rolled and drove a knife into one of the hounds. The other went for Caitlin as battle cries erupted.

Caitlin watched the hound close on her, and she found herself focused, her breathing steady. When the hound leapt, she stepped aside and drove her knife down as hard as she could. The blade sank into the dog's back and drove it to the ground with a whimper.

Blind rage boiled over and she stabbed into the beast, over and over and over again. Soon, she couldn't even see her hand in the cloud of darkness.

Then the knife sank into earth.

As the cloud of lights drifted away, she turned on the hunt and Cernunnos. Cernunnos got to his feet and looked to his hounds, only to find they'd both faded into nothingness. He cursed and thrust his spear at Brendan, who twisted, ducking beneath the thrust, and slashed with his knives. Cernunnos blocked one with his shield, but the other cut across his stomach. He swiped out with the spear, and it slashed across Brendan's chest. His shirt tore, and blood escaped from the wound. Knocking the spear aside, Brendan tumbled backwards and came to his feet in a ready stance.

The hunt charged forward.

Caitlin's heart skipped a beat as she watched the stampeding tide of nightmares. Three screaming warriors broke from the group attacking Brendan and came at her.

She walked backwards, struggling to find the focus and confidence from moments before. Her heel caught an uneven tile and she fell onto her backside. The first of the three smiled as he charged at her and drove the gleaming point of his spear down at her chest.

Caitlin swung desperately with her knife.

It connected with the haft, managing to drive the spear up and away from her chest. The tip cut across her cheek before driving into the ground beside her head.

The warrior drew the spear back, readying another thrust.

In that moment, instinct took over, and Caitlin screamed in rage. She kicked with all her strength, driving her heel into the warrior's knee.

There was a wet popping sound, the man's leg buckled, and he dropped his spear as he bellowed and began to fall. Pivoting, Caitlin drove her foot into his throat. The hunter's cry died in a gasp, and his eyes went wide. He gripped his neck and landed hard on his back.

Caitlin scrambled for her knife and drove it into the warrior's diaphragm, or rather, where a mortal's diaphragm would be, and up. The blade pierced the furs and sank into tender flesh. Then the tip bit into the earth on the other side of the warrior. He vanished in a puff of darkness.

Yanking the blade from the ground, Caitlin stared hard at the other two hunters.

They stopped, looked at each other, then back to her. Both smiled and took a step forward.

"I challenge!" Brendan screamed, and everything stopped.

Caitlin blinked as the two warriors abruptly lowered their weapons, turned, and rejoined their group. She took a hesitant step forward as the remaining hunt stepped back, opening up a circle around Brendan. At one end of the circle, Cernunnos struck the ground with the butt of his spear.

"So, a score gets settled this night after all," Cernunnos said. "Long overdue is this battle, Fian."

"If it's a settling of scores you're wanting, come and take it," Brendan answered. He spun his blades and smiled. "If you can."

In the blink of an eye, they were on each other. Like the hunt, she couldn't help but watch. It wasn't wild, brutal fighting. These were two masters of their art, fierce but graceful, purposeful and somehow elegant.

There were flashes of steel as knives and spear slashed out. The two combatants twisted and turned, barely avoiding each other's attacks. Even Caitlin could tell they were well matched, but then, Cernunnos wasn't injured.

The spear swept out in a wide arc at Brendan's legs, and he leapt over it. Cernunnos came around with his shield. It slammed hard into Brendan's chest, the blow knocking him onto his back and sending the knives from his hands.

Continuing his turn, Cernunnos drove the spear down, but Brendan rolled to one side and dodged. As

Cernunnos went to draw it back, Brendan grabbed the haft and held it.

"You're weakening, Fian." Cernunnos tried to pull the spear back. "This fight is mine, and soon, so shall be your ma—"

Brendan grabbed the shaft with his other hand and leaned back. This drove the tip into the ground, and he heaved it up. The haft caught Cernunnos under his arm, lifted him clear of the ground, and hurled him over Brendan.

Cernunnos crashed face-first into the ground.

Before Cernunnos could recover, Brendan was on his back, knee pressed into his spine and the spear tip pressed against his neck.

"It's done," Brendan said between labored breaths. "You've lost. I said our quarrel wasn't with you or your hunt."

The mass of warriors had gone still, as had Caitlin.

"What she said was true," Brendan said. "We're getting her child back, and for that we're after the man himself."

Caitlin held her breath and watched.

"You're noon fae," Brendan said. "You must answer a summons from either court, but you alone amongst the fae can choose to ignore it. Go, and leave us to our business." He pressed the tip into Cernunnos's neck a little more. "Or stay. Your choice, Cernunnos."

Everything was still for several long seconds. Finally, Cernunnos tapped his hand to the ground. The hunt, and Caitlin, let out a collective breath.

Brendan stood, and when Cernunnos rolled onto his back, Brendan offered his hand.

Cernunnos took it, and Brendan hauled him to his feet. They stared at each other then, and Brendan handed him his spear.

"You fight like Fionn himself," Cernunnos said. He said something to the hunt in a guttural tongue. In response, a horn sounded again with several short calls. The mob began to disperse the way they'd come, disappearing into the mists and shadows.

Brendan picked up his knives, but he never took his eyes from his opponent.

"Farewell, Fian," Cernunnos said to Brendan, then bowed to Caitlin. "Milady." He turned and walked away, but after a few steps, he looked over his shoulder. "We are not the last you will face this night. You know well, a third challenge awaits you. I for one wish you success so that one day we might battle once more."

With that, mists blew in, masking Cernunnos and the remaining hunters from view. When the fog passed, the hunt was gone.

Brendan dropped his knives, and he fell to his knees.

"Brendan!" Caitlin rushed to his side.

"The bastard caught me ribs with that fecking shield," he said between short gasps. "Just give me a minute."

Caitlin helped him to his feet.

Slowly, he straightened and drew some breaths. Before each got too deep though, he winced and exhaled.

He forced a pained smile. "Don't worry, love. I

thought this might happen." He pulled the necklace out from his shirt and lifted the wood carving to his lips. He kissed it and whispered something. A tingle went through her as the wood crumbled into dust. Brendan straightened and took several long, deep breaths.

"What was that?"

"Painkillers, of a sort. I'll be all right. I've had worse, to be sure."

Even though she could still see a slight wince when he drew a breath in too deeply, she didn't say anything.

"What about you?" he asked. "Are you all right?" He looked her over for a moment, then smiled wide. "That was bleeding deadly, that was."

She smiled. "I got lucky. I know what bones break most often and easily."

He turned her head and saw the cut. Wiping the trail of blood from her cheek, he looked at her. "Got a piece of you I see, but not too bad, I think."

"I'll be okay." Her eyes went wide as she realized what had just happened and the rush began to subside.

Brendan laughed. "You did fine. Luck can be as important as skill."

She closed her eyes and started laughing, too. "I can't believe I did that." As she put her hands to her face, she looked down. Brendan's shirt was torn in several places, and it was soaked with blood. Her laughter stopped.

Brendan looked down. "Ah, hell, I really liked this one." He sighed and pulled the shirt off. His chest was covered in fresh cuts and bruises. The arrow had struck the shoulder with the elfin bandage, and the bandage seemed to have closed over the wound after he pulled the arrow out.

"Let me look," she said.

He didn't fight her.

Most of the wounds were superficial, and only a couple of the cuts were still bleeding. There was, however, a nasty bruise over his ribs. When she touched it, he drew in a breath.

"Easy there, love. The pain is just lessened, not gone, and it didn't do nothing for the injury, I'm afraid."

"Sorry," she said, then continued her exam. Taking what was left of his shirt, she wiped blood away. "Are you sure you're going to be all right?"

"And if I'm not? What, we just turn around and head to the doctor?" He shook his head. "No. I'm not a hundred percent, but I'm not done in either."

She swallowed and looked him in the eye. After a moment of him staring back, she handed him the shirt.

He wiped the last of the blood away, then pulled a lighter from the pouch on his belt and set his bloodied shirt aflame. "I'll not be leaving me blood laying about here."

Caitlin swallowed and felt a twinge in her stomach as she thought of hair vanishing in fire and a brownie falling dead. Soon there was nothing left of the shirt but a small pile of ash. Standing there, shirtless, tattooed, and kilted, Brendan looked every bit the Celtic warrior of legend come to life. Caitlin found it more than a little inspiring.

"That was powerful fighting. You stood against them despite the dangers to yourself. You found the warrior inside you," Brendan said.

"I'm not—"

"Courage and the willingness to stand for those who can't, that's what makes a warrior."

Caitlin picked up the knife and smiled at the approval she saw in his eyes, but a sudden thought interrupted the moment.

"What did Cernunnos mean when he said another challenge?"

"Threes, everything is about threes. We faced Fergus's guard, then the wild hunt."

Caitlin opened her mouth, but Brendan continued before she could speak.

"The first two hounds were part of the hunt, as well. We've still got one more to deal with before we can get to the man himself."

Caitlin drew in a breath. "I'm ready. And for the first time I can remember, I really mean it."

"Let's get to the end of this, then, aye?"

Caitlin nodded.

Brendan continued down the path. Caitlin followed him, her steps a little surer than before.

CHAPTER THIRTY-FOUR

Caitlin found her senses becoming more acute with each step. Every sound or flash of movement caused her head to turn. Even the smells seemed to speak to her about their surroundings.

Brendan, however, seemed almost relaxed. His knives were in their sheaths, and he was walking calmly. The only telltale sign of his awareness was the small movement of his head. Even his slight limp was hard to spot. However, the calm of the woods didn't lessen the sense of menace—quite the opposite, actually. The stillness and quiet only put Caitlin more on edge, waiting for the inevitable trap to spring.

In a blur of movement, Brendan sprang toward the woods and grabbed something from the shadows. Before Caitlin could blink, he had a wriggling form pinned against a tree with his left forearm, a knife in his right hand held to the creature's throat.

"You have the keenest senses of anyone I know," the form said in a high-pitched, giggling voice. "Even most of the fae can't find me if I don't want them to."

Caitlin gripped her knife and stared at the pinned creature. It looked like a small, furry man-cat thing, no bigger than a six- or seven-year-old child. Its whole body was covered by black fur, and it had shimmering golden eyes. It grinned wide, showing bright white teeth. With the exception of prominent fangs, they were almost normal.

"You know," Brendan said, "after the hunt, I would've expected more from Fergus."

"Now that isn't very nice," the creature said. "I've only come to help you and this is the thankkkk—"

Brendan pressed his forearm into its neck. "You think I'm thick as all that, then? We've no time for your games, Puck."

"Puck?" Caitlin asked. "As in Robin Goodfellow? 'If we shadows have offended' Puck?"

Puck wriggled and gripped Brendan's arm, struggling as he gurgled something unintelligible.

"That's one of the little ape's names, aye," Brendan said. "He's captain of the pùca and Fergus's little trained monkey. Aren't you?"

"Is he the third challenge?" Caitlin asked, looking closer. Puck's eyes were beginning to bulge, and he was kicking more insistently.

"Not likely." Brendan laughed. "If he is, Fergus has gone wonky in his old age."

"Should we just kill him and be done?" Caitlin

asked. The ease with which she said those words surprised her. However, it quickly burned away under the anger that still smoldered in her.

"Naaahghk." Puck shook his head side to side so fast that his face blurred.

"What do you want?" Brendan asked and eased the pressure on Puck's neck.

Puck took in several deep gasps and began panting. "Is that any way to repay kindnahck—"

Brendan leaned in again. "You're as useless as a lighthouse in a bog, you are."

Puck struggled more, and his eyes almost doubled in size.

"*Dar fia,*" Brendan said. "Stop with the acting already. We both know you don't need to breathe."

The struggling stopped. Puck pursed his lips and glowered at Brendan. "You're no fun at all, Fian. You know that?"

"I'm only going to ask you one more time," Brendan said and set the point of his knife just above Puck's chest. "What the bloody hell do you want?"

"Fergus sent me to guide you," Puck said in a short, clipped tone, not unlike a pouting child, then crossed his arms. "He wanted me to lead you to the hall of doors. From there, if you're worthy, you can make your way to his court."

"Bollocks," Brendan said. "What are you doing here?"

Puck gritted his teeth and narrowed his eyes, and Caitlin almost thought she heard a growl come from him. "I've been sent to assure your safe passage through my lord's darkened woods," he said in a low tone. "And to ensure you arrive safe and whole at the hall of doors."

"Third time," Caitlin said, having figured out what Brendan was doing.

"Aye, you heard the lady. What are you doing here, you furry little shite?"

Puck made a sound that would've been more fitting coming from a Chihuahua, and his eyes seemed to light with fire. "I'm here to take you two to the hall of doors," he said. His eyes looked to one side, then the other. "Safely and unharmed," he added in a mocking tone as he bobbed his head from side to side.

"Fine, then," Brendan said, releasing him. "Lead on."

Puck dropped to the ground and landed on his backside. "Ow!" When he got to his feet, he scowled up at Brendan with his tongue out, then turned to Caitlin. "You know, I expected this big lummox to be lacking any manners or sense of fun, but you mortals are usually so much more entertaining."

Caitlin raised an eyebrow. The thought of killing him was becoming less bothersome.

Puck began walking down the trail ahead of them. "See what happens when you spend too much time with him?" he muttered.

"Come on," Brendan said to Caitlin as he sheathed his knife. "He's an annoying little bugger, but he's bound now."

"I heard that!" Puck shouted from down the trail.

"We're going to regret not killing him, aren't we?" Caitlin asked.

Puck stood several paces ahead, waiting with crossed arms, foot tapping the ground, casting glances at an imaginary wristwatch.

"Trip's not over yet, is it?" Brendan said with a smile.

"I heard that, too!" Puck shouted.

CHAPTER THIRTY-FIVE

"Good Lord, do you ever shut up?" Caitlin asked, rubbing her temples. A persistent throbbing had taken up residence behind her eyes and apparently had an extended lease.

"Not that I've ever heard." Brendan smacked Puck on the back of the head. "How close are we, Tinker Bell?"

"Do you see wings?" Puck asked and stamped a foot. "No, you don't. Why? Because I am not a pixie! I'm a pùca. Pùca! Pùca! Pùca!" He began jumping up and down, increasing the volume every time he repeated the word.

"You'll be a cloud of twinkling lights if you don't shut your gob!" Brendan said. "If you're lucky, I'll only boot your arse across the bleeding woods. Now, how close are we?"

Puck glared back over his shoulder at Brendan and

began bouncing his head back and forth. "Booot yer arse acroos da bleedan wood," he said in an exaggerated brogue and flashed Brendan a dirty look.

"Oh, you're claimed now!" Brendan reached for his knife.

Puck let out a squeak and ran toward a marble structure. "Here it is! Here it is!" he shouted as he reached the building. Then he bounded up into a tree and was gone in a rustling of branches.

"Oh, thank God," Caitlin said. "He isn't nearly so annoying in the play."

"I think old Billy Shakespeare was afraid the little bugger wouldn't stop pestering him if he'd made him as he was."

Caitlin chuckled, then looked at the building. "Is it me, or does that look just like the Parthenon?"

In fact, that was exactly what it looked like, though smaller in scale. The white marble still gleamed, but dead, brown grass and vines grew over it and up the columns.

"The fae contributed to a lot of architecture in mortal history," Brendan said. "You'll find things like this all through the Tír."

"So, what now?"

"We go inside." Brendan led the way up the stairs.

"Is Puck gone?" Caitlin asked. "Or do we need to worry about him jumping out of the shadows?"

"Well, he did say until we got to the hall of doors," Brendan said as he reached the top. "So, he's no longer bound to do no harm, but he's a bleeding coward. I'd say we need to worry more about the doors at this point."

"The third challenge?" Caitlin asked as she joined Brendan at the top of the stairs.

He nodded.

Inside, dirt covered the marble floor between dried, dead plants, vines, and scattered leaves. As Caitlin stepped inside, she saw walls lined with huge wooden doors set right into the marble.

"I don't remember ever hearing about a hall of doors. What is it?"

"The Dusk Court uses it to torment mortals they've brought across. Each door offers something you truly desire in a different way."

"And what's the catch?" Caitlin asked, looking at Brendan with a raised eyebrow.

"It's EXACTLY what you want, but in the worst possible circumstances," Brendan said. "If you opened a door wishing to be famous, it might be because you were hated and loathed."

"Infamous."

"Aye, and if you wanted money, it would be in a place where it had no value. Things like that and much, much worse. The Dusk Court takes great pride in coming up with new and clever ways to twist your deepest desire into your worst nightmare."

"So what are we doing here?"

"One of these doors will take us to Fergus's court."

"Which one?" Caitlin looked from one door to another. They were all different woods in all different states of disrepair, ranging from fresh oak to nearly rotted pine.

"I don't know. That's up to you, love. You're going to have to outsmart Fergus by wanting something he can't twist."

"What?"

"I can't open a door. This is your journey, and she's your *girseach*. I'll back you no matter what happens though."

"I still don't understand. What am I supposed to do?" Caitlin's palms were wet, and her heart was beating faster.

"You have to focus on Fiona, on getting her back. Do it so strongly, without doubt or ambiguity, that nothing about it can be turned on you."

"Any door?"

"That's where you trust your instincts." Brendan went to his knees and crossed himself.

"Are you praying?"

"Aye." He looked up at her. "I figured it couldn't hurt, but I can stop if you don't think we could use the help—"

"No." She shook her head. "By all means, go right ahead."

Brendan lowered his head again and began to mutter something in Latin as Caitlin looked at each door.

Which one?

First choice, she thought. Don't second-guess yourself. She closed her eyes, took a breath, and opened them again. She looked from one door to another. Her eyes passed over several, finally stopping on one that was dark red and well maintained. She walked to the door and swallowed as she reached out a trembling hand.

She touched the handle, and her breathing became more shallow and rapid. She closed her eyes and tried to think like a lawyer writing a contract.

"*In nomine Patris*," Brendan whispered.

Caitlin tightened her grip on the polished handle.

"*Et Filii.*"

She pushed the handle down.

"*Et Spiritus Sancti.*" Brendan crossed himself.

The door opened, and a gust of wind rushed past her face. All she could see was a blinding white light. At the last moment, she thought, I just want this to be over.

Caitlin sat up in bed with a start. She took several shuddering breaths as she looked around the darkened room. Cold sweat drenched her, causing her thin shirt to cling to her body.

"Are you all right, love?" a soft voice tinged with an Irish brogue asked.

A warm hand touched her shoulder, and she turned.

James looked at her with his brow knitted. "It were just a nightmare. That's all."

"Nightmare?" she stared at him.

"Aye, all's well now." He sat up and touched her face.

Something churned in her stomach. "No." She

shook her head, closed her eyes, and turned away. "This isn't—"

"Isn't what?" Edward asked.

Caitlin opened her eyes and looked at him. His smile was as comforting as ever.

"Was it a bad one?" he asked.

"She was alive," Caitlin said.

Edward wrapped her in his arms, pulled her down to him, and held her close.

She closed her eyes, rested her cheek on his bare chest, and fought the gnawing emptiness in her heart.

"It's okay," Edward whispered, then he kissed her head. "It was just a dream. It can be hard for your mind to accept, but she's gone."

A tear escaped and ran down Caitlin's cheek, landing on Edward's chest. "I miss her so much."

"Me, too." He squeezed her. "But just think about the good things—"

"Good things?" she asked. "What good things?"

"I don't mean it that way. Just think of all the freedom you have now, that we have. It wouldn't be like this if Fiona—"

Caitlin sat up and looked at him. The words bit like an icy dagger, but images came to her mind; walks with Edward, quiet dinners, and the sweetness of them falling in love.

She shook her head. "I'd have thought you'd tell me to take all the time I need. That losing a child is the hardest thing—"

"I have, a thousand times, and I will, but there

comes a time when you have to let the past go and see—"

"No," she said.

Edward's face became stern. "You know I love you, but I can't share you with a ghost."

Caitlin's stomach turned. She opened her mouth, but no words came out.

"All we've done, all we've become, and you still can't—?"

"She's alive!" Caitlin said.

Edward let out a breath. "She's not. Caitlin, you saw her body. You're the one who found her. It wasn't your fault, gas leaks happen."

There was a flash of memory; a cold room, a morgue. Caitlin stood over a table and looked down at the discolored face of her daughter.

Tears poured down Caitlin's cheeks. "No!"

"Damn it, Caitlin!" Edward threw the blanket aside and got to his feet. "This is the last time I'm having this conversation!"

"No, no, no, no!" She shook her head and covered her ears. "This is wrong, all wrong."

"You've got that right," Edward said.

"No, Eddy, please." She reached out for him, but he backed away. "She's alive, I know she is. I can feel it! Please believe me!"

"Would you listen to yourself? Do you have any idea how crazy you sound?"

"Yes, but I—" She stopped.

"But you what?"

"You didn't correct me," she whispered.

"What are you talking about?"

"You always react when I call you Eddy," she said. "I don't know if you're even aware of it anymore. Sometimes it's just a look, or a smile, but you didn't this time."

He scoffed. "You've lost it. I got over that a long time ago."

Caitlin pulled the blanket up to cover herself. "Who are you?"

"Wow." He sighed. "Okay, I'm calling the hospital. We need to get you admitted."

"What happened the day we met?" She climbed off the bed and blocked his path to the phone.

"What?"

"You heard me."

"Get out of my way." His eyes turned to stone. "I don't want to hurt you."

Caitlin smiled. "You just proved my point. Eddy is the gentlest person I've ever known. There's nothing I could do, nothing, that would make him hurt me."

Edward sneered and cursed, then the room spun.

Caitlin landed hard on her back. She looked around, and everything was blurry.

"Easy," Brendan said. She couldn't make his image come into focus. It took her a moment to realize that it was the tears pooling in her eyes.

"I'm right here," he said.

Caitlin wiped her eyes and sucked in a breath as her vision cleared.

"What did you see?"

She sat up with Brendan's help and chided herself for the mental slip.

"Can you hear me, love?"

"No, I mean yes, I can hear you. I'm an idiot. I had it figured out, then at the last moment . . ." She shook her head.

"It passes," he said, finishing for her. "That is what these—these bastards rely on. They can find the part of you that isn't quite dark and twist it just so. That's part of the torment. They delight in it, making you face something like that."

"So I failed?"

Brendan shook his head. "If you had, you wouldn't be here. Now, you try again."

Caitlin felt a rush of panic, and she looked at the doors. She was about to say that she wasn't sure she could do it again, but she stopped herself. She couldn't screw up again. She had to focus.

"Don't you see, you beat it, love," Brendan said. "They found something and taunted you with it, but you got the best of them."

"How do you know?"

He laughed. "Because you're here."

The nagging doubt began to vanish under a current of confidence. "I beat it."

"Aye."

Caitlin got to her feet.

"Find that fire, and focus on Fiona so hard there's nothing else. You have to block out those little thoughts and worries. You can't let nothing sneak in. Now get to it—it's nearly done."

She looked at him. "Nearly?"

"Threes, always in threes."

A stab of cold tried to settle in her stomach, but she squashed it before it could. She walked over to a faded pine door. Reaching out, she took the handle.

I want Fiona, my child. I want her back and I want her safe.

She focused on that thought as she turned the handle and opened the door.

A warm summer breeze blew across Caitlin's face, and she couldn't help but smile. Everything in the world felt right, and she couldn't remember the last time she was so relaxed. When she opened her eyes, she saw Fiona, eight years old and playing on the monkey bars. She reached out for one bar then another, smiling and laughing the whole time.

"Mommy, look at me, watch!"

"I see you, peanut."

Fiona dropped down and headed across the playground. An older boy, maybe thirteen, beat her to the last open swing.

"That's mine," Fiona said in a flat tone, her smile gone.

"Beat it, shrimp, I got it first," the boy said.

Caitlin walked over to intercede. She stopped when she saw Fiona grip the chain of the swing and stare at the boy.

"I said, it's mine," Fiona said.

Caitlin blinked, then shook her head. "Honey, just wait your—"

"NO!" Fiona screamed at her. "He can't have it, it's mine!"

"Fiona," Caitlin said in a stern tone. "I said, wait your turn."

The boy laughed and stuck out his tongue as Caitlin took Fiona's arm.

Fiona pulled from Caitlin's hold and tore the much larger boy from the swing. Caitlin watched in horror as Fiona took the boy's head and twisted it until there was a cracking sound, then dropped the limp body to the ground.

Caitlin's heart lurched, and her blood ran cold as Fiona stepped over the body and climbed into the now vacant swing.

"Oh, my God, Fiona," Caitlin said just above a whisper. "What did you do?"

"I told him it was mine," Fiona answered. "He should've given to me."

"You . . ." Caitlin swallowed. "You ki—" She tried to say the words, but she couldn't.

Fiona stopped the swing, looked at Caitlin, and blinked. When her eyes opened, her sparkling green irises were replaced by solid black orbs, devoid of anything human.

Caitlin shook her head. "No."

"He would've hurt me," Fiona said, her voice now cold and melodic. She took a step toward Caitlin.

Caitlin stepped back. "No, that isn't possible."

"You wouldn't want him to hurt me, would you, Mother?"

Caitlin shivered.

"Tommy!" another boy shouted.

Caitlin and Fiona turned to see a group of four boys ride their bikes over. After seeing the dead boy, they turned on Fiona.

"What did you do to him?" one of the boys asked.

"I killed him," Fiona answered.

"He's my brother," the boy said and pushed the bike into Fiona's path. "I'll kill y—"

Fiona, moving in a blur, grabbed the front of the bike. With the boy still on it, she swung it in a circle and hurled it at the jungle gym. Boy and bike sailed through the air and struck the metal bars. Several snapping sounds echoed through the air as the tangled pair fell to the ground, never to move again.

The others turned to flee, but Fiona bared rows of sharp teeth and leapt on one, shoving him to the ground.

"Fiona, no!" Caitlin shouted as she went after her daughter. With effort, she pulled Fiona off the boy, who bolted once he was free. "What are you doing?"

"They'll tell!" Fiona roared. "They'll take me away, they'll hurt me!" Fiona tore free and turned to go after the boys, but her foot caught on a bike, causing her to trip and fall. The exposed edge of the handlebar scratched her face.

Caitlin instinctively went to help Fiona up, but Fiona was on her feet before Caitlin got there. Darkness and tiny white lights seeped from the scratch on her face.

Caitlin swallowed. "No, no, this isn't right. Brendan was certain I was Dawn Court."

Fiona pushed Caitlin with both hands. Despite Fiona's previous display of strength, Caitlin wasn't prepared for the force of the shove. She went more than ten feet through the air, landing hard on her back.

"You are," Fiona said.

Before Caitlin could suck in a breath, Fiona was on her, and Caitlin was struggling to hold the little girl at bay.

"You're like them!" Fiona screamed through sharp teeth as she fought to tear at Caitlin with clawed fingers. "You'll hurt me, too!"

"You're not Fiona!"

"Oh, but I am, Mother."

As Fiona pushed Caitlin harder into the ground, Caitlin felt something pressing into her back. With a heave, she tossed Fiona off and rolled to one side. She reached back and felt the warm, wooden handle of the knife on her belt.

As Fiona came at her, Caitlin drew the knife and drove it forward. The girl groaned, staring at the knife as she sank to the ground.

"Mommy," Fiona said. "Why are you doing this, Mommy?"

Tears poured down Caitlin's face as she pulled the blade out. It was coated in thick, black blood that was evaporating into darkness and lights. "No," she said. "You're not my daughter. My daughter isn't a monster."

"I am your daughter," Fiona said. Her hand covered the wound, but trails of darkness and dancing white lights slipped through her small fingers.

"NO!" Caitlin screamed and stabbed the little girl over and over.

The last things to fade were Fiona's eyes. She blinked one last time, and they returned to their familiar green. "Why, Mommy?" a tiny voice said.

"No!" Caitlin sobbed and fell to her knees. "You're not my baby, please, God, no."

Caitlin could swear she heard, somewhere in the distance, someone laughing.

There was a rush of wind and Caitlin was back in the hall, still on her knees and still weeping. The knife fell to the floor as she brought her hands to her face. "No, no, no," she repeated. "Not my baby! No!"

"Easy, love." Brendan dropped down and took Caitlin into his arms. "It's okay, you're safe now. Whatever it was, it's over."

Caitlin threw her arms around him and buried her face in his chest. "You were wrong. I wished for Fiona and he used her face. He put it on some monster. It wasn't her, it couldn't have been her," she said between sobs. "I killed her, it, I had to—"

"Shh, it wasn't her. It was just a trick." Brendan tightened his hold. "That wasn't your Fiona. Your Fiona is waiting for you still."

Moment by moment, inch by inch, Caitlin came back to herself, but she couldn't stop crying or rid herself of the image of her baby being eaten away by darkness at her own hands. "I didn't wish for that, not even for a moment, ever."

Brendan pulled back and wiped tears from Caitlin's face. "I don't know what happened, but do you see now what he's capable of? You see now what kind of thing we're dealing with here? Fergus is no man. He's a devil, and that's no one to leave your girl with, is it?"

Caitlin's stomach twisted as she fought the images in her head. "It wasn't her. God, please, it couldn't have been her, could it?"

"Caitlin!"

She blinked and looked at him.

"Listen to me and listen well," he said. "This game has gone on long enough. It's time to get Fiona back, yeah? It's time to get her away from that *mac mallachta*, time to stop playing his bloody games, and long past time to get her back home." He looked at her with steel in his eyes. "You're the only one what can do that. Stoke that fire in your heart. The anger is what you need to get you past this."

She blinked at him.

"Get angry! He did this to you! To her! He means to keep her from you!"

Caitlin dug for anger, for rage, for the blind fury

from before, but it was gone. What she did find was a mother's love for her child. Caitlin knew that Brendan could use anger, but she couldn't. She had something else, and she knew it was the way to beat this game.

When she looked up at Brendan, the tears had stopped.

"That's it," Brendan said. "Hold on to it. Remember it. He took her from you. He tried to trick you, to keep you here and away from your little girl." He set his jaw. "He made you watch her die, yeah?"

She swallowed the memory down and focused on Fiona, not just her name, or an image, or a memory. She focused on the intangibles, the things that made Fiona who she was. Her laugh, the way she snuggled close to Caitlin on the couch when they watched a movie, the way she could melt Caitlin's heart with just a smile. These were the things that defined Fiona, and, paradoxically, they were all completely indefinable. They were indefinable and untwistable.

"Aye, there it is, then." He pulled away and stood up. "Now, on your feet."

Caitlin stood, and Brendan was right with her, his eyes still locked on hers. At that moment, she wished that he could've known this kind of love, the love of a parent for a child, even if for only a moment.

"Don't let him win." Brendan waited a moment. "You ready?"

Caitlin felt herself smile. "I really am."

"Good. Now, open a door and let's get your girl back."

Caitlin walked to another door, gripped the handle, and pulled it open.

Beyond the door was a path similar to the one that had brought them here, but not as aged. At the end of the trail, she could see a huge circle of tall stones. It looked like nothing less than a restored Stonehenge.

"Well done, love," Brendan said from behind her. "It's time to finish this, then."

Caitlin gripped her knife with white knuckles and stepped through the doorway.

"I'm coming, baby," she said to herself.

CHAPTER THIRTY-SIX

Caitlin took a long, deep breath as she looked down the
path. Brendan stepped up beside her, and the door closed
behind them with a hollow sound. They walked down
the path, side by side, each step slow and purposeful.

"Remember what I told you," Brendan said. "You
mightn't have much time or warning. You can't think
about what's going on around you. You can't let her
stay here." He took the knife from her hand and tucked
it back into the sheath, then pulled her jacket down
over it.

"All of us are leaving, Brendan."

"Don't be stupid, love." He came around to look her
in the eye. "I'm all for that, but if it comes to it, you
need to get out."

She stared at him for a long moment, then finally
nodded.

They continued along the path in silence until it led

them up to the circle, where two upright stones carried a third massive stone atop them.

They stepped into a pristine courtyard tiled in shining white marble. Lounging about the outer edge was every kind of nightmarish faerie imaginable, including winged pixies that flitted around, casting a cold glow about them. Their colors were all dark, ranging from purple to blue. Their wings, likewise, ranged from small bat wings to what looked like spiderwebs stretched over bones.

Caitlin saw goblins and old women draped in gray cloaks, with tortured faces and burning red eyes. She saw those fae that looked like elves, but without the allure of Dante and his kind. These were as frightening as they were beautiful. Their hair was of dark blues and blacks, their skin, the pale blue of moonlight, stretched over gaunt faces. When they turned to Caitlin, she saw that instead of radiant eyes of blue or green, there were only dark, empty sockets. At the far side, Puck leaned against a large marble throne, smiling. Several oíche clustered near him, and none looked pleased.

On the throne sat a dashing man in his late thirties, dressed in a deep blue robe. His hair and well-trimmed beard were both of the same light-consuming black. His left hand rested on a purple crystal, and on his lap sat Fiona.

He smirked as they approached.

"Mommy?" Fiona asked in a sleepy voice.

Caitlin set her jaw and forced a smile. "I'm here, baby. Are you all right?"

Fiona nodded woozily. "Uh-huh."

"See, I told you, darling," the man said to Fiona. "Your mommy is here." His voice was deep and resonant. There was a faint accent to it, the kind Caitlin imagined British professors had.

Fiona looked at the man, smiled, and nodded. "Yep, you said."

Grinding her teeth as she watched her daughter's sleepy eyes drift back to her, Caitlin fought back the urge to yank Fiona away. Again, she put on a smile.

"Now, Mommy and I need to talk," the man said and turned cold eyes to Caitlin.

"It's going to be all right, sweetie," Caitlin said, struggling to hold the smile on her face. "We'll be going home soon."

"Home?" Fiona asked, the trace of a smile coming to her little face.

"That's right," Caitlin said. "I promise." While she was glad that Fiona wasn't more scared, Caitlin had to wonder what Fergus had done to get her that way. Whatever it was, he'd pay for it, with interest.

Fergus eyed her and Brendan from his throne, then smiled and chuckled. "Careful, breaking promises here carries all kinds of consequences."

Caitlin wanted to spit venom, but she could feel every eye in the courtyard on her, watching every move. She bit her tongue and clenched her fists tighter, digging her nails into her palms. With a deep breath, her jaw eased a little, and she leveled her gaze on Fergus.

"You know why we're here," Brendan said. "Give us the girl, and we'll be gone. That'll be the end of it."

Fergus looked around the court. "These Fianna have no manners at all."

The court laughed.

"You bring iron into my lands. You kill my lieutenants. You butcher my warriors." Fergus motioned to Puck. "Assaulted my servant, sent only to offer you safe passage, and now you expect me to answer to demands? In my own court?"

"I think Cernunnos would disagree with being called your warrior," Brendan said. "As for your servant there," he said, and nodded to Puck, "well, he's the most annoying creature in twelve worlds. How you haven't killed him yourself is a mystery to me."

Fergus laughed. "I will grant you that much, I suppose."

"As for your lieutenants," Brendan said, "I came under the old treaty. I tried to pass peaceably, but one denied me that claim and insulted me on top of it. That left me no choice." He smiled. "You above all should know better than to give a Fian reason to fight."

Fergus let out a rumbling laugh that shook the courtyard like thunder, and once more, the whole court joined him.

"Indeed, Fian," Fergus said, and the laughter stopped. "Even so, you know full well iron is forbidden here. My lieutenant was enforcing the laws of my lands. Just because you were once Fianna doesn't give you leave to ignore my rule." He sighed and rolled his eyes. "Of course, I should know better than to expect a Fian to remember something like that." He turned to the court. "After all, we're lucky when we can get you to remember to go outside to relieve yourselves."

He and the court laughed again.

"We're here to claim the child. She's this woman's daughter," Brendan said over the laughter. Then he pointed at the assembled oíche. "Taken in violation of the Oaths, by them. I say again, give the child back, and we'll be on our way."

The laughter stopped, and Fergus stared at Brendan. "First, to your accusation," he said. "My loyal servants are not bound by the Oaths. You know that only the Rogue Court is." He motioned to the oíche. "And they are Dusk Court."

"They was Rogue Court when I spoke to your lieut—"

"Second," Fergus said, his tone louder and harsher. "I will not be releasing my daughter to anyone."

"What?" Caitlin said. She couldn't have heard that right. "What're you talking about? She's my daughter." She turned to Brendan, who was looking back at her with a furrowed brow.

Fergus smiled. "Ah, what's the matter, love? Don't you even recognize me, then?" he said in a thick Irish brogue.

Caitlin felt her stomach drop to the floor and her knees go weak as his voice rang in her head. The world seemed to stop, but somehow she was falling.

"You're as lovely as the dawn," Fergus said. His appearance shifted, and in place of the robed Fergus sat a young man with blond hair and blue eyes, dressed in jeans and a white T-shirt.

Caitlin stared. She wanted to scream, but her voice wouldn't come. She wanted to charge him, to drive her knife into his chest and take Fiona, but she couldn't move. She could only shake with fury and frustration.

"What is it, love?" Brendan asked. "What's he on about?"

Caitlin closed her eyes and thought back to the hall of doors. It all made sense now, and the true horror, the complete torment it was meant to be, finally set in. She seethed at how easily she'd been duped.

"Go on, love," Fergus said. "Tell him."

Caitlin swallowed back bile. "James," she said. "God help me, he's Fiona's father."

"She's saying I'm in the right, bucko," Fergus said and winked at Brendan.

"Why?" Caitlin asked, her voice shaking.

Brendan took her hand in his and held it tight. "I'm right here with you," he said.

"Well, my dear, the blood of the Milesians—or the Irish, if you prefer—is strong," Fergus said, the brogue now gone. "Even more so when mixed with our own. Yet, sadly, I couldn't find any native Erin women who would have me. Nor could they be charmed. They knew me, even if they couldn't name me."

"I've got a name for you," Caitlin said.

"That's not very lady-like, my dear." Fergus laughed. "The answer came to me, quite literally. This child of the Diaspora, with Dawn Court blood in her, no less, she found me."

"Dawn Court?" Brendan asked. "Why would you—" Color drained from his face. "*Darfia*, you mean to replace Teagan."

Fergus smiled, and his blue eyes glinted.

Caitlin looked at Brendan. "What's that mean?"

"Fiona is of both courts," Brendan said. "He'll use her to bring down Teagan and seize the Dawn Court for himself."

"As my queen, of course," Fergus said. "In retrospect, Teagan was a poor choice. Fiona will make a much finer consort."

"But she's your daughter!" Caitlin's stomach twisted. "You sick bas—"

"You have such a mortal view of blood and lineage," Fergus said. "Who better than my own child? I can raise her to be the queen I want. And her blood line is pure." He looked at Caitlin, lifted an eyebrow, and smiled. "Well, mostly."

"You—"

"So, you see, my dear," Fergus said, "I'll not be letting my daughter and future queen go."

Brendan took a step forward. "Fergus, you—"

"I've had quite enough of you, Fian," Fergus said. "This doesn't involve you." He waved his hand and a silver cord appeared from nowhere. It wrapped around Brendan's arms, pinning them to his sides, then around his legs, bringing them together. "There now, that's much better."

"*Téigh i dtigh diabhai*, you faerie bast—"

"Oops, almost forgot." Fergus held his hand up like a puppet and closed his fingers. Brendan went silent as his mouth was forced shut.

The whole court began laughing, and Caitlin looked at Brendan.

Think, damn it. He'd gotten her this far; she knew it was time for her to step up. She had to do something.

Fergus stood and set Fiona in the huge chair. "Mommy and Daddy need to talk for a moment, my dear," he said to her. "Wait right here on Daddy's throne. But don't get too comfortable."

A chuckle bubbled around the court.

"Okay, Daddy," Fiona said with a smile, her voice still sleepy.

The word struck Caitlin like a sledgehammer. "You are not her—"

Fergus picked up the purple crystal from beside his throne and began walking across the now silent courtyard. Caitlin noticed he held it in a tight grip and kept it close to his body.

"Caitlin," he said, his voice soft and gentle. "My sweet, sweet love."

He stepped close, and Caitlin fought back nausea.

"There is another option." He reached out with his free hand and caressed her face. "You needn't lose our child."

His touch made her wince, but she resisted pulling away.

"Stay here, with Fiona."

"What?"

"Think of it. Fiona will be safe." He put slight emphasis on *safe*. "She'll never get sick, never grow old, and neither will you. She will be a queen, wanting for nothing. Think what a life that will be for her."

There was something in his voice, something that tried to draw her in. But everything she'd faced, everything she'd done to get here, made her immune.

"If you worry over your wizard," Fergus said, "don't. He's dead."

Caitlin's head snapped up and her heart stopped for a moment. "What?"

"Oh, yes." Fergus nodded. "He died quite bravely, but died he did."

Caitlin saw the smug smiles on the faces of the oíche. One even licked his lips. Pain and regret coursed through her. She closed her eyes and saw Eddy's smile. Tears escaped her eyes as she opened them, doing her best to ignore the hole in her heart.

"All need not be lost," Fergus said. "I'll set the Fian free if you stay. No others need die."

Caitlin looked at Brendan as he struggled uselessly against his bonds.

"There's no choice," Fergus whispered in her ear. "Refuse me, and I'll kill the Fian. I'll make it last centuries, and I'll have Fiona anyway."

Caitlin drew in a breath and looked at her baby. Fiona was sitting quietly, and her eyes drooped, as if in a drug-induced haze. Caitlin smiled, realizing that they'd had to enchant her. Fiona must have fought them.

That's my girl, she thought.

Caitlin's eyes wandered over the court. She looked at the creatures of the dusk who would be Fiona's company if she stayed: her friends and servants. Fiona would surely become that monster from the hall, but she'd be safe. That was the taunt. Fiona would be safe, but she wouldn't be Fiona. Caitlin had been so focused on safe that she hadn't realized what that really meant. She'd worried about physical safety, not protecting who Fiona was.

As Caitlin closed her eyes, more stray tears ran down her cheeks, and she forced herself to think of killing the monster in the hall of doors.

Whatever it takes to save my child.

She knew Fergus was lying about Brendan. Oh, he'd set Brendan free, but Brendan would never leave these lands alive. Caitlin thought of what she might have to do if she couldn't get Fiona out. It was unthinkable, but it would be the only way.

A final tear rolled down her cheek, and she wiped it away as she made her decision. Fergus was right. There was no choice to make, not when it came to Fiona. Caitlin's hand drifted into her coat pocket, where she found Paddy Bear. Her heart began to pound. She swallowed, pulled out the bear, and, opening her eyes, turned to Brendan.

"I'm sorry, Brendan," she said. "I have to."

Fergus smiled wide and held his hand out to Caitlin. "Come, my dear."

Caitlin swallowed and stepped forward, taking Fergus's hand.

He drew her into his arms and whispered into her ear, "Oh, how I've longed for you."

Caitlin took her free hand and pulled the knife from the sheath hidden beneath her coat. She brought it around and drove it into Fergus's back. She yanked it back out as Fergus pushed her away. Stumbling, Caitlin slashed the knife. Fergus grunted in pain as the blade cut across his right hand. It came open on reflex, and the purple crystal fell.

Time seemed to slow, and Caitlin saw all the oíche's eyes go wide and their mouths turn up into grins. Fergus tried to catch the crystal, but he missed and it struck the tiles, causing a piece to break off.

"No!" Fergus roared. "You insufferable, mortal *striapach*!" He backhanded Caitlin, then picked up the crystal and broken shard.

Caitlin landed on the hard stone a step away from Brendan. The silver cords holding him seemed to be fading in and out. Caitlin looked from the bindings to the crystal with satisfaction.

Fergus turned murderous eyes to Caitlin, but he almost looked tired. "I'll show you pain and torment you never dreamed were possible."

"No," Caitlin said, wiping blood from her lip. "You made a promise. You swore to me. Don't you remember?"

Fergus narrowed his brow. "I made no promise."

Caitlin blinked her wet eyes, and the last of her tears escaped. "You promised me and you promised her. I need you to keep it, now."

Fergus's eyes went wide in realization, and he turned to Brendan.

"Brendan," Caitlin said through a sob. "You promised to save my little girl!"

Brendan's eyes blazed with the all the fires of all the hells. He threw back his head and let out a roar that shook the standing stones surrounding the courtyard.

Even Fergus took a step back.

There was a loud crack as the silver cords snapped and vanished.

"*Tar amach, a Bháis!*" The whites of Brendan's eyes vanished, filling with a bright blue that flared with unbridled rage as his muscles swelled and claws emerged from his hands.

For a moment, time froze, and the whole court stared in wide-eyed disbelief.

"*Fág an bealach!*" Brendan screamed, and in that split second of confusion, he drew his knives and hurled them. They streaked through the air, little more than a blur, and hit two oíche so hard they were lifted clear off the ground. Clouds of darkness and sparks trailed them as they flew back behind the throne and vanished.

Caitlin rolled to her feet, grabbed her knife, and sprinted past the stunned Fergus toward Fiona. Fergus reached out for her, but Brendan sprang on him and knocked him to the ground.

Caitlin ran faster.

"*Díoltas!*" Brendan yelled, and his knives leapt into the air, streaking past Caitlin.

She didn't turn; she just ran faster.

As she reached for Fiona, a hand grabbed at her shoulder. She whirled on her attacker, slashing out with her knife and burying it deep into his shoulder.

Fergus screamed, and she felt his grip on her slip away.

Leaving the blade, Caitlin grabbed Fiona, pushed the bear into her little hands, and turned. Fergus reached for her, but again Brendan seized him, claws sinking into flesh, and hurled the Dark King across the courtyard and into the frantic mob.

Brendan's burning blue eyes turned on Caitlin and Fiona.

Caitlin's heart stuttered as Brendan took a step toward them, murder in his eyes. She turned her body, shielding Fiona. "Brendan, remember!"

Her eyes met Brendan's and held them. She didn't move.

Brendan began to shake, and his eyes changed for just an instant.

"Please, remember," she said again.

Brendan clenched his fists and looked from Caitlin to Fiona. "GO!" he screamed, though his voice was barely recognizable. Then he leapt into the whirling cloud of darkness and twinkling lights.

Caitlin pulled the seeking stone from under her shirt and gripped it in her hand. She gasped as she saw a clawed hand lift out of the darkness, then come down in a strike. It was huge, covered in dark red fur and dripping with black gore.

Then the world spun, and she and Fiona were gone.

CHAPTER THIRTY-SEVEN

When the world stopped spinning, Caitlin found herself on a grassy hill. The sun hung high in the sky, and below her was the faerie market. The seeking stone crumbled to dust in her hand, and she looked down at Fiona in her arms.

The little girl blinked up at her as she gripped Paddy Bear. Tears were welling in her eyes, and her lower lip stuck out. "Mommy, I wanna go home."

"Me, too, baby. Let's go right now." Caitlin ignored her own tears and ran as fast as she could for the sidhe mound.

Faces stared at her as she ran through the market. As she sped past the stalls, it dawned on her what she'd forgotten when she and Brendan came through the first time. She looked at Fiona but pushed the panic aside and charged on, not daring to look behind her.

Adrenaline pumped through Caitlin, and the burning in her legs and lungs didn't matter. Fiona's weight didn't matter. The terrain didn't matter. Only reaching the mound mattered. So she ran as fast as she could through the market and up the hill on the far side.

The trail and scenery blurred by until at last she could see the mound in the distance and finally had to slow. When she risked a look back, she saw something in the distance approaching at a superhuman speed, and she knew it was Fergus. She didn't know how he'd caught up to her so fast, but he had.

Cold panic surged through her, and she turned to flee.

In her path now stood the most strikingly beautiful woman she'd ever seen. Her hair was the brown of chestnuts and her eyes the color of a summer sky. She smiled, and the sun would've been envious of her light and warmth.

"Peace, child," the woman said in a soft voice that sounded more like song than spoken words. She looked behind Caitlin.

Caitlin stared, her mouth going slack, then she turned around to see Fergus charging forward with hate and fury burning in his eyes. She went for her knife, but it was still buried in his shoulder. Her jaw tightened, and she drew Fiona closer to her.

The woman stepped forward, putting herself between them and Fergus.

Fergus stopped a few paces away, and his eyes moved from Caitlin to the woman and back again several times. "Wife," he finally said in a tone saturated in contempt.

"Husband," Teagan replied. She smiled again, but

this time it was tinged with delight. She looked at the knife protruding from Fergus's shoulder and raised an eyebrow.

Fergus tore the knife from his shoulder, threw it aside, and wiped his hand over the wound. The wafting darkness and blue lights ceased as the wound closed.

"Step aside, Teagan. This is no concern of yours." He pointed at Fiona. "That child is mine."

"Dear husband," Teagan said in a reproachful tone. "The mother, and hence the child, are mine."

Caitlin blinked. "What?"

Fergus's eyes went wide. "No, you can't—"

"My court was the first to her family line," Teagan said. "I have claim on her and all who follow." She smiled at Fiona. "And that you would presume to use this little one to usurp and replace me—" She looked at Fergus and shook her head. "—well, that most certainly is my concern."

Fergus's jaw tightened.

Teagan laughed. "My dear husband, I simply refuse to be replaced."

"The child is bound to me," Fergus said. "She partook of my food and drink." There was only smug satisfaction behind his smile.

"I see," Teagan said. "Well, that is a problem, isn't it?" She pursed her lips and turned to Caitlin. "I'm afraid the laws are clear."

Shaking her head, Caitlin pulled Fiona even tighter against her and took a step back. "No, I'll never allow—"

"We must resolve this matter." Teagan lightly dragged her finger over Fiona's forehead and left behind a soft golden glow, which faded a second later.

Fiona giggled. "That tickled."

Teagan looked at Fergus, and a wry smile emerged. "There, she is bound no more. The matter is resolved."

Caitlin could almost hear Fergus's teeth grind as he fumed.

"No!" Fergus said.

"Fear not, child," Teagan said to Caitlin, ignoring Fergus. "These are the lands I gave to the noon fae. Even were my husband's power not weakened by his own mischief," she said and glanced sidelong at the crystal still in Fergus's hand, "I still hold dominion here. You are of my blood, and as such, you have my protection while here."

Caitlin let out a deep sigh.

Teagan's face turned sad. "Your father was—" She smiled, but it was tinged with regret. "Well, he was very dear to me. Until he met your mother, that is."

Caitlin stared. "So you called him because—"

"I did." Teagan's eyes were soft. "I'm truly sorry. I never imagined how deeply he loved your mother. My vision beyond these lands is limited."

"Teagan, I will not be den—"

"Let me give this child a gift as recompense," Teagan said. Once more, she touched Fiona's forehead. This time the light trail was soft green. "Hidden will she remain, from all not of my court or blood, until such time as she has decided for herself how she will live."

Caitlin dared to feel elation. "Hidden?"

"You needn't worry this will happen again." Teagan put a hand on Caitlin's shoulder. "This child is very special. Both courts in her and mortal blood as well. That is truly rare."

"She's special for more than that," Caitlin said, looking at Fiona, who smiled back.

"Even so." Teagan looked at the little girl and sighed. "She has your father's smile. Did you know that?"

Caitlin shook her head, but now it was obvious to her.

"Go now." Teagan ran a hand down Caitlin's face. "Your role in this dispute is over." She cast a quick glance at Fergus and again to the crystal. "My husband and I have private matters to discuss." Teagan waved her hand and a swirling pool of light appeared. "This will return you to the sidhe mound you used to cross. I wish you both long life and joy."

Caitlin looked at Teagan. "What about Brendan?"

Teagan shook her head. "I cannot speak for him or his fate. What happens in my husband's lands is unknown to me and beyond my influence. But the Fian are a noble clan; you should honor him and his choice. Take your child home."

A cruel smile played across Fergus's lips, and it sent a shiver through Caitlin.

"Mommy," Fiona said, yawning. "Me and Paddy Bear are tired and hungry. Can we go home now?"

Caitlin nodded. "Yes, honey. We're going." She walked to the portal, holding Fiona tight in her arms.

When she reached it, she looked back one last time, but Brendan was nowhere to be seen.

Caitlin wanted to believe he could've made it out, but even if he had . . .

She closed her eyes, losing a few tears, and fought back a sob. Teagan was right. Brendan had made his choice, even after knowing what lay ahead and what it might cost him. Of course, Caitlin had made a decision too, and the weight of it was already settling on her shoulders.

Thank you, she thought. I'll tell her about you, about the brave and good man who saved her. She'll know what you did for her, what you sacrificed for her and for me. I swear it.

Blinking away the tears, Caitlin stepped through the portal.

CHAPTER THIRTY-EIGHT

Caitlin emerged at the foot of the mound and fell to her knees as the portal vanished behind her. Holding Fiona close to her, she began to sob.

"Caitlin?" Edward shouted. "Fiona?"

"Eddy!" Fiona shouted.

Caitlin's heart skipped a beat as she saw him, battered but alive, rushing to them. He was limping, his right arm was in a sling, and the left side of his face was covered by a bandage. Dante and two other elves followed him.

Caitlin let Fiona loose, and the little girl ran to Edward.

Amidst the maelstrom of emotions that raged in Caitlin, relief and joy surged to the surface as Fiona reached Edward and clung to his leg. He smiled and plodded on until he reached Caitlin. There, he pulled the little girl loose, knelt down, and wrapped his good arm around them both.

"Thank God you're okay," he said and squeezed them.

Caitlin kissed his cheek and buried her head in his neck as tears, now of joy, flowed down her face. Her hand went up, into his hair, and she ran her fingers through it, just wanting to be sure he was really there.

"You're squishing me!" Fiona said.

Edward and Caitlin pulled back, and they just looked at each other, smiling.

Caitlin's smile faded as she reached out and put a hand on his bandaged face. "What happened to you?"

"It doesn't matter." He put his hand over hers and pulled it away from his face. "You're back, both of you. That's what matters."

"But Fergus said the oíche had—" She swallowed. "That you were—"

"I nearly was."

"He stopped a ceremony that would've freed the oíche," Dante said. "Once that was done, we sent them packing. They've since rejoined the Dusk Court."

"He also rescued the other wizard from the demon controlling him," Faolan said.

Caitlin looked at him with tear-filled eyes. "A demon?"

Edward smiled his dimpled smile. "Piece of cake."

She ran her hand over his face and frowned, tears still running from her eyes. Then she leaned forward and kissed him. His lips were soft, and it felt like coming home.

When she pulled back, she looked at him. "You're sure you're okay?"

"I've never been better." He smiled, but he saw something in her eyes. He looked around, and his face went pale. "Where's Brendan?"

Caitlin bit her lip. The mention of his name did it for her. Sobs began to escape so hard that her body shook.

"I had to leave him." She sucked in a shuddering breath. "I had to, Eddy. I didn't want to, but it was the only way—"

Edward pulled her close, and she melted into him.

"It's how a Fian would want to go," Faolan said.

The finality of those words struck Caitlin hard.

"It's what he wanted," Dante said. "He wasn't just a Fian. He was the best of them." He wiped away a stray tear before looking across the field. "He was stubborn, and infuriating, and he was my best friend."

"He was also a man of his word," Caitlin whispered and wiped her own tears away.

"Come on," Edward said. "Let's get you two home."

Once Caitlin and Edward got to their feet, they looked at each other. She finally saw him now. She caressed his cheek and leaned in close, kissing his face.

"I love you," she whispered. "I always have."

He smiled. "And I've always known."

"Mommy?" Fiona said.

"Come along, little one," Dante said, offering Fiona his hand.

"No, Mommy says I can't go with strangers," Fiona said.

Caitlin couldn't help but laugh.

Fiona smiled, then said, "My name's Fiona Brady. What's yours?"

"Well, I'm Dante." He did a little bow. "It's very nice to finally meet you."

"Now we're not strangers." Fiona offered Dante her hand.

Dante accepted it, chuckled, and smiled at Caitlin. "Arlen will take you home." He sucked in a breath. "Faolan and I will see to Brendan's truck."

"He's a hero, you know," Caitlin said as they walked to the waiting SUV.

"Oh, I know that. I just wish he would've known it," Dante said. "Perhaps now he'll finally find some peace."

Caitlin stopped at the SUV's back door. "Not exactly happily ever after, is it?"

"Caitlin," Dante said, opening the door for her, "this is just the beginning of your tale." He lifted Fiona into the backseat, then helped Caitlin in as Edward climbed in the other side. Dante closed Caitlin's door, and she leaned against Edward.

"Mommy," Fiona said. "You're squishing me again!"

"Sorry, munchkin." Caitlin kissed Fiona's head and stroked her hair. "I just missed you so much."

"We'll be around if you need anything," Dante said

through the open window. "Or not, if that's what you choose."

"Absolutely not." Caitlin reached out and squeezed his hand. "You're family now."

Dante smiled and stepped back.

There was a shared glimpse between her and Dante then. It lasted only an instant, but it was obvious in his eyes. He knew more about Brendan, and what he was, than even Brendan himself did.

Caitlin didn't know what to feel as they pulled away and bounced down the trail, headed for the main road. So much lost and so much gained. She just held Fiona, leaned into Edward, and promised Brendan that she and Fiona would live good lives.

So help me, you'll never be forgotten in this family. Not ever.

EPILOGUE

Dante gripped the leather box in his hand and looked from it to the sidhe mound.

"You really think he's dead?" Faolan asked.

"I do," Dante lied.

Brother, I hope you found the redemption you were looking for. If you did live, I hope that you escaped. Heaven help you if you didn't.

"You didn't tell her," Faolan said as he watched the SUV vanish from sight.

"Somehow, I just didn't think the time was right." Dante didn't look from the mound. He slid the box into a pocket. "She's been through enough already. The last thing she needs right now is hearing what role her daughter might play in the future of our court." He patted Faolan's shoulder. "We have plenty of time."

"I suppose."

"It's hard enough for a mortal to raise a child who

thinks she's a faerie princess." Dante looked down the trail. "Let alone one who actually is."

Dante retrieved the keys from the box in the bed of Brendan's truck. He opened the driver's side door, and Faolan climbed into the passenger side. Dante hesitated, looking at the mound for a long moment.

"What is it?" Faolan asked.

"Nothing." Dante climbed in and started the engine. Reluctantly, he put the truck in gear and drove down the trail, leaving the mound shrinking in the rearview mirror.

"Now, tell me about what's happening in Seattle."

ACKNOWLEDGMENTS

My deepest gratitude goes to all those who helped this book, and me, reach this point. Thanks to all my friends who are characters enough to fill an epic series: Ed, Gabe, Ned, Kenda, Mike, Dustin, Casey, and Kristin. To the editors and staff at The Editorial Department: Renni, Shannon, Peter, Ross, and Jane, thanks for giving me the confidence to make the story my own. Susan E. Kennedy, MFA, thank you for your hard work and insight in polishing the story and characters and making them shine. Thank you to Rebecca Lucash and everyone at HarperCollins for your work in bringing it across the finish line in such a short period of time and so spectacularly! Thanks to my agent, Margaret Bail, for your hard work and support. Last but not least, my deepest thanks to Dr. Deborah Hayden, junior research fellow at Christ Church, for her assistance with the Irish language translations.

GLOSSARY

A bhitseach dhaonna *Irish/Fae* — "mortal bitch"

A ghrá mo chroí *Irish* — "my heart's beloved, my darling"

Ádh mór, mo dheartháir *Irish* — "good luck, my brother"

Agor y ffordd *Welsh* — "open the way"

Anghenfil *Welsh* — "monster/ogre/beast"

Atgyfnerthu *Welsh* — "to reinforce/fortify/strengthen"

Bastúin *Irish* — "bastard" or "an uncouth/aggressive/stupid man/ boy"; plural of *bastún*

Cac ar oineach *Irish* — "shits on honor"; a mean, low-down person

Cailín *Irish* — "girl"

Ceapa *Irish* — "protector"; *ceap* (singular) is a homophone of *cop* and thought to be a possible origin of the word

Codail *Irish* — "sleep"

Craic *Irish* — "news, gossip, fun, entertainment, and enjoyable conversation"

Cyrydu *Welsh* — "corrode"

Damnú air *Irish* — "damn it"; an oath or curse

Damnú ort *Irish* — "damn you"

Dar fia *Irish* — "by God"; expletive in line with the British *bloody hell* or more vulgar English words, also an oath or curse

Dia ár gcumhdach *Irish* — "God preserve/protect us"; an oath or curse

Dia ár réiteach *Irish* — "God save us"; an oath or curse

Deamhan buile *Irish* — "demon of madness/frenzy"

Dewin *Welsh* — "wizard/sorcerer"

Díbeartach *Irish* — "exile/reject/outcast"

Díoltas *Irish* — "vengeance"

Diwedd *Welsh* — "end"

Dóú craiceann *Irish/Fae* — "second skin"

Drochairteagal *Irish* — "bad/dangerous person"

Et Filii *Latin* — "And the Son"

Et Spiritus Sancti *Latin* — "and the Holy Spirit"

Fág an bealach *Irish* — "clear the way"; battle cry

Feck/Fecking *Hiberno-English* — gentle form of *fuck*

Girseach *Irish* — "young girl/lass/damsel"

Gobdaw *Hiberno-English* — "idiot"

Go hifreann leat *Irish* — "curse of God upon you"; an oath or curse

Haearn *Welsh* — "iron"

I mi *Welsh* — "to me"

In nomine Patris *Latin* — "in the name of the Father"

Lluosi tân *Welsh* — "multiply the fire"

Llyfr y tylwyth teg *Welsh* — "The Book of Faeries"

M'anam *Irish* — "my soul"; an oath or curse

Mac mallachta *Irish* — lit. trans. "son of a curse"; also means "limb of Satan/son of perdition"

Míle buíochas *Irish* — "a thousand thanks"

Mo mhallacht ort *Irish* — "my curse upon you"; an oath or curse

Nghalon *Welsh* — "heart/core/center"; name Edward has given to the voice that sometimes talks to him at home and his office

Peidio *Welsh* — "cease/refrain"

Skawly *Irish* — "bad/horrible."

Slán agat *Irish* — "good-bye"; spoken to one who is staying by someone who is leaving

Slán go fóill *Irish* — "good-bye for now"; carries the expectation of seeing the receiver again

Striapach *Irish/Fae* — "whore"

Tá grá agam duit, m'aingeal *Irish* — "I love you, my angel"

Taid *Welsh* — "grandfather"

Tân *Welsh* — "fire/flame"

Tar amach, a Bháis *Irish* — "come forth, Death"; used to release the demon in Brendan

Téigh i dtigh diabhai *Irish* — "go to the house of the devil"; an oath or curse

Tenebrae *Latin* — "darkness"

Tír na nÓg *Irish* — "Land of Eternal Youth"; Land of Faeries

Trwy dy enw, yr wyf yn eich gorfodi *Welsh* — "by your name I compel you"

Tymestl *Welsh* — "storm"

Wojus *Hiberno-English* — "bad/poor"

Ymdeithio *Welsh* — "journey/travel/venture forth"

Yn dangos i mi beth sy'n cuddio. Dangos i mi Fiona *Welsh* — "show me what is hidden, show me Fiona"

ABOUT THE AUTHOR

BISHOP O'CONNELL is a consultant, writer, poet, blogger, and member of the New Hampshire Writer's Project. Born in Naples, Italy, while his father was stationed in Sardinia, Bishop grew up in San Diego, California, where he fell in love with the ocean and fish tacos. While wandering the country for work and school, he experienced autumn in New England. Soon after, he settled in Manchester, New Hampshire, where he collects swords and kilts. But he only dons one of those two in public. He can be found online at A Quiet Pint (*www.aquietpint.com*), where he muses philosophical on the various aspects of writing and the road to getting published.

Visit www.AuthorTracker.com for exclusive information on your favorite HarperCollins authors.